D0495058

BIRMINGHAM
DISCARDED
BOOK
SH
LIBRARY SERVICES

11 N
22

2

- 2

Ch
or
wv
wv

5

CHURCHILL'S PEOPLE

In 1941 Churchill led his people in the fight against Nazi Germany, inspiring a determination to succeed whilst growling defiance to Hitler.

The Adams family continue to play their part in the war effort, and meet changes in the family with their usual optimism. Emma and Jonathan marry at last, while Boots' son Tim helps Felicity, his fiancee, blinded in the bombing. Rosie is set to marry Matthew Chapman, but Chinese Lady is uneasy. Is he the ideal choice for such a special young woman as Rosie? And newly-married Boots and Polly have some very unexpected news...

CHURCHILL'S PEOPLE

CHURCHILL'S
PEOPLE

by

Mary Jane Staples

Magna Large Print Books
Long Preston, North Yorkshire,
BD23 4ND, England.

British Library Cataloguing in Publication Data.

Staples, Mary Jane
  Churchill's people.

  A catalogue record of this book is
  available from the British Library

  ISBN   0-7505-1524-4

First published in Great Britain by Bantam Press
a division of Transworld Publishers Ltd., 1999

Copyright © 1999 by Mary Jane Staples

Cover illustration © Nigel Chamberlain by arrangement with
Transworld Publishers Ltd.

The right of Mary Jane Staples to be identified as the author of
this work has been asserted by her in accordance with the
Copyright, Designs and Patents Act, 1988

Published in Large Print 2000 by arrangement with
Transworld Publishers Ltd.

All Rights reserved. No part of this publication may be
reproduced, stored in a retrieval system, or transmitted in any
form or by any means, electronic, mechanical, photocopying,
recording or otherwise without the prior permission of the
Copyright owner.

Magna Large Print is an imprint of Library Magna Books Ltd.

Printed and bound in Great Britain by
T.J. (International) Ltd., Cornwall, PL28 8RW

All the characters in this book are fictitious, and any resemblance to actual persons, living or dead, is purely coincidental

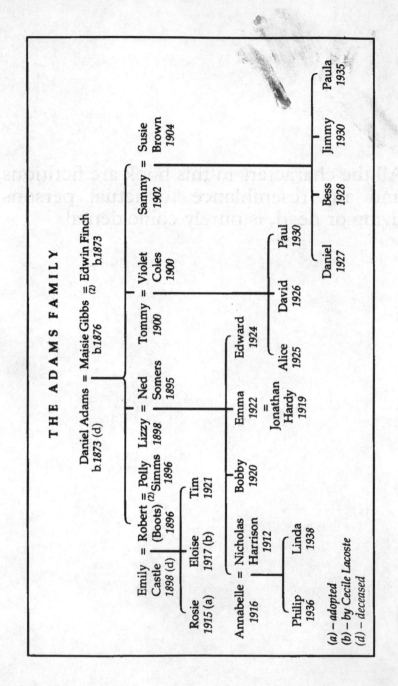

THE ADAMS FAMILY

Daniel Adams = Maisie Gibbs = Edwin Finch
b.1873 (d)   b.1876 (2)   b.1873

Emily = Robert = Polly   Lizzy = Ned   Tommy = Violet   Sammy = Susie
Castle (Boots) (2) Simms 1898   Somers   1900   Coles   1902   Brown
1898 (d) 1896   1896   1895   1900   1904

Rosie   Eloise   Tim   Bobby   Emma   Alice   David   Paul
1915 (a) 1917 (b) 1921   1920   1922   1925   1926   1930
                                      =
                            Jonathan   Daniel   Bess   Jimmy   Paula
                            Hardy   1927   1928   1930   1935
                            1919   Edward
                                      1924

Annabelle = Nicholas
1916   Harrison
            1912

Philip   Linda
1936   1938

(a) – adopted
(b) – by Cecile Lacoste
(d) – deceased

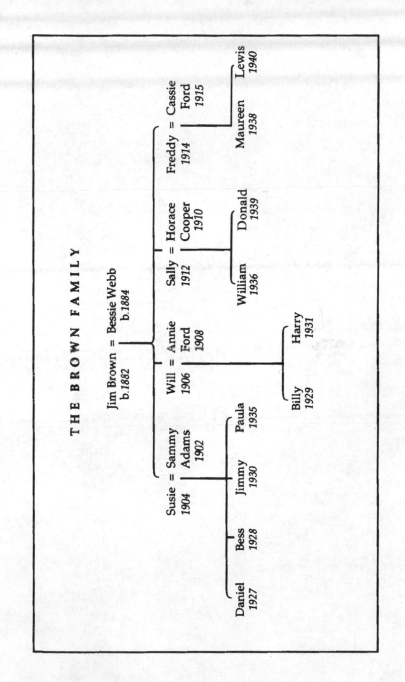

THE BROWN FAMILY

Jim Brown = Bessie Webb
b.1882   b.1884

Susie = Sammy
1904   Adams
         1902

Will = Annie
1906   Ford
        1908

Sally = Horace
1912   Cooper
         1910

Freddy = Cassie
1914   Ford
           1915

Daniel
1927

Bess
1928

Jimmy
1930

Paula
1935

Billy
1929

Harry
1931

William
1936

Donald
1939

Maureen
1938

Lewis
1940

Chapter One

'Go!'
'Go!'
'Go!'
From the air/sea rescue boats which had brought them across the Channel during the night, British Commandos, faces blackened, leapt out to wade ashore in the darkness of early morning. They had come from Dover to make their first strike against the German-occupied coast of Northern France. The objective was an aerodrome south of Le Touquet, and it was necessary to complete the strike and power their way home before dawn broke to expose their craft to German E-boats operating out of Boulogne harbour.

Out leapt Corporal Tim Adams, followed by Major Bill Lucas, a rugged and forceful artillery officer who had transferred from guns in favour of the blood-and-thunder type of operations special to Britain's growing strike units. He belonged, like Tim, to 4 Commando group which had combined with 6 Commando to mount a successful raid on the German-occupied Lofoten Islands earlier in the year. The only

11

resistance then had come from a contingent of *Luftwaffe* personnel, and was easily taken care of.

The strike against the coast of Northern France was expected to meet stiffer opposition. The Commandos, reaching the beach, swarmed through the darkness and at once ran into a German foot patrol. The patrol, hit from all sides by what seemed at first to be rushing shadows, lost men quickly. The rest scattered. On went the Commandos, Tim and Major Lucas in the van of one detachment. They came up against a guard hut manned by two sentries. This unfortunate duo of Germans died in a matter of seconds. The surprise element had been lost, however, for the garrison had already been aroused by the raiders' brief but noisy encounter with the patrol. Klaxons blared the alarm, Very lights sailed up to illuminate the drome and its perimeters, and a German machine-gun opened fire.

The Commandos silenced it with grenades and rushed to do as much damage as possible to the garrison and the buildings. Sten guns and Tommy-guns fired bursts at aroused but disorganized Germans, who had no idea what was going on apart from realizing some kind of hell had broken out. Several men were caught by the fire. The rest went to ground to oppose the rushing invaders from cover. More gun bursts made them keep their heads down. A storehouse loomed up. A Commando lobbed a grenade at the locked door. It struck the door hard, bounced back and landed at Tim's feet. Men flung themselves down. Tim reacted like a flash of lightning and took the risk of kicking the grenade. It shot away, skittering at speed, and exploded close to the storehouse door. Tim was flat on his face by then, even though the incident had lasted only seven seconds.

Major Lucas scrambled up, extended a hand and yanked Tim to his feet.

'What the hell d'you mean by trying to get your bloody leg blown off, Corporal Adams?' he shouted above the noise of mayhem.

'Reflex action of sheer panic,' said Tim.

'Just the job,' said Major Lucas, who featured prominently in the life of Tim's French-born half-sister, Eloise. 'Right, let's get this place blown up.'

Up it went, while elsewhere other detachments did what they could to show the Germans that blood, thunder and havoc weren't going to take place on a one-sided basis in future. On stormed Major Lucas and Tim with their platoon. A man stumbled, fell in front of Major Lucas and almost brought him down, besides knocking his Sten gun from his hand. Major Lucas, recovering, let the clumsy idiot know what he thought of him. The fallen Commando got up, received a shove in his back from the Major to get him moving, and away he went. Major Lucas stooped to retrieve his weapon. A German officer and a corporal, not as confused as the rest of the garrison personnel, came out of a pall of smoke and cut him off from his now distant detachment.

The German officer, instantly aware that here was a chance to take a prisoner and bring him in for interrogation, hissed instructions to his corporal, and bullets from machine-pistols smacked into the ground at the Major's feet, followed by a shout in German to stay where he was. But a burst from a Sten gun behind them smacked into the backs of their legs, and they staggered, crumpled and fell.

'Come on, Major!' shouted Tim, who had darted back to see what was keeping his detachment commander. 'Come on! Time's nearly up!'

Major Lucas skirted the wounded Germans at a rush and came up with Tim.

'Giving orders on top of bloody well showing off tonight, are you, Corporal Adams?' he said, but there was a grin on his face as he and Tim raced away and caught up with their men.

The raiding detachments were creating

havoc. But the signal came to withdraw. It was time to call off the action and to get back to the boats before the dark sky became touched by dawn's first light. Away the Commandos went, leaving fires burning. The garrison, rocked and disordered by the unexpectedness and shattering nature of the assault, went on firing at empty shadows for long minutes before they realized the raiders had vanished.

The Commandos left a number of Germans dead or wounded. There were a few lightly wounded men among their own ranks, but no fatalities. They poured down onto the beach with dawn not far away, and out they waded to climb aboard their waiting craft. Adrenalin was high, exhilaration prevalent as the air/sea rescue boats got under way.

A few minutes later they were holding their breath, for an E-boat, speeding out of Boulogne harbour, was scouring the waters. It was cutting a wide arc, its searchlight blazing. But the powerful beam passed above the British craft, which ran under it. The E-boat sped on, and the Commandos made for Dover. Dawn broke and by the time they were halfway across the Channel, daylight was flooding the sea. The helmsmen held course, and the Commandos searched the sky for German fighter planes.

Tim pushed his way through ranks of

packed men until he reached Major Lucas. He liked this officer and his aggressive, inspiring leadership.

'Fairly good show, would you say, sir?' he said.

'Would have been if we'd landed an hour earlier,' said Major Lucas tersely. The crossing from Dover had taken longer than expected.

'We'll get that right next time,' said Tim.

'We better had, by God,' said Major Lucas, at which point the sky erupted as British fighter planes arrived to escort the returning raiders the rest of the way to Dover. The sight and sound induced exhilaration in the contingent, and when they reached Dover every ship in the harbour was crowded with cheering men. Every ship had been waiting to witness the return.

Tim, along with other men of 4 Commando, arrived back in Troon on the 2nd of May. It was 1941, the second year of the war. He had missed the wedding of cousin Emma and Jonathan Hardy five days previously, and he knew the happy couple were now on their honeymoon. He felt a bit irked at his enforced absence on Emma's big day. However, on Friday at a special parade he received a direct commission as a first lieutenant. He had known he was in line for a commission, but not for two pips all at once. He was given a rousing time on being inducted into the rites of the Officers' Mess that evening, but later, when he managed to reach his billet, his motherly landlady, Mrs Maggie Andrews, scolded him for not being able to get up the stairs to his bedroom without her assistance. Tim did his best to assure her it had never happened to him before.

'I canna hear a word you're saying,' said Maggie.

'I think my engine's packed up,' said Tim, whose legs felt about as useful to him as two well-stewed sticks of rhubarb.

'Whisht, you're mumbling, laddie,' said Maggie, steering him into his room.

'Is there a bed somewhere?' asked Tim.

'Aye, it's there,' said Maggie, and he fell on it. Maggie shook her head at him, but deciding he needed more help, she undressed him down to his singlet and short pants and got him beneath the sheets. 'Weel now, there you are, Lieutenant McAdams,' she said, 'and I'm thinking I'd be in there wi' you given I was a young woman again.'

Tim didn't hear that. He wasn't meant to. He was already sound asleep. Maggie let a smile show then. She understood perfectly. A man didn't drink water on being commissioned, not in Scotland he didn't.

Tim phoned his dad the following evening. His dad, Major Robert Adams,

17

known as Boots, was living in a requisitioned Dorset cottage near 7 Corps headquarters with his new wife Polly, an ATS
captain now stationed at the headquarters
herself. It was Polly who answered the call.

'Hello?'

'Hello yourself, Ma, Tim here.'

'Ma?' Polly laughed. She was a woman
still in a happy state after several weeks of
marriage, finding life with Boots a delight
and a challenge while they both awaited the
inevitable. Rumours that the Corps would
embark for the Middle East before May was
out were blowing in the wind, and everyone
was certain the wind would land them as
official orders on the desk of the Corps
Commander, Polly's father, sooner or later.
'Heavens, Tim, you're not going to call me
Ma, are you?' she said.

'Polly, then?' suggested Tim.

'Pleasure, I'm sure, me dearie,' said Polly,
taking off Nellie Wallace, the old-time
cockney stage star presently entertaining the
troops in company with other old-timers.

'Well, you're a typical Polly,' said Tim.

'What's a typical Polly?'

'A load of fun,' said Tim. 'Listen, I've got
my commission. A first lieutenant. Let Dad
know, would you? He ought to have
something to make him feel his years as a
father haven't been wasted.'

'Tim, you and Rosie and Eloise made

18

every year worthwhile for him,' said Polly. 'Congratulations and many of 'em on your commission, old sport, I know you deserved it.'

'I like that coming from you,' said Tim. 'Well, I like you, and I'm delighted you married Dad.'

That touched Polly. She knew how devoted he and Rosie and Eloise had been to Emily, and if she was sensitive about anything it was how they regarded her for taking Emily's place.

'Well, thank you, Tim, that's made me very happy,' she said. 'So has your promotion. My word, the family is doing well, isn't it? You, Bobby and Rosie all commissioned, and Eloise halfway there, I fancy.' Eloise was currently at an ATS officers' training unit. 'In a moment, I'll let you talk to your father, my lord and master.'

'Your lord and master?' said Tim. 'How has that come about?'

'Oh, from the natural way he wears his ermine robes,' said Polly. 'One simply can't fight it.'

'I bet,' said Tim.

'Well, I do my best to answer him back,' said Polly, 'but it all bounces off him.'

'That's what Rosie calls his airy-fairy defensive system,' said Tim.

'Oh, it's a laugh a minute,' said Polly.

'Married life?' said Tim.

'It is with your father,' said Polly.

'It's putting the war into second place?' said Tim.

'Almost,' said Polly. 'By the way, Tim, were you one of the Commandos who made a raid on the French coast some days ago and caught the headlines?'

'All over now,' said Tim.

'Stirring stuff, though,' said Polly. 'Oh, how's the ATS officer who's taken your fancy?'

'I'm going to marry her this summer,' said Tim.

'Tim?'

'Fact,' said Tim.

'My word, old scout, that's a lovely piece of news, coming on top of Rosie getting married in July,' said Polly. 'Congratulations again. Yes, you'd better talk to your dad now, he's right here. So long, soldier.'

'So long, Polly,' said Tim, and Boots came on the line.

'Tim?'

'What-oh, Dad,' said Tim, 'thought I'd let you know I've been commissioned as a first lieutenant, and that I intend getting married.'

'Say that again,' said Boots. 'No, never mind, I think I heard, and I understand now why Polly's looking for a bottle of something. I'm delighted about your commission, old chap, and I'm pretty sure the family's going to stand on its head about another wedding. I take it that the lady in question is Lieutenant Felicity Jessop, whom we've heard about?'

'That's the lady, Dad,' said Tim, 'but what you haven't heard is that she's an air raid casualty.'

'Tell me,' said Boots.

Tim went into details. Felicity, on leave, had left a London theatre in company with friends one night, and their car ran into the path of a bomb. With her were two naval officers and a Wren officer. One man was killed, the other and the Wren officer were badly injured but now recovering. Felicity herself was blinded by an explosion of glass.

'And it's permanent,' said Tim.

'God Almighty,' said Boots.

'Yes, you'd know, wouldn't you, Dad, what losing your sight is like.'

'It leaves you desperately in need of help,' said Boots.

Tim went on to say he'd seen Felicity. Much to his admiration she was fighting like hell to cope with her disability, and much to his pleasure she'd agreed to marry him. She would share his billet and they'd both be under the roof of his treasured landlady, Mrs Andrews, who had promised to be a help and a companion to Felicity.

'There'll be no serious problems, Dad.'

'There'll be a few at first, old son,' said

Boots, 'but I think you'll win.'

'Well, you and Mum won your battle years ago,' said Tim, 'and Felicity and I will win this one.'

'I'll bet on that,' said Boots. 'All understood, Tim.'

'You sure?' said Tim. 'I'm not marrying her out of pity.'

'No, that would be a mistake,' said Boots. 'Would you like me to inform the family of all this?'

'Yes, would you? In a few days, I'll feel better able to deal with any letters that might come flying at me from home,' said Tim. 'By the way, it'll be a quiet wedding. Just Felicity's family, and you and Polly. You're my best friend, Dad, so be my best man. Sometime in late July or early August. Felicity will have adjusted to some extent by then, although we haven't fixed the exact date yet.'

Boots wondered if he would still be in the country by then. 7 Corps was undoubtedly being fully equipped for overseas duty, and General Sir Henry Simms expected embarkation orders within two weeks or so. He had, however, confided to Boots his suspicions that his deputy, Lieutenant-General Montrose, might be given the overseas command of the Corps, since he himself at sixty-six might be considered too old. The CIGS had expressed satisfaction at the way he and his deputy had licked the Corps into shape, while at the same time reminding him in friendly fashion of his age. It was the friendly tone that aroused Sir Henry's suspicions. Boots, however, supposed that he himself would go in the event of embarkation, although he'd be sorry to part from his father-in-law. Not that their relationship was that of father and son. It was one of a firm and long-standing friendship.

'I'll be delighted, Tim, to act as your best man, but bear in mind the family will want to meet Felicity sometime,' he said.

'I'll give that some thought,' said Tim, 'but I'd first have to consider how Felicity would regard the family running an eye over her.'

'Give her feelings priority,' said Boots.

'Well, again, you'd know, Dad,' said Tim. 'Thanks, you're a good old sport. By the way, what's Rosie's favoured bloke like? She told me in a letter he's her idea of happy ever after. Well, something like that.'

'He'll do, Tim, he's a very acceptable and good-natured bloke,' said Boots. 'I think Rosie sees him as Dorset's Gary Cooper – he looks a bit like him, with the same kind of easy-going outlook. We've just received word the wedding's fixed for the fifth of July.'

'Well, good for Rosie,' said Tim, 'if anyone in the family deserves a happy ever after

23

with Gary Cooper, she does.'

'No-one would argue with that,' said Boots. 'Keep in touch, Tim, and tell Felicity I wish her luck in climbing her mountains.'

'Will do,' said Tim. 'So long, Dad, see you at Rosie's wedding in July, then.'

'Hope so,' said Boots, and they rang off.

Tim then put a call through to Rosie at her headquarters in Dorset, but she was off duty. However, he managed to get hold of Eloise at her unit near Carlisle, where she was in training for a commission. His half-sister was delighted to hear of his promotion, and he asked her how she was getting on herself. Eloise said that as she was naturally good at everything, she was earning maximum marks. That raised a smile in Tim. Eloise's belief in herself never had a doubtful moment. She had, she said, long been fed-up at being merely a sergeant, and she certainly didn't feel inferior to the senior ATS officer in Troon, Pauline Cary, recently promoted to captain. Captain Cary was one more fussy officer. Fortunately, she said, Lieutenant Jessop was a much more agreeable woman.

'True,' said Tim.

'Oh, yes, you really are keen on her, aren't you?' said Eloise.

'True,' said Tim again.

'So is Captain Coombes,' said Eloise.

'Captain Coombes is hairy,' said Tim.

24

'Oh, is he growing a beard?' asked Eloise.

'Not in the Army, unless he's got permission,' said Tim.

'But has he got permission?' asked Eloise.

'Not as far as I know,' said Tim.

'Tim, are you actually in love with Lieutenant Jessop?' asked Eloise, fond of her half-brother.

'Enough to marry her,' said Tim, disinclined at the moment to repeat all he'd told Boots. Eloise would react too melodramatically, and he wasn't going to be able to cope with that.

'Have you asked her?' enquired Eloise.

'Yes, and the wedding'll be late July or early August,' said Tim. 'Well, it'll certainly be after Rosie's wedding on the fifth of July.'

'Oh, yes, Rosie wrote to me about hers,' said Eloise, 'but I'm amazed that Lieutenant Jessop is going to marry you.'

'Thanks a million,' said Tim.

'No, I mean I thought she was one of those Englishwomen devoted to hockey and cricket,' said Eloise. 'She really wants to marry you?'

'She's agreed it'll be a good idea,' said Tim, 'and I know I'm against her marrying anyone else.'

'Tim, how exciting, you and Rosie both getting married,' said Eloise happily.

'Looks like it,' said Tim. 'Does that make you feel you're being left behind? If so, there are any number of Commandos here who'd be willing to church you.'

'Those cannibals? Oh, you beast,' said Eloise, 'no girl is safe when they're off duty, especially after dark. Believe me, Tim, I felt I've been fighting for my honour even when certain men were only looking at me.'

That raised another smile in Tim. Eloise's imaginative output was pretty constant.

'In the dark?' he said.

'No, no, in broad daylight,' said Eloise, 'and I expect it will go on even when I'm an officer. They have no shame, some of your Commandos, and Major Lucas is no help.'

'Why, is he expected to be?' asked Tim.

'Of course,' said Eloise. 'He was responsible for bringing me to Troon.'

'I thought you asked for the transfer,' said Tim.

'He practically dragged me there,' said Eloise, which statement was a bit of a terminological inexactitude. 'But of course he has always found me indispensable, and when I return as an officer I shall be more so.'

'More so?' said Tim. 'That's a fact, is it?'

'I am sure of it,' said Eloise. 'I expect Major Lucas has mentioned to you that he's missing me, hasn't he?'

'Not yet,' said Tim. 'He's hoping, like the rest of us, that we'll get the chance of mounting a prime raid on the French coast that'll mean knocking off a squad of German gunners and spiking their heavies. The buggers are shelling Dover.'

'You don't have to swear,' said Eloise.

'Swear? Don't make me laugh,' said Tim.

'Are you celebrating your commission with Lieutenant Jessop?' asked Eloise.

'I'd like to,' said Tim, 'but she's away at the moment.' He was going to leave it to Boots to let her know why Felicity was away. He really didn't feel like going all through it again himself. 'Well, nice to have talked to you, sis. I did get through to Rosie's unit, but she was off duty.'

'Oh, imagine she's going to be married to a landed Dorset gentleman,' said Eloise.

'A what?' said Tim.

'Yes, isn't that what they call a man with property in an English county?' said Eloise.

'As far as I know, the property's an old wayside garage,' said Tim.

'No, no, it couldn't be,' said Eloise. 'You have no romance in your soul.'

'All the same, Rosie's wedding is one I don't want to miss when it happens,' said Tim. 'I've got to be home for that, you bet. Anyway, watch your maximum marks in case a bit of carelessness leads to the minimum. Um, shall I give your love to Major Lucas?'

'What do you mean?'

'Well, shall I?' offered Tim.

'I admire Major Lucas as a soldier,' said Eloise, 'but he's not a man I could fall in love with. Like Rosie, I would prefer a landed country gentleman.'

'OK, scatterbrain, wish you luck, then,' said Tim.

'Tim, I must go now,' said Eloise. 'Thanks for letting me know you're going to get married and that you're now a lieutenant. I'm proud of you. Goodbye.'

'So long,' said Tim. He hung up and left admin. He'd been using the phone in Colonel Foster's office with the connivance of the ATS duty NCO, a sergeant. She gave him a wink as he made his exit through the orderly room. 'Ta,' he said.

'Oh, you're welcome, sir,' she said, and Tim smiled. He wasn't used to being called 'sir'.

He walked to his billet, where Maggie received him in her cosy kitchen and put the kettle on.

'Laddie,' she said, 'I'm thinking your lady officer might be wishing to know you're now an officer yoursel'.'

'I'll try to get her on the phone during daytime tomorrow,' said Tim.

'Now I'm thinking the puir wee lass canna tell night from day,' sighed Maggie.

'Maggie, don't let's regard her as a poor wee lass,' said Tim.

'Aye, you're right,' said Maggie, 'I willna

call her that again. She wouldna want it. Tim, are you sure this house will do for you and her? It's no' anything special.'

'Well, it's special to me, Maggie, and so are you,' said Tim. 'Until you boot me out, or the unit moves, this is my home from home, and for Felicity too in a couple of months, and there couldn't be a better. Maggie, I owe you.'

'You dinna owe me a farthing,' said Maggie, smiling. She had quite an affection for this personable and good-humoured Commando. A Sassenach he might be, but he was as much of a man as any true-born Scot, especially in choosing to stand side by side with his blind lady officer. Which was why she often called him McAdams. 'Will you be at the bottle again tonight?'

'Not after what it did to me last night,' said Tim. 'Was I half-scuppered?'

'Drunk as a blue-nosed laird,' said Maggie.

'I don't have a clue as to how I got myself into bed,' said Tim. 'Must have been instinct triumphing over leglessness.'

'Och, aye,' said Maggie, and smiled again.

The Commandos were out the following day, practising difficult landings on the Isle of Arran in company with marines of the Special Boat Section. The landings launched them into dangerous and awesome ascents of precipitous Goat Fell. Such training was turning tough and rough men into death-defying opponents of the foe across the Channel.

There were inevitable accidents, however, and when 4 Commando returned to Troon in the late afternoon, there were a few broken bones. These casualties were hospitalized. Major Lucas was far from sympathetic.

'Rank bloody carelessness,' he said to Tim.

'Bloody hard going, though,' said Tim. 'Lucky some of us didn't break our necks.'

Major Lucas, blue eyes glinting in his brown rugged face, said, 'Luck of the devil, you mean? Is he on our side?'

'Hope so, Major,' said Tim, 'or there'll be brimstone scorching our tails when we sail up the Rhine.'

Major Lucas laughed. He liked Tim, an entirely straightforward and uncomplicated young man who was also a tough Commando, and thoroughly deserved his commission. And his decision to marry Felicity Jessop was that of a man and a half. But the Major's feelings for Tim's sister Eloise were beset by teeth-grinding frustration, for that young woman was the most provoking and discouraging he had ever met.

'A dose of brimstone will speed us up,' he said.

'I'm not sure how fast I'll be able to go with a scorched backside,' said Tim. 'By the way, I was speaking to my sister Eloise on the blower yesterday. She sent you her regards.'

A sceptical smile appeared on Major Lucas's rugged face.

'If your sister gets her commission,' he said, 'she'll do her best to take over the running of 4 Commando.'

'She's a bit of a character,' acknowledged Tim.

'That's only half of it,' said Major Lucas, giving Tim the impression that this redoubtable officer considered Eloise a bit of a handful. Well, a lot of women were like that now. They'd come out of their homes to work in the factories of war, to toil in the Land Army or to serve in the Forces, and they'd discovered how much they were worth to the country. That and a natural talent for outwitting blokes by fair means or foul were turning all of them into handfuls. It's a gorblimey social revolution, thought Tim, and I don't know if I'm for it or against it. 'How's Lieutenant Jessop getting on?' asked the Major.

'If I could use Colonel Foster's phone right now, I could find out,' said Tim.

'Go ahead,' said Major Lucas.

The girl on the switchboard of the military convalescent hospital let Tim know private phone calls to patients weren't allowed.

'We've got rules too, where I hang out,' said Tim, 'but if you can't break one or two at times, you might as well stay in bed all your life. Anyway, be a sport, and ask Sister Forbes if I can talk to Lieutenant Jessop.'

'Hold on a tick,' said the girl.

Tim held on for a long minute before Sister Forbes came on the line.

'Who is that, please?' she asked.

'Lieutenant Adams,' said Tim, 'even if I was only a corporal when I called before in person.'

'Oh, yes, I remember you,' said Sister Forbes. 'Did you really make lieutenant straight from corporal?'

'Yes, they thought I was a good bet for downing Hitler,' said Tim.

'Hold on,' said Sister Forbes, 'I'll get a nurse to fetch Lieutenant Jessop.'

'Bless you,' said Tim. He waited quite a while again, and then Felicity was on the line.

'Hello, Tim.'

'Well, that's fine,' said Tim, 'you know where the phone is.'

'I know where everything is as long as I'm led to it,' said Felicity.

'Rattling good show, then,' said Tim. 'How are you, my beauty?'

'Don't lark about with questions like that, you goof,' said Felicity, 'I can't give any brave answers. But I'm having a happy time at the moment.'

'There's a party going on?' said Tim.

'No, I'm talking to you,' said Felicity.

'That makes you happy?' said Tim.

'Of course,' said Felicity. 'You're my lifeline, and that means a lot more to me than a funny hat. Well, a funny hat is just like any old hat when you can't see them.'

Tim, detecting the brittle note that was so reminiscent of Polly, said, 'I'll look after what hats are right for you when we're married.'

'You'll probably have to help me dress sometimes,' said Felicity, 'in case I put my pants on back to front.'

'OK, we'll do a dummy run when I next see you,' said Tim. 'How's therapy?'

'Helping,' said Felicity.

'But you get down in the dumps every so often?' said Tim.

'Too often,' said Felicity, 'but I'm not going to shoot myself, not now I know you're going to hold my hand. Tim, are you still sure you want to take me on?'

'Certain sure,' said Tim, 'and I hope it lasts a lifetime.'

'Well, you're a girl's best friend, and it's lovely of you to phone me,' said Felicity. 'How are all my Commandos?'

'Missing you,' said Tim.

'Bless the hairy apes,' said Felicity. 'Oh,

my bandages are off now, but I know my eyes are bloodshot, and I'm having to wear dark glasses. I imagine I look frightful.'

'What do the doctors say?' asked Tim.

'About my looks?' said Felicity.

'About the bloodshot condition,' said Tim.

'That it's only temporary,' said Felicity.

They talked some more, Felicity brittle and bright by turns, and then they said goodbye.

'I'll stay in touch,' said Tim.

'Tim, don't be a hero, take care,' said Felicity.

He picked up a letter from the orderly room on his way out. It was from Grandma Finch and written to acquaint him with the news Tim had already received from Boots, that Rosie was engaged to be married to a Mr Matthew Chapman of Dorset. 'That I haven't met yet,' wrote Chinese Lady in a somewhat pained vein. All the same, she was happy for Rosie, of course. The wedding was to take place on 5 July, and it was hoped Tim would be there, since he hadn't been at Emma's wedding.

I'm not going to miss Rosie's, thought Tim. Rosie's been my best friend all my life. If his grandma hadn't met Matthew Chapman, neither had he, but he and Rosie wrote regularly to each other and she'd frequently mentioned her Dorset man in favourable terms.

34

The next thing he'd get from Grandma Finch, he supposed, would be a letter asking questions about Felicity and his own wedding day.

He wrote to Rosie, expressing congratulations, pleasure and affection.

Chapter Two

Saturday, 3 May.

Mr Edwin Finch, a distinguished-looking man of sixty-seven, frowned as he listened to the evening news that was coming so calmly from the BBC announcer, Frank Philips.

Hitler's iron hordes were sweeping Europe. After the conquest last year of Norway, Denmark, Holland, Belgium and France, they had this year forced the surrender of Yugoslavia, Albania and Greece. The British and Empire divisions sent to help Greece had evacuated to Crete, and Crete would be the next target of the war-crazy German Führer. That was certain.

Further, General Rommel and his Afrika Korps had a foothold in Egypt and were posing a dire threat to the British Eighth Army.

The rest of the world was looking on, leaving Britain and its Empire allies to stand alone against the monstrous menace of a merciless tyranny and its pitiless Gestapo.

Mr Finch's frown deepened.

'Edwin?' His wife made herself heard.

'Yes, Maisie?'

'That wireless is worrying you,' said Mrs Maisie Finch, known to her family as Chinese Lady because of her almond eyes and the fact that she had taken in washing during her days of poverty. 'I don't know why we ever bought it, there's never much good coming out of it. I can't hardly remember the last time it had something cheerful to say.'

Mr Finch could not help smiling. His wife, born a cockney and owning no more than an elementary education, never failed to touch an affectionate chord. She was as resilient and enduring as all her kind, and quick to show disapproval of anything she considered dubious or suspect, but no-one knew better than he did what a warm heart beat beneath her proud bosom. Proud bosom. Mr Finch smiled again. That was an unequivocal English expression, denoting firm and unyielding respectability.

'One does wish for better news now and again, Maisie,' he said, and switched off the set.

'Well, at least we've had some nice fam'ly news on top of a lovely fam'ly wedding,' said Chinese Lady. She was sixty-three, with very little grey in her dark brown hair, and still looked upon by her sons, her daughter and her grandchildren as the steadfast matriarch. The marriage of granddaughter Emma to Jonathan Hardy of the Royal

37

Artillery had taken place last Saturday week. Three days later she had received word that another family wedding was in the offing. Her granddaughter Rosie was engaged at last, at the age of nearly twenty-six. The news, arriving through Chinese Lady's receptive letterbox, spread from her to encompass the various branches of the family by word or letter. If she didn't know a lot about the man, Matthew Chapman, she felt she could rely on Rosie to have picked someone who deserved her.

'Who the hell's he?' Tommy Adams had asked of his wife Vi. 'Does anyone know him?'

'Well, I suppose his friends do,' said Vi, a soft-eyed and equable woman of forty, whose major complaint about the war was that it had taken her children away from her. Alice, David and Paul were all living in Devon as evacuees. 'I've been hearing rumours about Rosie, haven't you?'

'There's been rumours about Tim as well,' said Tommy, 'about him goin' weak at the knees every time a certain ATS officer crosses his line of fire.'

'That's not a rumour, love, that's how it is,' said Vi. 'He said so in a letter to us. Well, he didn't actually say anything about goin' weak at the knees, he said he was having serious thoughts about her.'

'All right, fair do's, I wish him luck,' said Tommy, 'it's not the same as Rosie gettin' engaged to a bloke none of us 'ave ever met.'

'Oh, I think Boots and Polly have,' said Vi.

'Nobody else has, not even Chinese Lady, which must be a blow to the old girl,' said Tommy. 'D'you suppose he's the genuine article, Vi?'

'Tommy, you silly, Rosie wouldn't ever pick the wrong kind of man,' said Vi. 'Not Rosie. She's like Boots, she can sum up a person very correct.'

'Funny, that,' mused Tommy, 'how much Rosie and Boots are like each other, when she's only his adopted daughter. If she'd been born of him and Em'ly you could understand it, but she took after Boots just as if he'd been her natural dad.'

'Well, Rosie's always admired Boots,' said Vi, 'and I expect she sort of grew into takin' after him. She's waited a long time to start a life of her own, but I'm glad she's doing it at last and not staying single for ever. Never mind that most of the fam'ly don't know Mr Chapman, I'm sure none of us'll be disappointed in her choice, especially if Boots approves, and we haven't heard he doesn't.'

'Well, if that's what you think, Vi,' said Tommy.

'Oh, I do,' said Vi.

'That's my girl,' said Tommy, a typical Adams in that, along with the other mature members of the family, he considered he had proprietary rights in respect of the doings and goings-on of the younger generation.

'Rosie at last, would you believe,' said Lizzy of the Somers branch to her husband Ned.

'I do believe,' said Ned, instigator of the Somers branch. At forty-six, he had a touch of grey in his hair, and still owned a souvenir of the Great War, a tin leg.

'But fancy it being someone we don't know,' said Lizzy. 'I mean, Rosie of all people, when she's always been so fam'ly-minded. Wouldn't you have thought she'd have brought him home to meet everyone at Polly and Boots's wedding, or Emma's?' Emma was presently on honeymoon with her happy-go-lucky country chap, Jonathan Hardy.

'Perhaps Mr Chapman's underneath a car at weekends,' said Ned. 'After all, he does car repairs, doesn't he?'

'Now how could anyone stay underneath a car all through a weekend?' asked Lizzy.

'If the repairs were urgent and the feller was conscientious?' offered Ned.

'Are you making a joke?' asked Lizzy.

'No, just a suggestion,' said Ned.

'It still sounds like a joke,' said Lizzy. 'Still, I'm pleased for Rosie, I must say. Well, she'll be twenty-six soon.'

'That's not actually old,' said Ned, whose position as manager of a wine merchant's in Great Tower Street sometimes hung in the balance because of air raids and reduced imports. Imports from France were nil, but the firm was finding South African wines surprisingly good. 'There's no-one in the family you could call old yet, not even Grandma and Grandpa Finch. Mark well their continuing vigorous contributions to life.'

'Mark what?' said Lizzy. 'Ned Somers, are you doing Shakespeare or something?'

'Or something,' said Ned. 'In the way of a neat turn of phrase, I thought.'

'Crikey, you and Boots,' said Lizzy, 'what a pair of toffs.'

'Don't mention it,' said Ned. 'Regarding Rosie, I'm as pleased for her as you are, even if Matthew Chapman is an unknown quantity at the moment. But it's a co-incidence, isn't it, that she and Emma have both chosen what Emma calls country chaps?'

'Oh, new blood might be good for the fam'ly,' said Lizzy.

'New blood or country cider,' said Ned.

'Oh, very comic,' said Lizzy.

'Get Emma to make a note in her diary if Jonathan fizzes,' said Ned.

'I hope you're not making vulgar insinuations,' said Lizzy. 'Anyway, Emma always

41

says that what she puts in her diary is for posterity.'

'I'll read it when I'm ninety,' said Ned, 'I'll be shaking hands with posterity by then.'

'Queen Victoria kept a diary,' said Lizzy.

'Yes, and posterity's had an interesting time reading it,' said Ned.

'You know, love, I sometimes thought Rosie would never get married,' said Lizzy, 'she's always been very attached to Boots and very happy just as one of the fam'ly.'

'I don't think any of us would have wanted Rosie to turn into a lifelong spinster,' said Ned.

'Ned, be your age,' said Lizzy, 'no-one says spinster now. It's bachelor girl. Spinster's been thrown into a wastepaper basket, and blessed if that isn't the right place for it.'

'Along with flannel bloomers,' observed Ned. 'I suppose that means good old cockney sayings like "winter drawers on, gal," have gone out of fashion too.'

'Yes, like some of your jokes,' said Lizzy who, in her forty-third year, still owned a handsome figure, favoured stylish under-wear, and shuddered at the thought of the bloomers of long ago. 'I wish this war and the air raids would go away,' she sighed. A week after the RAF had given the morale of the British people a long-awaited boost by mounting a massive raid on Berlin on 9 April, Goering sent his *Luftwaffe* on a revenge raid to London, inflicting the worst damage yet. 'No-one should have to suffer bombs all the time.' Actually, since the revenge raid, the onslaught from the air had lightened. 'If the raids stopped, we could bring Edward home from the country, and Annabelle could come home with the children.' Edward, their youngest, was completing his schooling as an evacuee in Wiltshire, and his elder sister Annabelle was living with her two children close by. 'And Tommy and Vi could bring theirs home too, and so could Sammy and Susie. Oh, well, never mind, at least we've got Rosie's wedding to look forward to.'

'I've a feeling that things really are going to quieten down at night,' said Ned. 'They were quietening down just before that last big raid. Well, damn it, Eliza, the Germans have got to call a halt sometime, or their bomber crews will collapse under the strain. Some must be at breaking-point by now.'

The *Luftwaffe* command, in fact, was slyly moving formations of bombers and fighters close to the border of Soviet Russia, and Prime Minister Churchill, apprised of this by British Intelligence, was alert to the possibility that Hitler was planning to do what he had always threatened, invade Russia and grab the Ukraine for Germany.

But Goering still had enough bombers based in Northern France to pose a constant menace to London and other cities. In any case, the air crews of the Third Reich did not permit themselves to suffer weaknesses. They were dedicated to their Führer and to unyielding heroism. If ordered to, they would bomb London until they fell heroically out of the sky.

Ned had heard Mr Finch recently declare that the Germans had reverted to iron-souled Prussianism. He was unaware of the fact that if anyone in the family knew the Germans well, Mr Finch did, for he'd been born a German and had once worked for German Intelligence. Boots, however, was the only member of the family who had knowledge of that, and was a faithful keeper of the secret.

Susie Adams and her husband Sammy had also talked about Rosie's engagement over supper. Sammy opened the discussion by saying he was disapproving.

'Oh, dear,' said Susie.

'I've got to be disapproving, seeing I don't know Matthew Clapham any more than I know Buffalo Bill,' said Sammy.

'Oh, dear,' said Susie again. 'It's Chapman, by the way, as you well know.'

'He could be anybody,' said Sammy.

'Well, when I was young and striving, I was anybody,' said Susie, 'and so were you.

No-one knew us.'

'Mummy, what's anybodies?' asked little Paula, now six.

'Well, nobodies, really,' said Susie.

'Crumbs, is Daddy nobody?' asked Paula, slightly alarmed.

'He was, darling,' said Susie, 'but not now. Now he's Mr Sammy Adams, a well-known businessman who keeps an eye on his over-heads.'

'Granted,' said Sammy.

'Oh, that's good,' said Paula, 'I don't want to tell my friends you're nobody, Daddy.'

'That's right, young Plum Pudding,' said Sammy, 'tell 'em I'm somebody. Listen, Susie, I'm not only disapproving on account of not being intimately acquainted with Rosie's bloke. It's also on account of him being a hard-up geezer with a run-down garage in the middle of nowhere who talked to Rosie about needing a bit of capital, you remember.'

'Oh, dear,' said Susie yet again. 'Sammy, I don't think Rosie would like you referring to her bloke as a geezer.'

'Well, I ask you, Susie, our Rosie livin' a poverty-stricken life, can you think about that without turning pale?' said Sammy. 'You and me, Susie, we've had some of that and it ain't recommendable, especially not for Rosie. Further, and what's more, suppose she ends up livin' down in Dorset?

45

Who's going to like that?'

'Rosie might,' said Susie. 'Anyway, it's not Australia.'

'Good as,' said Sammy. 'I'll have to think of something.'

'Don't you dare,' said Susie. 'Where Rosie lives with her husband is none of our business, and if I remember right, I had to tell you so once before.'

'Mummy, I like cousin Rosie,' said Paula.

'We all do,' said Sammy. 'She's fam'ly. So we don't want her livin' in the wilds of Dorset, do we? It could be Indian country out there. Susie, if I could come up with–'

'No, Sammy,' said Susie.

'Susie–' The phone rang then and Sammy answered it in the hall.

'Uncle Sammy?' said a well-known warm voice.

'Well, if I'm not mistaken, that's you, Rosie,' said Sammy.

'Yes,' said Rosie. 'Am I in the news?'

'You're in your grandma's favourite fam'ly magazine,' said Sammy, 'and we've all had a copy.'

'Are you pleased about Matthew and me?' asked Rosie.

'Surprised,' said Sammy.

'But you're pleased too, aren't you?'

Sammy, owning a very soft spot for Boots's adopted daughter, chucked his reservations aside.

46

'Highly tickled, in fact,' he said, 'and so is Susie.'

'You'll both like Matthew, I know you will,' said Rosie, 'he's a lovely man and makes very light of his lame leg.'

'Pardon?' said Sammy.

'Oh, he broke his ankle when he was young and it was never properly set,' said Rosie. Holy Joe, thought Sammy, the bloke's a cripple as well as a pauper? 'But it doesn't really hamper him,' said Rosie, 'although it keeps him out of the Army. That doesn't bother me at all. I like it that he's exempt.'

'That he won't be called up?' said Sammy.

'Yes, why not?' said Rosie. 'The Army's conscripted a million men, and I want this one for myself.'

'It's like that, is it?' said Sammy.

'Afraid so, Uncle Sammy. He's kind, he's gentle, he's amusing, and when we're married there'll be another branch to our family, the Chapmans.'

'He might think he's starting a Dorset branch of his own fam'ly,' said Sammy.

'Oh, Matthew has as much in common with the Adams' as Uncle Ned has,' said Rosie blithely. 'You'll see.'

'Half a mo,' said Sammy, 'what happens if you get sent overseas with your piece of the Army?'

'As a married woman I'll be excused

overseas duty,' said Rosie.

'Glad to hear it,' said Sammy.

'So am I now,' said Rosie. 'Uncle Sammy, I want to ask a favour.'

'Ask away, Rosie.'

'You know your retired designer, Lilian, made Emma's wedding gown from a stock of pre-war white silk you hold?'

'Mrs Lilian Hyams that was, Mrs Lilian Chambers that now is, married to her Walworth milkman and him a Gentile?' said Sammy. 'Yes, I know. Emma talked about getting a gown from our Oxford Street shop when the time came, but I talked Lilian into comin' to see her and offering a design in our white silk, which sent Emma dotty with old-fashioned jumping up and down. Lilian came again to fit it when Emma and Jonathan were able to fix their wedding date, and as you saw last Saturday, Emma poured herself into it with style and a plum.'

'Aplomb, Uncle Sammy?' said Rosie.

'Well, something French,' said Sammy. 'By the way, why didn't you tell the fam'ly then that you had a wedding date of your own?'

'Matthew had reservations,' said Rosie. 'He kept saying he shouldn't marry me, that it wouldn't be fair to because his income from the garage was so limited. So when I drove back to headquarters on Sunday, I called on him and gave him an ultimatum. He said he couldn't cope with ultimatums, so we fixed the date. I then wrote to Grandma and asked her to let everyone at home know.'

'Regarding limited incomes, Rosie,' said Sammy, 'it'll pain me considerable if you have to live off bread and cheese.'

'Uncle Sammy, of course I won't.' Rosie laughed. 'Listen, is there enough silk left to make a wedding gown for me?'

'There'd always be enough for you,' said Sammy.

'There's lovely you are,' said Rosie with a Welsh lilt.

'You want white silk, you're not getting married in your uniform?' said Sammy.

'Uncle Sammy, how can you even think I would?' protested Rosie.

'Well, of course, you're an Adams,' said Sammy, 'and you know what your grandma would expect, seeing she doesn't hold with female women in uniform. What's your present height and measurements?'

'Five feet eight, thirty-six, twenty-four, thirty-six,' said Rosie promptly.

'Rosie, my compliments and admiration,' said Sammy. 'Right, I'll get Lilian workin' on the design and let you have a sketch of it. She designed for Annabelle, Sally and Cassie, and she'll jump at the pleasure of designing for you.'

'Bless you, Uncle Sammy, and bless Lilian too,' said Rosie.

49

'Believe me, Rosie, it'll help take Lilian's mind off that specimen of German measles name of Henry Himmler,' said Sammy.

'A creature of dark and slimy repute,' said Rosie.

'And so say Lilian and our old friend Rachel Goodman on behalf of all the sons and daughters of Abraham,' said Sammy. 'Let's see, I believe your auspicious day is the fifth of July, right?'

'Yes, five weeks after the wedding of Matthew's sister,' said Rosie.

'Well, I'm now happy all over for you,' said Sammy. 'I like what you've told me about your Dorset bloke, that he's one of us, like your Uncle Ned.'

'Not everyone is, of course, and we have to be discriminating, don't we?' A warm little laugh arrived in Sammy's ear. 'After all, we're a very select lot, and only the right kind of people can join.'

'How about this ATS officer Tim's taken a fancy to?' asked Sammy.

'Felicity Jessop?' said Rosie.

'Would you repeat that, Rosie?'

'Felicity Jessop.'

'Is that a label for someone's home-made pickle?' asked Sammy.

'No, it's the name of Tim's fancy,' said Rosie, 'and I think he wants to make her the best part of his post-war future.'

'I've got post-war business diversification

on my own mind,' said Sammy.

'Pardon, Uncle Sammy?'

'On the lines of a property company that'll provide promising futures for Tim and Bobby,' said Sammy. 'I see 'em as a couple of bright sparks with initiative who'll be glad to shake hands with salaries that'll help keep their wives in style, such as is the pleasure of your Aunt Susie, your Aunt Vi and your stepma, currently your dad's legal bosom chum.'

Rosie's laugh travelled over the line again.

'Uncle Sammy, I'm delighted to know the war hasn't damaged your batteries,' she said. 'You're still charged with electricity and optimism. We all need any amount of that. I sometimes feel appalled by what we're up against, that terrifying Nazi war machine. It's overrunning Europe.'

'It'll overrun itself one day, Rosie, accordin' to Grandpa Finch,' said Sammy.

'Yes, he's always so calm and reassuring,' said Rosie, 'and he always seems to know so much about the minds and attitudes of the Germans. Oh, I'd like you to know that Boots, my lovely dad, is in favour of Matthew.'

'Your Aunt Susie and me wondered if they'd met,' said Sammy.

'Yes, and on level terms,' said Rosie. 'Boots wore an old civvy shirt and trousers, and Matthew was in his overalls. They met

51

at the garage and got on famously.'

'Well, if Boots is in favour,' said Sammy, 'who's goin' to argue?'

'Quite right, Uncle Sammy, who would dare to?' said Rosie. 'Goodbye now, thanks for being a darling, and love to Aunt Susie.'

''Bye, Rosie,' said Sammy, and when he rejoined Susie and Paula he was smiling. Susie asked what he was pleased about. Sammy said he'd been talking to Rosie, and that she'd convinced him her Dorset bloke was up to scratch. Susie asked how much up to scratch, and Sammy said he'd been informed in words various that Matthew Chapman would fit in with the family as easily as Ned did.

'Pardon?' said Susie, blinking.

'Yes, she informed me he's like Ned,' said Sammy. 'She actually called to know if I'd get Lilian to design a wedding gown for her, out of our pre-war stock of white silk. I said Lilian would fall over herself to oblige. By the way, there's something else concerning Rosie's intended. He's got a gammy leg.'

'He's got what?' asked Susie.

'He's lame,' said Sammy

'How strange,' said Susie.

'Strange?' said Sammy.

'Yes, Ned's lame too,' said Susie, while little Paula wondered if Rosie's sweetheart was a nobody or a somebody.

Down in Dorset that night, a man born with an inferiority complex and a negative outlook, whom people had considered a nobody all his life, set fire to a shop in Dorchester. It was his second successful venture into arson, and made him glow with the triumph of a positive man. He had long been excited by newspaper pictures of the roaring fires raised by the Germans in their air assaults on London and other cities, and it eventually occurred to him that any man could accomplish some fire-raising of his own, without having to drop bombs from a plane. His first success had been in Wareham, when he fired a newsagent's shop very satisfyingly. The Dorchester achievement went beyond being satisfying, however. It inflamed his senses, for he torched a hardware shop that contained a stock of paints. As the shop turned into an inferno of flame, he heard the tins explode and saw the resulting balls of fire bursting through the roof.

No wonder he glowed.

Chapter Three

Sunday morning, 4 May.

Major Robert Adams came back into the bedroom after washing and shaving. His wife Polly, dressing, was in her underwear, her regulation stockings sleek, her bare thighs as smooth and pearly as a young woman's, although she was in her forty-fifth year.

'Knock, knock, who's there?' she said, fixing a suspender.

'A friend,' said Boots.

'Some friend,' said Polly, 'you didn't knock.'

'Should I have?' asked Boots.

'We made an agreement that the mysteries of my person half-dressed or in the altogether should remain sacred,' said Polly.

'Did we make such an agreement?' asked Boots. 'Did I sign something?'

'You gave me the word of an officer and gentleman,' said Polly. Boots smiled. Her body was still smooth and firm. Her dark brown hair, worn for many years in a face-framing bob of piquant style, was longer now and dressed in curling fashion. Boots favoured her feminine qualities, and Polly, for all her sophistication and her sense of being any man's equal, was entirely feminine. 'Look here, you cad,' she said, 'any officer and gentleman whose wife is an officer and lady should sign something that will guarantee she's not caught unawares. One has one's modesty and military standing to consider.'

'I'm not signing anything like that,' said Boots, 'I like you in a state of unawares.'

'Do you swear to that?' asked Polly.

'Without hesitation,' said Boots.

'Oh, well, help yourself to a look at what the butler saw,' said Polly.

Boots laughed and slipped off his dressing-gown. In just his brief pants he reached for his singlet. Polly swooped. Boots twitched but stood his ground.

'What're you up to, Captain Adams?'

'Catching you unawares, Major Adams,' said Polly, and wondered if he had had interludes like this with Emily. Emily. Yes, thoughts of his former wife did intrude occasionally. 'Well, sauce for the goose, you know,' she said.

'That's fair,' said Boots.

They were living in a requisitioned cottage not far from Corps headquarters, and only the war prevented Polly from being totally in love with life. Boots as a husband was an adventurous, stimulating and playful lover. Sometimes she thought they were both

55

absurd in behaving like young and adolescent newly-weds, but what did it matter? Absurdity was a sweet luxury for a man and woman in their forties.

The batman, Lance-Corporal Higgins, called up from down below.

'Major? Breakfast on the table in five minutes.'

'Right, five minutes,' called Boots. 'We'll be there.'

He and Polly finished dressing.

They took breakfast in a pretty little dining-room, with pretty lace curtains and pictures of pretty country scenes, which made Polly suspect the owner of the cottage must be a pretty old lady, particularly as there were intriguing little moments when she was sure she could detect a faint smell of lavender.

Over the meal, she and Boots talked about Rosie and her fiancé, Matthew Chapman.

'I'm glad you found you liked him, Boots,' she said, not for the first time. 'It was necessary to Rosie and important to you that you did.'

'He's instantly likeable,' said Boots.

'Yes, I thought so too when I first met him,' said Polly. 'But you haven't yet told me how you feel about the fact that he owns virtually nothing.'

'You haven't asked,' said Boots.

'I suppose I thought that concerned Rosie

more than you and me,' said Polly. 'All the same, how do you feel?'

'I owned even less than virtually nothing when I married Emily,' said Boots. 'Certainly less than Matthew, who owns his cottage, a distinct asset to any couple. No mortgage repayments mean no big hole in his earnings.'

'But they're uncertain, his earnings, aren't they?' said Polly. 'His garage is only doing a minimum amount of business.'

'Rosie informed me it's got post-war prospects,' said Boots. 'But in regard to the present, does it occur to you that he could be useful to the Army?'

'With a lame leg?' said Polly.

'His qualifications as a motor engineer are first-class,' said Boots. 'I.Mech.E.'

'What does that mean, old love?' asked Polly.

'That he passed the exam that made him a member of the Institute of Mechanical Engineers,' said Boots. 'The Royal Army Ordnance Corps could make excellent use of a man like that, and turn a blind eye to his lame leg. He wouldn't be asked to run at the enemy, but to help make sure our mobile armour didn't break down. This war is one of machines and technicians. The Germans proved that in Poland and France. Their machines were always in the field first, and the infantry followed up. I'm

57

damn sure RAOC would take Matthew, providing he was able to sidestep the conventional medical and get himself a direct interview with the right kind of company commander.'

'Which you could wangle?' smiled Polly.

'Which might be arranged,' said Boots. 'If accepted, he'd go in with at least the rank of staff-sergeant, if not lieutenant. There are any amount of mechanics in the Army, there aren't all that many I.Mech.E. men.'

'Am I getting the picture?' asked Polly. 'Are you thinking of trying to pull some strings that'll mean a commission for Rosie's hard-up bloke?'

'It's a thought if his garage business runs into real trouble,' said Boots.

'Just a thought?' smiled Polly.

'In passing,' said Boots.

'Chiefly for the benefit of the Army?' said Polly.

'Good point, Polly. Is he more useful to the country keeping farm tractors going or running a team of tank maintenance men?'

'Fifty-fifty, old sport, unless you're thinking that his Army pay and an allowance as a married man would provide a more reliable income than his garage,' said Polly.

'A reliable income must have some attractions,' said Boots.

'How do you genuinely feel about Rosie marrying a hard-up man and Tim marrying

58

a blind woman?' asked Polly.

'I feel they both know exactly what they're doing,' said Boots, who had several times discussed with Polly the drama of Tim's news.

'Tim's very young,' said Polly.

'No younger than I was when I married Emily,' said Boots, 'and you know as well as anybody that on active service in wartime Army men and ambulance drivers grow old quickly.'

'I do know,' said Polly, 'it's something I can never forget. When are you going to tell the family about Tim?'

'I'll phone home this evening,' said Boots. 'Tim has too much on his mind to cope with family reactions himself.'

'The news will stagger some of them,' said Polly. 'It staggered me.'

'It was that kind of news,' said Boots. 'Now eat your toast.'

'I've eaten it, thank you, and finished up the marmalade,' said Polly.

'Finished it?' said Boots.

'Yes, rotten hard luck, lover,' said Polly.

'Marriage means equal shares,' said Boots.

'Yes, I know, darling, but sometimes my shares are more equal than yours,' said Polly. 'Wife's privilege, don't you know.'

'I spy another jar,' said Boots.

'Yes, you jammy old devil,' said Polly, 'and it's from Dorothy.'

'Your stepmother?' said Boots.

'Yes,' said Polly. 'It came out of a Red Cross parcel she sent us, and now your share is more equal than mine. Blow that for a lark.'

Sunday afternoon.

In the Western Desert, General Rommel was conducting another offensive against the British and Empire troops, who were coming to regard him as a bit of a pain in the elbow. He was a different proposition altogether from any of the Italian generals. He took war seriously, and his Afrika Korps, superbly equipped, and supported by a formidable air force, was proving an alarming threat to Egypt. Prime Minister Churchill, who had shared in his country's elation over Wavell's defeat of the Italians, now began to worry about whether or not Rommel could be held. General Wavell had been sent to command the British troops in war-torn Greece, but a combined German-Italian assault had forced a British evacuation that was uncomfortably similar to Dunkirk. General Auchinleck had taken charge in Egypt, where Britain simply couldn't afford another defeat, especially one that would lose them control of the Middle East and its oilfields. More men, armour and planes were needed to strengthen Auchinleck's army, which had been weakened by the transfer of some divisions to Greece.

Not far from Bere Regis in Dorset, a dogcart was ambling along a country lane. Matthew Chapman and ATS Lieutenant Rosie Adams had become addicted to this kind of excursion, which induced in both a feeling of being empathetic with the tranquillity of the countryside.

The early May afternoon was bright, Dorset lush with green growth, the landscapes picturesque and undulating. Away to the right, a tractor was travelling in a straight line over a field. Rosie conjured up thoughts of bygone times, when noisy internal combustion had not yet become one of man's more infernal inventions. Her vision made everything to do with the war seem remote and unreal, and what was it if not an impossible and ugly madness when set against God's gift of a world green and beautiful?

'Matt, stop a moment,' she said, and Matt whistled at his nag, which ambled to a halt.

'Something bothering you, Rosie?' he said.

'No, I simply want to feast my eyes,' she said, and took a long look at the panorama of Dorset in early summer. 'It's exquisite, isn't it, Matt?'

'Ar, that it is, m'dear,' said Matt.

'Don't go native,' said Rosie.

'Still, there it is,' said Matt. 'Dorset come by God's good hand, but 'tis man's own plough that tills its land.'

'Well, God's good hand and man's plough seem to have enjoyed a long and fruitful togetherness,' said Rosie.

'There's another kind of togetherness,' said Matt.

'You and your garage?' smiled Rosie, liking his well-defined profile and his healthy weathered look.

'I wasn't thinking on those lines,' he said.

'The togetherness of men and women, then?' said Rosie.

'Happy and long-lasting for some, quarrelsome for others,' said Matt.

'Quarrels are forbidden in my family,' said Rosie.

'Who forbids them?' asked Matt.

'My grandmother,' said Rosie. 'One is allowed to speak one's mind, and to argue, but never to quarrel. All married couples in our family have to put up with each other's faults.'

'But unless your grandmother's around at the time, how can she prevent a quarrel?' asked Matt.

'Oh, her invisible presence is always around,' smiled Rosie.

'Breathing fire?' said Matt. 'She's a dragon?'

'Certainly not,' said Rosie. 'How dare you

suggest that of my much-admired grand-mother, you shocker? Go to the bottom of the class.'

Matt laughed.

'I've been there more than once in my time,' he said.

'Haven't we all?' said Rosie, and she laughed too. They looked at each other. But in this kind of rural atmosphere, there didn't seem much point in merely looking. So they elected to kiss, and did so in such a heady and exciting way that each thought the other suspiciously well-practised in the art. When she was able to draw breath, Rosie demanded to know who else Matt had been kissing lately. No-one else, Rosie, only you, said Matt, and followed that up by asking if there'd been another man in her life recently. Rosie said there'd never been any other man at all. Matt, of course, at once suggested there had to have been some chap who'd taught her to kiss like there was no tomorrow.

'Yes, you have,' said Rosie, 'but I've been a very willing pupil.'

'Not much of the pupil about you, Rosie,' said Matt, 'you're all of a woman. What kind of togetherness d'you think we'll enjoy? Historical?'

'I'd prefer hysterical,' said Rosie. 'Well, there should be a few laughs in every marriage.'

'To put a smile on the face of the ups and downs?' said Matt.

'Well, I think so, don't you?' said Rosie. No traffic disturbed them. Sunday quiet prevailed. Somewhere the individual battalions that made up the 17th Infantry Division had their camps. Somewhere the camps of each battalion were scenes of movement, even if only the lazy movements of a Sunday, the accepted rest day of men training up to the limit on all other days. Time went by, then Matt took up the reins and set his good-tempered nag in motion. The dogcart reached the main road at a moment when two Army troop-carrying lorries went by, a scout car leading.

'Men travelling to their work?' said Matt.

'Their real work will be when they come up against the Germans,' said Rosie. 'Would you like to be with them?'

'Not while I'm with you,' said Matt, 'not at anytime when I'm with you do I want to be elsewhere.'

'But you regret sometimes that your leg keeps you out of the Army, don't you?' said Rosie.

'It's the way of a man, I suppose, to feel a call to the colours in a war like this one,' said Matt. 'But then, without this old leg of mine, I'd never have met you. I'd have missed the best moment of my life. Would I have opted for that? Blow my shirt off if I would.' He turned into the main road. 'I wonder at what you've opted for yourself, spending the rest of your life with me.'

'Well, you dear man, I like what I've opted for,' said Rosie, 'except that I didn't strictly opt for it. It rushed up and overtook me.'

'Let me tell you,' smiled Matt, 'the first time I laid eyes on you, I fell from a great height, and damn all if I'll ever recover. Now we'll go home and have some new-laid eggs for tea, soft-boiled.'

'All by ourselves,' smiled Rosie. His sister was out for the day with her fiancé, Constable John Rawlings.

'I'll play fair, I'll do some gardening,' said Matt.

'I'll get the tea,' said Rosie.

'That's very fair,' said Matt.

Rosie hoped events would also be fair, that orders from London wouldn't compel the departure of the 7th Corps overseas before her wedding. She and Matt had agreed that it should take place several weeks after his sister's, to give him time and space to do some interior work on his cottage, and to fit it up as a marital home. The work and the preparations were to include the installation of new furniture, especially for their bedroom.

Rosie needed her adoptive father to give her away. Of all people, he had to be there. She had written to her natural father,

Colonel Sir Charles Armitage. Sir Charles had inherited his title on the death of his own father several months ago, not long after his ailing wife had passed away. He was presently serving in the Middle East. Rosie had informed him of her forthcoming marriage, and asked him if he would like to attend, providing he could get leave. It would be a little while before she could expect an answer, and in any case, as things were in Egypt, she doubted his chances of leave. His absence, however, would be a small thing compared to not having her adoptive father give her away. She had made it clear to Sir Charles in the nicest kind of way that Boots must have precedence in this matter.

Rumours concerning a Middle East destination were flying about, and had been ever since General Rommel's offensive had carried his Afrika Korps from Libya into Egypt. In Libya, Tobruk was still held by the British, and part of Rommel's army was besieging it.

Rosie knew, of course, that her personal wishes were at the mercy of the demands of war, but she still hoped her wedding day would be as she wanted.

She smiled as she realized she was presently heading for Matt's cottage and a tea featuring soft-boiled eggs.

She wondered, when an engaged couple

were alone in a country cottage, what followed soft-boiled eggs?

What did follow, as a matter of fact, was nothing more than a relaxed hour or so listening to music from the radio. That is, until Matt suddenly came to his feet.

'Shan't be long,' he said.

'Are you going somewhere, then?' asked Rosie, jacket off and legs curled up under her on the sofa.

'Yes, up to look at the chickens.'

'You're what?'

'Going up to look at the chickens. It's safer.'

'Safer than what?'

'Being alone with you,' said Matt. 'Chickens don't play the devil with my feelings. I could look at a thousand hens without wanting to pull a single feather off any of 'em.'

'Matt, come back.'

But out of the room he went. He obviously felt their wedding night was the one right time to first make love to her. Bless the man. Rosie glanced down at herself. With her jacket off, her light khaki shirt was very defining. What had he meant about pulling feathers? That he was tempted to undo her shirt buttons? She wasn't sure if King's Regulations allowed an ATS officer to give permission for that kind of thing.

'Well,' she said to her well-fitting shirt,

67

'what shall we do now?'

Play a waiting game until he returns?

But she went to join him by the chicken run. He put an arm around her, a warm and caressing arm.

'I can wait for the right time, Rosie,' he said.

'I know that,' she said, 'but do you like how I look in my shirt?'

'Yes, both of you,' he said.

She laughed, and the sound was touched by the excitement of a young woman in love for the first time in her life.

The chickens clucked.

Chapter Four

Chinese Lady reflected on the state of family affairs. She was commonsensical enough to realize the war had to be fought overseas once the RAF had put paid to an invasion attempt by that lunatic warmonger Hitler. If ever there was a madman who ought to have been drowned at birth, or better, not to have been born at all, it was Hitler. He was going to be responsible sooner or later for several of her family being sent abroad again. Boots, Tim, Bobby, and Emma's husband Jonathan. Then there was Annabelle's husband Nick, he'd have to go for the first time. And what about Rosie, Polly and Eloise? They were all women soldiers. Lord, she'd been told there were ATS girls being trained to fire anti-aircraft guns. A fine thing that would be, if Boots's wife and daughters all ended up firing cannon shells. And a fine thing too if, when Boots did have to go overseas again, Polly went with him. Chinese Lady was blessed if she could understand a wife going off to war with her husband. Next thing there'd be a message to say Captain Simms – no, Captain Adams – had won a medal for charging into battle and having her leg blown off. Chinese Lady hoped such an outrageous message, or an even worse one, would never arrive. It just wasn't natural, turning women into soldiers, especially if they were wives. It didn't matter to Chinese Lady that various members of her family had assured her no Servicewomen would be thrown into a battle. That was all very well, but she didn't trust those generals at the War Office. After the way they'd used men in the Great War, she wouldn't put it past them to make women man the trenches against Hitler's Germans. Not blind to what was obvious, that Polly was remarkably attached to Boots, Chinese Lady supposed she would want to go overseas with him, never mind what might happen. But what kind of life was that for a couple not long married?

Or for Emma and Jonathan, now back from their honeymoon. Everyone knew Jonathan was on embarkation leave and that he'd be going overseas tomorrow, Monday. That was what war did to lots of young couples. Criminal, that's what it was. As for Emma's brother Bobby, and his French lady friend Helene, Bobby was with his unit, as far as she knew, and Helene was doing useful work in a women's First Aid company or something. She had no idea, any more than the rest of the family did, that Bobby and Helene were actually just beginning their time at an SOE training centre in the New Forest, and that it was their first step towards becoming agents who would work with a French Resistance cell.

Then there was Rosie and her wedding. Everyone wanted to be there. Well, Rosie was a dear girl. Chinese Lady hoped the devil of war wouldn't cause any inconvenience, like Boots not being able to attend. Inconvenience was the sort of thing that was always waiting to poke its nose into family affairs. Goodness knows how often it had walked through her front door in her own lifetime, and without being asked. It was one of the devil's regular aggravations, and nobody ought to actually invite such, like Boots had by going back into the Army. He ought to go up to the War Office and talk to them about making sure his wife and daughters didn't have to fire guns or charge into battle. If not, perhaps Edwin could go.

'Edwin?'

'Yes, my dear?' Mr Finch was enjoying a Sunday evening read.

'I think someone should go up to the War Office to make sure Polly, Rosie and Eloise don't have to fire guns or go into battle,' said Chinese Lady. 'Perhaps you could go in from your work one day.'

'I don't think Polly, Rosie and Eloise will have to fire guns or go into battle,' said Mr Finch.

'Well, what about those ATS girls that's being taught how to fire anti-aircraft guns?' asked Chinese Lady.

'Ah,' said Mr Finch.

'What's that you're saying, Edwin?'

'Ah,' said Mr Finch.

'That's not saying anything,' said Chinese Lady.

'By the way,' said Mr Finch who, like Boots, could divert Chinese Lady from one subject to another with practised ease, although in the knowledge that she only dismounted temporarily from a hobby-horse, 'did you know that the sister of Rosie's fiancé has the same name as you, Maisie?'

'Oh, yes, I remember it was mentioned,' said Chinese Lady. 'I hope the name doesn't get too common.'

'It's a name I'm very fond of,' said Mr Finch.

'Well, it's nice of you to say so,' said Chinese Lady. 'Would you like a cup of tea, Edwin?'

'Thank you, Maisie,' smiled Mr Finch.

'I'll have one myself,' said Chinese Lady. A nice cup of tea somehow always managed to put the war into the background.

Sammy mentioned to Susie that he'd got a foreboding. Susie asked if that was something he ought to see the doctor about.

72

Sammy said his foreboding was a feeling that Boots would be drafted overseas before very long, which meant he might miss the wedding. Susie took the foreboding in her stride, pointing out that Boots was never the sort of man to miss the wedding of someone very dear to him, as Rosie was. He wouldn't go sailing off before it happened. Sammy said he didn't think Boots would be going sailing, and Susie said well, he would be going on a boat somewhere, so there wasn't any need to quibble. Rosie wants him there, and so would I, she said, if Boots was my dad. I adore Boots, she said. Sammy pointed out it was illegal for her as his married wife to adore any bloke except himself, and that he'd had to tell her so before. Susie said a girl couldn't pick and choose about that sort of thing, like she could when buying apples. Adoring someone just happens, she said. Sammy told her to stop getting his goat. Susie said only teasing, love, let's write to the children and tell them we're going to bring them home definitely for the wedding if there still aren't any air raids to worry about. Tommy and Vi will want to do the same with their children, said Sammy. Susie asked what about Tim, Rosie's brother, and Bobby, her cousin? Yes, said Sammy, and what about Sir Henry and Lady Simms? They're on the guest list, but if my foreboding's correct, Sir

73

Henry might have to give it a miss.

'Well, lots of people had to give Emma's wedding a miss,' said Susie. 'That sort of thing can't be helped in wartime. Look at Jonathan. He and Emma were back yesterday from their honeymoon, but he's going overseas tomorrow, so he won't be there. I expect Emma's very down.'

Sammy frowned.

'Shouldn't be allowed, and I feel for Emma,' he said. 'Still, she'll buck up, she's got her dad's various fortitudes.'

'His what?' smiled Susie, who wore her thirty-seven years in a kind of challenging way. She was going to fight the onset of forty with spirit and subtle make-up. 'His what, Sammy?'

'Character,' said Sammy, 'Ned's got a lot of that. Tell you what, Susie, we'll help Chinese Lady and Stepdad with all the arrangements for the wedding. It'll be a worthwhile job and give us something to do.'

'I'll love to help,' said Susie, 'but I didn't think we were actually hard-up for something to do.'

'Well, the fact is,' said Sammy, 'business is all routine these days. In fact, I was thinking–' He stopped and coughed. Susie eyed him suspiciously. 'I was thinking of gettin' Tommy to run the business as it is at this particular time, which is an easy time

74

and won't give Tommy any worry. Well, it's hardly a strain on my own brainbox at the moment, if you see what I mean.'

'No, I don't see,' said Susie. 'Try a straight line instead of going round the mulberry bush.'

'Well, Susie, I was thinking – only thinking, mind – of offering my services to an Army quartermaster's department and takin' up a military challenge.'

'Oh, you were, were you?' said Susie. 'Sammy Adams, go to the kitchen and fetch me the egg saucepan.'

'Now, Susie—'

'Fetch it,' said Susie. 'I'm going to hit you with it and knock silly ideas right out of your daft head.'

'I don't think I'll do any fetching, Susie.'

'You won't do any more silly thinking, either,' said Susie. 'Boots is in the Army, and so are Tim and Bobby. So are Rosie and Polly and Eloise. So is my brother Freddy, and my brother-in-law Horace. And Annabelle's husband Nick is in the RAF. How many is that?'

'Quite a few,' said Sammy.

'Nine,' said Susie. 'That's more than enough. Have you got that, Sammy, are you hearing me?'

'Um – well,' said Sammy. Susie's blue eyes issued a warning. 'Yes, loud and clear, Susie.'

'Sammy, you silly man, you don't think I

want to see this war through without you, do you? You don't think I'll let you go off when there's already nine members of the family doing their bit, do you?'

'Well, Susie, it's just that I think Hitler's more of a Hun than Kaiser Bill ever was,' said Sammy, 'and I–'

'Boots and his like, and Mr Churchill, will deal with Hitler one day,' said Susie, even if she couldn't think how the British Army could get at Hitler in his German fortress. 'You can keep doing your own bit, Sammy, by making sure the business stays on its feet. Tommy's got a lot of commonsense and honesty, but he doesn't have your natural talent. Well, I'm glad we've settled that. What's that funny look for?'

'I can't tell a porkie,' said Sammy, 'I feel I've just been done over by your egg saucepan.'

Susie smiled. If she sometimes had to put her foot down with Sammy, that didn't alter the fact that she was still exceptionally fond of him. Anyone who suggested that a man as physically fit and energetic as Sammy ought to be doing more for his country than fulfilling Government contracts and carrying out ARP duties, would have received short shrift from Susie.

Besides, as a normal and healthy woman, she liked the fact that Sammy could still be very operative as a lover.

Boots rang Chinese Lady, who immediately asked what he was phoning for. Boots said just a chat. Well, thank goodness, she said, I thought it was to tell me you're going overseas again. You went in 1914 and 1939, she said, and it's time you stopped doing things that turn the family upside-down. Boots, who knew that Polly's father, General Sir Henry Simms, commanding the 7th Corps, was in London attending a conference with other corps commanders, might have said something urgent was in the wind, but merely asked how everyone was. Chinese Lady gave him a resumé of everyone's health, all of which was a lot better than it had been, she said, now that air raids had stopped for a bit.

'Pleased to hear it,' said Boots, 'but I think you'll have to prepare yourself for some of us being drafted overseas before very long.'

Chinese Lady did a bit of a carry-on then.

'You said you'd phoned just for a chat. I don't call that kind of talk just a chat, especially over the phone when you know I never trust what the contraption might do to me. I don't know what to make of you, you're always goin' overseas against the Germans as soon as you put a uniform on. It's very upsettin'.'

'One of those things that can't be helped,' said Boots.

'Can't be helped?' said Chinese Lady, and did a bit more carrying-on. 'You're as airy-fairy as you always were, and of course you never take any notice of me. I hope you're not going to tell me that Polly will go with you. You'll have to do something about that if it happens.'

Boots said he'd hold Polly's hand. Chinese Lady asked if that was supposed to be funny. No, supportive, said Boots. That won't do either of you much good when cannon shells start exploding all round both of you, said Chinese Lady, who simply couldn't be brought down from this particular hobby horse. I'd like it better, she said, if you and Polly had proper war jobs as a married couple, like working for the Red Cross. You'd better make sure you'll both be at Rosie's wedding, she said. Well, I know Emma was pleased you were at hers, she said, so I won't keep on at you about other things. Thanks, old girl, said Boots, which of course made Chinese Lady tell him, for the hundredth time, not to call her old girl.

'By the way,' said Boots, 'Tim's got his commission and is marrying the ATS officer we've heard so much about.'

'Lor',' said Chinese Lady, 'what's the war doing to everyone, I'd like to know. First Emma, then Rosie and now Tim. Not that I'm not pleased, except no-one told me things had got this far with Tim and his lady officer. And Tim didn't say anything in his last letter to me except someone had told him he could expect to be an officer himself soon. And now he is. I just don't hardly know what to say about my family having so many officers, it's not what I've ever been used to, and your late dad was happy enough as a corporal and was very respected as such. I hope being officers don't make any of you get above yourselves. Is Tim thinking about him and Rosie having a double wedding?'

'Tim wants a quiet wedding,' said Boots. 'That's because his young lady, Felicity, was caught by a bomb blast during an air raid on London. Tragically, old lady, it blinded her.'

There was a long silence at the other end of the line. At Boots's end, Polly was standing by his elbow.

'Boots?' Chinese Lady's voice was very quiet and a little emotional.

'Tim's going to make sure that blindness isn't the end of the world for Felicity,' said Boots, and clearly heard a deep sigh from his mother.

'I don't know what to say,' she said just as quietly, 'except I can't help thinking how you got blinded and how Em'ly was a godsend to you and the fam'ly all those years before you got unblinded.'

'I think Tim had my problem on his mind,' said Boots, 'I think he's now going to be a godsend himself. To Felicity.'

'It's a nice name,' said Chinese Lady in a slightly shaky and slightly irrelevant way. 'Oh, the poor young lady, I don't know when I've felt more upset. But I understand about a quiet wedding.'

'Be sure of one thing, it's a love match,' said Boots, 'and a pretty splendid one. I'm letting Rosie and Eloise know. Would you like to talk to Lizzy, Tommy and Sammy, or shall I?'

'I'll ask Edwin to,' said Chinese Lady, 'I'm too sad for Tim's young lady to do it myself. Still, I know one thing, we've all got to be proud of Tim.'

'Let's be proud of both of them,' said Boots, unusually sober, 'it's probably going to be even more difficult for Felicity than for Tim. She'll have to cope with not wanting to be a drag on him. She'll find herself thinking a great deal about that. I hope to God Tim's unit stays permanently based in Troon, where they're going to live.'

'Boots, she'll be alone a lot of the time,' protested Chinese Lady.

'Not alone,' said Boots. 'Tim's landlady will keep her company and give her any help she needs.'

'We all ought to go to church on Sunday and do some praying,' said Chinese Lady. She sighed again. 'Well, I'd best say goodbye now, Boots.'

'Goodbye, old lady,' said Boots.

'Well?' said Polly when he hung up.

'It was a blow to her, of course,' said Boots. 'Knocked her sideways, but give her a couple of days and she'll be as resilient as ever, with ideas about going to see Felicity.'

'Would Felicity want that?' asked Polly.

'Probably not,' said Boots, 'but if she's going to be family, there's no way she'll be able to keep Chinese Lady off her doorstep between now and the wedding.'

'Darling, your irreverence is a shocker,' said Polly. 'Is there no way of persuading you and your family to refer to your admirable mother in a more gracious fashion?'

'I doubt it,' said Boots. 'She considers the name a gracious compliment to the Chinese and to someone who was a friend of hers when we were all young kids.'

'Who was someone?' asked Polly.

'Mr Wong Fu, who ran the Chinese Laundry off the Old Kent Road,' said Boots.

Polly laughed.

Chinese Lady passed the unhappy news of Tim's fiancée to her husband. Mr Finch received it and it disturbed his calm. He wasn't sure, he said, whether or not Tim at twenty could handle the stress and emotions of what he was taking on, particularly as his first commitment was to the Army. I know, said Chinese Lady, and that's why I told Boots we all ought to go to church and pray for those two young people. I'd like you to talk to Lizzy, Tommy and Sammy, she said, I don't feel up to it myself. It's brought back all the years when the family had to live with Boots's blindness, she said, when it was painful to watch a proud man fighting his helplessness. Boots has always been a proud man under his airy-fairy self, and I expect Tim's young lady, being an officer, is just as proud as anyone, and Tim's going to feel pain like we all did.

'Maisie,' said Mr Finch quietly, 'I know few women more understanding of life and people than you. I'll talk to Lizzy, Tommy and Sammy, of course I will.'

'Thank you, Edwin,' said Chinese Lady and left the sad element alone then to take a different tack. She asked her husband to do what he could with the Government about making sure Boots and Polly didn't get sent overseas before Rosie was married.

'Tricky,' said Mr Finch.

'We'd all be grateful,' said Chinese Lady, 'especially Rosie, and especially if you could get the Government to give them safe jobs with the Red Cross.'

'Ah, yes,' said Mr Finch, and cleared a bone in his throat.

'I don't suppose you could actu'lly get to see Mr Churchill,' said Chinese Lady, 'but someone important that could do something.'

'I see, yes, someone important,' said Mr Finch.

'When you've got time, Edwin.'

'Of course, Maisie, when I've got time,' said Mr Finch. 'Um, I'll deal with Tim's news first.'

Ten minutes later he began the phone calls to Lizzy, Tommy and Sammy in turn. Lizzy was shocked by what had happened to the young lady about whom the family had heard so much, but thought it lovely of Tim to want to marry her. If anything could really help her, a caring husband could. When Tommy was told, he said oh ruddy blimey, that's a hard one to take, the poor girl must feel like committing suicide. Still, we'll all wish her and Tim all the luck going, he said, and anything Vi and me can do to help we will. Sammy was of the same mind, assuring his stepfather that he and Susie would back Tim in every way they could, and if, for instance, Tim needed a bit of funding, the family would be only too pleased to oblige, and that he himself would be ready to start the ball rolling.

In short, the initial reaction of Lizzy, Tommy and Sammy to Tim's intention to become a husband and a help to Felicity was one of admiration, and Ned, Vi and Susie were of a similar mind when the news was passed to them. Subsequently, of course, they all gave sober thought to the difficulties the young couple were bound to experience.

That night the man with the negative outlook, the man who had achieved something positive on two occasions, made an attempt on a third objective, a printing works in Weymouth. Unfortunately for his hopes, he was interrupted by a sailor and his lady friend just as he was about to gain entry by breaking a window. He disappeared fast, on his bicycle, and under his breath he put together some bitter words about the inconsiderate nature of people wandering the streets so late at night.

The sailor could have told him the reason. So could the sailor's lady friend.

Chapter Five

Monday morning.

London looked battered, scarred and wounded. Some of Wren's loveliest churches were no more than gaunt shells, but his cathedral still stood in towering defiance. The people were out and about, skirting the rubble of the last raid in mid-April, the revengeful one mounted by an infuriated and mocked Goering. Prior to that, the capital had for months suffered a sustained blitz from the air, and thousands of its citizens had died under the nightly hail of bombs, but at no time had Prime Minister Churchill ever suggested that he and the people were ready to surrender.

However, for over a week now there had been no raids, and London was taking a welcome breather in the kind of early May sunshine that suggested capricious summer had decided to put in a welcome appearance.

At King's Cross station, young Mrs Emma Hardy was saying goodbye to her husband Jonathan. They had been married for nine days. His leave had been for ten days, and Emma had soon found out that that length of time meant embarkation leave. Along with other men, Jonathan was now about to rejoin his regiment, which was assembling in Liverpool prior to embarking for the Middle East, where General Rommel and his Afrika Korps were giving the British forces many more punishing headaches than the Italians had. There had been a fierce engagement when the Germans attempted to breach the defences of Tobruk, determinedly held by the British and Empire troops. The Germans were driven back, but not before they'd inflicted a number of fatal casualties.

Emma was far from happy about Jonathan's departure, especially as she suspected his regiment would end up as artillery reinforcements for Tobruk.

'I mean, we simply don't know when we'll see each other again,' she said, thinking he now belonged more to the Army than to her. The honeymoon had been lovely, a week of exciting togetherness, during which time Jonathan had discovered that Emma, once she was over all the little yelps and blushmaking hurdles of their first act of togetherness, was a bride with a tendency to be saucy. For her part, Emma had dis- covered what a thrill he was to a girl.

'Jonathan, oh Christmas, is this really you?'

'Emma, you sure as a well-brought-up girl

you know what you're doing to me?'

'Well, if there's a law against it, it's a silly law. Jonathan, are you shy?'

'No, I don't be shy, I reckon, Emma, just disbelieving.'

'Jonathan, oh, you lovely chap, aren't you manly?'

'Going up in smoke, more like. D'you know what a saucy surprise packet you are, Emma Hardy?'

'But I like it, don't you, Jonathan?'

'Well, I hope you'll like what's going to happen next, Emma.'

'Heavens, are you going to have your wicked way with me again?'

'Well, I'm going to have a good try at doing what comes naturally, Emma.'

'I'll be happy to help, Jonathan.'

Those moments were all gone now. The long train was filling with soldiers and airmen, all destined for Liverpool and the troopships. Several contingents of WAAF and ATS personnel, laden with kit, were already aboard. They too were bound for troopships, troopships that would be part of protected convoys.

'Cheer up, Emma,' said Jonathan, standing on the platform with her and thinking this kind of event shouldn't happen more than once in a feller's life. 'I'll be back.'

'Yes, but when?' said Emma, thinking that if Shakespeare really wrote parting was

87

sweet sorrow, it wasn't one of his best lines. Parting was frankly painful. 'Have you got a pain, Jonathan? I have.'

'Well, something's hurting me, I know that,' said Jonathan. He hadn't wanted her to come to the station with him, but she'd insisted. Damn this old war, he thought. A whistle was blowing and doors were being slammed. The crowded platform was thinning out as men said their goodbyes to their nearest and dearest, and boarded the train. Emma suddenly threw her arms around Jonathan.

'Come back soon,' she whispered.

'You bet I will,' said Jonathan, and kissed her. She clung for long seconds before letting go.

She was biting her lip as he dumped his kitbag aboard and stepped up. It simply wasn't fair, a parting like this after a honeymoon like that. The whistle blew again, and the train's engine issued great hissing jets of steam that mushroomed. The last of the open doors were shut by porters, and the guard signalled with his green flag. Slowly the wheels of the train began to turn. Jonathan, standing in the corridor, had his head out of the window.

Emma, eyes misty, face lifted, swallowed and said, 'Could you come back tomorrow?'

'I'll write from Liverpool and let you know,' said Jonathan. 'Love you, Emma.'

'Take care, Jonathan, take care.'

She watched as the train pulled out. The scene reminded her of pictures of men departing for France during the Great War. Heads were at open windows, hands were waving, and from the platform emotional girls and women waved back and called their last goodbyes. Jonathan was receding, slowly but remorselessly, and Emma wondered when she would see him again. Her face felt stiff in her effort to control her own emotions. She lifted her hand. She waved, and Jonathan waved back. The guard's van passed Emma, and the train rattled over points as it began its journey north with its complement of Servicemen, Servicewomen and civilians.

Jonathan disappeared from her vision, and she stood still for long minutes before turning to make her way out of the station and into a life that had suddenly become empty. She was a girl who favoured self-control, but the bright wetness of her eyes was visible at that moment.

Chinese Lady was keeping Lizzy sympathetic company, commiserating with her over the enforced parting of Emma and Jonathan, which she was sure no-one was happy about. Lizzy said it was very hard on Emma. Chinese Lady said it was near to criminal, a husband having to leave his wife after only nine days of marriage. She felt sure God was frowning down on this kind of thing, which was happening to many young couples, and simply wasn't right or proper. Lizzy said war wasn't right or proper, either, except in this case.

'I mean, we had to stand up to Hitler, Mum. Ned says the country's taken on a responsibility that the whole world ought to share. He agrees with Mr Churchill that the whole world will be in a sorry mess if Hitler wins.'

'Well, I'm sure myself that the Lord is standing side by side with Mr Churchill,' said Chinese Lady. 'All the same, it's shameful, Jonathan being sent overseas. But I don't know who's to blame. Perhaps it's the Army's fault at not arranging things better.'

'I don't know if it is or not,' said Lizzy. 'Well, it's a very trying war for the Army, the Germans having a lot more guns and a lot more men. We're lucky we've got men of the Empire fighting on our side.'

'Oh, your late respected dad was fond of our Empire,' said Chinese Lady. 'Well, being a regular soldier, he did a lot for it. Still, someone's to blame about Emma and Jonathan, and I wouldn't be surprised if it was someone in the Government. I don't mean Mr Churchill. Mr Finch said only this morning at breakfast that Mr Churchill would sorrow very personal for the young couple if he knew. Well, he said something like that.'

She chatted on with Lizzy, but neither of them could definitely decide who was mostly to blame. However, they finally agreed, although in an uncertain way, that the fault could be laid at the door of someone in the Ministry.

Which Ministry?

They couldn't make up their minds about that.

Chinese Lady then talked about Boots and Polly probably having to go abroad sometime, which she hoped wouldn't be before Rosie's wedding. If she was sure of one thing, she said, it was that war wasn't good for family life. And look what it had done to Tim's young lady, blinded her and made it certain that Tim would have a very trying marriage, although, of course, she respected him for what he was going to do.

'Oh, we all do, Mum,' said Lizzy, 'but even if no-one likes what's happening to people, we've got to fight the war, and as I told Dad when he phoned last night, it's wonderful of Tim to take on a blind wife as well as doing his bit against the Germans.'

'Oh, I couldn't be more admiring, except it shook me up a bit when I remembered about Boots being blinded in the last war,' said Chinese Lady.

91

'Oh, Ned and me think there'll be problems for Tim and his young lady, but Boots, remember, managed ever so well with Em'ly's help,' said Lizzy. 'Anyway, about Boots and Polly goin' overseas, as long as it doesn't happen until after Rosie's wedding, we'd best not complain too much. Besides, going together would be what they'd want.'

'But it's just not right, women being sent overseas and ordered to man the trenches,' said Chinese Lady.

'Mum, I don't think there's going to be any trenches,' said Lizzy. 'Well, not according to Ned. He says this is a different kind of war.'

'Lord Above,' breathed Chinese Lady, 'you don't mean women soldiers are driving those great iron contraptions called tanks, do you?'

'Oh, I believe most of them just do office work, cooking and things like that,' smiled Lizzy, thinking it wiser not to mention that many ATS personnel were drivers, mechanics and motorcyclists, or that other women, like Amy Johnson, were piloting planes from factories and delivering them to the RAF.

'Well,' said Chinese Lady, 'I did hear some were learning how to fire anti-aircraft guns, which I'll never hold with. As for my new daughter-in-law Polly, that I must admit I admire, if she does cookin' for a whole company of men, I'll never be more surprised.'

'Nor me,' said Lizzy, 'especially as she told me, the day she married Boots, that she's never cooked a meal in her life.'

Shocked, Chinese Lady said, 'Lizzy, I never heard anything more unbelieving. A woman that's a wife can't cook? What's Boots doing about that?'

'Oh, he's done something already,' said Lizzy, 'he's bought her a cookery book.'

'I never learned any of my cookin' out of a book,' said Chinese Lady.

'Well, Polly hasn't lived your kind of life, Mum, or mine,' said Lizzy.

'I just hope Boots is gettin' some kind of proper meals while Polly's doing her learning,' said Chinese Lady.

'Oh, the Army's seeing to that,' said Lizzy.

'H'm,' said Chinese Lady doubtfully. She had reservations about Army food and Army cooking. 'Still, I suppose that's not very much to worry about, not when you think of what happened to Tim's poor young lady. Lizzy, have you heard from Bobby lately?'

'Oh, he writes very regular, but doesn't say much about what he's doing,' said Lizzy.

'Is his young French lady with him, Lizzy?'

'Yes, they're sharing life in some unit together,' said Lizzy.

'Well, I suppose that's all right,' said Chinese Lady. 'After all, Helene's a farmer's daughter, not one of them fast French-women from Paris, and Bobby's been brought up very proper.'

Lizzy smiled, knowing her mother was inclined to carry on about things improper. She'd been a formidable opponent of things improper all her life.

Down in the wilds of the New Forest the white-sweatered PT instructor addressed the men and women in shirts, shorts and gym shoes.

'Ladies and sirs, I'd be obliged if you'd kindly follow my movements, as previously requested. It's not part of my duties to get cross or spiteful, so I'm asking you to be nice to me, which means doing as I do. I realize, ladies and sirs, that you're all finding you've got muscles you never dreamed about, and that these exercises are punishing them, but I assure you that what you're imagining is pain you'll come to know as a tickle. By comparison.'

Second Lieutenant Bobby Somers let a grin slide across his face. His French lady love, Helene Aarlberg, a FANY officer, rolled her eyes. As far as she was concerned, all the English were crazy, full stop. A lot were also stuffy.

'Is there any good news?' asked a man.

'Not right now,' said the instructor, and resumed what was necessary, the daily exercises that would produce the desired end result, the feeling in these men and women that their bodies were made of india-rubber, their joints of elastic.

They were all volunteers, all willing to become part of the backbone of French Resistance.

Bobby and Helene had travelled down to the SOE (Special Operations Executive) training theatre in the New Forest after an interview with a Captain Jepson in London, following a previous interview with an anonymous kind of bloke. Everything about their meeting with Captain Jepson seemed informal, even casual. There had been no heroic pointing up of the honour, valour and glory of serving Britain by serving France. Just some friendly questions about themselves, and answers that told Captain Jepson the kind of young man and young woman he had before him. Their reputation for bravery and resourcefulness had gone ahead of them, and Captain Jepson only required to know what kind of people they were outside of that. Pleasant? Awkward? Inarticulate? Free-speaking? Intelligent? Or merely sensible? And so on.

He favoured their answers. He asked a final question, a simple one.

'Are you both certain you want to do this?'

Help France? Bobby and Helene looked at each other then at Captain Jepson.

'Yes,' said Helene.

'Yes,' said Bobby, although nothing had been said about what they would be specifically asked to do. That, he supposed, was to be left to their imagination for the time being. 'We're both certain.'

'Good,' said Captain Jepson and then told them that while being trained as operatives each would be known only by a single name. They could choose for themselves. Helene chose Fifi, which made Bobby smile. *Fifi* was the name of her sailing dinghy, the boat that had taken them halfway across the Channel before capsizing. Bobby chose good old Charlie.

Training at the New Forest school meant there was not only muscle-racking PT to endure, there were seminars that encouraged discussions about France, the French and the occupying Germans, and lectures that were extremely frank about the enemy and the enemy's ramifications of security. There were discouraging facts given about what any operative might expect from the Gestapo in the event of capture, and every kind of advice concerning how to achieve mental, as well as physical, resistance to interrogation. There were sudden questions, questions that were barked at the trainees.

'You, Josephine, how would you react if you fell foul of a suspicious SS officer?'

'Call him "mon Capitaine", answer all his questions like an advocate of Vichy France, and lie like the devil whenever necessary,' said a woman who had chosen the name Josephine for herself.

'And if he didn't believe you?'

'I would repeat all I'd said before to convince him it was true.'

'You, Charlie, what would you do if two Gestapo officers stopped you in a street and attempted to arrest you?'

'Put myself in a position of being able to escape,' said Bobby.

'How?'

'That would depend on the circumstances,' said Bobby.

'Well, let's assume there'd be German soldiers nearby.'

'Tricky,' said Bobby, 'and not something I'd make up my mind about in advance. I'd wait for the actual moment before I decided. See how the land lay. I'd be a ruddy idiot to rely on a fixed plan. But I know, of course, that since I wouldn't want to risk being taken to Gestapo headquarters, I'd have to take some sort of positive action, short of killing the Gestapo officers. I've been told that that kind of thing can lead to bloodthirsty reprisals.'

'You, Fifi, any comments?'

'Yes,' said Helene, 'I'd run as soon as the Gestapo pigs made themselves known to me.'

'You'd run?'

'Yes, of course,' said Helene. 'I've discovered the English have a very wise saying in an emergency. "Don't hang about, you bloody fool, run."'

'Can you run?'

'Faster than Gestapo pigs?' said Helene. 'Yes.'

The comprehensive training tested everyone to the limit. It could exhaust these volunteers mentally and physically. They had to return, over and over again, to absorbing everything concerning the art of resistance to interrogation and the rack. They had to learn Morse, and those who liked fiddling with wires, knobs and valves had to learn how to transmit and receive radio messages. All of them, the women included, had to become expert in the use of a Sten gun, in finding their way through a forest at night, and in the art of surviving if they ever had to go to ground. Tim would have sympathized with cousin Bobby and Helene in regard to the physical tribulations. He'd had months of similar stuff, though for a different purpose.

However, the trainees were housed very comfortably and the food was good. There was not a great deal of easy-going frater-

98

nization during rest periods, for every trainee was individualistic, with his or her own thoughts about Resistance work, and most were inclined to keep these thoughts to themselves.

One evening, when dinner was over, and relaxation a hard-earned luxury, Helene drew Bobby out of the common room and exchanged discreet whispers with him.

'Bobby–'

'Charlie.'

'Oh, Charlie, then.'

'Well, you know it's part of our training to only use our chosen names. Anyway, you want to ask something, Fifi?'

'Yes. Do you want to sleep with me?'

'Of course.'

'And make love to me?'

'Of course. But we haven't been trained for that yet, and I'm not sure if it's part of the course.'

'Trained? Trained? Part of the course? Oh, what an idiot you are, Bobby.'

'Charlie.'

'Oh, shut up. I'm learning many things here. How would you like it if I learned how to hate you?'

'Why would you want to learn that?'

'Because when you should be serious with me, you still talk like a crazy man.'

'If I remember right, you hated me when we first met–'

'That's a lie!'

'–and it grieved me a lot, I can tell you.'

'I was worried about France, that's all. You know I was.'

'Sorry, Fifi. But I'm not up to my usual self, not since hearing about Tim and his blinded fiancée.'

'Oh, that was such sad news, yes, I am dreadfully sorry.'

'I've written to him. Anyway, what was the question?'

'Do you want to sleep with me tonight?'

'Yes but no.'

'What do you mean, yes but no?'

'Yes, I want to sleep with you, Fifi, but no, I don't think I should. I promised your parents to take care of you, not to take advantage of you.'

Helene thought that absurd. Well, although she was a farmer's daughter and not a Paris sophisticate, she was still French, so she said, 'But we're in love and are going to be married one day.'

'I think I need help,' said Bobby.

'You need help to make love to me, a man like you?' she said.

'I need help to avoid temptation,' said Bobby. 'But look here, don't you share a room with the woman called Josephine?'

'Yes, but she's never there, she's sleeping every night with the man called Harold.'

'Saucy old Harold. Hope he doesn't get

poked in the eye on a night when she's not in the mood. Tell you what, I'll be at your door at twenty-three-hundred, and we'll have some hot cocoa and a talk about it.'

'A talk about what?'

'About if I ought to take advantage of you,' said Bobby, certain sure he shouldn't take any advantage of the daughter of Jacob and Madame Aarlberg, who had been so good to him and trusted him to take care of her. 'I'm supposed to be your guardian.'

'Crazy.'

'Well, let's see how we proceed with things from twenty-three-hundred onwards,' said Bobby.

When he quietly tapped on Helene's door at the appointed time, she at once opened it, took hold of his arm and pulled him quickly into her room.

'Bobby darling.'

'Holy Moses,' breathed Bobby. His French lady love was wearing nothing more than a shortie nightie. 'Blind me,' he said, and all his reservations went up in smoke.

If Matthew Chapman was too sensitive a man to take advantage of Rosie, Bobby was too full of a young man's vim and vigour to start another conversation about do's and don't's when his French lady love was clad in something that was hardly anything at all.

Not that it made a weak young woman of

her when they were bedded. Helene was supple and strong-bodied, and experienced excitement in turning the overture into a prolonged and provocative wrestling contest, during which one would have thought she was fighting for her honour. Bobby asked her in an exasperated whisper what she was after, a boxing match or a love match. Both, said Helene. God help you, then, said Bobby.

But of course it all became a lovers' get-together from that point, Helene's strength running away and Bobby's virility ascendant. He conducted the rest of the overture himself, and did so in such a winning way that when the curtain went up the opening duet was already in full song. And very musical it was too.

'Bobby – oh, *mon cheri.*'

'Join the club, you darling, I feel the same way.'

They pleased each other immensely.

Afterwards, Helene whispered, 'Why did we wait so long to do something so good?'

'Well, I've been brought up in a family that only does what's ordered by God, and God doesn't order anything like this for un-married people,' said Bobby.

'Ordered by God?' breathed Helene. 'What are you talking about, you idiot?'

'I'm talking about my maternal grand-mother,' said Bobby. 'She's a stern believer

102

in God's orders.'

'Ah, all you English are crazy,' said Helene, 'but I will still let you marry me.'

'Good on you, Fifi, you're lovely,' said Bobby, but he still thought that in this kind of war, with all kinds of relationships under strain, marriage should wait, especially for two people earmarked for undercover work in France. Quite soon they would be going to Manchester, to the Parachute Training School.

'Bobby, do it again,' said Helene after quite some time had elapsed.

'Pardon?' said Bobby.

'Yes, make love to me again,' said Helene.

'Well, all right, but I don't know what God's going to say,' said Bobby.

Chapter Six

In Troon, 4 Commando group were being prepared for another raid that, in concert with other groups, would be aimed at the destruction of a German-occupied port in Norway. The co-operation and assistance of the Royal Navy and the RAF were required in an attempt to severely shake the Germans, to deal a psychological blow that London hoped would make the enemy uneasily aware that they could be hit hard from Britain, and that they might be hit damned hard sometime in the future.

Up from the promontory came Major Lucas and Lieutenant Tim Adams. Behind them trudged a detachment of other ranks. It had been one more long and exhausting day. Tim was looking forward to a pot of his landlady's reviving tea and a hot bath, after which he would write to Felicity. The letter would be read to her by a nurse, of course. He'd received one from her, written by a nurse.

Tim darling,
I'm in the dark, can you send me a light? Not a box of matches. Your left eye would do, if you

can spare it. We could make history as a one-eyed couple on our wedding day. My parents, by the way, aren't too sure I wouldn't be better off living with them, but I need some recreational PT as well as help, and only you could provide that. Mr Lancaster, the eye surgeon, and Dr Langdale, the physician here, both tell me that by August I'll be a well-adjusted case, fit enough and fighting enough to go through the ceremony, so how about Saturday, 9th August? That's if you won't be doing one of your circus acts. You know what I mean.

Love, Felicity.

Tim thought he also knew what she meant by recreational PT.

As for Major Lucas, he was looking forward to a large whisky, a bath and an evening in Irvine with Captain Cary, the senior ATS officer in admin who, despite her officious exterior, was proving quite sociable. For all his masculine ruggedness, Major Lucas enjoyed female company. He would have favoured the company of Tim's sister Eloise most of all, but she was away training for her commission, and in any case, that precocious young lady had let him know she had no personal interest in him whatever.

He and Tim passed admin on their way to their respective billets, the sinking afternoon sun at their backs. Not long since, a flight of

Hurricane fighters based at Leuchars had scrambled following a radar warning that bandits were heading due south-east from the direction of German-occupied Norway. The Hurricanes climbed high and fast, streaking through the sky in the hope of intercepting and falling on a formation of Messerschmitt fighters escorting a flight of Stuka dive-bombers. The German planes were heading directly for Troon and the Commando base from which impertinent and insufferable raids had been mounted. German Intelligence had not been idle.

As Troon's air raid sirens sounded, the weary Commandos heard the noisy approach of the Stukas, low in the sky. The sun caught them and flashed them. The Commandos saw them quite clearly, coming in from the east and already their struts were howling and shrieking as they hurtled into the sun and crossed the outskirts of Troon. Above them, the Messerschmitts provided a protective umbrella. A klaxon blared a warning, and the Commandos scattered.

The Hurricanes arrived, peeled off and screamed down on the Messerschmitts. All hell happened then as the leading Stuka began its dive above Troon. Down it shrieked and let go its bombs, one after the other. One after another the bombs struck, and great eruptions mushroomed following the explosions, which ran in a straight line along the promontory.

The formation of Hurricanes split up. Some took on the Messerschmitts, the rest broke through the protective umbrella, hurtled down on the oncoming procession of Stukas and opened up with cannon fire. A second Stuka, following the first, was committed in its howling descent. Its bombs, propelled, created another running line of eruptions. High explosives gouged great holes in the promontory and the parade ground, hurling redhot debris and splinters in all directions. Running Commandos staggered under the bombardment of stone and metal. One explosion burst open the doors to admin and turned them into matchwood. Windows, taped, were sucked out.

A third Stuka stuck to its shrieking line of descent to unload its bombs. The Hurricanes were at the remainder of the flight then, and the Stukas seemed to turn into a flock of clumsy flapping pigeons scattering before ravenous hawks spitting fire. Above them, the Messerschmitts and other Hurricanes were engaged in an aerial dogfight that scarred the sky and drew streams of white across the blue. A fighter, its tail a plume of flame and smoke, fell twisting and turning into the Firth of Clyde, creating a huge upheaval of foaming water

107

as it plunged in. Another plummeted straight down north of the base and exploded.

A smitten Stuka broke up in mid-air and fell in blazing pieces that struck the hillside and set fire to the undergrowth. A second, a Hurricane on its tail, was doomed. Messerschmitts' breaking away from the fight above, descended fast to cover the retreat of the rest of the dive-bombers, which were scurrying and rushing in an attempt to take up a north-east course for Norway. The Hurricanes, superbly manoeuvrable, wheeled in the sky and came round to engage with whatever bandits appeared in their sights, fighters or bombers.

Suddenly, the combat above Troon vanished. The aerial mêlée was elsewhere, east of the town. Messerschmitts and Stukas, mission aborted, were heading for home, with the fiery Hurricanes in pursuit.

Commandos came to their feet, broke cover and strained their eyes in an attempt to discern what was still going on in the sky. But all they could see were the streams of white.

'Bloody hell,' said Tim to Major Lucas, 'that was a daylight raid on us, that was a strike against 4 Commando.'

With men shouting and running, Major Lucas spat words.

'We've got casualties on the promontory, so don't hold a bloody conversation with me.'

'I'm not,' shouted Tim, going at a run, 'I'm on my way.'

There were a dozen casualties. Six men were badly injured, four had open but less serious wounds, and two were dead. The admin staff were badly shaken but unhurt. Colonel Foster, second-in-command of the group, was swearing profusely about the lateness of the air raid warning, and the probability that it had cost the lives of the two unfortunate men.

'That's the everlasting curse of war,' said Major Lucas, 'it's always a pattern of errors and omissions.'

'Such as the charge of the Light Brigade?' grated Colonel Foster.

'Someone blundered there as well,' said Major Lucas.

Tim's landlady, Maggie Andrews, was distressed about the raid. Along with almost every other resident in Troon, she knew there had been casualties among the Commandos. Tim, whose toughening-up process had begun during the retreat to Dunkirk, gritted his teeth, and did his best to cheer her up. He persuaded her to have a wee nip of Scotch for her upset condition. Four nips later, she was scolding him for making her take to the bottle.

'McAdams, will you no' stop trying to turn a sober woman into a drunk when twenty of your braw laddies are lying dead out there?'

'Two,' said Tim.

'Two? It's no' twenty as I heard?'

'No, thank God, just two, even if that is two too many,' said Tim.

'Aye, it is thank God,' said Maggie. 'Ah, weel, then, perhaps I'll have one more wee nip.'

'I'll join you,' said Tim, hiding the bitterness he felt about dead and wounded comrades. Gritted teeth did not mean a bloke could easily resign himself to the fortunes of war.

Later, he managed to write his letter to Felicity, agreeing the wedding date, but including nothing about the daylight bombing raid on Troon.

The following morning, Felicity spoke to her most caring nurse, Clara Dickens.

'Any letters for me that you'd like to read to me?'

'Not this morning,' said Clara.

'Is the war over yet?'

'Not yet,' said Clara. 'And what d'you think? Those troublesome Germans made a daylight bombing raid on the west coast of Scotland yesterday evening.'

'The blighters are still at it?' said Felicity.

'Exactly where did they drop their filthy bombs?'

'It didn't say exactly where, just the west coast of Scotland, but they lost some planes, and only one of ours failed to return.'

'Only one?' said Felicity, wondering if Troon had been affected. 'I'm rapturous,' she said drily.

'That's good,' said Clara. 'We'll go for a little walk this morning.'

'Bloody hell, what fun,' said Felicity.

Tim's letter arrived the next day. Clara read it to her and gave Felicity a few minutes of welcome entertainment, as well as confirmation that Tim would be happy to marry her on the ninth of August.

'He's as good as a tonic,' said Clara.

'Doesn't he say anything about the daylight bombing raid on the west coast of Scotland?' asked Felicity.

'It probably wasn't near enough to Troon to take his mind off the more personal matter of letting you know he was blissful about the wedding date,' said Clara.

'Some wedding it'll be if I fall flat on my face going up the aisle,' said Felicity.

'Let's be cheerful,' said Clara.

'What are my eyes like today?' asked Felicity.

'They're better, they're better with each passing hour, believe me,' said Clara.

'I'm beginning not to look like a vampire?'

said Felicity, removing her dark glasses.

'You're beginning to look lovely,' said Clara, choosing to ignore the scarred condition of her patient's eyes.

'Take a letter,' said Felicity, replacing her glasses. 'Start with, "Darling Tim, I'm beginning to look as if I've got sex appeal."'

'You want me to write that?' said the nurse.

'Yes, why not?' said Felicity. 'Let's be delirious as well as cheerful.'

On Friday, Chinese Lady received a chatty letter from Cassie Brown, wife of Freddy Brown, Susie's younger brother. Chinese Lady was fond of Cassie, even if Freddy had once declared she was as barmy as a rockcake that thought itself a cream bun. Cassie was an entertaining and lively chatterbox to the Adams family, and Chinese Lady knew that Boots and Sammy both had very soft spots for her. In any case, she was a wife and mother now, and living sensibly down in Wiltshire with her two children and her dad. Her dad's sister, her Aunt Win, was putting them up. Freddy, of course, was away in the Army. Yes, and who wasn't, thought Chinese Lady.

In her letter, Cassie asked how everyone was, and said she hoped no-one had been bombed out, that it was a relief whenever she heard no-one had. Life was ever so quiet in the country, but the people there were ever so good, and her dad was happy in his job at the Swindon railway yards. Sally Cooper, Susie's sister, was living in the same village with her two boys, but missing her husband Horace a lot. Cassie said you don't think about what it's like to miss someone until they're not there. Sally and me heard about Emma getting married, she said, and we both wished we could have been there. Did Emma and Jonathan have a knees-up at the reception, like she and Sally did at theirs?

Cassie went on to say she missed Walworth and being able to make visits to all her friends and relatives. It was awful last year when she heard about Emily's death. She'd written a letter of sorrow to Boots, and Boots had written ever such a nice reply. It was very consoling to know he was graced with a new wife, especially as Polly Simms had always been such a good friend to the family. Sally had given her the news that Rosie was now going to get married, said Cassie, and went on to say she'd love to be able to go to the church, and she would, if she could. What she'd like most of all was to have Freddy go with her.

The children were well, she said, daughter Muffin was now three and into everything, and one-year-old Lewis was as good as gold. Well, nearly as good as gold, if no-one took any notice of what a palaver he set up when he was yelling.

Addicted to letter-writing, Chinese Lady replied at once, telling Cassie among other things that if she could get to the church she must come to the house afterwards for the reception. Perhaps Cassie could get her Aunt Win to look after the children for the weekend. The invitation included Freddy, of course, if he could manage it, though no-one could trust the Army to be anything but contrary about special leave for a soldier.

Chapter Seven

Since mid-April, when Goering, in revenge for the RAF's heavy raid on Berlin, had sent five hundred bombers to pulverize London, the capital had known several welcome nights of peace. By the second week in May, the people were beginning to feel the German air raids were at last tailing off. But on the full-moon night of the 10th of May, the capital suffered another major assault that lasted several hours. High explosives blasted the City and surrounds, and cascades of incendiaries set buildings ablaze.

Casualties were grievous, damage extensive and crippling. The Houses of Parliament were hit, the Commons' debating chamber totally wrecked. Westminster Abbey, the British Museum, five hospitals, various churches and many public buildings all suffered. So did many places in London's boroughs and suburbs. However, a number of German bombers were brought down by innovative RAF night fighters, and if that was only a small consolation to the injured and to families mourning their dead, it was a nasty shock to the Luftwaffe and to Goering.

Prime Minister Churchill came out to inspect the mountain of rubble that had once been the House of Commons, and his body language was of a kind that boded ill for the Germans if the British and their Empire allies ever managed to turn the tide. Further, Britain might find another ally in Soviet Russia, for Churchill, by reason of the fact that British Intelligence had acquired entry into Germany's code systems, knew that Hitler was preparing to go to war against Stalin. Stalin refused to believe it. He turned his nose up at anything emanating from the British Prime Minister. He trusted Hitler more than Churchill. If Mrs Susie Adams had known that, she'd have said Stalin ought to see the kind of doctor who was good at examining people's brains. Susie admired Mr Churchill, especially as he had once sent a very nice reply to a letter she'd written to him.

Churchill might have growled to Stalin, 'Be it on your own head, then,' but the last thing he wanted was for Germany's awesome Panzer divisions to mop up an unprepared Russia as they had mopped up other nations. Britain needed Russia as a powerful ally, not a shattered one.

It was London that lay in a shattered state on this May morning. Its numbed citizens emerged from shelters to survey scenes of destruction all too familiar to them. Despair might have been their primary reaction had it not been for the fact that their hatred of Hitler and his gloating war machine transcended all. Churchill, the glowering bulldog, fed that hatred and made a necessary weapon of it, while the appearance of the King and Queen effected a lift of spirits.

It was mid-morning when Mrs Jemima Hardy left her home in Lorrimore Square, Kennington, to do some shopping. Like all her neighbours and everyone else who had known months of the German blitz from the air, Jemima wondered how many more bombing raids London and its people could endure. Last night, her husband Job had been out on ARP duty until the small hours before snatching some sleep and going to work as usual. She and her eighteen-year-old daughter Jane had spent most of the night in their Anderson shelter, but Jane too had gone to her work at a war factory. People did that, they went to their places of work after every raid, simply because they knew it was the one way of fighting back.

Jemima's younger daughter Jennifer was an evacuee in the country, as was her brother Jonas. Jemima's elder son Jonathan was on his way overseas, having had to embark with his regiment almost immediately after his honeymoon with Emma, which Jemima thought downright hard on the couple.

It was more than ten years since Jemima and her family had left their quiet Sussex village to make a new home among the cockneys of South London. The house they chose, in Stead Street, Walworth, proved a happy abode, despite strange little happenings supposedly caused by the presence of an Irish leprechaun. However absurd that supposition was, the little happenings ceased after an Irishman called in 1939 and took the leprechaun away, or so he said, and with a warning that the house would come down around the family's ears if they stayed there.

Jemima took that warning seriously, and the family moved to Kennington. Sure enough, the house in Stead Street was subsequently destroyed by a German bomb.

Last night's raid had been terrible noisy and downright wicked, in Jemima's estimation. Kennington had suffered, along with other neighbourhoods, and Job had said that one bomb dropped straight down on a garden shelter in Kennington Park Road, killing its four occupants. That kind of thing really upset Job. It put him in a helpless rage. Born and bred in his Sussex village, he couldn't understand, any more than Jemima herself could, why the people of one country made war so barbarously on the people of another.

'It's a wicked sword Hitler's drawn,

Jemima,' he had said at the time of a massive raid in late December, 'and it'll be a terrible one he'll perish by. That'll be the way of things in the end. It's the devil's way, and it's the devil's own world Hitler's building and lording it over. Aye, he be Satan's son for certain.'

'But would Satan let his own son perish, Job?' asked Jemima.

'That he would, and take pleasure in it,' said Job. 'It's the way of Satan.'

'Well, I wish he would hurry it up,' said Jemima.

If the world had turned itself over to the devil, today's bright May sun gave her the impression that God's gifts were still evident. It was as if Satan's darkest nights could not prevail over heaven's morning light.

In Chapter Road, next to Lorrimore Square, she met a neighbour, Mrs Gladys Skinner. Jemima thought it a very suitable name, because the lady, buxom and beefy, was known to threaten to skin her husband regularly once a week. Well, Arthur Skinner was a bit of a boozer, and since he was earning good money as a foreman in a war factory, he was inclined to open his wage packet on Fridays and pop into a pub on his way home. That kind of thing was a punishable offence in the eyes of women who had been brought up to believe

119

husbands were strictly obliged to hand over wage packets intact. Mrs Skinner was definitely one such woman. Aggravatingly, Mr Skinner was one of several husbands who were regular offenders. His disobedience of the unwritten rule brought him into damaging conflict with his trouble and strife, and he was often seen going off to work on Saturday mornings in a bruised and wounded condition.

'Good morning, Mrs Skinner,' said Jemima in her friendly way. 'What a terrible night it were.'

'Gawd 'elp us,' sighed Mrs Skinner, blouse straining around her capacious frontage, 'I thought me house was comin' down on top of our shelter. That old man of mine, 'e didn't move a muscle. Asleep 'e was, like 'e was livin' in fairyland. So I woke 'im up and give 'im an earful. Well, I ask yer, Mrs 'Ardy, is it right 'aving yer husband sound asleep while you're suffering 'orrible anxieties? I told 'im it wasn't, I told 'im 'e 'adn't got no right to be asleep while I was wideawake waitin' for the 'ouse to fall on our shelter. If 'e nodded off again, I said, I'd murder 'im. And d'you know what 'e said, the saucy bugger? 'E said if I murdered 'im 'e wouldn't even wake up for breakfast and I'd 'ave to eat me porridge all by meself.'

'Oh, dear,' said Jemima 'you be a suffering woman, Mrs Skinner.'

120

'I give 'im another earful then,' said Mrs Skinner, the cherries on her old-fashioned hat quivering a bit. 'I told 'im that if 'e talked to me like that in the middle of an air raid, I'd chuck 'im out of the shelter and let the bombs fall on 'im. And d'you know—'

'I must go and do my shopping,' said Jemima, not wanting to be a listening-post for the rest of the morning.

'Yes, d'you know what me old man said then?' persisted Mrs Skinner. "E said 'e thought he'd pop into the 'ouse, anyway, and make hisself a pot of tea. Course, I 'ad to do me best to knock 'is saucy 'ead off then, but there's not a lot of room in them shelters to swing a copper stick. Still, wait till 'e comes 'ome from 'is work, I'll learn 'im. Mind, I won't say 'e don't stand up to air raids like a man should, nor will 'e let them Germans get 'im down, either. Nor will I. It's being cheerful as keeps us goin', that's what we both say.'

Jemima offered agreement, then made her escape. Because it was May, the first month of summer, and because country-born people always celebrated summer's arrival more wholeheartedly than town people, she was going to buy herself a new dress. For that purpose, she was on her way to the Adams dress shop near the Oval, which specialized in stylish clothes at good prices. Besides, Jonathan had married into the

Adams family. Well, Emma's mother was the sister of Sammy Adams, the founder of the family firm. They were very outgoing and talkative, all the Adamses. Jemima, with husband Job, had met a lot of them before the wedding, and more of them at the wedding and the reception. They all seemed to want to know everything about herself and her own family, as if they were trying to find out whether or not she and Job, and their offspring, fitted into the world of the various Adams families. In the end, they all seemed approving, without apparently worrying one bit if they themselves needed to be considered acceptable. Their belief in their own worthiness was very evident, although one of Emma's uncles, an Army major whom the family called Boots, seemed a whimsical man able to laugh at himself and his relatives. His wife Polly was a fascinating woman, and Jemima liked them both, very much. She also took to the younger brother, Sammy, such a vital man.

Jemima smiled to herself as she crossed Kennington Park Road and walked to the shop in Harleyford Street, close to the Oval cricket ground. There was a gentleman present. Well, he looked like a gentleman in his well-cut grey suit and Homburg hat. He was talking to the manageress, Miss Lomax, whom Jemima an occasional customer, knew. She heard her speak.

122

'People have got more money these days, Mr Adams, and they're buying for the summer and autumn before everyone's issued with clothing coupons next month.'

'Well, that's it, is it, that's why sales are jumping at the moment, Miss Lomax, which I suppose is like people having a ball while the orchestra's still in tune,' said Sammy Adams, and Jemima recognized him then. He turned as she advanced, and recognition became mutual. His blue eyes brightened. He had quickly acquired a liking for Emma's comely mother-in-law. 'Upon me soul,' he said, raising his hat, 'here's a welcome surprise. Good morning, Mrs Hardy.'

'Good morning, Mr Adams,' smiled Jemima.

'It wasn't to begin with, not after the night,' said Sammy. 'It looks better now on account of the pleasure of seeing you again. Miss Lomax, meet Mrs Jemima Hardy, a lady I'm now related to on account of her son Jonathan having married my niece Emma just recent. But–'

'I know Mrs Hardy,' said stylish Miss Lomax, smiling, 'she's a customer. Good morning, Mrs Hardy.'

'Good morning,' said Jemima.

'Customers,' said Sammy, 'happen to be my fav'rite people, Mrs Hardy, some more than others, such as any relatives by marriage. Where was I?'

'Here,' said Miss Lomax.

'Glad to hear it,' said Sammy. 'If I was somewhere else, I'd be in the wrong place. But what was I about to say? I know. I was about to say, Mrs Hardy, that I'm sorry Jonathan had to go overseas so soon. My respected mother, Emma's grandma, called it a criminal liberty on the part of the Army, with which sentiment I agree.'

'All the blame belongs to Hitler,' said Jemima.

'The madman,' said Miss Lomax, who had once had Sammy's sister-in-law Sally as an assistant. Now she managed with a part-timer, who worked from eleven until five. 'If the Germans had had any sense, they'd have locked him up in an asylum years ago, and kept him there until he was old and tooth-less.'

'Well, as things are,' said Sammy, 'he represents rotten hard luck for Jonathan and Emma.'

'Downright sorrowful, Mr Adams,' said Jemima.

'And for all kinds of other people,' said Sammy, thinking of parents whose kids were evacuated, and what a major hole it would make in the family if Boots and Polly went overseas.

'My husband thinks it'll be worse luck for the Germans one day,' said Jemima

124

'One day next week won't be too soon for me,' observed Sammy.

'Mrs Hardy, can I help you?' asked Miss Lomax.

'Well, I do be thinking of buying a summer dress,' said Jemima.

'That's the kind of thinking I'm partial to,' said Sammy. 'Miss Lomax, kindly note Mrs Hardy is now entitled to fam'ly discount.'

'How kind,' smiled Jemima

'Was last night worrisome for you?' asked Sammy.

'I were more downright angry with the Germans than worrying,' said Jemima

'I like that, Mrs Hardy,' said Sammy. 'I like the thought of you standing up and shakin' your fist at the bombers. I'll stand with you anytime, so will my fam'ly and every other fam'ly. So will Miss Lomax. We've all got too much to live for to be licked by Hitler the Hun. Accordin' to my educated brother Boots—'

'Such a reassuring man,' said Jemima remembering the pleasure of meeting Boots and his wife Polly at the wedding reception.

'Tower of strength, you might say,' said Sammy. 'Well, accordin' to him, we won the biggest battle of all for civilization, the battle of Britain, now highly historical. And we'll win the last battle, the one that'll settle things. As my wife Susie says, that'll be when Winston Churchill will make Hitler wish he'd never been born. Am I performing a speech?'

'Yes, and nearly as good as one of Mr Churchill's,' said Miss Lomax.

'It's very cheering to listen to,' smiled Jemima

'Well, better than givin' the Hitler salute,' said Sammy, and looked at his watch. 'Excuse me if I push off now, I've got to see an old business friend of mine, Mr Eli Greenberg, about a new cuttin' machine for our factory. Pleasure to have met you again, Mrs Hardy. Miss Lomax, look after the lady.'

Out he went, a man of energy, and Jemima thought that he and Mrs Skinner had both put new heart into her. Yes, and so had Job. He'd placed money on the kitchen table just before going off to his work, and she asked what it was for. For you, Jemima he said, to buy yourself a new dress, a summer dress. She asked if there was a special reason. Aye, said Job, to show no-one's going to spoil the summer for you, and because you're a good wife and no man had a better or braver. Job, that be a very pretty thing for a man to say to a woman, she said. Ah, well, he said, it be women like you, Jemima that'll help to make sure we win this ugly old war.

I don't exactly know how we're going to win, she thought now, but I'm certain sure we won't lose. Then she gave her attention to the pleasure of selecting a new dress, Miss Lomax sharing the pleasure.

'Sammy, a cutting machine?' said Mr Eli Greenberg, Sammy's old and trusted business friend, now with grey rampant in his bushy black hair on which rested, as always, his round rusty black hat. 'A cutting machine, you said?'

'So I did, Eli old cock,' said Sammy. They were in Mr Greenberg's new yard at Camberwell. His long-established premises in Blackfriars had been bombed months ago. 'I come to you with confident expectations.'

'Vell, and ain't I pleased to see you, Sammy?' said Mr Greenberg, the grey streaking his beard. 'Vhen vasn't I pleased, even on the occasions vhen you left me poorer in striking a bargain? But a cutting machine at a time like this, Sammy?'

'All I'm asking for is a first-class second-hand machine that's goin' spare somewhere,' said Sammy. 'Could I get hold of a new machine? I could, providing I didn't mind waitin' several months, which I do mind, on account of it would give me a headache I don't require.'

'Times are hard, Sammy,' said Mr Greenberg, shaking his head, 'and ain't mercy itself in short supply, ain't it shorter vith every bomb that drops? But as to vhat you're after, vhy, don't I know of a varehouse in Barnet that might be obliging as long as you don't ask for an invoice?'

'Understood,' said Sammy. 'It's a black market warehouse full up with salvage from a shipwreck.'

'Sammy my friend, not so loud,' urged Mr Greenberg.

'Understood,' said Sammy. 'And no paperwork, of course, just some loose cash.'

'It ain't going to be got for a mere song, Sammy.'

'All right, what about "Land of Hope and Glory", six encores and a band in addition to the required amount of dibs?' suggested Sammy.

'Plus commission for the sake of friendship?' said Mr Greenberg.

'Fair enough,' said Sammy, 'and I'll throw in the National Anthem and stand to attention.'

Mr Greenberg smiled. He loved Sammy like a father, and would have scoured every rag-and-bone yard and every black market source in the kingdom, for whatever he wanted.

'That's fair for both of us, eh, Sammy? I know you vouldn't take the shirt off the back of a poor man like me. Vhat about delivery?'

'Tomorrow?' said Sammy.

'Tomorrow?' Mr Greenberg threw up his mittened hands. 'Sammy, Sammy, vhat d'you vant to give me, a veek's headache?'

'Just treat me to one of your minor miracles,' said Sammy.

'Sammy,' said Mr Greenberg, shaking his head again, 'ain't I mentioned it before, that I ain't Jesus and don't valk on vater?'

'Leave it to you to do your best, Eli,' said Sammy.

'Vell, so I vill, Sammy,' said Mr Greenberg. 'Now, vill you take a glass and a sandvich vith me at the pub, vhere I have to meet a friend later?'

'I'll be happy to, Eli old cock,' said Sammy, and Mr Greenberg's dark eyes turned liquid with pleasure.

'Sammy, ain't I been many years in this old country, ain't I seen its people go through good days and bad days?' he said. 'Now their bad days are their vorst days, and sad, Sammy, sad.'

'Don't I know it,' said Sammy. 'Don't I have a nephew whose young lady's been blinded by a bomb blast right in the middle of London? And didn't our Em'ly pass on last year on account of another bomb?'

'The Lord rest her soul,' said Mr Greenberg, and dabbed with his large handkerchief at a sincere tear in his eye. 'But vith all the bombs, never did I know more neighbourliness or more kindness, and ain't I proud to belong?'

'Glad to have a bloke like you as one of us, Eli,' said Sammy.

'Ain't that my good fortune, Sammy?' Mr Greenberg blew his nose. 'Ain't I heard stories about the Jews of Poland and Germany that turn my blood cold, stories about vhat men like Himmler are doing to them?'

'I've heard Mrs Rachel Goodman talk about Nazis moving Jews into labour camps and beating them to death,' said Sammy.

'Labour camps?' Mr Greenberg, dark and soulful, shook a sad head. 'No, death camps, Sammy, and vhat do men of affairs say about it? They say they have no proof.'

'Eli old lad,' said Sammy, 'if it's all true, proof will hit us all in the eye one day. Come on, blow your nose again and I'll give you a lift to the pub. By the way, who's paying?'

Mr Greenberg came out of sadness to eye Sammy with a smile.

'A kind offer of yours, Sammy,' he said, 'but it vas my offer first.'

'Highly sociable of you, Eli,' said Sammy, his prevailing mood amiable. He had recently done himself a good turn by having a few telling words with his assistant, a Miss Symonds, who had an embarrassing habit of rubbing up against him. She took instant umbrage at his address, drew herself up and gave notice in a proud and dignified way, which notice Sammy was honoured to accept and acknowledge by paying her off on the spot. Subsequently, Susie said she'd

130

think about coming back to work part-time for him, during the hours little Paula was at nursery school. Sammy said he'd be very appreciative, as long as she took note that at the office he was boss. Susie just smiled. Sammy lapsed into a mumble. He didn't know any female woman whose smile was more undermining than Susie's. He'd first met her when she was only fifteen. She'd done it to him then, and had been doing it to him ever since. It was a fair old miracle that he could still stand up straight.

He spoke to her that evening about what forthcoming clothes rationing was likely to do to the business.

'Knock holes in it?' said Susie.

'Our retail side, yes,' said Sammy. 'Susie, have you got the same kind of horrendous feelings that I have?'

'No, I don't think so, Sammy love,' said Susie. 'Sit down and fan yourself for a bit, you've gone all flushed.'

'What with old Fatty Goering's bombers and clothing coupons, I'm likely to lose all me hair and go bald,' said Sammy.

'Sammy, don't you dare go bald,' said Susie. 'There's no such thing as a bald Adams, and if I find one next to me when I wake up one morning, I'll go home to my mum.'

'Be serious, Susie.'

'I am serious,' said Susie. 'If any of your hair starts falling out, stick it on again.'

'That's serious?' said Sammy. 'Susie, believe me, once clothes rationing hits our shops, the Army and Air Force contracts will be our lifeblood. Without 'em, we'd only be one step away from closing down. Could I hand Bert and Gertie and the girls that kind of unfortunate information? Not on your Nelly. I'd have to start thinking about black market clothing coupons for under-the-counter distribution to our customers.'

'I'll divorce you if you do,' said Susie.

'It's no time for joking, Susie.'

'I'm not joking,' said Susie.

'I'm speakin' of a legal black market, naturally,' said Sammy.

'A legal black market?' said Susie. 'What's that, might I ask?'

'I'll work something out on paper,' said Sammy.

'Don't bother,' said Susie. 'D'you know what black market people are being called? Spivs. That's horrid. Sammy Adams, there's going to be no black market business or spivs in this family, d'you hear me?'

'Is that a considered decision of yours, Susie?' asked Sammy.

'It's my final decision,' said Susie. 'Anyway, what about your idea of forming a property company?'

'That'll happen, you bet it will,' said

Sammy, 'but we'll have to accumulate a bit more capital from profits before I can start some serious buying. Meanwhile, concerning what clothing coupons might do to us, I'll think of something.'

'Something?' said Susie.

'Um – something else,' said Sammy, and went a bit sober. 'You know, Susie, it's a bloody awful war.'

'I do know,' said Susie, 'it's murdering women and children. It's Hitler's own kind of war, and I shudder to think what he might do next with his bombers if we don't give in.'

'Susie, if we give in,' said Sammy, 'it's my belief he'll make this country a hell on earth, and God knows what he'd do to Rachel, Lilian and the rest of our Jewish fraternity. Eli Greenberg reckons that if we all knew what he's doing to his own Jews, it would freeze our blood.'

'I'd believe anything of that man,' said Susie. 'Sammy, go up and take a look at Paula.'

'She's asleep,' said Sammy.

'Yes, but if you went up and took a look at her,' said Susie, 'I think you'd know why we must never give in, never.'

'Meaning it'll make me realize we can't ever deliver innocence to the devil?' said Sammy.

'Sammy, you love, even Boots couldn't

have said anything better than that,' smiled Susie.

'I think I'll go up and look in on Plum Pudding the Second,' said Sammy.

The little girl was sound asleep, innocence personified. Now I know what 'Land of Hope and Glory' is all about, thought Sammy. Or is it 'Rule Britannia'?

Well, whatever, the mad Pied Piper of Berlin's not going to get you, my angel, or any of our kids.

A dark shadow flitted across the North Sea that night in the direction of Scotland.

Chapter Eight

'What?' said Prime Minister Winston Churchill. 'What?'

The news was unbelievable. Rudolf Hess, Hitler's deputy, had landed in Scotland, baling out from his crashing Messerschmitt fighter plane. At his request, he was taken by a Scottish farmer to the Duke of Hamilton, an RAF wing commander who happened to be on night duty, and whom he had met during the Olympic Games in Berlin in 1936. Hess declared to the Duke that he had come to negotiate peace with Britain, but not through the medium of Churchill, known to the rest of the world, he declared, as a warmonger who had been planning for years to attack Germany. The Duke thought the man quite mad, and it was certainly true that Hess was erratic in his behaviour and muddled in his thinking.

Churchill gave some credence to the story, however, since British Intelligence had gathered enough information to confirm that which Stalin refused to believe, that Hitler's planned invasion of Russia would definitely go ahead. His armies would cross the border some time in June. Accordingly he would want to avoid a two-front war. Peace with Britain would mean he could move the bulk of German forces in France to join the attack on the Soviet Union. In turn, that would mean Stalin having to face a colossal war machine.

Nevertheless, and much to his rage, Hess was denied all contact with any representatives of the British Government. The Duke of Hamilton told him he was insane to imagine Britain would give in to Hitler and his gang of criminals. He was treated not as a dove of peace, but as a prisoner of war. It sent him off his unsteady rocker, and when the news of his landing broke worldwide on 12th May, it didn't do Hitler's mental equipment much good, either, for he'd known nothing of Hess's intentions.

But it caused a grin or two among the bombed and battered cockneys of London, and the people of other suffering towns and cities.

Chinese Lady didn't know if what was coming out of the blessed old wireless was good news or bad.

'What's it all mean, Edwin?'

'That this man Hess and other Nazis are uneasy about our refusal to surrender, Maisie,' said Mr Finch.

'I hope I never live to see the day when we give in to them aggravating Germans,' said Chinese Lady. 'All my life they've –

they've–' She searched for the right words.

'Been rattling their sabres?' said Mr Finch.

'Yes, I've read words like that somewhere,' said Chinese Lady.

'I'm sure you have,' said Mr Finch, and thought about the tendency of the German people to go along with ambitious warlords. Never had Germany's military might been greater than now, and part of it lay just across the English Channel, throwing a dark shadow over his adopted country. God in heaven, one day a titanic battle would have to be fought, either on the beaches of Britain or the shores of Northern France.

'Edwin, you're doing a lot of frowning lately,' said Chinese Lady. 'You're not worrying about that man Hess, are you?'

'Least of all about him, Maisie.'

'Then what?'

'Oh, the war generally,' said Mr Finch, 'but they're not serious worries. This country, represented by the Welsh, Scots, English and Northern Irish, four of the toughest peoples in the world, has only ever lost one war of note, that against the American colonists, mainly of British stock themselves, aided by the French. Had it not been for that, the British Empire would have been far too powerful even for Hitler to provoke.'

'Well, I'm sure our King and Queen will be pleased to hear that,' said Chinese Lady.

'I'm sure they're having a troublesome time, Buckingham Palace having been bombed and all.'

'Bless Their Majesties,' said Mr Finch, and Chinese Lady smiled. She liked to hear her husband say that sort of thing. Her dislike of Russian Bolsheviks and German Nazis made her very much a monarchist, and greatly in favour of kind kings and queens. Which meant, of course, that she naturally disapproved strongly of Henry the Eighth, who had chopped his wives' heads off like a common maniac, and she thought now that perhaps in some outlandish way Hitler was a descendant of his.

The days went by. There were sporadic air raids on towns and cities in Britain, and Rommel's Afrika Korps still held the initiative in Cyrenaica. The fighting in the desert was fierce, the tank warfare dominated in the main by the superior armour and superior tactics of Rommel's army. To make matters more critical for Winston Churchill and his War Cabinet, the Germans, having vanquished Greece, were openly preparing for their expected airborne landings in Crete. There, British and Empire troops were making their own preparations for a fierce resistance, and in them Churchill rested his hopes.

In the West Country the arsonist, having been thwarted in his attempt to fire a printing works in Weymouth, examined another target, one which he was sure would bring no interruption and which offered the promise of an exhilarating conflagration. Such promise positively thrilled the blood of the man who was no longer a negative being.

For Felicity, there was another letter from Tim. He was writing regularly.

'Shall I read it?' asked Clara, the caring nurse, out in the sunshine with her charge, whose dark glasses hid the condition of her sightless eyes, still a little bloodshot. The condition, however, was definitely improving daily.

'Well, you dear woman,' said Felicity, 'you're not thinking of eating it, are you? You've had your breakfast, haven't you?'

'Now, now,' said Clara, 'don't let's be grumpy.'

'I'm not grumpy,' said Felicity who, on waking up each morning, gritted her teeth at being in a world she couldn't see. 'I'm simply ratty, that's all, a much more honest state. It's my privilege. Anyway, go ahead.'

Seated on a bench next to the unfortunate ATS officer, the nurse began to read,

'Dear Sexy–'

'Hell's bells, he hasn't started like that, has he?' interrupted Felicity.

'It's in black and white,' said Clara, 'and is probably a response to your telling him you were beginning to look sexy.'

'All the same, what a bounder when he knows you have to read me all his letters,' said Felicity. 'Sexy, he says? It's not true, of course, I'm not that kind of girl.'

'Oh, I'd like to be considered a bit sexy myself,' said Clara.

'I've heard that some patients think you are,' said Felicity. 'Read on.'

'I'm happy to know you're progressing so well. Up here I'm going downhill fast, having taken a tumble off a rockface for the second time in two days. I think I've bruises in places I didn't know about, but Major Lucas said I'm only one of many, so don't fuss, and having thought about you and your problems, I'm not fussing at all. Maggie said what I need is a good woman to apply hot poultices, so I reminded her I'm getting one. She says to give you her regards, and hopes to have the pleasure of your company every day when you eventually get up here as Mrs Adams the Fourth. Did I tell you there's already Mrs Adams One, Two and Three? That's dad's wife, Uncle Tommy's wife and Uncle Sammy's wife. They're all lovely women in looks and character, and they'll give you a warm welcome if you can condition yourself to becoming Mrs Four.'

'The man's drivelling,' said Felicity.

'Well, I've seen him,' said Clara, 'and my word, six feet of good-looking whipcord. Imagine waking up next to all of it, so if you don't want him, I'll have him.'

'You'll be lucky,' said Felicity, 'and look here, you're supposed to be a therapeutic influence, not a nutmeg grater rubbing me up the wrong way. Is there any more?'

'A little,' said Clara, and read on. *'I'm thinking about you every day, Puss—'*

'Puss?' said Felicity.

'Does he mean Pussy?' asked the nurse.

'Don't be disgusting,' said Felicity, and smiled. That's her first real smile, thought Clara. 'What a clown,' said Felicity, 'but who's complaining? I'm not, except about bomber Fatty Goering and what he did to me. Come on, then, let's hear the rest.'

'I'm thinking about you every day, Puss, and I'd like to be with you, giving you what help you need. On the other hand, I'm still betting you're strong enough to give yourself the best kind of help, although I know that's easier said by me than done by you. Everyone up here sends you their best wishes. Here's looking forward to the ninth of August and to a quiet happy wedding. Believe me, Puss, I can hardly wait. Love, Tim.'

'I'll give him Puss,' said Felicity, and laughed.

141

'By letter or when you next see him?' asked Clara.

Felicity stopped laughing and said, 'I think you'd better rephrase that.'

'So sorry, but seeing wasn't meant literally, and you actually need to accept it in conversation,' said Clara. 'When you can, you're mentally on the mend.'

'Forget it,' said Felicity, and had one of her naturally bitter moods. One couldn't be heroic all day long, especially when one's anchor was up in Scotland and one's parents fussed and fretted whenever they visited.

Tim wasn't like that, thank God. He was much more a tower of strength. Well, being blind didn't mean she couldn't be exciting to her tower of strength. Physically, she had a splendid body, and she knew it.

She also knew Tim had a fine body. She'd seen him in nothing but brief pants, and she hadn't been able to fault him.

Oh, curse it, she was never going to literally see him again.

Her mood blackened.

By reason of experience and understanding, Clara did not attempt to jolly her. She had a warm admiration for this personable ATS officer and her fighting spirit. She was entitled to her moments of rageful bitterness.

Thursday, 15 May.

Captain Polly Adams emerged from the surgery of a doctor in Corfe village. She had elected to consult him instead of the Medical Officer at Corps Headquarters.

There was a dazed look on her face, and disbelief in her eyes.

It couldn't be true, but Dr Graham had assured her it was. She was seven weeks pregnant. She was in her forty-fifth year, and was going to have a baby. Impossible. She didn't want a baby, not when she would be sixty by the time the child was fourteen. What child of that age wanted a sixty-year-old mother? God, she'd have wrinkles by then, and Boots would look grandfatherly.

What was he going to say, and what would happen when the Corps embarked overseas? He'd have to go, but she'd have to stay behind. That wasn't the idea at all, it never had been. After so many years of wanting him and never having him, she was now enjoying every day of being married to him. He had a way of making her feel young again, of making her body course with pulsing life. Oh, hell, how could she stay behind?

Yet there were other feelings. She had always said that if he had married her instead of Emily long ago, she would have given him four children because he was such a family man. Emily had given him only one, his son Tim. He had been swift to adopt Rosie, and delighted to have found Eloise, daughter of the Frenchwoman he made love to during the Great War.

Ye gods, thought Polly, he may like my gift to him. I know him so well, he'll laugh our ages off, he'll make nothing of the fact that we're both in our forty-fifth year. But at my age can I carry for nine months? Dr Graham said I could, and damn it, I don't feel old, I simply don't. I'm going to have Boots's child and I feel triumphant. Blow any wrinkles.

But if I declare I'm pregnant, I'll be left behind. Boots won't be there when I have the child. I've got feelings all over my body and they're fighting each other. Think, Polly old girl, think.

There was a surging flap on when she reached headquarters. Orders had finally come. All units of 7 Corps were to embark over a period of three days, from 25 May to 27 May. Arrangements for embarkation leave had already been set in motion for most fighting and admin personnel.

Polly discovered something odd as she studied orders concerning headquarters personnel. She discovered she'd been on the list of ATS officers scheduled for departure, but that her name had been crossed out. Further, Boots's name, along with two other officers on Sir Henry's personal staff, had also been crossed out of the main list. She asked the adjutant for an interview with her father, 7 Corps commander.

'Now?' said the adjutant, a file under each arm and one in his right hand.

'Well, immediately, if possible,' said Polly, 'so be a sport.'

'Why not talk to your husband, Major Adams, instead?'

Polly knew some regulations had been set aside to allow her to serve in the same establishment as Boots, although she was never in direct contact with him.

'Where is he?' she asked.

'With Sir Henry, now I come to think,' said the adjutant. 'Look, if you're thinking of commiserating with Sir Henry–'

'Commiserating?' said Polly.

'I haven't got time to go into details,' said the adjutant, 'just enough time to tell you Lieutenant-General Montrose is taking over command of the Corps and Sir Henry will have the responsibility of knocking a new corps into shape. Fact is, London thinks he's too old for an active service command. Sorry, Polly.' The adjutant disappeared.

Polly went directly to her father's office and knocked.

'Yes?' Her father sounded testy.

She entered. Sir Henry was standing at his desk, and with him were three officers, two of them colonels, the third one Boots.

'I'm interrupting?' she said.

'Yes, damn it,' said Sir Henry. 'Major Adams, take her away and talk to her.'

Boots took her out of the building and talked to her in the sunshine, confirming that her father would not be going with the Corps, that he'd lost his command to his Scottish deputy, and would be taking up the challenge of welding together an appropriate number of units to form a new corps. London had referred to this as a challenge, but Sir Henry, of course, knew the word had been used as a sop. Sir Henry, said Boots, was still swearing his head off.

'But why have you and I been crossed off the draft list?' asked Polly.

'Sir Henry informed London he'd only accept the new command on condition he was allowed to retain three of his immediate staff,' said Boots. 'Colonel Briggs, Colonel Newton and myself. London issued a cancellation of our draft orders, and that led to you being taken off the list of ATS officers.' Boots found a reason to smile. 'Well, naturally, I wasn't going to let you disappear in the direction of the Eighth Army. Chinese Lady would have chewed my ear off on the grounds that I'd made a mess of God's orders, which, in her mind, strictly forbid a man to let his wife go to war without him. Go to war at all, in fact.'

Polly felt giddy. The Corps as a whole had

been impatient for embarkation. Her father had looked forward to it, and for a chance to prove himself in the field of modern warfare. Boots had seen the necessity of getting at the Germans overseas. And she had only been concerned with a need to go with him. All those years when she had been on the outside, because of Emily, had suddenly ended, and fulfilling years had begun for her. She would have fought like a tigress if she had been taken off the overseas draft and Boots had remained on. But they were both to stay on home service. If there was disappointment at not going with the Corps to the Middle East, there was sweet consolation. She could tell him now.

'My father's swearing about developments?' she said.

'Believe me,' said Boots, thinking her as trim in her uniform as any of the younger ATS officers.

'Are you swearing too?' asked Polly.

'Not out loud,' said Boots. 'My chief feelings amount to sympathy for your father, who's done such a good job with the Corps.'

'Then if you're swallowing your disappointment like a gentleman,' said Polly, 'I've some different news for you.'

'Have you?' said Boots, aware that unit commanders were arriving one after another. 'Give it to me, then.'

147

'Darling,' said Polly, 'you're going to be a father again.'

'I'm what?' said Boots in disbelief.

'You're going to be a father again,' said Polly. 'I'm seven weeks into happy expectations according to a doctor I consulted in Corfe this morning. Do you mind?'

Boots stared at her.

'Good God, is it possible?' he said.

'It's true,' said Polly.

'Good God,' said Boots.

'Say something else,' said Polly, 'or I'll think I'm embarrassing you.'

'Polly, you beauty,' said Boots. He laughed out loud, put his arms around her, drew her close and planted a delighted kiss on her mouth. A brigadier, arriving, glanced in shock and disapproval at an Army major and an ATS captain engaged in a tight embrace and a lingering kiss. He knew the former, Major Robert Adams, and on entering the mansion he ran into Sir Henry. He delivered an immediate complaint. Sir Henry, very much out of sorts, delivered a riposte.

'None of your business,' he said, 'forget it.'

Outside, Polly was radiant.

'Boots darling, you really don't mind, you're actually happy about it?' she said.

'What man of my age wouldn't be?' said Boots. 'Love you, you wonderful woman. God help me if you aren't a walking miracle.'

148

'You don't mind, either, that this walking miracle will be old and wrinkled by the time our son or daughter comes of age?' said Polly.

Boots laughed again.

'I shan't give a damn about your wrinkles or mine,' he said, 'and nor will our son or daughter. Holy angels, Polly, are you thinking what I'm thinking?'

'What are you thinking?' asked Polly, delighted by his reaction.

'That if we've done it once, we can do it again,' said Boots.

'Boots!'

Another senior officer, stepping from his car, raised his eyebrows at the sight of an Army officer and an ATS officer laughing their heads off.

Polly was able to see her father later. Sir Henry, suffering bitter disappointment, was nevertheless always Polly's affectionate father, and her news sweetly coated his pill.

'Incredible. Marvellous. Damned wonderful, Polly, and so are you.'

'Boots is delighted,' said Polly.

'So am I,' said Sir Henry. 'By God, if any news could console a superseded corps commander, this could and has.'

'Well,' said Polly, 'you might be superseded, but you're still one of the best as a supportive father and a thinking soldier. As

149

for brasshats, blow their glass eyes if they can't see what you're worth to the Army. I can and so can Boots. He's your number one fan.'

'The loyalty and support I've always had from Boots won't go unrecorded in my papers,' said Sir Henry. 'I'm damned glad I'll still have him on my staff when I take up my new command. He'll be Colonel Adams then.'

'Heavens,' said Polly, 'what his mother will say to that should be worth listening to.'

'Polly – um – er–'

'Yes?' smiled Polly.

'Um, shouldn't you be resting?' asked Sir Henry.

'Darling, I'm as strong as a horse, and not even Boots is going to make me lie down morning and afternoon,' smiled Polly. 'Exercise is the thing, didn't you know?'

'No, by gad, I didn't,' said Sir Henry. 'Are you sure?'

'Of course,' said Polly, as if being on close terms with pregnancy was familiar to her.

Boots phoned Rosie. Rosie knew all about the embarkation orders. Divisional head-quarters, she said, were buzzing. She herself was not on the list. She was to stay and be taken on the staff of a new division due to move in. But was it true that Sir Henry wasn't going, that the Corps was to be commanded by his deputy? Boots said yes, and Rosie said most of the senior staff officers of the 17th Division were sympathetic, but not surprised. Boots said probably because they had felt Sir Henry's age would count against him when the crunch came. He'd suspected that himself.

'By the way, Rosie, I'm staying with Sir Henry.'

'Are you? You're not going?' Rosie was far from disappointed. 'Well, I'm all in favour, Daddy old love. And does that mean Polly isn't going, either?'

'Yes, poppet, it does mean that,' said Boots, 'and something else means she wouldn't have gone, in any case.'

'What something else?' asked Rosie.

'Hold on to your hat,' said Boots. 'Polly's expecting.'

'She's what?' gasped Rosie.

'There's an infant on the way,' said Boots.

'Oh, my sainted aunt,' breathed Rosie, 'is she sure?'

'A certain doctor is,' said Boots, 'and now I know why she's been sick some mornings.'

'Daddy, I suppose you realize Polly's the third woman you've put in the family way?' said Rosie, and her laughter travelled like a series of warm vibrations down the line. 'You shocker. Did Polly thump you when she found out what you'd done to her?'

'On the contrary,' said Boots.

'She's happy about it?' said Rosie.

'As a lark,' said Boots. 'She's a walking miracle as far as I'm concerned.'

'Did you tell her so?' asked Rosie.

'I did,' said Boots.

'And who's going to tell Grandma Finch?' asked Rosie.

'I will,' said Boots.

'No, let me,' said Rosie, 'I'd love to hear how she takes it. I can tell her at the same time that you and Polly aren't going overseas. Daddy old thing, let me phone her.'

'That'll tickle you, will it?' said Boots.

'I'm tickled already,' said Rosie, 'but I don't know if it'll tickle Nana or collapse her.'

'Go ahead and find out,' said Boots.

Chapter Nine

'What?' said Chinese Lady, and held the receiver away from her as if the blessed contraption had bitten her. Then she put it cautiously to her ear again. 'What did you say, Rosie?'

'That Polly's going to have a baby, Nana,' said Rosie, making the call from her office at 17th Division.

'Rosie, I don't know what gets into these telephone things,' said Chinese Lady. 'It must be electricity or something, which didn't ought to be allowed. It's making you say something I can't believe or didn't hear properly. You didn't say, did you, that Polly's going to have a baby?'

'Yes, I did say that,' said Rosie. 'I've just had the news from Daddy, and I knew you'd want to know.'

'Lord Above,' breathed Chinese Lady, 'what this war's doing to people I can't hardly credit. Polly, you said?'

'Yes, Nana.'

'Oh, my goodness,' breathed Chinese Lady, 'what got into her at her age?'

Rosie, fighting laughter, said, 'I think you'd better rephrase that, Nana, in case someone's listening.'

'What?' Chinese Lady was struggling to collect herself, since she wasn't sure if what Boots and Polly had done was actually decent at their age. 'What, Rosie?'

'Never mind,' said Rosie. 'It's lovely, really, isn't it, and a delicious surprise?'

Chinese Lady, finding ample breath at last, said, 'I don't know what to say, and I certainly don't know what the fam'ly's going to say, especially your Aunt Victoria. She'll come round as soon as she hears and put me into a flushed state about it. Rosie, Boots hasn't had a child since Tim was born twenty years ago. What come over him, for goodness sake?'

'Fatherhood?' suggested Rosie.

'I've got palpitations,' said Chinese Lady, 'and I wouldn't be surprised if Polly didn't feel the same. D'you know how she's taking it, Rosie? Is she in shock?'

'According to Daddy, she's over the moon,' said Rosie, 'and they're proud of each other.'

'Proud?' said Chinese Lady. 'They'll get people looking at them, and I don't suppose the fam'ly will ever stop talking about it once everyone knows.'

'Will you tell them, Nana?' asked Rosie.

'I'll have to,' said Chinese Lady, 'it's a bit too delicate for Edwin to. Lor', I never did hear the like.'

154

'Oh, and there's something else,' said Rosie, 'Daddy and Polly won't be going overseas. They're excused.'

'Well, that's something to be thankful for,' said Chinese Lady. 'Rosie?'

'Yes, Nana?'

'You're sure it's true about Polly?'

'Quite sure,' said Rosie, and thought she heard just the faintest little laugh from the other end. 'Nana?'

'That only oldest son of mine,' said Chinese Lady, 'now look what his airy-fairy ways have done for him, and with a war on too.'

'Nana, did I hear you laugh?' asked Rosie.

'Well, Rosie, it's come to me sudden that it's nothing to cry about,' said Chinese Lady.

'Love you,' said Rosie. 'Must go now, everyone here is rushing about because of draft orders and I'm the only slacker. 'Bye.'

'Goodbye, Rosie love.' Chinese Lady put the phone down. My goodness, Boots and Polly, she thought, who'd have thought it at their age? Still, I won't let cousin Victoria go on about it, and there's one thing that's certain. Boots will be able to give Rosie away at her wedding, even if he does get looked at.

She picked the phone up again, studied it to make sure no sparks were coming from it, and then rang Lizzy. She imparted the news

155

of Polly's condition.

'What?' shrieked Lizzy, and that was the start of a conversation full of exclamation marks from the Somers' representative. Lizzy, disbelieving to begin with, was still disbelieving to finish with, her parting shot being that if it was true, then Boots ought to have his credentials examined.

Subsequently, Vi took the news in much more equable fashion, and even said wasn't it lovely for Boots and Polly, celebrating their marriage in such a happy way? She would write and congratulate them, she said.

Susie was next to be informed.

'Mum, it's certain, positive and official?' she said.

'Well, we can't disbelieve our Rosie,' said Chinese Lady.

'Let's have a party,' said Susie.

'Susie, a party?' said Chinese Lady.

'Yes, to celebrate Boots's achievement, Mum,' said Susie. 'Not many men could do for a woman of forty-four what he's done for Polly.'

'Susie, I don't know what's up with this phone, the things I seem to be hearing on it today,' said Chinese Lady. 'I never did trust it, not from the time the GPO men came and fitted it. Susie, you didn't say something vulgar, did you?'

'No, Mum, of course not,' said Susie, 'I

only sort of mentioned you must be proud of your oldest son.'

'Well, I can't make up my mind if he's a surprise or a shock to me,' said Chinese Lady. 'Or what,' she added. 'Lizzy's unbelieving, but Vi said she was pleased for Polly.'

'I'm delighted myself,' said Susie.

'Oh, that's nice,' said Chinese Lady, 'I wouldn't want anyone in the fam'ly to actually be disapproving.'

Susie simply had to tell Sammy. She rang him at his office and delivered the news. There was a muffled sound and then nothing.

'Sammy? Sammy?'

'Fell off me chair,' said Sammy. 'Now listen, Susie, are you telling me fairy stories during me office hours?'

Susie assured him she wasn't, that she'd got the news from his mother, who'd received it from Rosie, who'd had it from Boots himself. Sammy said bloody hell.

'Now, Sammy love.'

'Well, I ask you, Susie, Polly and Boots at their time of life?'

'Yes, isn't it lovely that they managed it?' said Susie. 'It's a record for the family.'

'Who's lookin' for that kind of record?' said Sammy. 'Seems to me Boots is the kind of bloke who's only got to give a female woman the glad eye and click-bang, she's in

157

the club, never mind how old she is.'

'Sammy, he's only done it three times in his life,' said Susie.

'Well, you keep your distance in future, Susie,' said Sammy, 'I don't want him chalkin' you up as the fourth.'

'Let's see, would I like another baby?' murmured Susie. 'No, I don't think so, I'm happy with the number I've had. You're right, Sammy, I'll dodge getting bosom to bosom and eye to eye with Boots.' A funny sound reached her ear. 'Sammy, you there?'

'Just pickin' myself up, just fell off this gorblimey chair again,' said Sammy.

'Who's a clever boy, then?' said Susie.

'What a war,' said Sammy. 'Good old Boots,' he said.

'Lucky old Polly,' said Susie. 'Over forty, and click-bang.'

'Boots darling,' said Polly over supper that evening, 'you know the destination of the Corps, I suppose?'

'Yes, I know,' said Boots. 'So do you, minx, you got it out of your father last thing this afternoon.'

'Yes, the dear man, it's—'

'Not in front of the children,' said Boots. His batman, presently in the kitchen, could still make use of his ears. Batmen were generally the first of other ranks to find out what was in the wind, and there was always a possibility that they'd retail the information to mates over a drink in a pub. German agents had an ongoing interest in the destinations of troopships, which were, of course, among the prime targets of U-boats.

'Well, wherever,' said Polly, 'we'll have the consolation of being able to attend Rosie's wedding.'

'And there's Tim's,' said Boots.

'Oh, my hat,' said Polly, 'I feel rotten each time I think about the blind young lady. How was it for you exactly during the years you were blind?'

'You can't guess?' said Boots.

'Yes, of course,' said Polly. 'Sorry, old scout, but I'm still giddy. It's understandable why Tim wants a quiet wedding.'

'Just you and me and Felicity's parents,' said Boots. 'Polly, how'd you feel?'

'About being at Tim's wedding?' said Polly. 'We must go, of course, we must give him and Felicity all the support we can.'

'I meant how'd you feel about your condition?'

'As lively as a cricket,' said Polly, 'and utterly blissful that you're pleased with me, you darling man.'

'Do I deserve such happy words?' asked Boots. 'And what's this we're eating?'

'The answer to your first question stumps me,' said Polly. 'The answer to your second

159

is fish in parsley sauce.'

'I fail to recognize it,' said Boots, and
called. 'Higgins?' Lance-Corporal Higgins
put his head in.

'Sir?'

'What's this fish?' asked Boots.

'Whitefish,' said Higgins.

'Which species?' asked Boots.

'Dunno, sir,' said Higgins.

'Something that got torpedoed?' said
Boots.

'Probably, sir,' said Higgins. 'It's this here
war, y'know. Mind if I get back to stirring
the custard?'

'Give it a go,' said Boots, and Higgins
disappeared. Polly smiled.

'How's your fish now?' she asked.

'Still unrecognizable,' said Boots.

'Is something doing funny things to your
taste buds?' asked Polly. 'I mean, are you
lightheaded?'

'Yes,' said Boots.

'So am I,' said Polly, 'and if someone told
me I was eating a boiled cricket ball, I
wouldn't argue. Tell me, how old do you
feel?'

'About nineteen,' said Boots.

'So do I,' said Polly. 'Aren't we wonderful?'

'You certainly are,' said Boots. 'What
d'you put it down to?'

'A flash of lightning during the first week

of our marriage,' said Polly.

'Baked apple and 'ot custard comin' up, sir,' called Higgins.

'Hope we recognize it,' said Boots.

'What's that, sir?'

'Oh, just something about boiled cricket balls, Corporal Higgins,' said Boots.

'You got me there, sir, I ain't too sharp lately.'

'Try a flash of lightning with Mrs Higgins,' said Boots.

Polly laughed. God, she thought, all the years I didn't have with the man I was born for. Life let me down there.

Rosie phoned later, wanting to talk to Polly. Polly received congratulations on her condition and compliments on her fertility.

'Steady, ducky,' said Polly, 'don't let's get biological.'

'Still,' said Rosie, 'you're a lovely example of flourishing womanhood. By the way, I've been told that if I don't want to join the admin staff of the new division which will be moving in, I can exercise the option available to a married woman, and apply for a discharge.'

Which made Polly say, 'You'd have to, Rosie, if you and Matt started a family.'

'Oh, feeling motherly, are we?' said Rosie. 'But if I tell you Matt's talking about turning one bedroom into a kind of nursery, would you think he's got something on his mind that I ought to know about?'

'Hasn't he mentioned the patter of tiny feet, then?' asked Polly.

'He mentioned he liked kids,' said Rosie, 'so I asked if he meant other people's. He said ask him another.'

'I don't think it'll be long, ducky, before you apply for a discharge,' said Polly.

'Have you applied for yours?' asked Rosie.

'Not yet,' said Polly. 'Would you like to talk to Boots now?'

'For a few minutes,' said Rosie. She and Boots had a very affectionate chat that didn't get emotional until she suddenly said, 'I'm so happy you're not on the draft. I really wasn't looking forward to you and me being far away from each other. Well, you've always been somewhere around, you've always been reachable, and I've always loved you for it. Don't forget that, will you?'

'Rosie, there's no way I could ever forget anything about all our years together,' said Boots. 'They've been a joy to me, and so have you. You've a new life in front of you now, and I hope it'll be all you want and deserve, but wherever I am I'll be reachable in one way or another.'

'Well, if I have Matt beside me and you within reach in one way or another, what more could I ask for?' said Rosie.

162

'There's always the moon,' said Boots, 'but if any of us had it what could we do with it except build a shed for it?'

'Matt's coming home with me for a few days sometime in advance of the wedding,' said Rosie. 'He'll be able to meet the family before we take him legally to our bosom.'

Boots laughed.

'Well, I think your grandma would feel the family bosom always has room for one more, although she'd never mention it,' he said. 'On the grounds that bosoms are sacred.'

'Quite right, so they are,' said Rosie, and laughed.

'Goodbye for now, poppet,' said Boots.

'Au 'voir, Daddy old love. Bless us, what a man.'

Boots made his weekly phone call to Eloise the following evening. She was delighted to talk to him, to tell him that as an officer cadet she was the recipient of many compliments from instructors and lecturers. She was confident she would be commissioned and back in Troon in three weeks.

'And how about Rosie's wedding?' asked Boots.

'Oh, I'll ask for forty-eight hours special leave from the Friday to Sunday,' said Eloise, 'although a certain po-faced officer might look down her nose about it. I don't think she believes women need to have husbands.'

'What does she believe they should have instead?' asked Boots.

'Horses and dogs,' said Eloise.

'Well, better than a parrot, I suppose,' said Boots.

'Papa, listen,' said Eloise, 'what do you think about Tim getting married so soon after Rosie?'

'I think he obviously prefers a wife to a horse,' said Boots.

'Well, of course, you silly,' said Eloise. 'But he's not inviting anyone except you and stepmama. Yes, that is what you said in a letter. Why does he want such a quiet wedding?'

'Some people prefer it,' said Boots.

'Well, when he next phones me I will speak to him,' said Eloise.

'Good idea, it's what phones are for,' said Boots, 'but perhaps I should let you know now the reason for a quiet wedding. It's time you did know.' He explained. Eloise was aghast. Lieutenant Jessop, the nicest ATS officer at Troon blinded in an air raid? How terrible, how tragic, but how wonderful of Tim to be marrying her. Yet how could he take proper care of her when so much of his time was with the Army, the Commandos? Boots said his landlady, a Mrs Andrews, was going to provide support and company, and that Felicity had settled for the arrangement, since she wanted to be in Troon.

'Oh, I do wish them good luck and happiness,' said Eloise, 'and I admire both of them, yes, very much, and yes, how proud I am of my English family. I am very glad you loved my mother, Papa.'

'Your mother, Eloise, was very lovable,' said Boots, and changed the subject to one that amazed her.

'Mother Mary, what have you done, Papa?' she exclaimed.

'Would you like me to send you a book that explains everything about the consequences of marriage?' said Boots.

'No, no, of course not, but merciful heavens, you and stepmama are to have a child?'

'A bit of a miracle, would you say, my French chicken?'

'Well, you are very clever, Papa, yes, but very naughty.'

'Naughty, yes, I see.'

'All the same, I'm proud of you,' said Eloise, 'it's a pleasure to me to be the daughter of such an accomplished man.'

'You're very welcome,' said Boots.

Chapter Ten

Tuesday, 20 May.

German airborne troops had landed on Crete to immediately find themselves locked in battle with the British and Empire forces. Casualties were heavy on both sides, but this did not deter the Germans, and their landings were continuous.

Matthew's sister Maisie, sitting down to supper with him, said, 'Rosie's making you a happy man.'

'Was I a doleful fellow before?' smiled Matt.

'Only half a man you were,' said Maisie, 'being a disappointed one.' She was referring to the fact that he'd been as good as jilted two and a half years ago by Margaret Chaise of Bere Regis. 'Different now you've got Rosie, she being a lovely young woman with a nice nature and warm heart. You're treating her right?'

'Treating her right?' said Matt. 'What does that mean?'

'I mean, are you making her a happy woman like she's making you a happy man?' said Maisie. 'Only you haven't had much to do with women since Margaret went and married someone else.'

'What's your idea of making a woman happy?' asked Matt.

'Fuss and affection,' said Maisie, 'and letting her feel sure you love her, you being a mite conservative.'

'You're fishing,' said Matt.

'And what might I be fishing for?' asked Maisie.

'Details of my private life with Rosie,' said Matt. 'I don't fish into what you and John Rawlings are getting up to.'

Maisie emitted something very much like a giggle. Constable John Rawlings was the man she was going to marry in June.

'Well, I'm a widow and John's a man and don't we be going to the church in a few weeks?' she said.

'You naughty girl,' said Matt.

'There's the war,' said Maisie, 'and people don't waste time like they used to.'

'You're still fishing,' said Matt.

'Only talking,' said Maisie, eyes teasing. 'You and Rosie, you'll have the cottage all to yourselves after I'm married.'

There would be five weeks between Maisie's wedding and his own, and Matt intended to use that time to do some decorating, converting and refurnishing. He meant to make the interior of the cottage fit his and Rosie's ideas of a marital home.

That kind of work would take his mind off the temptations of what he saw as Rosie's extraordinary sex appeal. He was indeed a conservative man in certain respects. If he was healthy, he was not promiscuous. If he had a welcome sense of humour, he did not treat women lightly, and his regard for Rosie was of a kind that made him willing to stand off from her until they were married.

For her part, Rosie had moments of tingling anticipation. There were no undue advances from Matt, but there were still occasions when they were sensitively conscious of each other. There were undercurrents too in their dialogue, and when Matt pondered humorously on how Adam and Eve went about that of which they knew nothing, being the first of their kind, Rosie said she supposed they first removed their fig leaves. Matt said that was probably a simpler process than it was today. Rosie asked if he was referring to the modern equivalent of fig leaves.

'Pants?' said Matt, with the devil of a broad grin.

'Panties in my case,' said Rosie.

'Ar, pretty on civilian girls, so I've heard,' said Matt.

'Are you suggesting mine are unappealing?' said Rosie.

'Couldn't say,' said Matt. 'Regulation issue, I suppose, or so I've heard. And then

168

there's appurtenances, also pretty, I daresay, but nowhere near as simple as fig leaves.'

Rosie laughed. She enjoyed this kind of dialogue with him, the kind she'd never indulged in with other men.

'I must inform you, sir, that as an officer, my regulation issue and my appurtenances are sacred.'

'Well, they are at the moment,' said Matt, 'and I'm saying a prayer for them.'

Rosie laughed again, this time in sheer delight. Matt may have considered himself just another man, but Rosie thought him exciting, with a bit of the devil about him.

She had never allowed any man to make love to her. She had remained faithful to the principles laid down by Grandma Finch, who got them from God's ordinance. She had also taken note of the loyalties and faithfulness of all the married members of the family. Now, with her own marriage approaching, she did not need an explanatory booklet to tell her why it was that Matthew aroused her as no other man had. Simply, she was very much in love.

On duty, she was in such an anticipatory frame of mind that she sometimes found it difficult to concentrate on her work. That, however, was only of a clearing-up kind. Divisional headquarters was now a place of echoes of men and women gone – only a few remained behind. By tomorrow they would be gone too, and then the mansion would be waiting for its next occupants, the staff of a new division or brigade. She was to be attached, and the cottage was to be her billet when she was married.

The Parachute Training School at Ringway, close to Manchester, was not a place for fainthearts. It was not geared for such. Fainthearts indeed never reached the training theatre in the New Forest, let alone Ringway. The instructors, however, could be sympathetic, shaking their heads in sorrow over broken bones.

Bobby and Helene, on arrival at Ringway with other trainees, soon learned that the daily grind was tough and uncompromising. Lectures alternated with exercises that took in gym practice and drops from a standing mock-up Whitley bomber onto coconut matting. The latter were a strain on leg joints.

'This is killing my knees,' complained Helene.

'Well, I'll grant knees are a bit iffy, Fifi,' said the instructor, 'but we've never actually seen any die a death. Up you go again.'

Such practice jumps were to lead to being taken up in a balloon and launched into their first two parachute drops. During following days, they would take off on five occasions in a Whitley bomber for the drops that would complete their training.

'How many legs get broken?' asked Bobby.

'Good question, Charlie. Say one in five.'

'Is that a fact?' enquired Bobby.

'Ask the MO.'

Later, after another series of practice jumps from the standing model of a Whitley, Bobby and Helene were watching other trainees doing the same. Bobby put a question to Helene.

'How are your legs and so on, Fifi?'

'Ah, you want to look, Charlie?'

'I mean, how do they feel?'

'You terrible man, you want to feel as well as look?'

'No, and stop mucking about. Are your legs in a fragile state, that's what I want to know.'

'Of course. They are aching everywhere from jumping, falling, climbing, running and more jumping.'

'Fifi, d'you want to give up and go home?'

'Give up? Give up? When I haven't yet blown up a single German factory? Or killed a single German pig? I shall never give up.'

'Good on you, girl, but the idea is to commit sabotage, not assassination.'

'Yes, I know. Charlie, do you want to make love to me again?'

'Fifi, be your age. This hangar is full of people like ourselves, trained not to miss anything that's going on.'

'No, no, you idiot, do you think I want you to make love to me in front of thirty people?'

'Well, Fifi, I hope you don't, it's thirty too many.'

'Name of a clown, what a stupid woman I am to be crazy about an idiot like you. I'm ashamed of myself. Charlie, how many times have I had to call you an idiot?'

'Search me. Look out, here comes Captain Wagstaffe. He's going to send us up there for more jumps, you can bet your life on it, so flex your knees.'

'Well, I will do every jump, I am never going to give up.

'That's my Fifi.'

'Yes, I'm all yours, Charlie. Who cares that you are off your head? Myself, I am too, so what does it matter?'

'Right, up you go again,' said Captain Wagstaffe, arriving. 'Hold on, what's amusing the pair of you?'

'Fifi's just found out we're both crazy,' said Bobby.

'You think you're unique?' said Captain Wagstaffe. 'Look around you when you finally go aloft in a plane, and you'll see the whole world's off its flaming rocker.'

'Now, what's that?' asked the caring nurse.

'A spoon,' said Felicity. Dressed in her uniform, at her own insistence, she was sitting on a bench in the sunshine, the nurse with her.

'And this?'

Another object was put into Felicity's hand.

'A bowl of soup?' she said.

'Your jokes are killing me,' said Clara. 'It's a cup.' Felicity, the dark glasses protecting her still sensitive eyes from the sun, made a little gesture of irritation. 'What's this?' asked Clara, and Felicity groped and took hold of a face towel. She fingered it.

'Towel,' she said.

'Good,' said Clara. 'And this?' She took the towel and gave Felicity a box of matches. Felicity shook the box and gave the right answer. 'Good,' said Clara again, 'it's everyday things you need to be familiar with first.'

'Oh, righty-oh,' said Felicity, 'so now lead me to a gas cooker and see if I can light the oven before I gas myself or blow myself up.'

'You're not ready to play about with cookers,' said Clara.

'I'm not ready for boiling a potato, either,' said Felicity, 'but I've got to get there some-time or other. So keep going.'

'What're these?'

'Knife, fork and spoon. Oh, come on, let's try the more difficult stuff.'

'This, then?' said Clara.

'Reel of cotton,' said Felicity. 'You call that

difficult?' The nurse smiled and handed her something else from a tray of items. Felicity explored it with the fingers of both hands. 'You funny woman,' she said, 'it's a potato.'

'Yes, a very everyday thing,' said Clara.

'Right,' said Felicity, 'now give me that knife back and I'll try peeling the spud.'

'You need a proper potato-peeler for that,' said Clara.

'Well, find one,' said Felicity.

'Tomorrow, perhaps,' said Clara. 'For now, how about another little walk?'

'I'm game,' said Felicity, 'but, I don't want any white stick. If I have to use a white stick, I might as well put on a grey wig, a bloody Victorian black bonnet and an old woman's shuffle. I'll look like Tim's grandmother. That'll be jolly, won't it, Tim looking as if he's married to his grandmother?'

'Good for a laugh,' said Clara, liking her patient for her character and the unique way she was fighting her disability, even if she did have moments when she was a little savage about it. But the venting of feelings did more for the process of rehabilitation than giving in to periods of dark depression, 'dark' being the operative word.

They walked amid surroundings green and pleasant, surroundings that offered the freshness and scents of the open air to Felicity, but were invisible to her. She clenched her teeth, her hand on Clara's wrist, and she walked and endured. When it was over and without any setbacks or accidents, an orderly brought a letter out to Felicity. It had arrived by the midday post, and was from Tim.

'Not before time,' said Felicity.

'But you had one only three days ago,' said Clara.

'My good woman,' said Felicity, 'three days is a hell of a time to someone in my condition.'

'Shall I read it?' asked Clara.

'There's a lovely old pal you are,' said Felicity.

'*Dear Puss—*'

'I'll kill him,' breathed Felicity. 'You did put down in my last letter to him that he wasn't to call me Puss, didn't you?'

'Yes,' said Clara.

'I'll definitely kill him,' said Felicity. 'Read on, please.'

'*Dear Puss,*

I enjoyed your latest letter, it was full of fireworks and bloodcurdling threats, but I know you didn't mean them. It's natural that you're at war with the world, and so would I be if I'd lost my sight. You can't really want to break my legs for calling you Puss, so I'll accept you never wrote it, or at least your nurse didn't. Is she the one with a fetching cap and brown eyes? Give her my regards.'

175

'He's showing off again, the saucy bounder,' said Felicity. 'Wait a tick, have you been adding a PS to the letters, telling him you fancy him?'

'Certainly not, that would be an unforgivable breach of ethics,' said Clara.

'Women shouldn't take any notice of some ethics,' said Felicity, 'they all originate with men, like rules and regulations. If I'd taken any notice of regulations, I wouldn't have posed for Tim's camera in my saucy sweater and showing my legs.'

'Did you do that?' smiled Clara.

'He tied me up,' said Felicity. 'That was against regulations too, which is one of the reasons why I like him, the sexy bounder.'

'He tied you up?' said Clara. 'That's sadism.'

'I mean he had me all giddy,' said Felicity, 'that's as good as being tied up. Read on, Clara.'

'I'm recovered from my falls, but am being worn down to my bones by extra training. That worries me a bit, seeing that when I arrive here with you as my bride, I'd like to have enough muscle left to carry you over Maggie's threshold. I don't want to drop you, you've got worries and troubles in plenty already, and a bruised bum would be the tender end, you might say.'

'What a specimen,' said Felicity. 'Would you believe he could write down "bum" in a letter he knew was going to be read by you?'

'There's more to come,' said Clara.

'Righty-oh, give me hysterics,' said Felicity, wishing she could see the sun that was so warm to her face.

'Anyway, Puss, if it happens, which I hope it won't on account of having great respect for your derrière, *I'll give you a massage. We'll be married, so it'll be expected of me as your caring husband, but I'll understand if I see any blushes.'*

'He's a pervert,' said Felicity. 'Why am I marrying him?'

'I wouldn't mind one like him,' said Clara. 'Do you think he meant blushing face or blushing *derrière?*'

'I'll ask him,' said Felicity, 'I'll ask him in my next letter, and if he says *derrière*, I'll send him a bomb in a brown paper parcel. Is there any more?'

'Yes,' said Clara.

'I'd like to hear about your progress, and how you feel as time goes by, but don't want to press you about what you might think is obvious, that nothing can mean much to you and that I ought to realize it. You can give me more fireworks if that'll relieve some of your frustrations. Believe

me, I'd gladly present you with one of my eyes if it could be done, and it's a swine that it can't. I admire you for what you put into your letters, and that includes all the saucy stuff. Every letter convinces me you're a great girl, and it's a privilege knowing you, which I hope doesn't embarrass you too much. Everyone here wants to be remembered to you as usual, and Major Lucas sends his very special regards. God bless. Love, Tim.'

'Don't send a bomb,' said Felicity.

'Oh, good,' said Clara, 'I was wondering how we could get one into a brown paper parcel and into a pillar box.'

'Find out if anyone here has got an unused wedding dress lying around at home,' said Felicity.

'You don't mind that Tim's a pervert?' said Clara.

'Be your age, Clara,' said Felicity, 'who wants a Christopher Robin?'

Chapter Eleven

On the evening of 23 May, the British destroyers *Norfolk* and *Suffolk*, patrolling the cold waters north of Iceland, made a dramatic sighting of two German battleships entering Denmark Strait west of Iceland and heading south. One was the *Prince Eugen*, the other Germany's newest and most powerful warship, the *Bismarck*.

The British destroyers began to shadow the Germans, the while calling up two battleships, the *Hood* and the *Prince of Wales*, whose position was south of Iceland. With the German ships steaming south, the *Hood* and the *Prince of Wales* moved to intercept and engage.

About this time, Mr Finch heard a key turn in the lock of the front door. Out he went into the hall and at the open door he saw Tim.

'What-oh, Grandpa, how's yourself?' said Tim, putting his valise down.

'In the pink,' smiled Mr Finch, 'and delighted to see you.' He shook hands with Boots's son and thought how very much like his father he was in his looks, his physique and the easy way his smile appeared. Six feet tall and as fit as a fiddle, his uniform that of a first lieutenant, Tim in the eyes of Mr Finch was an impressive young man, with a maturity that belied his twenty years. 'To what do your grandmother and I owe the pleasure of this homecoming?'

'Oh, to a fall I had that nearly altered the shape of my body,' said Tim. He had indeed taken a fall during a rock climb, and although no bones had been broken, he was black, blue and bruised all over. Recovered, he'd taken advantage of Major Lucas's receptive ear and the Major had arranged for him to take three days leave. Confirmation coming this morning, he'd left for home. 'Tried to phone you from King's Cross, Grandpa, but there was a queue at every phone box. There always is. Everyone's chattering to everyone else these days.'

Out came Chinese Lady.

'Well, I never,' she said, 'look who's here, Edwin.'

'Yes, I'm aware, Maisie,' said Mr Finch, and Tim put his enduring grandmother into a proper tizzy and fluster by wrapping his arms around her, folding her against his lean chest and giving her a real smacker on her cheek.

'Good to see you, Gran,' he said, 'and younger than ever, I note. How'd you do it? There's us, all growing older, and you're growing the other way. Got a pot of tea going?'

'Bless us, you've got me wondering what's hit the house,' said Chinese Lady. 'But, my, look at you, as tall as your dad and an officer and all. I don't know what the fam'ly's comin' to. Oh, did you say you'd like a cup of tea? It's a quiet evening, no blessed bombs or anything, and we can have a nice sit down and a talk round the kitchen table.'

At the table, Tim told Chinese Lady why he'd been given three days rest leave, but hoped she wouldn't mind if he spent the last day with Felicity.

'Understood, Tim,' said Mr Finch.

'Yes, of course, Tim love,' said Chinese Lady, experiencing quite emotional affection for him because he was so staunchly committed to the welfare of that poor young lady.

Mr Finch drew from him some Commando anecdotes that brought Tim's sense of humour to the fore, although that didn't hide the obvious – the toughness of the specialized training and the kind of man it had made of him. Outside of all that, he said, the people of Troon, especially those like Maggie Andrews, looked after the Commandos as if they were their own when off duty. Maggie, he said, would be a godsend to Felicity. Chinese Lady understood that. She had always insisted Emily had been a godsend to Boots during his years of blindness.

Tim subsequently enjoyed a good night's sleep and a wartime breakfast of porridge and toast with his grandparents, towards the end of which Mr Finch switched the wireless on to catch the news before he left for work. His action made Chinese Lady fidget a bit. Moments later, fidgets counted for nothing, for what came out of the set grieved Chinese Lady, and stunned her husband and grandson.

The announcer, referring to the pursuit of the *Bismarck* and the *Prince Eugen*, spoke of the German battleships being caught and engaged by the *Hood* and the *Prince of Wales* early that morning. The action at sea was only a matter of minutes old when a shell from the *Bismarck* struck the *Hood*. It pierced the magazine, and the mighty *Hood* blew up with a tremendous roar and sank. It was feared the loss of life was almost total. While the *Prince of Wales* searched for hoped-for survivors, the German battleships steamed away, and the Royal Navy was mounting a new pursuit of them.

'Hell's bells,' breathed Tim, 'the *Hood*? Gone, just like that?'

'Just like that, Tim, it seems, and with all hands,' said Mr Finch, looking sombre. He and Tim both knew the blow to the Royal Navy was devastating.

'Edwin,' said Chinese Lady, 'I don't know how many times I've had to tell you nothing good ever comes out of that wireless. It ought to be put where no-one can switch it on. Look what it's done now, spoiled Tim's leave and given you a lot of gloom to take to your office.'

'I'll try not to wear it all day, Maisie,' said Mr Finch, and after he had gone, Tim phoned the convalescent hospital.

Felicity was out-of-doors again. She always fumed and fretted for the open air as soon as breakfast was over. Rain was a curse to her. It kept her in. She could sense the existence of walls, and walls made her feel hemmed in. She told herself that only in the open air would the miracle of light come to her eyes one day.

She sat on the bench which she had virtually made her own, discouraging all attempts by other patients to share it with her. Other patients with other kinds of disabilities wanted to sit and talk and be comforted, of course. How the hell could a blinded casualty of the bombings be expected to dispense comfort to someone who'd only lost a leg? Felicity didn't ask to be comforted herself. She was sure that could only come from her own inner strength, if she could find it and get it working.

'There you are, Felicity.'

Her caring nurse had come on duty.

'Yes, here I am. I'm just waiting for a bus. I thought I'd have a shopping trip to the town and then take in a cinema.'

'This isn't the bus stop, Felicity, and we're not up to that kind of outing yet,' said Clara. 'I came to tell you there's been a phone call. Tim's coming to see you tomorrow.'

'Tim? Tim?'

'Yes, you know, the dishy corporal who turned into a lieutenant and is slightly perverted,' said Clara.

'He's coming here?'

'That's what he said on the phone.'

'He's coming tomorrow?'

'About noon,' said Clara.

'What else did he say?' asked Felicity.

'"Give my love to Puss."'

'He's in form, is he?' said Felicity.

'Up to scratch,' said Clara.

'Tell me, how do I look?' asked Felicity.

'Lovely,' said Clara.

'No soft soap,' said Felicity, 'how do I look?'

'Lovely,' said Clara. 'You can leave your glasses off, if you like. There's no bloodshot condition at all now, you know that.'

'But I feel naked without them,' said Felicity. However, she took them off. Her caring nurse studied her scarred eyes, knowing it was Tim who would have to live with their blind look. Felicity would never know how they looked, unless someone was callous enough to tell her, or she guessed. Then she and Tim would both have to live with the scars. 'Well?' said Felicity.

'There you are, no bloodshot signs at all,' said Clara. 'Can I leave you for half an hour? I've notes to write up, then I'll join you and we'll have a few more lessons.'

'Could someone bring out one of the battery wireless sets?' asked Felicity, putting her dark glasses back on. 'I'd like to hear if the Navy's caught up with the filthy *Bismarck*.' The news of the *Hood* disaster had spoiled breakfast for staff and patients.

'That was terrible, wasn't it, the *Hood* blowing up?' said Clara. 'I'll see that a set is brought out to you, and I hope the ten o'clock news is of a kind that won't depress all of us.'

The morning was frustrating not only for Felicity but for the whole country. The *Bismarck* was leading the Royal Navy a dance, and the German heavy cruiser, the *Prince Eugen*, had slipped away and vanished. However, the *Prince of Wales* was on course in her pursuit of the *Bismarck*. Having recently acquired a very personal dislike of the enemy, Felicity hoped both German warships would be caught and blown up by the Royal Navy.

Was Tim really going to be with her to-morrow?

'What's this?' General Sir Henry Simms looked at the papers Boots had placed on his desk.

'History of the 222nd Infantry Brigade, the first of our new units,' said Boots.

'Never heard of it,' said Sir Henry tersely. He was still smarting from the blow dealt by London, although he knew that at his age an overseas command had always been doubtful. 'Tell me in a nutshell.'

'No history at all, Sir Henry,' said Boots, 'it's a newly-formed brigade of conscripts just out of their training camps.'

'Damn my breeches,' said Sir Henry, 'they're not even soldiers yet? What's their weaponry?'

'Enfield 303's, Browning machine-guns,' said Boots.

'No anti-tank weapons?'

'None,' said Boots.

'Boots, they're giving me tin soldiers to play with,' said Sir Henry.

'Well, they won't be the first you've turned into live ones,' said Boots. 'Here's a list of officers, complete with their records, from which to pick your new staff, sir.'

'I'll take my time,' said Sir Henry. 'Any news of the *Bismarck*?'

It was ten minutes past eleven, and the

pursuit of the *Bismarck* was engaging the fevered interest of the whole country.

'The eleven o'clock news only confirmed the *Prince of Wales* was still in chase,' said Boots. 'No contact yet.'

'I hope to God the Navy catches up, or morale will sink as low as the *Hood*,' said Sir Henry. 'Churchill can do without that disaster. Only the sinking of the *Bismarck* can compensate. How's Polly?'

'Marshalling an intake of new ATS personnel and examining their shoes for polish and their stockings for wrinkles,' said Boots.

'Tell her I'm going to have her discharged due to her delicate condition,' said Sir Henry.

'She'll come and talk to you if you do that,' said Boots. 'She's not ready to relinquish her uniform yet.'

'She knows the regulations, she knows they require her to apply for her discharge,' said Sir Henry.

'Have you ever had a serious talk with Polly about the necessity of observing regulations and rules, Sir Henry?' asked Boots.

'Have you?' asked Sir Henry.

'Yes,' said Boots, 'and it's a damned dangerous business, believe me. I've been lucky to escape alive.'

'Women,' said Sir Henry.

'Some are endearing,' said Boots.

Sir Henry smiled.

'Well, you've got your own ways with them, Boots,' he said, 'and I'm delighted at how your way with Polly worked out. Capital. Extraordinary, but capital.'

'Corporal Higgins is still with us,' said Polly over supper that evening.

'So it seems,' said Boots, regarding his food. Something was on his plate, along with new potatoes, green peas and roast parsnip. 'What is it?'

'Lamb chop,' said Polly.

'Looks dark and suspicious to me,' said Boots.

'That's probably because it's a mutton chop,' said Polly.

'Some old sheep fell foul of Higgins, I suppose,' said Boots, and the seven o'clock news came on then. The announcer referred to the Royal Navy's efforts to catch and engage the *Bismarck*. The *Prince of Wales* was closing in, and action was expected any moment. Other British warships were steaming at full speed in an attempt to cut off the German battleship's avenue of escape.

'They've got to catch it and sink it before they lose it,' said Polly. 'They must.'

'Yes, they must,' said Boots. 'By the way, your father suggested you should apply for your discharge.'

188

'He's fussing,' said Polly.

'So will I be in a week or so,' said Boots.

'Because of my age?' said Polly. 'Well, I can understand that, old sport, but I'll put myself under doctor's orders and follow his advice, I promise you. Darling, are you still happy about your expectant Polly?'

'I'm still thunderstruck,' said Boots.

'Thunderstruck?'

'In a devoted way,' said Boots, wrestling manfully with his chop.

'How can anyone be devotedly thunderstruck?' asked Polly.

'It's an odd feeling, I agree,' said Boots, 'verging on the impossible. What a wonderful woman you are, Polly.'

'Thank you, darling,' said Polly. 'Is there any other miracle I can perform for you?'

'Yes, my angel, you can finish up my mutton chop,' smiled Boots.

'I thought I'd like it, and I do,' said Polly.

'A Higgins mutton chop?' said Boots.

'No, being married to you,' said Polly.

Some women, Boots had observed to Sir Henry, were endearing. Polly was one of them. Oddly, for all her sophistication, her sharp wit and her belief that she was any man's equal, Polly was a more feminine woman than Emily had been.

The late news contained further details of events in the North Atlantic. A little while before seven o'clock, the *Prince of Wales*, sighting the *Bismarck* east of the southern tip of Greenland, closed and engaged. Gunfire of an awesome kind ensued, but the *Bismarck* chose to avoid the risk of fighting to a finish. Her captain was happy enough with the destruction of the *Hood*, and the German battleship issued a great smoke-screen that veiled her movements and hovered like a grey-black cloud over the surface of the ocean for long minutes.

The Prince of Wales lost the prey.

The Royal Navy had taken up a new search.

'It's criminal,' said Chinese Lady.

'Fair tactics, a smoke-screen, Grandma,' said Tim.

'I don't think your grandmother is referring to that, Tim,' said Mr Finch.

'I mean our blessed old wireless,' said Chinese Lady, 'it's been a misery ever since we had it. Ought to be given a year's hard labour. That would learn it not to upset people.'

'There's a lot more like ours, Grandma,' said Tim. 'My landlady, Maggie Andrews, has got one exactly the same.'

'Now what?' said Tommy to Vi.

'Don't ask me, love,' said Vi, 'I'm not in the Navy.'

190

'There'll be hell to pay if that German battleship escapes,' said Tommy.

'But it must be as big as a bus,' said Vi, knitting.

'Bigger than a fleet of buses,' said Tommy.

'Well, there you are, then, someone's bound to see it,' said Vi.

'Yes, right, someone would if it was goin' from the Elephant and Castle to Clapham Common,' said Tommy.

'It's serious,' said Ned, frowning at the news that the *Bismarck* had disappeared.

'We mustn't get gloomy,' said Lizzy.

'I'm past gloomy, I'm sunk in despair,' said Emma.

'Let's have a cup of tea,' said Lizzy.

'I'll have a nip of whisky,' said Ned.

'I'll have some Sussex cider,' said Emma.

'Afraid we don't have Sussex cider,' said Ned.

'Well, I call that graceless,' said Emma. 'We ought to have several bottles out of respect for Jonathan.'

'Jonathan has all my respect,' said Ned.

'Still, you ought to have a bottle of Sussex cider in the larder as well,' said Lizzy.

'It all comes from Somerset,' said Ned.

'Well, good enough, I suppose. Somerset's almost next door to Sussex.'

'Jane's young man is in the Navy,' said Emma. Jane was Jonathan's elder sister. 'I wonder if he's on one of the ships looking for the *Bismarck*?' And I wonder, she thought, where my Jonathan from Sussex is now?

Jonathan and his battery, in fact, were already among the guns of the Eighth Army, and finding the desert hot in more ways than one. The German armoury was fearsome, and their supportive combat planes made strikes that had the British gunners diving for cover.

'I'm goin' to have a heart attack if the ruddy *Bismarck* gets back scot-free to Germany,' said Sammy. 'Hitler'll give it the Iron Cross and make a speech lasting a week.'

'A week?' said Susie. 'Hope so. It'll put all the Germans in a state of collapse.'

'No laughing matter, y'know, Susie,' said Sammy.

'Who's laughing? I'm not,' said Susie, 'I lost my sense of humour as soon as we heard all those sailors had gone down with the *Hood*. Sammy, that was awful.'

'So it was, Susie, so it was,' said Sammy, and bit his lip.

'It was nice to see Tim again,' said Susie. 'Didn't he look all of a man, and so like Boots.'

'A chip off the old block, and I liked it that he made the rounds of the fam'ly,' said Sammy.

'I can understand him wanting a quiet wedding when he marries his ATS officer,' said Susie.

'Well, I don't suppose she's all that keen on havin' a crowd of us there,' said Sammy. 'And what could we say to a blind bride? "Hope the weather keeps fine for you"? She wouldn't know if it was sunny or foggy.'

'I feel desperately sorry for her,' said Susie.

'Don't we all,' said Sammy.

The night sky was quiet over Southern England, the *Luftwaffe* bombers heading for Liverpool and Scotland.

South-west of Iceland, the aircraft carrier *Victorious* made contact with the *Bismarck* half an hour after midnight, and despatched planes to deliver an attack. A hit was scored, but the German battleship steamed on apparently undamaged and unimpressed. HMS *Rodney* was on the alert well to the east of the *Bismarck*, and west of Ireland the aircraft carrier *Ark Royal* was making a bid to join the hunt.

The North Atlantic was not so quiet, nor was the British Admiralty.

Get the *Bismarck*.

Churchill, awake, chewed on his cigar.

He was dozing when, at three in the morning, the Admiralty reported that all contact with the German battleship had again been lost.

Chapter Twelve

25 May.

Felicity was walking with her caring nurse, Clara, whose guiding hand rested on her patient's arm.

'What's the morning like?' asked Felicity, her feet feeling the way over the path, her imagination conjuring up obstacles. 'And what time did you say Tim was coming?'

'It's a bright morning,' said Clara, 'and your fiancé will be here about noon.'

'Well, bless the man,' said Felicity. 'Look here, how far have we walked?'

'Oh, just around this side of the grounds,' said Clara. 'Say about a hundred yards in a circle.'

'A circle? No wonder I'm dizzy,' said Felicity. 'Still, carry on, Clara, and I'll try to wear you out.' She knew this kind of natural exercise was good for her. It put her on her feet and set her in motion, motion that under Clara's guidance was less cautious each day. 'What a swine that that bloody Jerry battleship has slipped the Navy.'

'Dr Samuels isn't far away,' said Clara. 'He's a courteous medical gentleman who doesn't like to hear a lady swearing.'

'Well, lah-de-dah and dearie me, poor old

gent,' said Felicity, 'and if I've given him or you the impression I'm a lady put it down to my feeble state.'

'You're not feeble,' said Clara, 'you're fit and strong.'

'I meant I'm feeble-minded,' said Felicity.

'If I believed that, I'd be brain-dim myself,' said Clara. 'My word, aren't we doing well this morning? We're really stepping out.'

'Hardly,' said Felicity.

'We are by comparison with a week ago,' said Clara, 'but we'll go back now and I'll see about having your lunch brought out. Will you need me?'

'Only to remind me where my mouth is,' said Felicity. 'If Tim turns up, can you find some lunch for him too?'

'I'll wangle it,' said Clara.

Felicity ate the meal outside, from a little table in front of her bench. She was able to bring everything to her mouth by her fingers, the sandwich that was cut into four, crisp lettuce leaves, a quartered tomato and some spring onions. She listened to the twelve o'clock news. The Royal Navy was still searching for the *Bismarck*.

'Well, come on, you saints and sinners, catch that Nazi tin can,' she hissed.

Unknown to her and the rest of the nation, the formidable German battleship

195

had altered its course at a point south-east of Greenland to head for Brest, the large French naval station on the tip of North-West France. The station was in German hands, and offered a refuge. It was an audacious move on the part of the battle-ship's captain, for it could mean running the gauntlet of prowling British warships.

Felicity took her temper out on a large spring onion, crunching it to destruction and death. The tingling juices spilled into her throat. She had an awful thought five minutes later. She groped and felt over the plate. It was empty, she'd eaten everything, including all the spring onions. Tim was due any moment and her breath would smell. She cupped her hand to her mouth, blew breath into it and smelled it. Oh, yuk. She stood up. Her knees made contact with the table, and the table quivered. She knew from her walks with Clara that the bench stood alongside the path that led past the rear entrance to the hospital building. One stood up, took two paces forward onto the path and turned right. She moved sideways away from the table, took her two paces, felt the tarmac surface of the path beneath her feet, and turned. She could hear other patients talking together, and hoped none would come up. She was always better by herself, hating the helplessness that aroused sympathy and an offer to assist. She was amenable only to Clara's care and attention. She began a slow blind walk, wanting to get to her ward, to her locker and her toothbrush and paste.

She heard footsteps, then a voice.

'Hello, Puss, can I help?'

Felicity expelled a little yelp, then strong arms embraced her and warm lips engaged lovingly with her own. After giddy seconds, the warm lips departed.

'Tim?'

'You've been eating spring onions.' said Tim.

'Oh, bloody hell, did you have to notice?' wailed Felicity.

'Why not?' said Tim. 'I like spring onions. How are you, Puss?'

'Don't call me Puss,' said Felicity, wishing quite desperately that she could see him. His embrace and his kiss had reminded her of how personable he was to look at. Touch, yes, she could still touch, but at this moment it wasn't enough. God, I'll go demented if I'm never able to see him again. 'Why do you call me Puss, anyway?'

'Well, you've heard of cheeky pussies, haven't you?' said Tim. 'You're one of them. I get more sauce from you in a week than some blokes get in a year. Anyway, delighted to see you. Ruddy happy, in fact. Look at you, sexy as ever, especially in those dark glasses. I've seen your nurse and she says you're the most fighting patient here. She's leaving me in charge of you for an hour or so. I don't suppose you'd know for certain, but is there some place around here where I could help you unbutton your uniform and have a bit of what the butler fancied through Lady Blushington's keyhole?'

Felicity laughed.

'Oh, you bounder, you're still after helping yourself to what an ATS officer is supposed to keep to herself,' she said.

'Stone me,' said Tim, 'aren't these ever going to see the light of my day?'

She felt him touch her jacket where it curved the most. She laughed again.

'Don't you care who's looking?' she asked.

'There's a killing war on,' said Tim, 'Jerry's bombed your eyes and blown up the *Hood*. So I don't care who's looking. I care only about you.'

'Well, bless you,' said Felicity. 'D'you want something to eat?'

'I had something in the station buffet at Farnham,' said Tim.

'Tell me, exactly what are these hospital grounds like?' asked Felicity.

'Extensive,' said Tim. 'Lawns and long grass all over the place, and any amount of shrubberies. But keep in mind an ex-soldier, Great War vintage, who's grubbing about on gardening duty.'

'Never mind him,' said Felicity, 'walk me

somewhere, find a place dangerously private.'

'Dangerously?' said Tim.

'Well, you're here, you're good for me, and I'm in the mood to risk facing up to what the butler fancied,' said Felicity.

'Take my arm,' said Tim, touching elbows with her, and she slipped her arm through his. He began to walk her, his guidance sure. The hospital was murmurous with sound, the ground murmurous with conversational patients enjoying the open air, and here and there, battery wireless sets, available to assist rehabilitation, issued lunchtime music for factory workers.

Felicity heard Clara's voice as she and Tim passed the rear entrance.

'Take good care of her, Lieutenant Adams.'

'Trust me,' said Tim.

'She might,' whispered Felicity, 'I don't.'

They walked, through darkness as far as Felicity was concerned, but her spirits had taken a lift, and it was good to be close to Tim, to feel his warmth and the firmness of his muscled arm. Tim was aware of the spacious grounds, the peacefulness, the atmosphere of convalescence and the apparent lack of complaint among the men and women trying to come to terms with disablement of one kind or another, including blindness.

199

'Ruddy awful about the *Hood*,' he said.

'Yes, and they still haven't caught the *Bismarck*,' said Felicity. 'The Navy must be boiling mad. Oh, well, I'm not the one who'll get the chopper from Churchill. God, he's having a lousy war, suffering all the slings and arrows of one setback after another. I know I've got my own problem, but he's got mountains of them.'

'He'd rather have his mountains than your particular problem, I'd bet my life on that,' said Tim.

'Glad you're here, Tim, glad you came,' she said. 'How did you manage it?'

'Major Lucas helped me get three days leave,' said Tim. 'I've been home, and seen the family. They all sent their best wishes, and they all understand we don't want a crowded wedding.'

'Well, as long as you and I are both there, that's all we'll need,' said Felicity.

'Plus a vicar and our parents as witnesses,' said Tim. He felt for her, for her blindness, her frustrations and her fighting spirit. Her walk was measured, exploratory, but not nervous. She was putting her trust in his guidance. The path wound away, and he took her to a bench where they were out of earshot of everyone else. 'Try this seat for comfort,' he said, guiding her movements. She sat down, and he sat beside her.

'What's my nurse like to look at?' she

asked.

'Plump,' said Tim.

'Fat plump?'

'Nicely plump,' said Tim.

'D'you like them like that?'

'Explain what you mean by them,' said Tim.

'Not what you've got in mind,' said Felicity, 'and look here, could you keep perversion out of your letters? It's making her feel sexy for you.'

'She likes a bit of perversion?' said Tim.

'She'd like a bit of you.'

'Don't let's talk about what bit,' said Tim.

'About you and me, then?' said Felicity, hip to hip with him because she needed physical contact.

'About you, anyway,' said Tim.

'I don't want to hear anything that makes me feel sorrier for myself,' said Felicity. 'I'm sorry enough.'

'We'll share your problems when we're mister and missus,' said Tim, 'and knock 'em on the head one by one.'

'First off, you'll have to teach me how to boil an egg without upsetting the saucepan,' said Felicity.

'We'll knock that one for six,' said Tim.

'Listen, if there's one thing that really makes me sorry for myself,' said Felicity, 'it's that I can't see you.'

'Is that one of your big worries?' asked

201

Tim.

'It has to be.' Felicity, one of England's jolly hockey sticks types who had always favoured a breezy approach to relationships, found blindness did not support that. Beneath her brittleness, she was more emotional. It was a surge of emotion that made her say, 'Don't you realize what it's like not to be able to see someone you love?'

That touched Tim.

'Well, we love each other, don't we, Puss?' he said. 'I like that, it'll help us in our marriage, won't it? Yes, it will.'

'I'll never be a burden, Tim, I swear,' said Felicity.

'How could you be?' said Tim. 'You're a fighter.'

'Were you ever a Boy Scout?' asked Felicity.

'A bit of a cricketer, but never a Boy Scout,' said Tim.

'Was it cricket, then, that taught you how to do good deeds?' asked Felicity.

'I can't remember any specific good deeds,' said Tim.

'You're doing one now,' said Felicity.

'Am I?'

'Yes, just by being here. You're good for me.'

'Mutual,' said Tim. 'By the way, when do you expect your discharge?'

'When a collection of old Army medical

buffers decide nothing can be done and that I'm useless to the ATS,' said Felicity. 'That's going to leave me shipwrecked unless I can be useful to you.'

'I don't want you to be useful,' said Tim. 'A cardboard box is useful, so's a kettle. You're not either, you're my idea of what I'd like to come home to every evening.'

'As Mrs Adams the Fourth?' said Felicity.

'That's it, a family treasure,' said Tim.

'You're expecting me to be a treasure?' said Felicity.

'Yes, just as much as Mrs Adams the First, Second and Third,' said Tim. 'I already treasure your sex appeal.'

'Visible sex appeal?' Felicity laughed. She felt high. 'I wouldn't know, would I?'

Tim wasn't going to tell her not to make references to her disability. As far as he was concerned, she could talk about it as much as she liked. He thought, in fact, that that might be as much of a help to her as all other forms of rehabilitation.

'You can take my word for it,' he said.

'Have you ever heard of mental therapy?' asked Felicity.

'Yes, every time I've fallen off a rockface and the MO has told me to tell myself I'm only imagining I hurt, to exercise my mind to my advantage,' said Tim.

'Well, what you've just said about my sex appeal is therapeutic,' said Felicity. She removed her glasses, and Tim looked at her disfigured eyes, the damaged pupils cloudy. Tim felt wrenched. 'How do I look?' she asked.

'Marvellous,' he said.

A patient, an infantry lieutenant who'd lost his speech through shellshock in the desert, suddenly ran amok, brandishing another patient's crutch. He made straight for the distant bench on which Felicity and Tim were seated. His face was red, twisted and contorted, and his mouth was issuing gurgling noises. A male orderly went after him, shouting at him. Tim saw him coming, whirling the crutch about like a hammer-thrower.

'Who's shouting?' asked Felicity.

'Nobody I know,' said Tim, and came to his feet. He advanced several paces, waiting for the onrushing man, whose eyes were bulging. On he came, still whirling the crutch. Tim ducked and dived. He went straight for the man's legs, wound his arms around them, used his shoulder to strike a blow, and brought the bloke down. Up came the orderly to wrench the crutch free.

'Sorry about that, sir,' he said. 'Now, Lieutenant,' he said to the writhing patient, 'what d'you think you're up to? Can't have that, y'know. Come on, up you get.'

The unfortunate patient went limp, and he allowed Tim and the orderly to bring him to his feet.

'What's going on?' called Felicity.

'Lieutenant Peebles wants his tea,' said the orderly, 'but it's a bit early for that. Come on, Mister Peebles, let's get back to your jigsaw puzzle. Much obliged, sir,' he said to Tim, and took the subdued patient away.

Tim acquainted Felicity with details of the incident, and Felicity sighed.

'I've felt like running wild myself sometimes,' she said. 'With a hammer.'

'Understandable,' said Tim, and they talked some more, Felicity very brittle at times. Tim didn't touch on anything too serious. He had a feeling that beneath her brittleness she was capable of a good cry if her emotions were aroused, and he was not sure he could cope with that. At three o'clock, Clara beckoned, and he went to collect a tea tray. There was a pot of tea and some cake for himself and Felicity.

'It's against the rules, of course,' she said.

'Well, it's up to some of us to fight them,' said Tim.

'How are you getting on with Lieutenant Jessop?' she asked.

'She hasn't called for help yet,' said Tim.

'Keep going,' said Clara, 'you're the best thing that's happened to her. Can I ask if you're really going to marry her?'

'I really am,' said Tim.

'You'll save her life,' said Clara.

'Any news of the *Bismarck*?' asked Tim.

'They're still chasing it,' said Clara.

Tim stayed until four, by which time he thought Felicity deserved a break. He was sure the strain of staying bright and cheerful for him was getting to her. It had to be an effort, sustaining that kind of front, although when he said it was time he went, she protested a little.

'Puss, you're tired,' he said.

'No, really,' she said.

'Well, a little tired?' he said gently.

'Only a little,' she said.

'Come on, I'll walk you back to your nurse,' he said, and she let him. He placed her in charge of Clara, kissed her, gave her bottom a surreptitious pat to let her know she really did have sex appeal, refrained from a drawn-out goodbye, said he'd be in touch and left. Felicity bit her lip as his going gave her a sense that cold empty air had taken his place.

'Would you like half an hour on your bed now?' asked Clara.

'I'd like a good howl,' said Felicity.

'Is that what his visit has done to you?' asked Clara.

'Well, of course it has, woman,' said Felicity. 'I'm not made of cast-iron. As for half an hour on the bed, what's the point of that now he's gone? Couldn't you have led us to some private bed while he was still here? God, what a lovely bloke. Do I deserve him?'

'You deserve an archangel,' said Clara.

'Don't be naive,' said Felicity. 'You kneel in divine prayer with an archangel, you don't go to bed with him. Oh, all right, I will have forty winks.'

'This way,' said Clara.

'Incidentally,' said Felicity, 'if ever Tim makes another visit here, don't give me large spring onions with my lunch.'

Chapter Thirteen

Arriving home in time for supper, Tim delivered to his grandparents details of his visit to Felicity. He was happy, he said, to let them know that throughout she was courageously bright. He had no idea exactly what it must be like to find oneself suddenly blind, except that it had to be a ruddy nightmare.

'Beg pardon?' said Chinese Lady.

'Yes, muddy nightmare, Grandma,' said Tim, tactfully corrective. 'Well, everything around you as clear as black mud. I've got so much admiration for her I could fill an Army troop carrier with it. Fortunately, she's in caring hands at the hospital, where they're experienced at looking after all kinds of difficult cases, and she has a very fine nurse helping her.'

'She's also got you, Tim,' said Mr Finch.

'Not much I can do personally for her at the moment,' said Tim.

'Poor young woman,' said Chinese Lady.

'Not poor in that sense, Grandma,' said Tim, 'she's a fighter. She'll win. She'll come to terms with the nightmare one day, and it won't take her a lifetime. Can we have the

208

news, Grandpa?'

Mr Finch switched on the wireless, and the seven o'clock news began to reach their ears. There was nothing to cheer them up in respect of the *Bismarck*. The Royal Navy still hadn't made contact, and Mr Finch hoped to God that the German battleship wouldn't escape.

The fact, not known, was that searching British warships had cut across the line taken by the *Bismarck* without realizing it was on a south-east course, and not until they were many miles directly south did they suspect they were chasing a shadow. They turned back. Meanwhile, the *Rodney* was closer to the quarry than her captain realized. Even so, no sighting was made, there being too much distance between hunter and prey. The *Bismarck* steamed on in the bright light of day, massive in its structure, but a mere dot on the vastness of the ocean.

The compulsory series of parachute jumps from a flying Whitley bomber had been made by Bobby and Helene, in company with other trainees. Intelligent, quick to learn and always willing to listen to advice, guidance and criticism, Bobby and Helene were also young people of an adventurous and courageous kind. Their jumps were made with confidence and boldness, their landings earning them praise. Helene had only one very definite point to make to Captain Wagstaffe before taking dinner that evening.

'When we are sent to France, I refuse to make a landing in a skirt,' she said.

'Well, you haven't made any in a skirt here, but when your time comes you'll be dressed according to what's suitable, Fifi,' said Captain Wagstaffe.

'Ah, you are going to infuriate me, yes, I know it,' said Helene.

'I'm only going to tell you that if you're required to be a Paris tart, you'll land in a slit skirt, black stockings and pink suspenders,' said Captain Wagstaffe, straight-faced.

'And frilly pants,' said Bobby as an aside.

'Never,' said Helene, 'never, do you hear, *mon Capitaine*?'

'Talk about it when you're summoned to London,' said Captain Wagstaffe, and departed. Helene appealed to Bobby.

'You wouldn't let them send me as a Paris tart, would you?'

'I wouldn't be in favour,' said Bobby, 'but if it's got to be one of us, it has to be you, Fifi. Come to that, I think I might fancy you in a slit skirt and pink suspenders.'

'Oh, filthy beast,' cried Helene, and went for him. Bobby beat a running retreat. His sensitive young French lady could pack a punishing wallop.

Staff and trainees at the Parachute School listened to the late night news. Battleships, cruisers and destroyers were still conducting a desperate search for the elusive *Bismarck*. Planes from the *Ark Royal* were continuously roaming the skies in their own search of the great grey waters of the North Atlantic. The BBC had representatives at all naval stations and at the Admiralty, but the measured tones of the announcer dispensing a summary of reports did not reflect the impatience and frustrations of the nation.

'What is the matter with the British Navy that it can't find that brute of a battleship?' breathed Helene into Bobby's ear.

'Looking in all the wrong places, obviously,' whispered Bobby, 'but there's a lot of sea out there. The *Bismarck* could be anywhere. It might even be just off Brighton Pier.'

'Brighton Pier?'

'Yes, and who'd look for it there?'

'Idiot, is this a time for joking?' whispered Helene.

'Far from it,' said Bobby. 'I was just pointing out that the hunt is turning into a farce. Well, that's how most people will see it if the *Bismarck* slips the Navy for good.'

'Everything is going the way of Hitler's filthy Nazis,' said Helene.

'Their luck will run out one day,' said Bobby.

'Would you two mind shutting up so that we can catch the rest of the news?' asked someone anonymous.

'Sorry,' said Bobby, and received a dig in the ribs from Helene for apologizing.

26 May.

Polly, having suffered another bout of morning sickness, crawled back into bed at the same time as Boots vacated it.

'Anything I can do for you, angel?' he asked.

'No. Go away.'

'Would you like breakfast in bed?'

'Oh, you fiend. Hate you. Go away.'

Boots made himself scarce. She took the morning off. Recovering, she ate a light lunch and listened to the one o'clock news. Coastal Command aircraft had sighted the *Bismarck* at a distance of five hundred miles from Brest. The formidable German battleship at that stage was two thousand five hundred miles from the point where it had first been spotted by the destroyers *Norfolk* and *Suffolk*. It was an epic voyage, but it was about to run the gauntlet now. British warships were rushing to the area.

Polly made her way to headquarters and informed Boots.

'Yes, we've all heard,' said Boots. 'Let's have a look at you.'

'What for?' asked Polly.

'Are you better? Are you fit for work? Can you walk about? How's tummy?'

'Private, thank you,' said Polly.

'Let's have a look,' said Boots.

Polly took hold of a rolled-up map and hit him with it.

'Take that.' She hit him again. 'And that. Stop playing the comic and stop fussing. Morning sickness is normal, you know that, or you should.'

Boots looked at his watch.

'I've an appointment with the GOC of Southern Command at Aldershot at five this afternoon,' he said. 'I'm to try to persuade him to release one of his senior tank officers to Sir Henry. Sir Henry wants him on his new staff, and suggested a personal approach. Five o'clock is the only time the GOC has offered. Care to come with me if you're brimming with health? We'll be late back.'

'Love to come,' said Polly.

'I thought, if we made good time, we'd drop in at the convalescent hospital near Farnham and find out if we can see Lieutenant Jessop,' said Boots.

'Boots, should we?' said Polly.

'If she's against visitors,' said Boots, 'we'll accept that, but shall we give it a go?'

'Tally-ho,' said Polly, 'I'd love to meet her.'

'It won't be a tea party,' said Boots.

'I know that,' said Polly.

213

The defenders of Tobruk were under renewed attack by the Afrika Korps. Fierce sorties by the Germans were beaten off, but casualties were heavy on both sides. Among the British dead was a man who was known to the Adams family.

Felicity was testing her touch again, Clara handing her one object after another.

'Salt cellar.'

'Try again.'

'If it's not a salt cellar, to hell with it,' said Felicity.

Up came an orderly. He spoke to Clara.

'Will Lieutenant Jessop entertain two visitors?'

'Will I nothing,' said Felicity. 'I'm not in the business of entertaining anybody. I'm a hospital inmate, not a performing monkey. Wait, are they my parents?'

'No, ma'am,' said the orderly,' a Major Adams and a Captain Adams.'

'Adams?' said Felicity. 'Adams?'

'Major Adams informed me he's the father of Lieutenant Tim Adams,' said the orderly. 'Captain Adams is his wife.'

'Bloody hell,' said Felicity, 'they've come to inspect me.'

'You don't have to receive them,' said Clara.

'I'm not going to run away,' said Felicity,

'I'll meet the challenge. Wheel them out here.'

'I'll fetch them,' said Clara.

Felicity steeled herself, and was on her feet when Clara returned in company with the visitors and made the introductions. Felicity felt there was a blank wall in front of her, a wall that was always going to be there. Boots and Polly saw a young ATS lieutenant quite upright and quite composed, apparently. A very good-looking brunette with a healthy complexion, she wore dark glasses and the hint of a polite smile.

'I'm so glad to meet you, lieutenant,' said Polly, and Felicity heard the note of the well-bred woman in her voice.

'We have to thank you for giving us the chance to,' said Boots, and Felicity thought his voice entirely pleasant with its masculine vibrations.

'What made you come?' she asked.

'The fact that my son Tim has spoken so much of you,' said Boots. 'We're on our way to Aldershot, and I thought that when we reached Farnham we shouldn't pass up the opportunity to call in at the hospital. My wife Polly wasn't too sure we should, but I said let's give it a go on the understanding that we wouldn't intrude if you preferred us not to. That's something we can both sympathize with. So we're delighted you received us, and promise to stay no longer

215

than a few minutes.'

The easy flow of the words, the natural-
ness, the note of warmth and the absence of
any awkward reference to her blindness,
made their appeal to Felicity.

'Major Adams, if you and your wife would
like to sit down, we can have the few
minutes together,' she said.

'I'll leave you to each other,' said Clara.
She gave Boots and Polly a nod and a smile,
and left. Polly watched as Felicity reseated
herself on the bench, her movements not in
the least hesitant.

'I don't think we'll address you as
Lieutenant,' said Boots, 'not under the circumstances.'

'The circumstances of the wedding?' said
Felicity.

'Right,' said Boots.

'Tim was here yesterday, did you know?'
she said.

'Yes, he phoned us before he left for Troon
this morning,' said Boots. 'We know you as
Felicity, and would like to call you so.'

'And what do I call you?' asked Felicity.
'Mum and Dad once Tim and I have signed
the register?'

'Dad will do for me,' said Boots, 'but I
have to warn you Polly has a standing
objection to being called anything but Polly.'

'You old tell-tale, is that something
Felicity is dying to know?' said Polly, and

Felicity heard the laughter in her voice. 'She and I will decide for ourselves.'

'We can work on it,' said Felicity. 'You're both coming to the wedding?'

'Along with your parents,' said Boots. 'Have you any idea what you'd like for a wedding present? We'd prefer to avoid duplicating a set of cutlery or a tea service.'

'Frankly,' said Felicity, 'I still haven't come to terms with Tim's offer to marry me, so presents are far from my mind. Would you say he's mad at taking me on?'

'Not on your life,' said Polly. 'Unlike his father, that young man has never done anything mad in all the years I've known him.'

'What mad things has his father done, then?' asked Felicity.

'According to his mother, Tim's grandma, he's twice rushed off to war while her back was turned,' said Polly. 'This war and the Great War.'

'There's one lunatic in every family,' said Boots.

'Tim told me you were blinded in the Great War,' said Felicity.

'A sad case of forgetting to duck,' said Boots, 'and a fortunate case in that it was a temporary condition.'

'It lasted four years, didn't it?' said Felicity.

'Then an operation cured me,' said Boots,

and Polly glanced at him. That left eye of his. Still lazy-looking, still practically blind, still his own particular souvenir of the Somme.

'What was it like for you during those four years?' asked Felicity.

'Pretty bloody,' said Boots, which frankness let her know there was no way she could avoid her long fight.

'And what was it like for your wife?' she asked.

'Emily? My first wife?'

'I know about her from Tim,' said Felicity.

'For Emily it was a constant trial,' said Boots.

'Major Adams, do you think I should let Tim marry me?' asked Felicity.

'He'll be cut up if you don't,' said Boots. 'So will I, so will Polly.'

'But–'

'Felicity, life isn't perfect for any of us,' said Polly, 'probably because we're not perfect ourselves. But it can be as much fun as our imperfections allow, providing it's spent with the one person who means most to us.'

'Fun?' said Felicity.

'You need a sense of humour, of course,' said Polly. 'Tim tells me you've got your share of that.'

'You approve of me?' said Felicity with her brittle smile.

'My dear young lady,' said Boots, 'do you think we're here to approve of you?'

'Aren't you?' said Felicity.

'Perish the thought,' said Boots. 'As far as Polly and I are concerned, all that counts is that Tim's made up his mind about you, and having met you I like the fact that he has.'

'I'm delighted,' said Polly.

Felicity smiled.

'Oh, rattling good show,' she said, 'and as for a wedding present, I don't think Tim and I will be ready for things like tea services until we're in a home of our own, and God knows when that will be. So I'd like a book of funny stories.'

'Would you care to repeat that?' asked Polly.

'A book of funny bedtime stories,' said Felicity. 'Tim can read them to me. I'm going for the laughs.'

'We'll do our best to help,' said Boots.

'I'm in favour of that kind of help,' said Polly.

'It's a quick way to the fun,' said Felicity.

'Haven't tried it myself,' said Boots, 'but it sounds promising. Felicity, I think we'll push off now.'

'You're welcome to stay a little longer,' said Felicity.

'It's been long enough, I think,' said Boots, 'and we've an appointment to keep in Aldershot. But thanks very much for allowing us to meet you.'

'Really thanks,' said Polly. 'Goodbye, Felicity.' She and Boots each shook her hand.

'Thanks for coming,' said Felicity. She smiled. 'Really thanks.'

'Our pleasure,' said Boots. 'Believe me.'

After they had gone, Clara returned.

'Well?' she said.

'What were they like to look at?' asked Felicity.

'Dashing,' said Clara. 'She's got vivaciousness written all over her, and he's my idea of what sex appeal is all about.'

'But aren't they middle-aged?'

'If they are, they're keeping it to themselves,' said Clara. 'Did you like them?'

'In ten minutes, how the hell can you like people you can't see?' said Felicity.

'You can like their approach,' said Clara.

'No complaints,' said Felicity, 'and they're going to give me a book of funny stories for a wedding present.'

'Whose idea was that?' asked Clara.

'Mine,' said Felicity.

'Bless you, my child,' said Clara.

'Well, there's got to be some fun,' said Felicity. 'Polly convinced me.'

'Polly?' said Clara.

'My future mother-in-law, God help us both,' said Felicity. 'Has the Navy sunk the *Bismarck* yet?'

'Not yet,' said Clara.

'Send a message to our admiral,' said Felicity. 'Tell him to get a bloody move on.'

Clara smiled. Her special patient was in her most fighting mood, which meant she wasn't too displeased with life at the moment.

'Well, lover?' said Polly, when she and Boots were on their way again.

'I liked her,' said Boots. 'No self-pity, no lament. Tim says she's a fighter. I think she is.'

'I think we were right not to fuss her,' said Polly, 'but to simply agree she's going to have a tough time.'

'A lovely young lady,' said Boots.

'Steady as you go, sailor,' said Polly, 'remember you're the father of my child.'

'What a fortunate old codger I am,' said Boots, 'and Tim's not going to do so badly, either. There'll be problems, we've talked about that, but they'll beat them, they'll knock the stuffing out of misfortune.'

'I second that,' said Polly, 'drive on, me old haricot bean.'

Boots had a very satisfactory meeting with the GOC at Aldershot, obtaining from him a promise to leave the decision to the officer in question. And the officer in question, a brigadier, professed himself very interested in a place on Sir Henry's staff. He'd make his decision inside two days, he said.

By the time Polly and Boots got back to their cottage in Dorset, Corporal Higgins had gone off in a sulk, leaving a note to say their meal was in the oven and that they'd have to make their own custard if they wanted afters of what was left of some apple pie.

'God, the rotter,' said Polly, 'he knows I've never made custard.'

'Good time to start,' said Boots. 'What's in the oven, anyway?'

'You tell me,' said Polly, bringing the plates in from the kitchen. On each plate was a warm congealed mass. 'Stew?'

'Looks like something that's been run over,' said Boots. 'I'll just have some warmed-up apple pie with custard.'

'Keep your fingers crossed,' said Polly, and took the plates back to the kitchen. Boots switched on the radio and caught the ten o'clock news. The *Bismarck* was under attack by warplanes from the *Ark Royal* and had been damaged, but it was steaming on. British destroyers were closing in on the beleaguered German battleship, Hitler's hammer of the seas.

'Got the tiger, have we?' said Boots.

'What's that?' called Polly.

'The Navy's up with the *Bismarck*,' said Boots, 'and I don't think they'll let her slip them this time.'

'Send the Navy my best wishes,' called Polly.

She brought the warmed-up apple pie in ten minutes later, together with a jug of hot custard.

'There's a clever girl,' said Boots.

'The things I do for England,' said Polly, and they sat down to the remains of the apple pie. Polly put half of it on Boots's plate. He took up the jug of custard and poured it over the pie. It issued reluctantly from the jug in blobs and lumps.

'H'm,' he said.

'Don't look at me,' said Polly guiltily.

'Well, it's hot,' said Boots, 'so you're halfway there, Polly.' He began to eat his way through the pie and the golden blobs.

'You old darling, you love me,' said Polly.

'So I do,' said Boots.

'You must,' said Polly, 'or you wouldn't eat that custard. What a sacrifice, all in the name of devotion.'

'Join me,' said Boots.

'I think I'll just have the apple pie by itself,' said Polly.

'Give my regards to your tummy,' said Boots.

During the night the *Bismarck* fought a battle with British destroyers. They crippled her, wrecked her steering and her captain lost control of his ship. Subsequently, after a pursuit lasting for several days over a distance of nearly three thousand miles, HMS *Dorsetshire* finished off the awesome, helpless giant with torpedoes, and the *Bismarck* followed the *Hood* to the bottom of the sea. The Royal Navy picked up survivors.

The relieved people of Britain celebrated the revenge. Churchill helped himself to a whisky and a new cigar. Tommy took a bunch of flowers and bottle of port home to Vi. Sammy, making use of a mild black market contact, took a box of chocolates home to Susie. Ned took a potted azalea of bright crimson home to Lizzy. Mr Finch presented Chinese Lady with a beautiful cameo brooch.

'Why, Edwin, what's this for?' she asked.

'It's a mark of my affection for you, Maisie,' he said.

'Well, you couldn't of given me anything nicer,' said Chinese Lady. 'It's been a nice day all round, Boots phoning to say he and Polly have met Tim's misfortunate young lady and taken kindly to her, and even that old wireless has been a bit more cheerful for a change. Thank you, Edwin.' She delivered a peck on his cheek.

'Well, to crown a nice day, Maisie, would you like a glass of port?' smiled Mr Finch.

'Bless me, yes, I think I would. Just a small glass.'

In Kennington, Mrs Skinner applied a sympathetic poultice to her husband's black eye, which she had landed on him for coming home as drunk as an Irish fiddler on St Patrick's night. And Job Hardy treated Jemima and his daughter Jane to the evening performance of the Crazy Gang in a West End theatre.

At Ringway, near Manchester, Bobby and Helene celebrated by making love, although Bobby offered to spare her blushes by sharing a mug of late night cocoa with her instead of taking advantage of her.

'That stuff?' said Helene. 'No, no, I would much rather suffer a hundred blushes.'

'All right, I'll join you,' said Bobby, 'I'll be blushing myself. It's my upbringing.'

Up in Carlisle, Eloise was one of several cadets who got squiffy – for the first time in her life. Much to her horror, when she came to her bra was among others flying from a pole above the office of the Commandant. At the foot of the pole was a placard on which some male wag had written, 'Who's collecting the empties?' For some alarming minutes, Eloise wondered if she was still a virgin. Well, she was a good Catholic. Her alarm was fortunately false.

The Commandant turned a blind eye. It was Nelson's day.

In Troon, the Commandos joined the civilians in crowding the pubs and knocking back the stuff for which Scotland was famous.

In Dorset, Matthew took Rosie out for an evening drive, and treated her to dinner in a Wimborne Minster hotel.

'I like you more and more,' said Rosie.

'Is that what a wartime menu does for you?' asked Matt.

'Isn't the human condition peculiar at times?' said Rosie. 'We've no control over it.'

'My peculiar condition is a trial to me,' said Matt.

'Will marriage cure it?' asked Rosie.

'I'm counting on it,' said Matt.

'Then it's not a peculiar condition, is it?' she said. 'It's a natural one, isn't it?'

'It's still terrible trying,' said Matt.

The arsonist put his fiery mark on the occasion by torching the objective that had been dancing in his disordered mind for some time, a large barn packed with bales of hay. The conflagration, while not the result of an explosion, was of the kind Guy Fawkes might have envied.

Chapter Fourteen

In early June, Bobby and Helene left Ringway in response to a summons from London. There they were interviewed by Major Buckmaster, head of SOE (French Section), a personable man notable for being understanding. He had their confidential assessments on his desk, and each assessment was a shrewd summary of their aptitude, their capabilities and their potential. Both assessments were complimentary, although there was a note to the effect that 'Fifi' was a little headstrong. However, if the two of them were sent into the field as a partnership, 'Charlie' could be relied on to be a restraining influence.

'Excellent,' said Major Buckmaster, tapping the reports with a light finger, his smile paternal.

'We've passed?' said Bobby.

'Let me say that when we find suitable work for you, we'll have confidence in what you can achieve,' said Major Buckmaster. 'You'll each receive details relating to appropriate identities with full background notes. You'll digest these with care until you're absolutely certain of every detail and every fact. You'll also be given new code names, from which you must never deviate. Thank you both very much for your admirable application to your studies and training. Now you can go home.'

'Excuse me, *mon Commandant*?' said Helene.

'You can go home,' smiled Major Buckmaster, 'and wait until you hear from us.'

'When will that be, sir?' asked Bobby.

'When we know exactly where and how we can use you. We'll then, with your help, begin to establish your new identities. When we're satisfied you can fit them perfectly, arrangements will be made to despatch you to France.'

'We must be sent together,' said Helene.

'That, I believe, has been your wish all along,' said Major Buckmaster, 'and I assure you we've taken due note of same. Goodbye, then, for the present, and thank you again. Oh, any questions?'

'None for the moment,' said Bobby, 'but I daresay we'll ask a few when we come under orders.'

'We usually make requests,' said Major Buckmaster. 'We never lose sight of the fact that all our people are volunteers.'

Leaving the building with Bobby, Helene said, 'Well, what do you think of that? We have nothing to do except wait.'

'Oh, we'll find something to do at home,'

said Bobby, 'something to pass the time.'

'Never,' said Helene. 'Do you think I would permit that in the home of your parents?'

'I wasn't thinking of that,' said Bobby as, carrying their valises, they began to make their way to the Baker Street tube station. 'I was thinking of some healthy walks around the Surrey countryside.'

'You must understand I could never permit you to make love to me under your parents' roof,' said Helene. 'It would dishonour your parents, and us too, unless we were married.'

'I wasn't thinking of that,' said Bobby, 'I was thinking of wandering around the fields and farms of my county, and showing you some native cows.'

'Ah, that is different,' said Helene. 'In a field barn, of course, with no-one looking, I could not say no.'

'I wasn't thinking of that,' said Bobby, returning the salute of a passing soldier, 'I was thinking we'll have to give my parents a good reason why we're spending time at home.'

'We must tell them we've been given leave until we're sent abroad with our unit,' said Helene.

'Great, that'll do,' said Bobby, as they entered the station. 'Pleasure to know you're a bright young lady.'

'Yes, I wish to be liked for my very fine mind,' said Helene.

'Which I admire more than I can say,' said Bobby, as they entered the station.

'Oh? What is wrong with my looks, then?' demanded Helene.

Realizing there was no sensible answer to that, Bobby busied himself buying tickets.

Lizzy, of course, was delighted to see them and to be told they were on indefinite leave while waiting for their unit's embarkation orders. Being her mother's daughter, she immediately made a pot of tea, and Helene, having become further Anglicized in her relationship with a teapot, happily accepted a cup of the steaming brew with milk.

Lizzy asked what their unit was. Not one, she hoped, that meant Helene would have to face up to German soldiers.

'Your grandma would have a fit, Bobby, if I had to tell her that,' she said. 'Weren't you in the artillery when you were in France?'

'I'm still artillery,' said Bobby, 'and Helene's attached to the unit. She and other women will be behind the lines, though, doing special work.'

'What special work?' asked Lizzy.

'Telegrams,' said Bobby. 'Can't say more, Mum. Himmler might be listening, and you know what he's like. He's got his nose into everything, and he'd get it into Helene's

230

shoulder bag, if he could.'

'A pig of a Nazi,' said Helene.

'Well, you both look healthy enough to stand up to him and all those Nazi gangsters,' said Lizzy. 'I've never seen any young people look more healthy. Do you both do special exercises?'

What a question, thought Bobby. Special, for God's sake.

'Oh, yes, very special,' said Helene.

'What sort of special?' asked Lizzy.

Ruddy gorblimey, thought Bobby, I'll have to marry Fifi, war or no war, and then questions like that from my own mum won't embarrass me.

'Physical co-ordination,' he said.

'What's physical co ordination?' asked Lizzy.

'Oh, an exercise that helps your muscles to cooperate with your reflexes,' said Bobby.

'But what does Helene want muscles and reflexes for?' asked Lizzy.

'Well, suppose our artillery got overrun by the Germans,' said Bobby. 'Helene would have to scarper quick by means of lightning reflexes and active leg muscles. Show them to Mum, Helene.'

'Bobby, she doesn't have to do that,' said Lizzy.

'Well, it's no secret I've seen her legs in her PT kit,' said Bobby, 'and she's got the kind of muscles you couldn't fault for running.'

'Madame – Mrs Somers, it's a lie,' said Helene, 'I don't have big leg muscles. That is what he means, big leg muscles. He's a terrible man, your son.'

'Full of nonsense sometimes,' said Lizzy, 'like his dad and his uncles. Would you like more tea, Helene?'

'Thank you, yes,' said Helene, and glanced at Bobby. He winked to let her know a bit of nonsense made his mum forget to ask more questions. Ah, such a crazy man, she thought, but when the war is over no-one shall have him but me. How weak a woman is to want to spend her life with an idiot, especially an English idiot.

She smiled her thanks at his mother for the refilled cup.

7 June.

Susie, seated at her kitchen table, was writing down the names of all the expected guests at Rosie's wedding. With Chinese Lady's willing approval, she had taken on the responsibility of seeing to the wedding breakfast, the reception being at Rosie's home. However, Susie had dismissed the idea of the family providing the food because of restrictions, and arranged for Williamsons, the caterers, to take care of everything relating to the breakfast, although they too would be limited in what they could provide. It was going to be a free-

and-easy occasion, not a formal seated affair, so she and the caterers didn't have to worry about table plans. Everyone would help themselves to the food, and the caterers would serve the drinks.

Susie looked at her list, made up of people who would definitely be present. The bride and groom, Grandma and Grandpa Finch, Boots, Polly, Lizzy, Ned, Emma, Tommy, Vi, herself, Sammy, bridesmaid Paula, Rachel Goodman, Mr Greenberg, Sir Henry and Lady Simms – crikey, the aristocracy – old Aunt Victoria and Uncle Tom, plus the groom's parents, sister and brother-in-law. Then there were Bobby and Helene, who were on extended leave and hoping it would last until the wedding day was over. Susie decided to put them down as possibles. Then there were Tim and Eloise, both of whom had said they were going to get a special forty-eight hours leave pass, come what may. Further, because of Chinese Lady's insistence that they were family and old friends, there were Susie's parents, Mr and Mrs Brown, and on the grounds that they were newly related, Emma's in-laws, Jemima and Job Hardy. Chinese Lady was always reaching out to embrace everyone with family connections.

After another quiet period, there had been a raid on London two nights ago, a brief but noisy one, and that had discouraged the family from thinking about bringing their evacuated children home for the wedding. No-one could trust those tormenting Germans.

Little Paula, watching her mother musing over the list, said, 'Mummy, have you put my name down?'

'Yes, of course, darling, yours was nearly the first,' smiled Susie.

'Crumbs,' said Paula, 'who was first, then?'

'Oh, it had to be cousin Rosie and her bridegroom,' said Susie.

'Oh, well, I don't mind them,' said Paula.

Susie phoned the caterers, gave them the number of definite guests, and asked them to allow for a dozen extra, say. Some of Rosie's old Somerville friends hoped to come, and there were always the unexpected faces to consider.

Sammy arrived home soon after, with a kiss for Susie and two for little Paula.

'I see who's favourite now,' said Susie.

'Pardon?' said Sammy

'You're not listening,' said Susie.

'I'll admit I'm not meself lately,' said Sammy. The truth was, so many things concerning the war and its effect on the family were making holes in his brainbox. And what a bomb had done to Tim's young lady was on everyone's mind. Nor did it help that his office never seemed to be rid of an overload of Government forms, popularly known as bumph. That was the price a business had to pay for securing Government contracts.

'Try to remember Bobby and Helene are popping in again this evening,' said Susie.

'Nice to be seeing them frequent while they're on leave,' said Sammy. Bobby and Helene were making regular rounds of the families. What a pair they were, always striking sparks off each other. A fine-looking female woman Helene Aarlberg was, and strong. Funny about a FANY officer being attached to Bobby's artillery unit. Still, nobody ever knew how the Army worked. In triplicate behind the lines, probably, like the Civil Service. Well, Bobby's young French FANY looked as if she could see off everything in Army triplicate.

He lightly ruffled Paula's hair. The little girl giggled. What a treasure, he thought. Wish my other kids were home. Not natural for any family to be split in half. He, Susie and Paula, together with Tommy and Vi, had travelled to Devon last weekend to see their evacuated offspring who, fortunately, looked healthy and had no complaints, although twelve-year-old Bess did ask him when he thought they might be able to come home.

It made Sammy hope the RAF could knock the *Luftwaffe* right out of the skies so that even if the war became a long and lousy one, there'd at least be no more air raids. Every evacuated kid could come home then.

17 June.

'Goodbye and good luck, Subaltern Adams,' said Commandant Hilary Watts-Wickham. She was saying a personal goodbye to all successful cadets.

'Thank you, ma'am,' said Eloise, uniform faultless, demeanour respectful. She saluted smartly before departing.

A commandant can be more gracious than a pofaced lieutenant, she thought. I shall be a gracious officer myself. Well, I am naturally that way, and would make a very suitable wife for an English landowner. But when am I going to meet one? I am already twenty-four. How worrying.

The following day she was back at Troon. Almost the first person she saw as she walked out of the station carrying her valise was Major Lucas, looking as rugged and vigorous as ever. He was just about to get into his car.

'Major Lucas!'

He turned and saw her, a fully-fledged subaltern.

'Good God,' he said.

'Well, really, what kind of a greeting is that?' she said. 'Aren't you proud of me, just a private when we first met, and now with a commission? How do I look?'

Too damned bewitching, thought Major Lucas.

'How'd you look?' he said. 'Pleased with yourself. Well, my compliments and congratulations, Subaltern Adams.'

'Thank you, sir, how kind,' she said.

'Hop in if you want a lift to admin,' he said.

'Sir, were you waiting for me, did you know I was arriving on this train?' she asked.

'No, I motored down to pick up some of my special tobacco from the station shop,' he said.

'Really, sir, that isn't very gracious,' said Eloise.

About to deliver a sarcastic rejoinder, he checked. Lucas, he said to himself, you're a prize belly-ache, you're playing a man scorned and you're worse than any scorned woman.

'Hop in, Subaltern Adams,' he said.

Eloise put her valise in the back of the car and slid into the passenger seat. He slid in beside her, started the car and headed for the Commando base.

'Oh, I was dreadfully sorry to hear about Lieutenant Jessop,' she said.

'The whole group was cut up,' said the Major.

'Did you know my brother Tim is going to marry her?' asked Eloise.

'Yes, I knew,' he said brusquely.

'Isn't that wonderful of Tim?' she said. Major Lucas muttered something. 'Well, isn't it?' she said.

'I find the whole thing painful,' he said.

'No, no, you mustn't look at it like that,' said Eloise, 'we must all be supportive and uplifting.' Major Lucas muttered again. 'You're saying something?'

'I can't reconcile myself to a woman like Lieutenant Jessop suffering such a devastating blow,' he said.

'Well, I'm sure you're as human as any of us, sir,' said Eloise. 'And I'm also sure you must be pleased that I'm back as your personal assistant and can do all your driving for you.'

'As a sergeant, it was suitable for you to be my driver,' he said, 'but as an officer you're more suited to drive a general.'

'I don't wish to drive a general,' she said, liking the familiar scenes of Troon. 'It was always agreed I should be your driver in between my admin duties.' She had a thing about that, about her special relationship with him, simply because she regarded him as the kind of man who'd be the first to get to Hitler and hang him. He wouldn't let protocol hold him back, he'd hang the monster on the spot before Army lawyers

238

arrived. 'I wish to continue,' she said.

'In that case, perhaps you'll drive me to Irvine this evening,' he said.

'Yes, sir, with pleasure,' she said.

'Be at my billet at seven,' he said.

'Yes, sir,' she said. 'I'm happy to know you're glad I'm back.'

Damned if she wasn't as cocky as ever. There was no end to her self-satisfaction. He couldn't help himself. He laughed.

'I'm overjoyed, naturally,' he said.

'There, I knew my return would be a pleasure to you,' she said.

One thing she didn't know, and that was his present inclination to stop the car, to take hold of her and eat her. For all her little conceits, she was so damned attractive and engaging she was almost irrisistible.

'I presume you found admirers in Carlisle,' he said.

'Yes, but none who really interested me,' said Eloise.

'Not distinguished enough?' said Major Lucas.

'They were all quite ordinary,' said Eloise.

'Like all of us here,' said Major Lucas.

'I shan't despair,' said Eloise.

'You'll land a prize one day,' he said, and drove on to admin. He pulled up.

'Ah, here I am again, where the west wind blows,' she said. She saw several Commandos coming up from the promontory,

239

laughing and joking. They all looked such resolute men, with their own air of self-confidence, but they were all bears, of course.

'Thank you for the lift, Major Lucas.'

Damn me, he thought, she's sitting there, she's waiting for me to get out, to go round, and to open the damned door for her. He tested her.

'Stay there and I'll come round and let you out,' he said drily.

'Thank you, most kind,' she said.

Resigned, if a little growling, he alighted, went round and pulled the door open. Perhaps he thought it was worthwhile then, for Eloise swivelled, her legs emerged and her trim tailored skirt slid back several inches. Clad in fine regulation stockings, her legs, shining, were a delightful picture.

A Commando whistled and Eloise came hastily to her feet.

'Why do such good soldiers have no manners?' she asked.

'Men who say sorry while they're throttling a German sentry don't get to be Commandos,' said Major Lucas.

'Ah, yes, I understand,' said Eloise, and let him pull out her valise and hand it to her. 'Thank you, Major Lucas, and I'll see you at seven.'

'Right,' he said, and watched her as she entered the admin offices, her poise that of a newly-commissioned ATS officer with a large amount of belief in her worth.

Eloise introduced her newly-commissioned self to Tim when he came off duty. He told her she looked top of her class, that he was proud of her, and that family members were performing wonders considering their more recent ancestors were only Walworth market barrow boys.

'What are barrow boys?' asked Eloise.

'Up-and-coming costermongers,' said Tim.

'Costermongers?' Eloise had heard of them. 'Of course not. No, no, they are common. Grandmama says so.'

'Good sturdy stock, y'know,' said Tim.

'Well, let us be proud of that,' said Eloise.

'By the way, there's a flap on,' said Tim.

'Oh, do take care, Tim, if there's another raid,' she said.

'I'm fully trained in the art of ducking at the right moment,' said Tim.

At seven precisely she arrived at Major Lucas's billet. His car was parked outside, and he himself emerged from the house at once, looking very well-dressed in his best uniform. Eloise, trim and composed, gave him a salute. He returned it, then seated himself in the back of the car. Eloise slipped into the driving seat.

'Drive first to Argyle House,' he said.

'Very good, sir,' she said, and drove the seventy yards to a large house that billeted several officers. As she pulled up, Captain Cary came out, she too looking exceptionally smart. Major Lucas alighted, held the door open for her, and smiling at him, she slipped in. He closed the door, went round to the other side of the car, slipped in beside her, then spoke to Eloise.

'Subaltern Adams? The Royal Restaurant, Irvine, please.'

The turn of events made Eloise sit rigid and furious at the wheel. What did they think she was, a taxi driver? She was to take Major Lucas and that snooty Captain Cary to Irvine to dine together? She had reported to her on her return, and received cool congratulations on securing her commission. Major Lucas must have very poor taste to want to entertain a woman as stiff and starchy as Captain Cary. And he expects me, now an officer, to drive them?

'Kindly get going, Subaltern,' said Captain Cary.

Eloise fought an impulse to leap out of the car and slam the door on them. She gritted her teeth and began the journey. Forced to listen to them exchanging conversation that she thought utterly trite and boring, she said not a word herself, not until she reached the restaurant and dropped them off. 'Many thanks, Subaltern Adams,' said Major Lucas, 'and would you pick us up at ten?'

That was her cue.

'Yes, of course, sir,' she said, 'you must know I've always wanted to be a taxi driver.'

'First I've heard of it,' he said. 'At ten, then.'

Throughout the five mile journey back to Troon, she was oblivious of the magnificent scenery and the softness of the summer evening. She was talking to herself, but saying only one thing over and over again.

'I'll kill him.'

She went to the mess for dinner, was greeted boisterously, congratulated rousingly, and bought everyone the drinks required of a new officer. But she simmered from the time she arrived until the time she left, and not even a reunion with Tim helped her to cool down. Although there was talk of another Commando raid being imminent, very little of it broke through her angry front. She arrived back in Irvine at ten minutes past ten, purposely late, and was not in the least displeased to note that Major Lucas and Captain Cary were outside the restaurant, that she'd kept them waiting. Major Lucas said nothing by way of a rebuke, however. In fact, he thanked her for turning up. As for Captain Cary, one could have said she was wine-flushed and full of wellbeing. Eloise, of course, chose to consider she looked silly and simpering.

She silently raged on the drive back to Troon, for the pair of them talked and laughed in the back of the car as if she herself was non-existent. She stopped outside Argyle House. Major Lucas accompanied the ATs captain up the stone steps to the front door. Probably because she's drunk, thought Eloise, and then her fury reached a peak. It was double summertime, the late twilight only just beginning to blur the clear outlines of day, and she had to suffer the abominable sight of Major Lucas kissing the woman before he said goodnight to her.

Returning to the car, he opened the driver's door and addressed Eloise.

'Drive yourself to your billet, Subaltern. You can leave the car there. I'll walk to my own billet.'

'Good,' said Eloise fiercely, 'and I hope you fall and break your leg on the way.'

'Would you like to repeat that?' asked Major Lucas.

'With pleasure, except that I hope you break both legs.'

'Are you drunk, Subaltern Adams?'

'No, I'm not,' she said. 'If I were I'd probably do my best to run you over.'

Major Lucas moved around the car. The passenger door opened and he slipped into the seat.

'What brought this on?' he asked.

'What do you think? You made a fool of me, yes, you did, and you know it. Do you imagine I would have offered to drive the car if I'd known Captain Cary was going to be with you?'

'Why should that have made any difference?' asked the Major.

'Why? Why?' Eloise was beside herself with anger and something else. Something like rageful jealousy. 'I'm not her chauffeuse, nor your taxi driver. You could have driven the car yourself instead of compelling me to listen to you drooling over her on the way back.'

'Drooling?' he said.

'Yes,' she said, 'and I despise you for it. I despise all men who drool. Oh, I didn't think as soon as my back was turned you would run into the arms of someone as starchy as Captain Cary.'

'She's not as starchy as you think.'

'She has no looks, nothing except thick ankles,' said Eloise, 'and it made me sick to see you kissing her.'

'Hold on,' said Major Lucas. 'As soon as your back was turned? What the devil d'you mean by that, you baggage?'

'Baggage? Baggage?' Eloise seethed. 'How dare you? I'm nobody's baggage, and I'm disgusted that you betrayed my loyalty to you while I was away by making Captain Cary your lover.'

'She's not my lover,' said Major Lucas, 'and stop all these melodramatics. Never heard such rubbish. In any case, if Captain Cary were my lover, why should you object?'

'Well, I would!'

'Don't talk nonsense,' he said.

'I hate you for being despicable and disloyal.'

'You saucy monkey, that's too much,' said Major Lucas, and did what all his inclinations urged him to. He reached, pulled her halfway out of the driving seat and kissed her resoundingly. Not just once, either. Eloise tried to kick him, but the lack of space hampered her. All kinds of emotions assailed her, among which was amazed reaction to being kissed so ardently. However, as soon as he released her, she attempted to smack his face. He caught her hand. 'What the devil are you up to now, you brat?' he asked.

'Brat? Brat?' Eloise could hardly believe her ears.

'Yes. For all your fine airs, you're a spoiled brat.'

'Oh, that isn't true! How can you say such a wicked thing?'

'Wicked?' he said.

'Yes! You've wounded me, mortally.'

'Mortally?' Major Lucas thought that laughable. Eloise, face flushed, eyes glittering, didn't think so at all.

'I hate you for it,' she breathed.

'Well, I accept you don't like me,' he said, 'so let's leave it at that. I've other things on my mind. Good night, Subaltern Adams.'

He was out of the car and away then, striding to his billet in a handsome house. Eloise was left in such an angry welter of mixed-up emotions that if a hammer had been to hand she'd have smashed his car into a wreck.

A spoiled brat, that was what he had called her? Oh, the pig, wait until I see him tomorrow, I'll have him charged for assault. Yes, I'll do that, I'll do it.

No, I won't.

I'll think of something else.

What other things did he have on his mind?

She was woken at one in the morning by the sounds of a marching column. 4 Commando group was on its way to the station to board a special train, as she found out at breakfast. It put Major Lucas out of reach for the time being, and she knew then what had been on his mind. Another raid, with all its dangers.

Tim would be there.

Eloise suffered worry, frustration and fretfulness, while presenting a cool front every time she came into contact with Captain Cary.

Chapter Fifteen

Wednesday, 18th June, and the massive German build-up of men and armour close to the border with Russia had reached a peak. British Intelligence knew it, and Churchill therefore also knew. Sir Stafford Cripps, British Ambassador in Moscow, tried to persuade the Soviets' Foreign Minister, Molotov, to warn Stalin that a German invasion was imminent. Molotov said the Soviet Union was in no danger from Nazi Germany. A non-aggression pact existed between them. Good day to you, Ambassador.

Matthew, having left his mechanics Ben and Josh in charge of the garage, began a journey to London, Rosie beside him in his car. Rosie, whose duties were presently minimal and would remain so until a new division or brigade moved in, was on four days special leave. Matthew was going home with her in order to give her family the pleasure of meeting him before the wedding on Saturday week.

They enjoyed their usual kind of free-and-easy dialogue, and when Rosie reminded

Matthew that their marriage was following that of her cousin Emma, and their own was being followed by that of her brother Tim to Felicity Jessop, Matt suggested three family marriages in the space of a few months was a mite uncommon. Rosie said yes, and that she'd be happy to receive a special award for being part of it.

'As I'm part of your part,' said Matt, 'do I get an award myself?'

'You don't need an award, you're getting me,' said Rosie in typical Adams fashion.

Meanwhile, the arsonist, having oiled the ballbearings of his bicycle, was looking forward to a night ride and another flareup.

'Be so good, chum, as to read it,' said Felicity, referring to a letter just received from Tim. She was lightly tanned from the time she was spending in the sun. Her sightlessness, however, still gave her restless nights and wretched waking-up moments, and the effort of coming to terms with what she was up against was never easy. But with gritted teeth she persevered, and Clara was always a great help.

'Here goes,' said Clara. *'Heavenly Puss–'*

'Delirious, poor dear,' said Felicity.

'Thanks for your last letter, and sorry not to have acknowledged it before but we've been out

*of sight of land for several days on an exercise,
and I can tell you anti-seasick pills don't always
work for a lot of the lads. Fortunately, they work
for me, so my stomach was one of those that
didn't land up in the sea. Major Lucas used a
bit of language on the blokes who'd thrown theirs
into the waves. and one groaning squaddy
answered back, "All right, chuck me overboard,
see if I care."*

*'Thanks for letting me know my dad and
stepma called on you, glad to hear they made a
good impression. Stepma wrote to me herself to
let me know they'd seen you and liked you. They
think we're made for each other, and Stepma
complimented me on my good taste. Incidentally, I don't call her Stepma, she won't let
me, so I call her Polly. You're welcome to do the
same, she'll like it. She was one of those Bright
Young Things in the Twenties, and she still is in
spirit.*

*'I really enjoyed seeing you, uplifting to know
you're fighting all the way. There's a flap coming
on up here – damn – got to go for a briefing –
buckets of love,*

Tim.'

'That's a bit sudden,' frowned Felicity.

'Fell off his chair, perhaps?' said Clara.

'I know what a briefing means,' said
Felicity.

'What does it mean?' asked Clara.

'That something's on,' said Felicity. If it's

happening now, she thought, for God's sake remember to duck, Tim. Your father mentioned he'd forgotten to in the last war.

Tim at this moment was in Portsmouth, having entrained overnight along with Major Lucas and other Commandos of 4 Group. They were waiting to board a warship. Major Lucas was fighting fit and in an aggressive mood. Tim asked him if he'd seen Eloise since her return.

'Your sister?' growled the Major.

'None other,' said Tim.

'I saw her, yes.'

'Happy reunion?' said Tim.

'More like a Victorian melodrama,' said Major Lucas.

'In what way?' asked Tim.

'Her way.'

'Know what you mean,' said Tim.

'Yes, feel my bruises.'

'Well, for God's sake,' said Tim, 'what goes on between you two?'

'Nothing I wouldn't rather miss,' said Major Lucas.

It was Chinese Lady who opened the door to Rosie and Matthew.

'Hello, Nana, bless you for being home,' said Rosie, stepping into the hall.

'Well, goodness me, of course I'm home, Rosie love,' said Chinese Lady, looking perky and upright. 'I wasn't brought up to go shoppin' when I was expecting.'

'Expecting, Nana?' smiled Rosie.

'Expecting someone in the fam'ly that's dear to me,' said Chinese Lady, who didn't often wear her heart on her sleeve. She regarded Rosie with visible affection, thinking what a lovely young woman she was, even in that Army uniform. Now a nurse's uniform or a Red Cross uniform, yes, either of them would be more suitable. Still, she didn't want to go on about it now, not when Rosie was home and was going to be married soon. Also, she'd brought her fiancé with her so that everyone could meet him, so a body didn't want to do any pinpricking. 'Blessed if I've ever been more pleased to see you, Rosie.'

'Blessed if it isn't mutual, Nana,' said Rosie, and kissed her. 'Oh, and this is Matthew. Matthew, meet my lovely grandma.'

They were curious about each other, Rosie's Dorset man and her grandmother by adoption. Matthew saw a slender elderly woman, with noticeably almond eyes, holding herself upright in a plain brown dress that gave her a neat, tidy and respectable appearance. For her part, Chinese Lady saw a man very masculine in his tanned and weathered looks, his eyes friendly and enquiring, his physique strong-looking. Much to her relief, she liked what she saw, especially his eyes. A woman could trust a man whose eyes were clear and didn't shift about.

'Well, I must say, Mr Chapman, I'm very taken with the pleasure of meetin' you at last,' she said.

Matthew didn't fail to catch her cockney accent, while at the same time sensing a certain carefulness in the way she delivered her words. Rosie could have told him it was her grandmother's acquired way of speaking 'proper'.

Knowing her name, he said, 'Believe me, Mrs Finch, the pleasure's all mine. It couldn't be otherwise.'

'It's very polite of you to say so,' said Chinese Lady, 'but of course we've all heard nice things about you.'

'I think they come from a source prejudiced in my favour,' smiled Matt, and Chinese Lady liked the mellowness of his deep baritone voice, which she supposed was to do with him being country-born.

'I expect you mean it's our Rosie that's spoken in your favour,' she said. 'Well, I'm sure that means you'll be very welcome to me and all my fam'ly as her lawful wedded husband, and I don't know why we're all standin' here like we're too formal to go and sit down. I'd make a pot of tea except it's nearly lunchtime. Oh, the designing lady was here earlier Rosie.'

Rosie blinked.

253

'Designing lady, Nana?' she said. 'Do we know one like that?'

'Yes, I met her first at Cassie and Sally's double wedding,' said Chinese Lady, 'and I must say she's very nice. She's brought your gown for a fittin', knowing you were comin' home today.'

'Oh, you mean Mrs Chambers,' said Rosie, 'Uncle Sammy's dress designer before the war.'

'Yes, that's her,' said Chinese Lady. 'She's gone to Brixton to see Rachel Goodman and have lunch with her. She's staying there for a few days so that she'll have time to give you a fitting and do any needful alterations. She'll be back here later for the fitting.'

'Then I'll take Matthew up to the spare room, shall I, Nana?' said Rosie.

'Yes, it's all ready,' said Chinese Lady. 'Everything's aired, and so's everything in your own room, Rosie.'

What a lovely old lady, thought Matt. Full of words, straightforward of manner and, he'd wager, a bit of a character who probably laid down the law in this large house. He had noted the impressive frontage and the handsome hall. It was a residence that made his cottage seem insignificant. This was Rosie's home, this was where she had lived for many years. It spoke of very comfortable circumstances, and it meant, in old-time parlance, that he'd have his work cut out to keep her in the manner to which she was accustomed.

'This way, Matt,' said Rosie, who was not making comparisons herself. To her, Matthew's cottage was cosy, charming and delightful, and her future home. She was perfectly happy about that. Like Boots, she had never asked for marble halls. It was Sammy with his flair for business who had provided the family with a stairway to the realms of middle class affluence.

Matt picked up Rosie's valise and his case, and followed her up to the first floor landing. Chinese Lady, watching, noticed his limp then. What a shame, she thought, it don't seem fair, a nice man like that being lame.

On the landing, Rosie took her Dorset intended into the spare room, as spacious as all the others in the house.

'There, will this do?' she asked.

'Well,' observed Matt, 'as Dorabelle the cow said when she was introduced to a new field of clover, I'm not going to complain.'

Rosie smiled. Matt put the bags down, placed his hands on the curve of her jacket and kissed her.

'I liked that,' she said.

'In that case,' said Matt, 'we'll do it seriously next time.'

'Promises, promises,' said Rosie, and laughed. Downstairs, Chinese Lady heard it.

'Well, bless me,' she said on her way to the kitchen, 'that sounds to me as if our Rosie's in love all right, and I must say I'm glad he's got manly looks.'

She prided herself that all the Adams men had manly looks. It was a shame, of course, about Mr Chapman's lame foot or whatever, but it didn't make him hobble a bit awkward or use a crutch, so nobody need think Rosie was marrying a cripple. That made her thoughts turn to Tim and his decision to marry a blind young lady. She supposed blind people could be called cripples in a way.

Was that sort of thing common in her family? Well, Lizzy's husband Ned had an artificial leg, Rosie's fiancé was lame and Tim's future wife blind. And even Boots, who had the kind of air and looks that could probably get him admitted to a duke's castle, especially with Polly on his arm, had only one really sound eye.

'Lor',' she said to the kitchen window, 'it's all very strange and coinciding, but I don't know I want to call it common.'

Then she got briskly on with her cooking.

Mrs Lilian Chambers, wife of her erstwhile Walworth milkman, Bill Chambers, was lunching with Mrs Rachel Goodman at Rachel's house off Brixton Hill. Rachel was almost thirty-nine, Lilian forty-three. They were similar in looks. Both had an abundance of dark glossy hair, and the velvety brown eyes of their race. Both were full-figured and blessed with warm, generous hearts.

'Benjamin's actually back at work?' said Lilian.

'Actually, yes,' smiled Rachel. Her husband Benjamin had suffered two broken legs when, after a massive air raid on London in late December, he'd entered a partly-destroyed house in an attempt to rescue a trapped woman. The house had collapsed on him. 'You know Benjy, only happy when he's at work. As soon as he was able to throw his crutches away, back he went. His racecourse business has stopped for the duration, but now he has an interest in the Victoria Club.' The Victoria Club had a gaming licence. 'And he's also into the loans business.'

'My life, isn't that the business where you can make two hundred per cent profit?' asked Lilian.

'I should allow him that kind of profit at the expense of unhappy clients?' said Rachel, and shook her head. 'Never. Such commercial indecency was always my Daddy's idea of bad business, not good. No-one ever committed suicide because of his hard heart, so I'll make sure Benjy doesn't drive any client to the kind of despair that will cause him to jump off Tower Bridge.'

'It's a long way down from there to the Thames,' observed Lilian. 'Is your father still away, Rachel?'

'Yes, still in Palestine with a delegation patiently waiting to hear that the Pope will intercede with Hitler on behalf of the Jews of Europe,' said Rachel. 'Lilian, the messages of tragedy and misery that are reaching Palestine are unbelievably heart-breaking.'

'You have heard, I have heard,' said Lilian. 'Every synagogue in this land is full of terrible whispers. Hitler and Himmler are destroying our race, murdering them, burning them, so the whispers say. My husband says such things can't possibly be true, that it must be some kind of anti-German propaganda. Such a good man he is, a Gentile who loves me. Do you know what it's like, Rachel, for a woman of my age to find a new husband who loves her? I shall convert, I think, and go to his Christian church with him.'

Rachel thought of Sammy, of how she had fallen in love with him at a very young age. Given the chance, given that her attachment to the Jewish faith had not been such a pleasure to her father, she knew she herself would have willingly converted to become Mrs Sammy Adams. Nevertheless, she had been true to her father's precepts and faithful to Benjamin. It had never occurred to her to be other than a faithful wife. That, however, did not prevent her from sighing sometimes.

She and Polly Simms had both known heartburning, she on account of Sammy, Polly on account of being desperate to have Boots for a lover. What was it about Chinese Lady's sons that made them so much more appealing than other men? What were they if not cockneys of the humblest beginnings, except that Boots had never been other than cosmopolitan, Sammy never less than electric, Tommy born to be the handsomest and kindest of men.

Polly had Boots now, all of him, because of the tragic death of Emily, and Polly at last was a contented woman, no longer restless, brittle and frustrated. Or so it had seemed to Rachel at Emma's wedding.

'Lilian, perhaps you have what you deserve, a husband who loves you,' she said. 'Perhaps we all have what we deserve, either happiness or disappointment. But do the Jews of Europe deserve such a monster as Himmler when we, the Jews of Britain, are favoured by living under the leadership of such a lion as Churchill? My life, Lilian, there is a man who will defy Hitler with his last breath.'

'Not his last breath,' said Lilian. 'Churchill was born to be the death of Hitler, not his victim. I should be happy about that? I am. They face each other across land and sea, and who is the one who screams like a frightened maniac? Hitler. Who is the one who roars? Churchill. Never did I think the roars of a man would sound sweet to my ears, but his do.' Lilian laughed. 'He isn't six feet tall, nor handsome, muscular and arresting, but all the same, I love him. He's the hope of the world, but the world has yet to recognize that. When the war is over, the Zionists mean to fight him and the British to make Palestine a Jewish state. Should I support them? Will you?'

'I'm not a Zionist, I'm British and a subject of King George,' said Rachel. 'I will always stand with my country.'

'Right or wrong?' said Lilian.

Rachel did not hesitate.

'We aren't wrong in fighting this war,' she said.

'That's the answer Germans would give about their own country,' said Lilian.

'But how pathetic they are, stupid victims of a brutal hypnotist,' said Rachel.

'Well, this lunch isn't pathetic,' said Lilian. 'May I have more salad? Have you met Rosie's fiancé?'

'No,' smiled Rachel, ladling out more salad, 'has anyone?'

'Well,' remarked Lilian, also with a smile, 'I'll be bold enough to say that after the whole family has met him, it'll be the grand-mother who'll pronounce him acceptable or not.'

'I should hope that that darling girl Rosie hasn't chosen the unacceptable,' said Rachel. 'You didn't say, but are you a Zionist yourself?'

'No, I'm my husband's wife,' said Lilian, 'and don't wish to be anything else.'

Chapter Sixteen

Chinese Lady served a light lunch of home-
made fish cakes and new potatoes, and
apologized that she didn't have any butter to
put on the potatoes because of the war.
Matt said don't apologize, people needed to
keep their own cows if they wanted a decent
supply of butter in wartime.

'Oh, I don't think we've got room in the
garden for any cows,' said Chinese Lady,
'and even if we did have, I don't know who'd
look after them. Mr Finch, my husband,
hasn't ever kept cows, and I only kept a
parrot once that my only oldest son, Rosie's
dad, brought home to me from somewhere.
That parrot, well, Mr Chapman, you should
of heard some of the things it said. It nearly
took away our respectability, and I always
had to cover it up if I had visitors, especially
the vicar's lady wife. I don't think I'd want
another one.'

'Don't worry, Nana, Matthew hasn't
brought you one,' said Rosie.

'Some eggs, some rabbits and some trout,'
said Matthew. 'They're in that straw bag
there, all wrapped up, with the eggs in a
box.'

'Well, I never did,' said Chinese Lady, 'how kind of you, I'm sure.' She regarded him with great favour. 'I must say I always thought Rosie would marry a gentleman.' Which reminded her that Eloise hoped to meet and marry that kind of man. Lord, what with Polly being upper class, family connections were likely to get confusing.

'Are you a gentleman, Matt?' smiled Rosie.

'Not very often,' said Matt, 'and hardly at all when I'm in my overalls and under a contrary car.'

'It's not clothes that make a gentleman,' said Chinese Lady, 'it's how he treats people.'

'That's right,' said Rosie. 'You can kick a car that's contrary, Matt, but as long as you're nice to the owner, you're as good a gentleman as the Lord Chancellor.'

'I see,' said Matt, 'and what makes a lady?'

'Her hats,' said Rosie. 'That's in times of peace, of course, not war. In war, the hats are awful, haven't you noticed?'

'I must say I'm fond of a nice hat,' said Chinese Lady.

'But what makes a lady in wartime if the hats are awful?' asked Matt.

'There aren't any,' said Rosie, 'we all get primitive.'

'Well, I'll admit I've had very unladylike feelings about Hitler,' said Chinese Lady.

'Oh, I don't usually do afters for lunch, Mr Chapman, but as I thought you and Rosie would want something extra because of comin' all the way from Dorset, I've done a roly-poly jam pudding.'

'I'll go for that,' said Matt.

'I'll go for a fair share,' said Rosie.

'Mind, it doesn't have any suet in it,' said Chinese Lady, 'you just can't get much suet now.'

'We'll still go for it,' smiled Rosie.

'Both of us,' said Matt.

Altogether, it was an agreeable lunch that allowed Chinese Lady and Rosie's man from Dorset to get to know each other.

Lilian returned from her lunch with Rachel and gave Rosie a fitting of her wedding gown. Some alterations proved necessary, but Lilian had allowed herself time to attend to them. In Rosie's room, she began the work.

Downstairs, in the room she always called the parlour, Chinese Lady entertained Matt, or it might have been the other way about. Whatever, Chinese Lady acquired a pleasing impression of Rosie's Dorset gentleman. That is, until she asked him about his country garage and received a reply to the effect that he was just managing to scrape a living from it.

Chinese Lady was shocked. No-one had

told her that Rosie's future husband had poverty on his doorstep. Lord, as his wife Rosie wouldn't know where the next shilling was coming from. Poverty might not be a crime, but it wasn't what Rosie was born for as a wife, nor what she went to university for. Not that she was the kind to want to live in luxury, but she ought to be able to go out and buy her groceries with a comfortable amount of money in her purse. If Mr Chapman was only scraping a living for himself, how was he going to provide for a wife? That was a husband's first duty, to be a proper provider. What about clothes for Rosie? Rosie always dressed very elegant, in nice clothes. At least, she had until she went into uniform. I can't hardly think it's right, she said to herself, a man asking a young lady to marry him when he wasn't able to provide proper for her. I know what a struggle it is, living in poverty, and what a blessing it was when the family got comfortably off. Imagine Rosie having to buy her clothes at a village jumble sale, and having to save crusts to make bread puddings. Yes, and now she realized Mr Chapman wasn't wearing a nice suit, but a mid-brown jacket with leather-patched elbows and dark brown trousers. She was sure the jacket was old.

'Something bothering you, Mrs Finch?' said Matthew.

'Oh, I was just thinking,' said Chinese Lady, hiding worry. 'I was thinking I expect your garage has prospects.'

'Yes, post-war prospects, when private cars come back on the road,' said Matthew. 'There'll be an immediate rush by owners to have their cars serviced after lying idle, as well as an immediate rise in petrol sales.'

'Will you be able to manage all right till then?'

'I'll leave that to Rosie,' said Matt, 'I've an idea she's a first-class manager.'

Chinese Lady was tempted to say a wife couldn't manage like she should if there wasn't much money coming in. However, it wasn't her place to interfere, and it would upset Rosie if she did. But she regarded Mr Chapman with more of a frown now, although that didn't mean her liking for him went through the door. You could like all kinds of people, even if they did have the fault of being unresponsible.

She meant irresponsible.

The Troon Commandos were aboard a warship, moving to rendezvous with groups in other ships. The expected new assault had been given the go-ahead, and Tim was wondering how long it would be before 4 Commando got back to Troon. He felt it imperative to keep in regular touch with Felicity. The combined assault force was due to reach its target in Norway early on Friday morning. The commanders were arranging for the committed groups to meet for a collective briefing at Scapa Flow.

Tim, at the warship's rail, stared fixedly at the rolling wake, sparkling in the sunshine. Major Lucas arrived beside him.

'Something bugging you, Tim?' he asked.

'Not seriously,' said Tim. 'We ought to be back well in time for me to contact Felicity again. I don't like missing out for too long.'

'It shouldn't be too long,' said the Major. 'So keep your mind on what's more important to miss, German fire-power. They're going to chuck it at us by the hundredweight. Then there's your wedding, which naturally means a hell of a lot to you, so keep your head down, or you won't get there.'

'I'd like it,' said Tim, 'if you'd try to cheer me up, not remind me of all the grim stuff. Believe me, I mean to be at my wedding, and my sister Rosie's too. Felicity's my future, and Rosie's my best friend. Always has been.'

'What about your other sister, then?' asked Major Lucas, sharing Tim's view of the perpetual wake.

'Eloise? Bit of French sauce about her,' said Tim, 'but she's another best friend.'

'Delighted to hear it,' said Major Lucas drily, and Tim wondered exactly what was going on between his detachment commander and his Anglo-French sister. He'd bet a fiver Eloise represented a challenge to a man like Major Lucas.

The warship steamed on, the Commandos already in tension, but high on adrenalin.

In Troon, Eloise found herself enduring the ever-present frustrations of a young woman waiting to settle a score with a man who was to lead a detachment of Commandos, including her half-brother Tim, into the fiery furnace of a German stronghold.

It's not fair, I'm worrying badly now. Everyone says it's going to be the most dangerous raid yet. Well, of course I should be worrying. About all of them. It's not unfair, it's natural.

Lizzy and Vi, having been shopping together, could not resist dropping in on Chinese Lady later that afternoon. The idea, of course, was to preview Rosie's intended.

'Is he here, Mum, is that his car in the drive?' asked Lizzy, immediately her mother opened the front door and showed herself.

'Yes, he's in the garden with Rosie just now, Lizzy,' said Chinese Lady. 'Lilian Chambers, the lady that's designed Rosie's gown, has been here doing one or two alterations, but she's just taken the gown to Rachel's, where she's staying. Was I expectin' you and Vi?'

'Oh, we thought we'd pop in after our shopping,' said Lizzy.

'Well, that's nice,' said Chinese Lady, and allowed her daughter and daughter-in-law to peck her cheeks.

'And how are you, Mum?' asked Vi, whose equability rarely took a wrong turning, although the sound of air raid sirens made her bite her lip, wince, and worry about Tommy being called out on ARP duty.

'Well, I can't say I'm not a bit concerned,' said Chinese Lady. 'Let's go in the parlour for a few minutes.'

In the well-furnished parlour, larger and grander than that which the family had known during their striving years in Walworth, Lizzy said, 'What's concerning you, then?'

'It's Mr Chapman,' said Chinese Lady, lowering her voice.

'Oh, don't you like him now you've met him?' asked Vi.

'I can't say I don't,' said Chinese Lady, 'but I'm worried that he's only scrapin' a living from his garage business. He said so himself. Lor', he come right out with it just like he was only telling the time. All these weeks, and no-one's said anything to me about Rosie marrying a man that can't hardly support her.'

'Oh, Ned and me did hear he wasn't comfortably off,' said Lizzy, 'but–'

'I didn't hear,' said Chinese Lady.

'Oh, I'm sure he and Rosie will have worked things out,' said Vi, 'I'm sure they'll be able to manage.'

'Yes, but Rosie shouldn't have to worry if she's got enough to pay the milkman each week,' said Chinese Lady. 'You and me and Lizzy have all lived through days of want, and I don't like the thought of any of my grandchildren havin' to scrimp and scrape. They're not used to it like we were. They've been brought up more comfortable. I've been thinking of Rosie havin' to buy her clothes at village jumble sales and save her crusts. It's – Lizzy, have you got a chest cold?'

'No, just a tickle in my throat,' said Lizzy, trying to visualize Rosie, the most stylish member of the family, rummaging through cast-offs at a jumble sale. Even in uniform, Rosie projected elegance. 'Mum, I don't think Rosie will have to buy secondhand clothes or save her crusts.'

'I should hope not, I'd be shocked if she did,' said Chinese Lady. 'I'd just like to know why no-one's told me Mr Chapman can't actu'lly afford a wife, especially not one like our Rosie, a born lady in my opinion and always a blessing to Boots and the rest of us. Does anyone know if Mr Chapman's cottage is a bit rundown? I'd get heartburn if Rosie had to live in a place with holes in the roof, doors off their hinges, and one of them outside places.'

'Mum, don't let yourself get prone to exaggerations,' said Lizzy.

'Let myself what?' said Chinese Lady. 'Lizzy, I hope you're not goin' to start sounding like Boots or Sammy with that kind of language.'

'Lizzy only means you mustn't imagine things are all that bad,' said Vi. 'I'm sure Rosie and Mr Chapman have talked about their finances and have decided they can manage. Me and Tommy did when we were first married and had to live with me mum and dad to save on rent.'

'I expect Boots knows a bit more about Mr Chapman than we do,' said Chinese Lady. 'He met him down at his garage. I'll have to talk to him when he gets here with Polly tomorrow for the weekend. He said they'd come tomorrow. Lord, with all the worries of the war, I never thought I'd have extra worries about Rosie livin' in a run-down country cottage and not havin' decent shoes on her feet after a while. Well, I suppose that's what scraping a livin' means, that she'd have to make do with old shoes, but I hope she doesn't come down to goin' about with holes in her stockings or takin' in washing, like I had to once – Lizzy, where you goin'?'

'Into the garden, to meet Mr Chapman,'

said Lizzy in a slightly strangled voice.

'I'll come with you,' said Vi, escaping the imaginative despair of her inimitable mother-in-law and joining the slightly hysterical Lizzy.

In the garden, they saw Rosie talking to her Dorset man. She was smiling up at him, and what she was saying was making him laugh.

Lizzy called.

'Hello, Rosie love.'

'We were just passing,' called Vi.

'Lovely you dropped in,' said Rosie, delighted. 'You can meet Matthew now.'

She walked over the lawn with him and over the short stone path dividing flower beds. Lizzy and Vi did not miss Matthew's limp. Introductions were made, and after a few minutes, neither Lizzy nor Vi could seriously fault Rosie's intended. They liked his tanned country looks, his fruity Dorset voice, his immediate friendliness and his easy-going style that was remindful of Boots. Yes, thought Lizzy, for Rosie perhaps there had to be something of Boots about a man she wanted to live with for the rest of her life.

Vi thought she would be able to tell Tommy that she'd been right about Rosie making a suitable choice. Mr Chapman seemed very suitable, except could it be true that he couldn't really afford a wife? Well, if anyone would know it had to be Boots, Rosie's protective dad.

For his part, Matthew noted the slight trace of cockney in the speech of Rosie's aunts, which was odd considering Rosie and her adoptive father, the brother of one of these women, delivered not a trace of it. Matthew also noted the excellent style and quality of Vi and Lizzy's clothes and hats. Lizzy had always owned a fine dress sense, and Ned had never failed to finance her wardrobe, much of it obtained from Adams Fashions at a family discount. And Tommy, generously salaried by Sammy, made sure Vi was always able to look as well-dressed as Lizzy and Susie.

It seems certain, thought Matt, that I'm marrying into an affluent family, and it's just as certain that Rosie isn't. Mangy foxes and hungry hounds, I own a garage and so does my father, but both of us haven't much to spare, and the new furniture for the cottage is going to make a hole in my modest bank balance. It'll blow my head off if there's no balance at all in the end, except on the wrong side.

'We've heard a lot about you having a garage, Mr Chapman,' said Lizzy.

'So I have,' smiled Matt.

'We all hope it's doing well,' said Lizzy.

'Oh, yes,' said Vi.

'It's short of business,' said Matt, 'but not

273

on the rocks yet.'

'We're just waiting for the tide to turn,' said Rosie. She was in her uniform, but without her cap, her hair golden in the sunshine, and she looks so striking, thought Vi, that it's easy to believe her natural father's an aristocrat. Eloise, who had met him, was certain about that. 'We're wallowing in the shallows at the moment,' said Rosie.

'Oh, I expect you'll manage,' said Vi, thinking she and Lizzy didn't ought to pry too much. 'Will you be leaving the Army, Rosie?'

'Only if I have to,' said Rosie. Matt had said that while the war was on he wasn't going to object to her staying in the ATS. He'd mentioned he had conservative views about some things, but he wasn't the kind of man to lay down Victorian laws concerning husbands, wives and marriage, or not to realize her officer's pay would be useful.

Chinese Lady appeared and let everyone know she'd just made a pot of tea, and perhaps they'd all like to have a cup while it was still fresh.

Matt came through the ordeal of drinking tea with four females of the Adams clan without once looking as if he'd prefer to be under a car. Rosie thought him very adaptable. Matthew, remembering his impressions of Boots's wife Polly, undeniably upper class, and of Boots himself, thought Rosie's relatives an extraordinary mixture. But they had one thing in common, an obvious belief that what counted most in their lives was 'the family'.

Well, that was what a good many people believed. The dissidents were those whose families were always on the verge of civil war.

Mr Finch, home from his work that evening, did not take long to make up his mind that Matthew Chapman would do very well for Rosie, despite Chinese Lady mentioning, confidentially, that Rosie might have to struggle with poverty. Mr Finch coughed, then said he thought the family could discount that. No two people like Rosie and Matthew Chapman would become the victims of poverty, he said. Chinese Lady still worried about it, however.

As for Matthew's impression of Mr Finch, he thought here's a man of distinction, obviously well-educated, and accordingly another typical ingredient of the odd family mixture. His attitude towards his wife, Rosie's cockney grandmother, was touched with the quiet and civilized affection of a cultured man. Blow my head off, thought Matt, will I add to the odd? That is, make the mixture odder? Probably.

He woke up halfway through the night. He slipped from the bed, crossed to the window, drew back the curtains and looked up at the night sky of London. It was brilliant with stars and a full white moon. It was a bombers' moon, flooding the capital with light, but not a single plane flew under the stars, and not a sound disturbed the sleeping people of the sprawling city. The house itself was wrapped in silence.

This was Rosie's home, built in Victorian times, the kitchen with a butler's pantry, the hall leading to a handsome staircase, the rooms high-ceilinged and spacious. Here, before the war, Rosie had lived with her adoptive family, her grandparents, her father, her late mother, her brother Tim, and her sister Eloise, who had been born of a Frenchwoman during the Great War. Only her grandparents lived here now. All the others were serving in the Army, except of course for the late mother. A bomb had taken her from life, and her husband, called Boots, an out-of-the-ordinary man, had married again. Matthew, having met him, thought him a man for all people, and could understand Rosie's attachment to him. He could also understand her affection for her fascinating stepmother, an ATS captain who often sounded as if she had come straight out of the Twenties.

Matthew grimaced as a twinge attacked his crippled ankle. Damn that old wrecked joint, he thought, for the fact is a war against Hitler and his devils is one for every man who counts freedom precious. Churchill hit the nail on the head every time he addressed Parliament or the nation. A great man. And what am I? A lame duck. Does a lame duck deserve a woman as lovely and vital as Rosie?

He grimaced again.

Well, witches and wombats, if I gave her up, who's to say she might not have the bad luck to be led by God knows what circumstances into the arms of someone even less deserving? What I have I'll hold, treasure my good fortune, and make that old garage pay its way and more.

He limped back to bed, back to sleep.

Chapter Seventeen

Rosie had a hundred and one things to do the following day, all relating to the wedding, so Matthew said he'd motor up to central London. Rosie asked why. I think I'd like to see what the bombs have done to our capital, said Matthew. I don't think you'll like it, said Rosie. It's something Dorset people should take a look at when they're up from the country, said Matthew.

'Off you go, then,' smiled Rosie, 'go and see the ruins that Germany's Oliver Cromwell has knocked about a bit. You'll come back with the thunder of revenge on your noble brow.'

Having parked his car on a cleared bomb site near the Bank of England, Matthew limped through the City. The scenes of devastation were even worse than he'd imagined. They pained the eye. Around St Paul's, the area was choked by mounds of bricks and stone, but the cathedral itself, relatively undamaged, soared majestically to the sky, its magnificent dome intact.

The City, the heart of London's trade and commerce, was hideously scarred, but still beating. The people, office workers in the main, were going about their business, skirting piles of rubble as a matter of everyday course. He could not say they looked depressed or defeated. Their step was brisk, their shoulders unbowed, and policemen on point duty were exchanging repartee with van drivers who wanted to know why such-and-such a street was still blocked off.

'Short of a broom round here, are they, mate?'

'And muscles, Claud.'

'Bleedin' disgrace in Watling Street, can't even ride a bike there this morning.'

'See the Lord Mayor.'

Matthew made his way up Aldersgate to the fringes of the East End, where cockney residents had known what it was to emerge from shelters at the sound of the All-Clear to find their homes blown to smithereens. The devastation was heartbreaking here, and spoke of Hitler's war against civilians, against women and children. Like so many people of the United Kingdom, Matthew felt the only way to discourage all future German militarism was for its leaders and citizens to suffer double doses of their own medicine.

A podgy bloke in shirt, pullover, trousers and flat cap came out of a house that was minus its roof, its upper rooms gaping and lifeless. By the open door, which was splintered, was a notice.

DANGER – KEEP OUT!

The podgy bloke was carrying a birdcage and a dust-covered, walnut-framed clock. He set them down at Matthew's feet.

''Ere, guard them for me, mate,' he said blithely. 'I got other stuff to bring out.'

'You'll get nothing if the house falls on you,' said Matthew.

'I'll be out quick as a flea out of a pepper-pot as soon as it starts shakin',' said Podgy. 'I'm doin' a clearin' job for me nearest and dearest, yer know, me old mum and dad that got bombed out. Anyway, keep yer eye on that there cage and clock, I don't want 'em nicked, me old lady's partial to the cage and me old man cherishes 'is chimer.'

Back in he went, and out he came again a minute later, carrying a dusty shopping basket full of china. He placed it carefully down beside the birdcage.

'Is this your home too?' asked Matthew.

'Well, it would be, mate, if it 'ud got its titfer on,' said Podgy genially, 'but as yer can see, it ain't, and the bleedin' rain comes in. Keep yer mince pies on me old lady's china while I git me old man's wireless set.'

Into the roofless house he went again.

A fulsome good-looking woman came along. She looked and stopped.

''Ere, 'oo broke that door down?' she asked aggressively. 'And what yer doin' with

Mrs Beadle's belongings?'

'Damned if I know,' said Matthew. 'Has Mrs Beadle got a husband and son?'

'No, she ain't, she's an old widder woman with four married daughters,' said the fulsome woman.

'Well, I know now what I'm doing with this stuff,' said Matthew.

'So do I,' said the woman, 'you're a bleedin' looter, and I'm goin' for a copper.' Off she went in aggressive search of a bobby. Podgy reappeared, carrying a dust-covered wireless set, plus a large sack.

''Ere we are, mate,' he said, ''old the wireless a tick, and then 'elp me load the sack, eh? Ta, you're a pal.'

'Take it back,' said Matthew.

'Eh?' said Podgy.

'All of it,' said Matthew.

'I'm 'ard of 'earing,' said Podgy.

'Take it all back,' said Matthew.

''Ere, listen, mate, live and let live, eh?' said Podgy.

'You're lifting Mrs Beadle's goods and chattels, you bugger,' said Matthew.

'Who's she?'

'Not your poor old mother, that's for sure,' said Matthew.

'Never 'eard of 'er,' protested Podgy, and tried to do a runner. Matthew yanked him back. 'Sod yer,' said Podgy, 'it ain't yer business.'

'And this stuff's not your business, either,' said Matthew.

The aggressive woman was back then, coming at a lively trot, a police constable striding along beside her.

'Ruddy 'ell, I'm orf,' said Podgy, and made another attempt to disappear. Matthew held on to him. Up came law and order and the woman.

'There y'ar,' she said to the copper, 'that's ''im.' She pointed at Matthew, and looked at Podgy. 'And that's 'is fat brother, I shouldn't wonder.'

'I recognize his fat brother,' said the constable, 'it's Swagman Stan. Gotcher, have we, Stan, and your brother?'

It turned into a long story before either the woman or the constable accepted that Matthew was an innocent party. Law and order then informed the culprit he would be taken to the station and charged with breaking, entering and looting.

'Well, I ain't in bleedin' favour,' said the culprit, 'but fair cop. What'll it be?'

'Tower of London and executed at dawn, probably,' said the constable.

'Well, I ain't in favour of that, neither,' said Podgy.

'Serve yer bleedin' right for robbin' a pore old widder lady that's been bombed out,' said the woman.

'There,' said Podgy to Matthew, 'see what

yer done, and me thinkin' I'd found a pal. 'Ope me execution is on yer conscience for the rest of yer natural.'

'Put the evidence in that sack and bring it with you,' said the constable. He took Podgy away with him after thanking Matthew and the woman for their help.

"Ere, mister, I'm sorry I misjudged yer, and you a pleasant gent and all,' said the woman, her florid good looks a bit coarsened by this, that and the other. 'Would yer like to come 'ome with me and 'ave a nice cup of tea?'

Matthew, quite intrigued by events, said he would. This was his first encounter with the East End of London and its cockney characters. Further, he was a fascinated observer of a ravaged and mutilated London that, despite so much bombing, still teemed with life, with people who dwelt there or worked there and could not be driven to seek holes in the hills of Surrey. It was a fact that Dorset and the West Country, apart from Plymouth, knew nothing of the sheer hell of assaults from the skies. He himself lived in what was a comparative oasis of peace, where striving farmers and the Land Army girls related more to the war effort than he did. He was suddenly disgusted with his disability.

Chattering, the woman took him through streets where bombs had created great jagged gaps in rows of terraced houses. Kids too young to be evacuated climbed about on mounds of rubble. Kids. They looked as if they were at play on the lifeless cratered moon. The woman reached a street where, by a miracle, there were more standing houses than collapsed dwellings. Her own house looked dust-covered, the windows grey with it. She said as her old man was in the Merchant Navy and only home once a year, like, she'd be better off living with her brother and his wife up in Hackney, except she couldn't stand the wife on account of she smelled of fish and chips. Well, she worked in a fried fish and chips shop.

'I like fish 'n chips, course I do, mister,' she said, 'but not livin' up against the smell. Besides, I got a little wartime business goin' for gents and the like. Daytime, of course, and mostly on account of being recommended. Well, people don't come around 'ere much at night, not since the raids started. Is yer limp a war wound, only you look like an 'andsome soldier, that you do.'

'It's the result of an old injury,' said Matthew.

'Well, that's a shame,' she said. ''Ere we are, come on in, in me parlour.'

Her front door was open and she went in, followed by Matthew. Dust seemed to have invaded the interior, but the parlour itself looked well-kept. A sofa against one wall

284

faced a mahogany table, and there were two armchairs, one on each side of the hearth.

'You've managed to live through all the bombing?' he said.

'Dunno 'ow long for if there's more to come,' she said. 'Still, it can only kill yer, can't it?' She issued a wheezy laugh, like a gurgle. She was very full-bodied, her eyes bright and knowing, her lashes thick. Her blouse had straining pearl buttons, and her long skirt hung from rounded hips. Matthew was beginning to sum her up, but couldn't help liking her. 'Well, if a bomb's got the address of yer shelter on it, there ain't a lot you can do about it.'

'Damned if I know how you people can stand it,' said Matthew, feeling the low ceiling of the parlour wasn't too far from his head.

'Well, it ain't easy to get used to, even after all these months,' she said, 'but it's been a bit better just lately. I'm Mrs 'Arriet Billings, and I must say you talk like a very nice-speakin' gent, and it'll be me pleasure to put the kettle on this minute, like. Sit down and make yerself comfy.'

Out she went and he heard her call.

'Maudie, you up there? We've got a gent visitin'. D'you want to come down while I'm makin' a pot of tea?'

'A gent?' said a trilling voice. 'All right, I'll be down in a tick. Don't let 'im get away.'

Matthew sat down to wait and to muse.

When Mrs Billings re-entered the parlour carrying a tray, she was followed by a young woman, a colourful brunette freshly made-up, and wearing a pastel pink wrap with a sash. She eyed Matthew speculatively. He was sitting on the sofa, and the young lady, having observed how personable he was, let go a brilliant smile.

'Well, 'owdyerdo,' she said, 'I'm Maudie, and Mrs Billings is me aunt. Well, a sort of aunt.'

'Guardian?' suggested Matthew, his air of good fellowship often deceptive. The young lady laughed.

'D'you 'ear that, Auntie?' she said.

'Well, he's a gent,' said Mrs Billings. 'Now there's the tray, Maudie. Tea for you and 'im. I'll 'ave mine in the kitchen. Well, two's company, three's a bit of a crowd. Is yer bed tidy?'

'Course it is,' said Maudie, and sat down by the table and opposite Matthew. She smiled as she crossed her legs. Her wrap parted and Matthew saw shining black stockings and black suspenders.

'Enjoy yer tea,' said Mrs Billings to Matthew. 'Maudie'll look after you very nice.' Out she went, winking.

'D'you take sugar?' asked Maudie.

'Sugar?' smiled Matthew, now summing up the obvious. He wondered what Rosie

286

would say. 'No, no sugar, thanks.'

'Just as well,' said Maudie, 'Auntie ain't brought none. Bet she's gone through the ration already.' She filled cups from the pot. 'D'you like me?'

'I've hardly had time to make up my mind,' said Matthew, 'but I'd wager you've got any amount of likeable ways.'

'Well, so I 'ave,' said Maudie, 'but you're a real gent for saying so. Real gents know 'ow to be nice to a girl, and I like yer looks, I must say. Well, 'ere's yer tea, and it'll be five quid.'

'Seems an expensive cup of tea,' said Matthew.

Maudie laughed again.

'It's the fruit bun you pay for,' she said.

'I see,' said Matthew. 'Um, what fruit bun?'

'Me,' said Maudie, and showed more leg.

'I'll get my wallet,' said Matthew and stood up.

'Where'd yer keep yer wallet, then?' asked Maudie.

'A friend's looking after it,' said Matthew, and departed from the parlour and the house at a fast limp.

Maudie waited a bit, then realized the rotten so-and-so had done a bunk. She yelled at Mrs Billings.

''Ere, 'e wasn't no gent, 'e's bleedin' 'opped it.'

'Oh, yer just can't trust no-one these days,' cried Mrs Billings, 'not even in daylight.'

Far from the London scene, warships were arriving at Scapa Flow, and Tim was wishing the whole thing was over and done with. He had Felicity on his mind. Major Lucas was itching for action, and more or less said so.

'Fatal,' said Tim. 'I'm bloody scared myself. That's a good omen.'

'Time we hit the Hun for real, Tim,' said Major Lucas.

On his way back to South London, Matthew found a café in Chelsea that served him a lunchtime snack of wartime sausages, baked beans and tinned tomatoes. Three recruits from Chelsea Barracks were having the same, in preference, he supposed, to what was being dished up in their mess. Or in addition? They were vigorous specimens, training to do their bit, and looked as if a large intake of food was a natural requirement.

His meal finished, he resumed his journey, only to pull up again, this time outside the recruiting centre. Damn it, why not go in? He did so. At the desk he was received by a veteran, moustached sergeant in his mid-forties, who listened politely to him.

'I see, sir. Well, whatever kind of job you

might be detailed for in the Army, and I won't say qualified motor mechanics aren't wanted, the fact is sometime or other you'd have to do a bit of marching, and I don't mean on the square. I mean according to circumstances, which could be of a kind where you'd have to footslog at the double.'

'I can ride a bike,' said Matthew.

The recruiting sergeant looked at him and couldn't remember when he'd last interviewed a volunteer who seemed to have more of the makings than this one. Fine upstanding bloke, that he was.

'Can't say there'd be a spare bike lying around in awkward circumstances, sir,' he said. 'Mind if I had a look at this here ankle of yours? Come round the desk into this office.'

In the office, Matthew took off his left shoe and sock, and the recruiting sergeant took a keen look at his misshapen ankle.

'Well?' said Matthew.

'You'd never get an Army boot on, which is necessary equipment,' said the sergeant. 'Even pimply orderly room clerks have to wear boots. Stock-in-trade of the Army, boots are, y'know.'

'No go, then?' said Matthew.

'Sorry, sir.'

'So am I,' said Matthew, and was back in his car a few minutes later.

'Matt!' Rosie shrieked at what Matthew was telling her about his morning trip to bombed London. 'Matt, you didn't get taken in first by a shifty looter and then by an East End madame, did you?'

'So I did, Rosie, blow my shirt buttons off if I didn't,' he said. It was mid-afternoon and they were out in the garden. 'Up to a point in both cases, that is. In the madame's parlour, I turned down the fruit bun.'

'Fruit bun?' said Rosie. 'Explain, please.'

Matt explained. Rosie shrieked again.

'Is it that funny?' smiled Matt.

'Riotous,' said Rosie. She was wearing a turquoise blue dress, classic in its simplicity, and Matt thought her clean, fresh and exquisite. 'Nearly arrested, nearly dragged into bed by naughty Maudie, what were you up to?'

'Seeing the sights of a bombed city,' said Matt, and looked sober. 'Damn all, Rosie, you'd think earthquakes had struck it.'

'I know,' said Rosie, 'I've seen some of it. The wonder is that Londoners aren't giving in, and won't – nor the people of Liverpool, Glasgow, Coventry and other cities. They can't, Matt, and we can't.'

'Oh, I can wave a flag, Rosie,' said Matt, 'but there must be something else I can do as well.'

'Well, you can first marry me,' said Rosie lightly. She knew what was bothering him.

The disability that exempted him from call-up. He looked as strong and healthy as the fittest soldier in the realm. Only when people noticed his limp could they understand why he wasn't in the Army. But he had his worth to the country, as did any man who could keep farmers' tractors from falling apart in the fight to increase the bounty of the land. 'We'll work something out when we're back in Dorset.'

'Like enrolling in the Home Guard?' said Matt.

'Home Guard?' said Rosie.

'That's something,' said Matt, who had said nothing about his interview with a recruiting sergeant. He was not a secretive man, far from it, especially with Rosie, but he did not want to make more than he had of his particular problem at a time when their wedding day wasn't far away.

Chapter Eighteen

Susie answered the ringing phone.

'Hello?'

'Susie?' It was Sammy, calling from his office.

'Sammy? Are the premises on fire?'

'Well, if they are no-one's told me and the fire brigade's not here,' said Sammy.

'Why are you calling, then?' asked Susie.

'Have you seen Rosie's Dorset bloke yet?' asked Sammy.

'No. Everyone's going round this evening,' said Susie, 'and I'm against poking my nose in until then.'

'Well,' said Sammy, 'I was wondering if the bloke can do office work. I'm still short of a managerial assistant, Miss Symonds havin' disappeared some time ago in a cloud of sniffy umbrage, and you still not havin' made your mind up about coming back. So I was thinking–'

'Sammy, you shocker, you're thinking again of interfering,' said Susie.

'Now, Susie, is a kind thought the same as interfering?' asked Sammy.

'It's the start of it,' said Susie.

'But think about it, Susie, a job for the

geezer in the fam'ly business—'

'Sammy, our Rosie's fiancé is not a geezer.'

'Fair comment, Susie, and duly noted,' said Sammy. 'But the job would save Rosie gettin' lost in the wilds of Dorset and give her bloke the means to buy a house just up the road from Chinese Lady, which would tickle Ma's fancy no end.'

'No, Sammy,' said Susie. 'You're sweet, but it's wrong to try to make Rosie and Mr Chapman live where you'd like them to. Besides, he'd probably see your offer of a job as charity.'

'Charity's highly thought of, Susie, and by such important people as our King and Queenie, bless 'em.'

'Oh, dear,' sighed Susie, 'then we'll just have to ask Their Majesties if they think highly enough of your kind of charity.'

'Well, to please you, Susie,' said Sammy, 'I'll drop 'em a line on me best notepaper.'

'Oh, very comical,' said Susie, 'but you're out of order, lovey, and you know it.'

'Thought I'd just mention it, though, before we went round this evening,' said Sammy.

'Bless you, Sammy,' said Susie, 'your heart's in the right place, it's just your thinking that's lost its way.'

'I'd better get Sherlock Holmes on the job of finding it,' said Sammy. 'It's been desertin' me a lot lately on account of the war, and it won't get better if bombs start falling again.'

'Yes, you need help, Sammy dear,' said Susie.

'It's partly me office workload, and partly fam'ly worries,' said Sammy. 'Oh, well, see you later, Susie old girl.'

'Same to you, Sammy old bloke,' said Susie, and thought for a while after she'd hung up. Then, before she went to pick up Paula from a friend's house, she phoned Rachel.

'Rachel, Susie here.'

'Susie?' Rachel was always careful with Susie. Susie knew she'd been Sammy's one and only girlfriend in the old days, and often had an eye on her.

'How are you, Rachel, and how's Benjamin?' asked Susie.

Rachel said she was fine, except that she was missing her daughters, evacuees in the West Country. And Benjamin was fine too, he was back at work. Susie said he'd been heroic. Rachel said he was simply grateful that the collapsing house hadn't smothered him to death. Susie said miracles like that were happening in every air raid.

'God is good to many of us,' said Rachel.

'Yes, we can't shut our eyes to that,' said Susie. 'Rachel, you're a director of the Adams firm, aren't you?'

'Yes, Susie.'

'Well, Sammy needs help,' said Susie, and went on to say he was short of a managerial assistant. She had thought about doing the job herself, but only on a part-time basis because of Paula. Even then, there were school holidays, which would mean she couldn't be at the office at all for weeks at a time. 'Rachel, you know the business, would you have time to do the job?'

'Susie?' said Rachel, taken aback.

'It wouldn't worry me,' said Susie. She had long been sure of Sammy's fidelity, long realized he was the son of his mother, as Boots was. She had always felt Boots had been entirely faithful to Emily, despite Polly's infatuation with him. 'And I'm sure you'd be as efficient as Sammy is himself. Would you like to think about it?'

Rachel experienced delight, not only because the idea appealed immensely to her, but because Susie trusted her.

'Susie, I'd be very happy to be a help to the firm, my life, yes,' she said. 'We must keep it going. Tommy and Sammy are performing wonders with the Army and Air Force contracts, and I really would be happy to help. My only commitment is to Red Cross work, but I could still do that in my spare time and at weekends.'

'I can tell Sammy you'll take Boots's old position of general manager?' said Susie.

'Yes, Susie,' said Rachel. 'I should say no?

How could I? I've had years of kindness and friendship from the Adams family, I'd never refuse a request for help, especially as I get director's fees each year. Susie, thank you for phoning me, and please tell Sammy I'll start as soon as he likes.'

'That'll help him put his brainbox together again,' said Susie.

'I should believe it's in pieces?' said Rachel. 'Sammy's brainbox?'

'That's what he says.'

'He's joking, of course,' said Rachel.

'Half-joking,' said Susie. 'Goodbye, Rachel, thanks for being positive. Sammy will be grateful.'

'Goodbye, Susie.' Rachel was smiling as she put the phone down. Working with Sammy for the firm and its war contracts? With Susie's blessing? How exhilarating, and neither Susie nor Benjamin would be given any cause to worry.

Boots and Polly arrived while Rosie and Matthew were still in the garden. Chinese Lady welcomed them. There might have been some restraint in her attitude because it was now Boots and Polly after years of being Boots and Emily. But she had accepted without any real quibble the inevitability of Boots's second marriage. After all, she was in her second marriage herself. But she hadn't ever thought Boots and Polly would have a child, and it was downright disbelievable that Polly was expecting. She wasn't sure that Boots oughtn't to be spoken to considering Tim, Rosie and Eloise had all been born of different mothers and Polly was going to be the fourth mother. Even the vicar, very Christian and tolerant, might raise his eyebrows and wonder if her eldest son didn't cast his seed a bit too wide. Of course, Rosie was adopted, but even so people would be bound to give Boots queer looks.

However, her greeting was typical in that it was honest rather than demonstrative. She said she was gratified to see them, that it was nice to know they weren't going off to the war, that they were home for the wedding, and how was Lady Simms? Busy, smiled Polly, and Chinese Lady said it was all that useful work she was doing for the Red Cross, which was very suitable work for women. But she didn't say it would be more suitable for Polly than manning a trench, although she had a fixed idea it would be. But then, Polly would be leaving the Army soon, of course. What a blessing.

'My, I never had more of a surprise than when Boots told me you were expecting, Polly,' she said, 'and Susie and Vi were very compliment'ry about how healthy you must be. Everything's all right with you?'

'Everything's in perfect order,' said Polly. 'That's if one counts morning sickness as part of perfect order.'

'Well, it's natural, but discomfortin', of course,' said Chinese Lady. 'Still, you do seem very healthy, and I don't know how you keep so young-looking. And you still don't look your age, Boots.'

'It's Polly's hot custard,' said Boots. 'Stirring stuff.'

Polly's sweet smile let him know she'd do dire things to him later.

'Lor', I never knew custard made people look younger,' said Chinese Lady.

'Not everybody's custard,' said Boots, and Chinese Lady gave him a look in case he meant her own was inferior. Then she said she had to mention this was only the second time he and Polly had come home to the house as a married couple. The first was on the occasion of Emma's wedding, which had made her feel it was nice to have other people in the house besides herself and Mr Finch.

'It's this blessed war that's making fam'ly homes feel empty,' she said.

'We'd be home more often if we could,' said Polly quite gently, and Chinese Lady thought it was very gratifying that Polly could speak so naturally of the house as her home. But Polly had a quite affectionate relationship with Boots's mother. Although she regarded her as a Victorian throwback, she had always liked her. In fact, they liked each other.

'Well, it is your home till you and Boots get your own house,' said Chinese Lady, 'which I expect you will after the war. Oh, Rosie's here. She's in the garden with Mr Chapman, if you and Boots want to go out and see them.'

'I'd really like to freshen up first and get into something fascinating,' smiled Polly.

Chinese Lady approved of something fascinating, like one of Polly's stylish frocks in place of an Army uniform.

'Yes, you and Boots unpack first,' she said. 'I must say Mr Chapman seems a very pleasant gentleman that looks like a country farmer.'

'An improvement on town farmers, would you say, old lady?' said Boots.

'I don't know I've met any town farmers,' said Chinese Lady. 'Well, I'm sure I've never met any in Camberwell, nor in Walworth. Never mind, Rosie seems very happy about Mr Chapman being here, except he'll be staying with Tommy and Vi when he comes again for the wedding. Well, it wouldn't do for the bridegroom to be living so close to the bride just before they go to the church.'

'How close so far?' asked Boots.

'What's that mean, might I ask?' said Chinese Lady, and Polly's elbow made hidden but pointed contact with Boots's ribs.

'Slip of the tongue,' he said.

'That tongue of yours has been slipping since I can't think when,' said Chinese Lady.

'And don't we all know it, Maisie?' said Polly.

Chinese Lady, never sure it was proper for her new daughter-in-law to call her by her first name, gave a little cough, then said that while they unpacked and freshened up, she'd make a pot of tea for everyone.

Upstairs in the bedroom that had once been exclusive to Boots and Emily, Polly said, 'Listen, old darling, I'm not sure I can sleep in that bed this time.'

'Lumpy mattress?' said Boots.

'No, Emily's ghost,' said Polly. 'It got in with us when we were here for the weekend of Emma's wedding.'

'That's a bit fanciful,' said Boots.

'Honest to God, she was there,' said Polly, 'and trying to push me out.'

'Not very friendly" said Boots. He rarely referred to Emily when in conversation with Polly, knowing that neither had been very popular with the other. He also knew that for all her resilience and strength of character, Polly was sensitive about that bed and the fact that he and Emily had shared it for years. 'What's the answer?'

'Chuck it out,' said Polly with a wry smile.

'We'll change it for the bed in the spare room,' said Boots. 'Will that do?'

'There's a good old soldier,' said Polly, 'but you'll have to face up to questions from your mother.'

'I'll tell her this bed creaks,' said Boots.

'You'll do what?' said Polly.

'She'll understand,' said Boots, 'she'll know we're still a couple of newly-weds.'

'Blow that for a piece of prize buffoonery,' said Polly, 'I'll be expected to blush.'

'But you're serious about not being in love with this bed?' said Boots.

'It's Emily's bed,' said Polly, 'and she knows it.'

Boots didn't suggest she was letting imagination take hold of her. He took a look at the bed, purchased with others when he and Emily moved into this house. His gaze shifted to the decorative headboard.

'Wait a moment,' he said. 'Hold on,' he said after another look, and went down to speak to his mother, just about to put the kettle on. 'Listen, old lady,' he said, 'has something happened to our bed?'

'Yes,' said Chinese Lady, 'Edwin and me changed it for the one in the spare room.'

'I thought there was a difference when I looked at the headboard,' said Boots. 'Why did you make the change?'

'When you were here for Emma's

wedding, I asked Polly how she slept and she said not very well.' Chinese Lady spoke quietly. 'I guessed it was because of Em'ly.'

'You guessed, did you?' said Boots.

'It was natural,' said Chinese Lady. 'I understood and so did Edwin. You and me don't have to have a lot of talk about it, Boots. Edwin and me made the change, not just for Polly but out of respect for Em'ly's memory. A wife that's gone might not take kindly to a new wife sleeping in the same bed, and nor might the new wife like it very much. I expect you and me can both see that.'

'I'm sure we can,' said Boots, 'and I suppose I should have thought about it when Polly and I came home for Emma's wedding.'

'Of course, it's not my place to interfere,' said Chinese Lady, 'but–'

'Understood,' said Boots, 'and you and Edwin have saved me the job of making the change myself.'

'Best it got done,' said Chinese Lady.

'Yes,' smiled Boots.

'By the way–' Chinese Lady touched his arm. 'By the way, Boots, make sure you take care of Polly. I mean, a woman her age, well, see that she looks after herself.'

'Fair comment, old lady,' said Boots, 'I'll keep an eye on her, believe me.' He gave her a light pat, then went up to rejoin Polly. She

302

was out of her uniform and slipping into one of the dresses she'd brought with her. 'It's been taken care of,' he said, and explained.

'This is the spare room bed?' said Polly.

'Not a lot of difference, but yes, it's from the spare room,' said Boots.

'Your mother understood?' said Polly.

'Fully,' said Boots.

'What a lovely old lady,' smiled Polly, 'and you're not so bad yourself, ducky.'

'And you're looking better,' said Boots, 'you were a bit peaky this morning.'

Polly had suffered another bout of morning sickness on waking up at six o'clock.

'Well, you heard your mother,' she smiled, 'it's natural, but discomforting. I can live with it, old sport. You can live with it too, can't you?'

'Sympathetically,' said Boots.

The pot of tea made, Rosie and Matthew came in from the garden as Polly and Boots came down the stairs, Polly in a jersey wool dress of beige. The meeting was in the nature of a very agreeable reunion. It was a pleasure for Polly and Boots to renew acquaintance with Matthew and, as always, a delight to see Rosie.

Over the pot of tea around the kitchen table, Chinese Lady let it be known she was getting flustered about these wartime family weddings, but hoped she would see them through without having an accident. Touching on the war, she delivered one of her typical homilies. She said she didn't know how the Government allowed it to happen in the first place. She said she could have told them that Hitler ought to have been arrested years ago, and that Mr Chamberlain should have taken some lawful London policemen with him to Munich, not a present of a bunch of flowers or whatever it was he did take. Boots said umbrella. A fat lot of good that was, said Chinese Lady, and it wasn't raining there, was it?

'If it was,' said Matt, 'I daresay Hitler had it stopped.'

'Beg pardon?' said Chinese Lady.

'I think there's something else coming,' said Rosie.

'Yes, haven't you all heard that Hitler made a visit to the Almighty?' said Matt.

'Beg pardon?' said Chinese Lady again, this time in shock.

'Yes,' said Matt, 'and as he approached the Almighty, the Almighty asked him who he was. "I'm God," said Hitler, "and that's my chair you're sitting in".'

Laughter ran round the table. Chinese Lady, however, looked as if she thought irreverence had made its mark in her kitchen. Then her mouth twitched, which was a sure sign of her liking for Rosie's intended. Liking induced tolerance, even tolerance of irreverence sometimes. It did not however, guarantee acceptance of a state of wedded poverty. Poverty was something that had existed in the past for Chinese Lady and her family, and she didn't want any of the younger people to be introduced to it in this day and age, especially when even ordinary people were earning high wages in factories.

'Lovely story, Matt,' said Polly, 'although when I first heard it, in 1915, it was Kaiser Bill.'

'Before that,' said Boots, 'it was Napoleon.'

'Aunt Susie once told me it was Uncle Sammy,' said Rosie.

'Well, whatever the Almighty might think of Sammy, we all know what He must think of Hitler,' said Chinese Lady, 'especially after what one of that man's bombs did to this fam'ly when—' She checked. She'd been going to say when Emily had been done to death. No, best not to in front of Polly. 'When Tim's lady friend was on leave, blinding her and all,' she said. 'I'm sure we all think kindly of him for wanting to marry her and take care of her, which I've said before.'

Matt asked if an active Army man could find enough time to do a complete caring job. Boots said Tim's Scots landlady had promised some sterling help. Matt said a military man and a Scots landlady sounded like a pretty useful combination, and that he'd like to meet Tim sometime.

'Oh, we're expecting him home for the wedding,' said Rosie, 'and you'll meet him then.'

'I'll look forward to it,' said Matt.

'Yes, do come,' said Rosie.

'Wouldn't be the same without you, Matt old sport,' said Polly.

'I'll make it a priority,' said Matt.

'Well, it's usual for both the bride and groom to turn up,' said Boots, 'and at the same time. Allowing, of course, for the bride to be a few minutes late.'

'I'll allow that,' said Matt, and Rosie gave him a smile. She was particularly pleased that he seemed to have a special empathy with Boots. I'd feel torn in half if they didn't like each other, she thought.

The pot of tea finished, Boots said he'd take a turn around the garden.

'A turn around the garden?' said Chinese Lady.

'Old familiar things have their appeal,' said Boots.

Rosie took the opportunity quite soon to corner him by the vegetable plot, leaving Polly and Chinese Lady to look after Matthew.

'Daddy old dear, I want to talk to you,' she said.

Boots surveyed her. Her turquoise blue dress was faultless. She looked exquisite. Boots thought what a delight she had always been to his eyes, right from her time as a deliciously enchanting child of five.

'I'm listening, Rosie,' he said.

'Yes, you've always done that, you've always listened to me,' said Rosie. 'Well, I want to listen to you now, I want you to tell me about the first time you made love to a woman.'

'I don't think I heard that,' said Boots.

'Yes, you did,' said Rosie, 'I'm going to be married and I'm innocent, excited and curious.'

'How old are you?' asked Boots.

'Just twenty-six, as you well know,' said Rosie.

'And you need to be told about love-making?' said Boots, gravity writ plain on his face, except that his eyes, even his impaired one, belied it. 'You need to be told how I got through my first experience?'

'I'd simply like to know,' said Rosie.

'Well, my first time was with a middle-class lady ambulance driver in France,' said Boots. 'Nineteen fifteen, if I remember right. She took me to a field of French clover in the moonlight, removed all her clothes, played the very devil with my

307

modesty, told me nothing at all about the birds and the bees, simply pointed me in the right direction and hummed "All The Nice Girls Love A Sailor" while it was happening, which lasted about as long as two rolls of thunder.'

Rosie's laughter bubbled.

'But it couldn't have been quite like that, it couldn't,' she said.

'Believe me, my mind was boggling,' said Boots. 'But the second time was better, I'll admit. I knew more about what I was doing then. Not a lot more, but enough.'

'But your feelings and your emotions,' said Rosie, 'they were affected, weren't they?'

'The feelings were all physical,' said Boots, 'and my personal belief is that you don't suffer deep emotions, Rosie, until you're experiencing your first time with someone you love. When I was sixteen, your Aunt Lizzy asked me to ask your grandma about what happened between newly-weds, exactly what it all came down to.'

'Daddy, you didn't ask, did you?' said Rosie.

'I don't think I would if I'd been twenty-six, but at sixteen you're a fount of ignorance and curiosity, and you burn with the need to know what adults know from experience,' said Boots. 'So I asked, and Chinese Lady told me to go and see the vicar. Then she said all I had to do was to remember to be nice to my eventual bride. That was all, be nice, she said.'

'So to make it as it should be, I tell Matt to be nice to me?' said Rosie.

'At your age and with your experience of life, even if not of love-making, I think you'll be able to get through it without having a nervous breakdown,' said Boots. 'Rely on Matt to help you enjoy your leap into the unknown. But haven't you ever talked to Polly?'

'Polly told me you close your eyes and think of your country,' said Rosie.

'She wasn't talking about what you and I are talking about,' smiled Boots.

'I know,' said Rosie. 'She was telling me about her years in France during the last war, when she let some soldiers make love to her because she felt so sad for them. She's spoken to me many times about that, and about how miserably unlucky she was not to have met you. I haven't asked how she felt when she made love with you as your wife.'

'Well, that's something just between Polly and me, isn't it, poppet?' said Boots.

'Do you love her?' asked Rosie.

'Yes,' said Boots.

'As much as Emily?' enquired Rosie.

'In a different way,' said Boots.

'How different? Tell me,' said Rosie.

'Emily was an undemanding woman on

the whole, Polly's challenging,' said Boots.

'And that makes her a more exciting woman?' suggested Rosie.

'All personable women of character are exciting in one way or another,' said Boots.

'Am I personable enough to be exciting to Matt?' asked Rosie.

Boots laughed.

'You can ask that at your age and with your looks?' he said.

'Well, you see, I love talking like this with you,' said Rosie. 'Daddy, you will take care if you should end up in the desert war one day, won't you?'

'I'll be taking care in an armchair behind the lines,' said Boots.

'I wouldn't bet on that,' said Rosie. 'Oh, damn the war, anyway, it's so much in the way of everything, and Lord knows who's going to win and how long it will last.'

'Hitler could shorten it for us if he went to war with Russia,' said Boots.

'What?' breathed Rosie. 'But Hitler has a pact with Stalin.'

'Hitler is a man who tears up pacts,' said Boots, 'and wouldn't think twice about tearing up this one. If he did, then Russia with its limitless manpower would become our ally. That would make winning far more likely than losing.'

'Would Hitler really go to war with Stalin?' asked Rosie.

'We're at the mercy of rumours, of course,' said Boots.

'Ordinary rumours or official rumours?' asked Rosie.

Boots smiled.

'Can't say, poppet, but they could mean watch out for summer fireworks,' he said. 'However, do me the favour of keeping this strictly to yourself.'

'Promise,' said Rosie, 'but heavens, old thing, what's Nana going to say if we all have to start cheering the Bolsheviks?' Everyone in the family knew that to Chinese Lady there had never been a scrap of difference between Stalin's Communists and Lenin's Bolsheviks, and she wouldn't have opened her door to any of them.'

'If it happens, and she hears the news on her wireless,' said Boots, 'she'll either reach for her smelling-salts or get rid of the set.'

'Someone will have to tell her that if Stalin comes in on our side, whether he wants to or not, we'll all have to learn to love him,' said Rosie. 'I don't think I'll risk telling her. You'll have to.'

Boots laughed. Rosie delivered a warm kiss on his cheek.

Clara, walking her patient, said, 'I know you hate the idea, Felicity, but you really should accept that you'll have to use a white stick to—'

'Oh, shut up,' said Felicity.

'Feeling rotten this afternoon?' said Clara.

'Well, I feel rotten every day, don't I?' said Felicity. 'I can't bloody well see, can I? If I've said that before, I'm saying it again.'

'If it helps, you can say whatever you like,' said Clara.

'Look here,' said Felicity, 'I'm going to be married, and I don't want to be one step away from uselessness.'

'You won't be, not by the time your wedding day arrives,' said Clara. 'You're not useless now, to start with.'

'Thanks,' said Felicity, 'you're getting to be my best chum.'

'I'd like to think you mean that,' said Clara.

'Get time off and come to the wedding,' said Felicity. 'Be my bridesmaid.'

'Is that a serious invitation?' asked Clara.

'Yes, be my help,' said Felicity. 'But don't dress up, wear something simple. And don't take too much notice of my foul moods.'

'I don't,' said Clara. 'I agree with Tim, you're a fighter.'

'Sammy love,' said Susie, when he arrived home that evening, 'you'd like someone very efficient as a new general manager, wouldn't you?'

'You've decided you'll come back and do the job?' said Sammy, giving Paula a cuddle.

'No, I've actually decided I can't,' said Susie. 'There's Paula and all her school holidays. So I spoke to Rachel.'

'Eh?' said Sammy.

'Mrs Rachel Goodman,' said Susie.

'Pardon?' said Sammy.

'Yes, we both know her, Sammy, and she'll be happy to help you out,' said Susie.

'Come again?' said Sammy.

'Rachel's a director, she knows the business and she'll know how to help you operate at a profit,' said Susie.

'Susie, are you telling me Rachel will take Miss Symonds' job?' asked Sammy, blinking.

'She'll start on Monday, if you like,' said Susie.

'Holy cows,' said Sammy. Paula wondered what holy cows were. Sammy came to. 'Well,' he said, 'I won't say Rachel wouldn't be useful, she's smart up top, like her dad. She's got the makings, that's for sure, but has she got your blessing, Susie?'

Susie looked him in the eye.

'I can trust you, can't I?' she said.

'On me soul, that's a question you don't ever need to ask,' said Sammy. 'You can trust me till the cows come home, Susie.'

'Crumbs,' said Paula, fascinated. She was used to the funny kind of talk that went on between her mum and dad, but this was the first time holy cows and cows coming home had been mentioned. 'Are they coming home here?' She tried to picture what it would be like. 'Holy cows,' she said.

'Paula?' Susie, in Sammy's lingo, was consternated. 'Paula?'

'Yes, Mummy?'

'What was that you said?'

'Only what Daddy said,' explained Paula. Well, she often quoted him, which was what caused her mum to suffer periodical consternation.

'I forbid it,' said Susie.

'Mummy, d'you mean me or Daddy?'

'I mean both of you,' said Susie.

'Yes, Mummy.'

'Sammy, your mother didn't bring you up to say what you shouldn't in front of little girls,' said Susie.

'Granted,' said Sammy.

'Daddy, what's holy cows, anyway?' asked Paula.

'Forbidden,' said Sammy.

'Well, I expect that's why I've never seen any at church,' said Paula.

Chapter Nineteen

That evening, after supper, at the invitation of Chinese Lady, various family members and friends turned up to meet Rosie's fiancé in advance of the wedding. Of the family, only Lizzy and Vi had had the pleasure so far.

Lizzy and Ned, together with Emma, Bobby and Helene, arrived first, then along came Tommy and Vi, with Vi's parents, old Aunt Victoria and Uncle Tom. Aunt Victoria always hoped to find something not to her liking within the realms of Chinese Lady's little world. She'd been very critical of Boots marrying Polly, and went on about it to Uncle Tom. She didn't, she said, expect Boots to cast off the memory of Emily so soon, seeing she'd always considered him the only gentleman in the family. She also said it was a bit of a shock that at their ages Boots and Polly were going to have a child. It wasn't very respectable, either. Uncle Tom, grown rebellious in his later years, told her to put a sock in it. If they hadn't got married, he said, the baby would be a little whatsit. Aunt Victoria went pale at what her neighbours might say about that, and hastily changed the subject.

Now she was finding it hard to fault Mr Chapman, who had healthy looks, pleasing manners and the kind of voice she vaguely associated with country squires. That was something to mention to neighbours in passing, a country squire.

Sammy and Susie put in an appearance, bringing little Paula with them. Five minutes later, Rachel and Lilian also turned up. Much to Rosie's amusement, she and Matthew found themselves surrounded by her intrigued relatives and friends. She did all the introductions, and he faced up to the music. The Adams men and women played their fiddles under his nose, as it were, and he sang all the right tunes. He really was splendid, thought Rosie, so natural in his manner, and not in the least at a loss with this extrovert, robust and life-loving family. They did love life, all of them, and showed they did. She was, delighted with the way Matt responded to them and to their questions, comments and quips. Eventually, Polly and Boots, deciding the man of the moment needed a breather, skilfully detached him from the benevolent inquisition.

'Well, Matt,' said Boots, 'd'you see what you're getting in addition to Rosie?'

'A large number of relatives?' said Matt.

'Yes,' smiled Polly. 'Well, you know there are more, don't you, some living in the West

316

Country and some serving in the Forces, and if I tell you they're all different in some ways but all the same generally, will that confuse you?'

'Yes, and does it confuse you?' said Matt.

'Oh, I'm an addict,' said Polly.

'I'm an untried recruit,' said Matt.

'I think you'll come to like the Company Commander,' said Boots.

'Your mother?' said Matthew.

'A jewel,' said Polly, 'and you can believe that, old bean.' Matthew, she thought, would find himself married into an extraordinary family headed by their Victorian matriarch. The Adamses did not stand off from one they accepted as their own. They enthusiastically embraced him or her. Matthew, however, might escape some of it if he and Rosie lived permanently in Dorset.

Sammy came up and addressed Matt breezily.

'What's your garage like, old man, and how's it doing?'

Matt said there were two garages, one in Dorchester owned by his father, one near Bere Regis owned by himself. Both were doing just enough business to keep going. Sammy said he trusted there were profitable prospects when the war was over. Matt said he'd eat his shirt buttons if he had to wait until after the war to make a profit.

317

'Are shirt buttons digestible?' asked Boots.

'Not as much as a saddle of Dorset lamb,' said Matt.

'Haven't seen one of those since the outbreak of war,' said Sammy.

'Well, if you're ever down our way,' said Matt, 'I'll let you have a couple of rabbits as a consolation prize. I'll drop them into your hat.'

'Why his hat?' smiled Polly.

'When he gets home, he'll be able to show his little girl where rabbits come from,' said Matt. 'Out of a hat.'

The little girl, Paula, skipped over at that moment to put herself beside Boots, a favourite with her. She extended a hand. Boots took it and gave it a gentle squeeze.

'Hello, poppet,' he said, and she smiled up at him. He thought if Polly gave him one like her, he'd enjoy his old age. 'Meet a new uncle, Uncle Matthew. Matt, say hello to Paula.'

'Hello,' said Matt.

'Oh, hello,' said Paula. 'Please, d'you do tricks?'

'Only this one,' said Matt. He took his hand out of his pocket, reached and, much to Paula's delight, brought a penny out of her ear. He gave it to her.

'Again, again,' said Paula, and he repeated the trick, making her richer by two pennies. 'Crumbs, I like you, Uncle Matthew,' she said. Then, enquiringly, 'D'you know about holy cows?'

'Oh, me gawd,' said Sammy in a palsied aside, and thanked his lucky stars that Susie hadn't heard.

'Holy cows?' said Matt.

'Yes, Daddy talks about them,' said Paula.

'Some new kind of business contacts, I suppose,' said Boots.

'With haloes?' said Polly.

'Us down in Dorset don't get to see too many cows of that kind,' said Matt.

'I've never seen them in our church, either,' said Paula. 'They're forbidden. Mummy says so.'

'So kindly don't mention them, young Plum Pudding,' said Sammy. 'Matt, can you make money catching and selling rabbits?'

'Hardly,' said Matt.

'Not much of a sideline, then?' said Sammy.

'Not much,' said Matt.

'I sympathize,' said Sammy.

'Why?' asked Polly.

'Well,' said Sammy, 'some sidelines can be highly lucrative, y'know, Polly.'

'Sammy, you old ratbag,' said Polly, 'sidelines might be fascinating to you, but they're irrelevant to the rest of us. The rest of us are only interested in some friendly but fiendish gadget that will blow Hitler and his Nazis sky-high. End of that hairy lot,

319

end of war. Enter peace and goodwill.'

'Well, I'll say this much,' said Sammy, 'peace and goodwill could do a lot for Adams Enterprises and Matt's garage.'

'And give the Land Army girls a chance to say goodbye to ploughs, cows, muck and breeches, and go home to their Sunday frocks,' said Matt.

'Happy thought, old scout,' said Polly.

Rachel and Lilian were talking to Rosie about Matthew.

'Rosie, having met him, I like him,' said Rachel.

'Ditto,' said Lilian. 'If I hadn't already found Bill, I'd look for one like Matthew. Where was it you said you discovered him?'

'In a country garage,' said Rosie.

'Under a car?' smiled Lilian.

'You met his legs first, Rosie?' said Rachel.

Rosie laughed.

'No, he was upright and on his feet,' she said.

'Lovely bloke,' said Lilian, refusing, like Rachel, to make any mention of the Dorset man's lameness. 'I'm happy for you, Rosie.'

Rachel caught Sammy's eye then. She detached herself, and up he came.

'I'm touched,' he said.

'My life, Sammy, you of all people?' said Rachel. 'Who touched you, and how much for?'

'Tck, Mrs Goodman, that's a bit naughty,'

said Sammy. 'I happen to be speakin' of your offer to work for the firm, which offer is very acceptable. Not that business is goin' to pot. On the contrary, our military contracts are humming. But the paperwork and the communicatin' that's always goin' on between us and the Government's Civil Servants can be considerably tryin' to yours truly, as well as takin' up time I could devote to post-war plans. If it wasn't for that, the business could run itself. Well, almost.'

'Sammy, I'd be glad to take on all the Civil Servants,' said Rachel.

'In triplicate?' said Sammy.

'Forms in triplicate proliferate?' said Rachel.

'If you mean what I think you do, you can say that twice over and some more,' said Sammy. 'I'm appreciative of what I know you can do for us. You can start Monday?'

'Happy to,' said Rachel.

'You're on,' said Sammy. Noting Susie was having a ladies' dialogue with Vi and Lizzy, he cleared his throat. 'Of course, always remembering you're a married wife and I've got a businessman's respectability to take care of.'

'Of course, Sammy,' said Rachel. She smiled. 'I cherish your respectability as much as I cherish my own. All the same, I'll enjoy being a cog in the wheels of Adams Enterprises.'

'Hope so,' said Sammy.

'At what salary?' asked Rachel.

'Friendly one?' said Sammy.

'Friendly on payday, businesslike otherwise,' said Rachel.

'Shall we discuss it on Monday?' said Sammy.

'With pleasure,' said Rachel. 'On the basis of five hundred a year?'

'Nothing friendly about that,' said Sammy.

'But businesslike?' said Rachel.

'Granted,' said Sammy. 'Um, what d'you think of Rosie's Dorset bloke?'

'Special,' said Rachel.

'How special?' asked Sammy.

'Enough to make him just the man for Rosie,' said Rachel.

'He's a bit hard-up,' said Sammy.

'What's that got to do with it?' asked Rachel.

'Ask me again next year,' said Sammy. 'That's if this island's still floating. You seen some of the holes the bombs have made? Overflowing with water. It's like the plugs have been pulled out. By the way, at the office, I'll be addressing you fairly constant as Mrs Goodman, and I daresay it'll do for you to call me sir.'

Rachel laughed.

'I understand, but you're still very droll, Sammy,' she said. Sammy let a grin come and go.

Boots had a chat with Bobby and Helene, wanting to know how it was that Helene, as a FANY officer, was attached to an artillery regiment.

'Special liaison duties,' said Bobby.

'Liaison between the regiment and what?' asked Boots.

'FANY,' said Bobby.

'I give up,' said Boots.

'Ah, so do I, many times,' said Helene. 'Yes, I am always giving up on Bobby. He is hopeless. You are much more sensible.'

'I'm not sure that's a compliment,' said Boots, 'since I know Polly considers sensible men pretty dull.'

'But you are not sensible like that,' said Helene, 'you are very pleasing.'

'If I'm in the way,' said Bobby, 'I'll push off.'

Helene laughed, and Boots thought these two shared an uncommon kind of togetherness. And what exactly did their indefinite leave mean? Helene had turned the conversation very adroitly from the subject of liaison. Boots, however, decided to mind his own business.

'Boots?' Vi detached him.

'Hello, Vi.' Boots had a great deal of affection for his two sisters-in-law, Susie because she was a roguish match for Sammy, and Vi because she was so equable and gentle-natured.

'Are you happy for Rosie?' asked Vi.

'Very,' said Boots.

'So am I,' said Vi. 'Matthew's really likeable, I think.'

'Well, if he's only half as likeable as you, Vi,' said Boots, 'no-one's ever going to quarrel with him.'

'Is that me you're talking about?' smiled Vi.

'Accept my compliments and blessings,' said Boots.

'Pleasured I'm sure,' said Vi.

At nine-thirty, a gradual departure of guests began. Air raids on London had diminished, but there was no permanent let-up, and everyone wanted to get home in case the Germans launched one tonight.

With Paula put to bed, Sammy confided to Susie that it might be a good idea next time they went down to Devon to take a look at Matt's garage on the way.

'What for?' asked Susie.

'Well, to see if it's genuine prospective and if a bit of capital is needed,' said Sammy.

'I forbid it,' said Susie.

'Susie, that sounds like a commandment,' said Sammy.

'Yes, I'm one of the Ten Commandments in this house,' said Susie.

'Granted,' said Sammy.

'So you can take that grin off your face,' said Susie.

'I like you, Susie, d'you know that?' said Sammy.

'Well, I like it that you like me,' said Susie, 'but you should be more worried about the war than Matthew's garage.'

Sammy went sober.

'I am, Susie, believe me,' he said, 'but my money's still on Churchill. It's got to be. Who else have we got? Further and also, I've an idea Winnie's a bit smarter than Adolf, and with more staying power.'

'That's not wishful thinking, is it?' said Susie.

'Well, if it is,' said Sammy, 'I put it to you again, Susie, who else have we got?'

'I know who you've got,' said Susie.

'Who?' asked Sammy.

'Me,' said Susie.

'Which makes me a fortunate bloke,' said Sammy, not for the first time.

'Yes, Sammy, I know,' said Susie for the umpteenth time.

'Well, you were right, Vi,' said Tommy, slipping into bed beside her when the day was over, 'he's got a nice touch of Dorset about him, a kind of farming gent.'

'He's excitin' too,' said Vi, 'don't you think so?'

'He don't excite me,' said Tommy, 'for which I'm thankful. If he did, I'd need a doctor.'

'Don't make me giggle,' said Vi. 'I meant I think Rosie would find him exciting. He's got something a bit sexy behind that smile of his.'

'He's got a garage,' said Tommy. 'Would Rosie find that a bit sexy?'

'No, you daft thing,' said Vi, 'garages aren't sexy. By the way, your mum's twice mentioned to me that she thinks he's a bit too hard-up to be ready for marrying Rosie.'

'Rosie can cope with not marrying a well-britched bloke,' said Tommy. 'She's never been in want, we all know that, but a bit of mild want won't worry her, and she'll 'ave her officer's pay till she leaves the Army. Anyway, Matt will make a go of things, I'll lay your best fur coat on it.'

'I don't have a fur coat,' said Vi.

'Would you like one, then?' asked Tommy.

'Nice of you, Tommy love, but I don't need one, especially not with a war on,' said Vi. 'I'd look like a profiteer's wife.'

'Like a cuddle instead, would you?' asked Tommy.

'Last time we arranged to have a cuddle,' said Vi, 'you got called out on ARP duties.'

'All right, I'll be quicker tonight,' said Tommy.

'If you don't mind,' said Vi, 'I like it better when you take your time.'

'He'll do,' said Ned to Lizzy.

'Yes, I think so too,' said Lizzy.

'So do I,' said Emma. 'Emphatically,' she added, then unconsciously echoed her Aunt Vi. 'He's sexy.'

'Sexy?' said Lizzy, who hadn't grown up in close communication with that word.

'Like Jonathan,' said Emma who, having discovered on her honeymoon just how exciting he was, lamented having to live a maiden's life. An empty bed was no fun at all.

'Like Jonathan?' said Lizzy.

'Yes, lovely,' said Emma.

Lizzy smiled.

'That's what sexy is?' she said.

'Ask Rosie after her honeymoon,' said Emma.

'I'll do no such thing,' said Lizzy.

'I'll ask her on your behalf,' said Ned.

'Don't you dare,' said Lizzy, and then thought that perhaps Ned could have been called sexy in his time.

'Mum, you're giggling,' said Emma.

'Me at my age?' said Lizzy. 'Of course I'm not.'

'I'm happy that there haven't been any air raids lately,' said Emma, and wondered if life was quiet for Jonathan at the moment. She was sure, when reading between the lines of his letters, that he was in the desert, facing the Afrika Korps.

Rosie's intended had been found acceptable all round. It was a fact that Rosie, although not a blood relation, had such a special place in the affections of the family that everyone had felt it necessary to make a keen study of her choice. It was a relief to be able to approve, even if Chinese Lady and Sammy both felt Matthew wasn't going to be able to keep her in style.

Polly and Boots retired to the bed from the spare room.

Tim was sailing north-east with the Commando raiding force, his mind on Felicity, on Rosie as well, and on the family weddings that were in the offing. Us Adamses, he thought, are a marrying lot. And seeing that Grandma and good old Dad have been twice married, it must be a bit of all right.

Major Lucas, even with the challenge of the Commandos' riskiest raid ahead, thought about Subaltern Eloise Adams, and toyed with the idea of smacking her bottom.

It was past midnight when the arsonist set fire to the place he had previously targeted as highly promising. Within minutes, he was exultant. Flames were beginning to leap. He exited by the way he had entered, through a window he had opened after smashing it. No-one heard the sound. The place stood alone, a quarter of a mile from the nearest habitation.

By the time he reached the front of the building the flames were roaring. Everything inside was inflammable. He took hold of his bike and retreated from the field of heat. He stood and watched, enthralled by the voracious nature of fire, which consumed all it touched.

The place was turning into a flaming hell. Wonderful. He could not stay long enough to witness total destruction, he had to be away before the blaze caught someone's attention. But he stood there, giddy with excitement and licking his lips.

Something exploded inside the building. A sliding door, closed and locked, burst apart and a great tongue of flame rushed and reached. It sucked at the arsonist, searing him. It embraced him. Something else exploded. He screamed as his clothes and hair caught alight. Blinded, he ran, but straight into a ball of fire, which turned him into a blazing orange torch.

'Boots, wake up.'

Boots awoke to the demanding whisper in his ear.

'Who's that?' he murmured.

'Me, of course,' breathed Polly. 'Did you think it was Emily, you stinker? Well, it could have been. This might be a different bed, but she's here again, doing her best to smother me.'

'Smother you?'

'Yes,' said Polly, 'I woke up with the bedclothes over my head. I never sleep like that, with my head smothered. She did it.'

'A delusion,' said Boots. 'But it's uncovered now, your head?'

'It is now, yes.'

'Good,' said Boots, 'let's give thanks we can both get back to sleep.'

'Oh, very funny, I don't think,' said Polly.

'Turn this way,' said Boots, and she turned and snuggled up. He put his arms around her. 'How's that as a cure for your imagination, Mrs Adams?'

'Promising,' murmured Polly. 'Oh!' she gasped a second later.

'What happened?' asked Boots.

'She pinched me, she pinched me!'

'Your bottom?' said Boots.

'Yes!'

'That was me,' said Boots.

'Oh, you fiend,' breathed Polly, 'you knew I'd think it was her.'

'It's curative, a pinch on the bottom,' said Boots.

'So's this,' said Polly, and bit his shoulder.

'Suffering cats, that's not a cure, it's a wound,' said Boots. 'And I think you're playing about.'

'In the middle of the night?' said Polly. 'I

suppose I could be imagining things, and I could be wrong about the bed. It could be the room, her room.'

'You'd like to change rooms?' said Boots.

'No, I'll put up with it, dear old thing, until the weekend's over,' murmured Polly. 'Would you like another bite?'

'Only if you'd like another pinch,' said Boots.

'I pass,' said Polly, and cast out the imps of her imagination. 'Would you like to know something?'

'Such as?'

'I like being in bed with you,' murmured Polly. Boots smiled sleepily. Polly was very much the feminine woman.

Chapter Twenty

The German corporal on lookout duty at the entrance to a Norwegian fjord blinked sleepy eyes. It was early morning and dark grey. Daylight wouldn't break for another hour or so. He looked again, then scanned the waters through his field glasses.

'*Mein Gott!*'

The dim outlines of ships passing the point shocked him. He rang the German harbourmaster's office at Vaargo port and reported to the duty officer the suspected presence of enemy warships in the fjord.

'No, no, they're merchant ships we're expecting today, a convoy.'

'But they're blacked out, showing no light, and don't look like merchantmen to me.'

'You're dreaming in the dark. Get off the line, you idiot.'

But ten minutes later the loud drone of approaching Hampden bombers alerted every unit of the strong German garrison. That garrison was the objective of the large Commando force. It was to be destroyed in a way that would demoralize the enemy and shake the commanders of every German stronghold guarding the west coast of

Norway and the harbouring fjords.

The RAF bombers were following the course of the British warships towards the particular anchorage of Vaargo. The German coastal batteries, quickly manned following the sounding off of air raid sirens, began firing, showering the sky with lethal flak.

The British destroyers were escorting troopships packed with Commandos, and their stealthy approach to the port had been unhindered through the unmined waters used by Germany convoys. The destroyers, reaching their destination at a prescribed distance from the harbour, manoeuvred to take up positions and begin a bombardment. The troopships edged forward inshore to discharge landing craft under the covering fire of the naval guns, which opened up the moment the warships were at the ready. Explosive shells began to pulverize German defences, the positions of which had been photographed weeks ago by RAF reconnaissance.

The early morning that had been humdrum and quiet in Vaargo a short time ago was no longer so. Above the disturbing drone of approaching British bombers, what was left of the quiet was being shattered by the violent noise of the bombardment.

The training exercises the Commandos had

endured and survived in Scotland were put swiftly into practice, the Navy and the RAF participating according to plan and briefing. The landing craft, touching water, headed speedily for the port amid the covering fire from the warships. German flak, however, continued to rake the sky and to threaten the oncoming Hampdens.

'Bloody hell,' breathed Tim, peering ahead and watching the flash of exploding shells, 'I think this is serious stuff.'

'Yes, count yourself a happy man, you lucky bugger,' said Major Lucas.

'Major, I'm not in the mood for jokes,' said Tim.

'Who is?' grated Major Lucas, adrenalin surging.

Their ploughing craft, with others, was only a hundred yards short of the landing point when a dozen red Very lights were fired by the commander of the assault forces. They represented the signal for the destroyers to cease firing and for the Hampdens to come in and drop smoke bombs. The guns fell quiet. The planes arrived on cue, and at such a low altitude that the men in the landing craft instinctively ducked as the bombers passed overhead. The roar of the planes was deafening, their bombs a fiery threat to the defending Germans. One after the other, and amid a hail of flak, the Hampdens

roared in and unleashed their loads. 1
bomb that fell and struck created an ins
ball of phosphorous fire which billow
upwards. A platoon of German soldiei
rushing to join others in the manning o
strongpoints, scattered frantically from the
onslaught of a low-flying Hampden. A fire
bomb hurtled down and exploded. Several
Germans died hideously.

Clouds of thick smoke, born of the fiery
bombs, began to roll. Flak tore into a
Hampden coming in from over the sea. It
fatally crippled the bomber. It wavered,
slipped sideways and went to its doom. One
of its bombs plummeted down and
exploded in ghastly fashion in the middle of
a landing craft. Commandos burned to
instant death in the cascading fire, and the
men in other craf watched in horror.

'Christ Almighty,' breathed Tim, appalled.

'Holy God,' said Major Lucas, and
clenched his teeth. This was red and bloody
war, the first real test of courage and
fighting spirit for the Commandos.

The remaining landing craft went on,
impelled by orders and discipline. The craft
beached, and out of each leapt a storm of
Commandos. They rushed forward, firing
from the hip at Germans running to
assembly points. Tim and Major Lucas, at
the head of their detachment, engaged with
darting shadows, shadows that resolved into

resolute defenders. The fighting men of the garrison were first-class combat troops, tenacious, experienced and fully equipped. They were a match for the British Commandos who, although superbly trained, had met relatively inferior opposition on their previous raids.

All the same, the Commandos, rough, tough and ruthless, had known that sooner or later they were going to come up against a formidable enemy, and their detachments stormed into the town to meet the challenge. The battle was joined in the streets and around individual houses. From the houses the German fire-power was deadly. Every burst from a British Sten or tommy-gun brought forth a ferocious response. British grenades exploded to smash walls, doors and windows, German grenades exploded at the feet of rushing Commandos amid the rolling smoke.

A house that had been turned into a defence post because of its position, came under attack. A fireworks display resulted as guns and grenades were used by the assailants and defenders alike. A Commando slapped a high explosive charge on a door. He was riddled by a German machine-gun operating at a window. The door disappeared, fragmented by the charge, and fire and smoke filled the passage. Tim, bent double, raced along the front of the house and flung in a fire bomb. It finished the house, which burst into flame, and Germans jumped or fell from windows to be either shot or taken prisoner.

Daylight came with the Commandos and the Germans locked in pitched battles in the streets or fighting at close quarters in house by house conflict, the latter a particularly ferocious form of dealing out death.

Casualties were high. Men blown up by grenades in the streets or blown from the windows of houses became dead bodies while still in motion. Nevertheless, the Commandos were achieving a blood-and-thunder advance under the driving inspiration of bold and mettlesome leadership. Warehouses went up in fire and flame, command posts were smashed, gun batteries put out of action. The German troops, shocked and surprised by the powerful weaponry of the Commandos, nevertheless fought every inch of the way, and if they had to scramble and scatter at times, they quickly regrouped.

A thick-roofed house, used as a battery headquarters, was fully manned by German troops, and they met the assault of Major Lucas and his detachment with concentrated fire-power. A Commando, hit, fell and sprawled, and the rest of the detachment dived for cover. From cover they raked the door and windows with bullets.

'Blow the bloody door in!' shouted Major Lucas.

The nearest man, Sergeant Watts, raised a head and an arm, a grenade in his hand. He was immediately shot through the head. The bullet blew his brains out, the grenade exploded under his body and Tim experienced a sickening blow at the gruesome death of a man he had known since joining the Troon group. He burst forward, and the rest of the detachment poured fire to cover him. He pulled the pin of a grenade and hurled it, then wheeled fast to make for the corner of the house and out of sight of the defenders. On the other side of the street a wall exploded and bricks flew. One struck Tim on his left shoulder. The impact, like the kick of a mule, spun him round and he fell on his back just as a German machine-pistol let go a burst. The bullets hit empty air above him.

A dozen men from another detachment arrived to reinforce Major Lucas's men, and the assault became savage. The Commandos fought their way in through the blown door. The house was taken and six surviving Germans were made prisoner. The shattered building was then completely destroyed. Immediately following that, Major Lucas, his right hand grazed by a bullet, ran to look down at Tim, who had moved himself clear of the melee, and was sitting with his back against a pile of rubble, grimaces of pain showing through his grease mask.

'For Christ's sake, Tim, did you have to get in the way?' grated the sweating Major, his hand dripping blood.

'Thanks for your understanding,' breathed Tim, conscious of a damaged shoulder, 'I'm sickening for something I'm not going to like.'

Major Lucas, regretting the disabling wound of a young man he regarded as a fighting soldier and a treasured comrade, ordered him to walk back to the harbour, while he himself rejoined what was left of his detachment.

In the early afternoon, after hours of street battles had ended in favour of the British, their withdrawal began. Landing craft were used to take off wounded men, German prisoners, volunteer Norwegians, and weary but triumphant survivors, transporting all to the assault vessels, where doctors and surgeons were kept busy attending to the wounded, the more serious cases given priority. Most of the dead were left to be buried by the Germans, and there were grim faces among the British commanders at the high number of men lost, among which were all too many quality officers, the kind who were born leaders of troops trained to attack.

The raid, however, had produced the hoped-for result. All primary objectives had been smashed or blown up. German admin blocks, the German barracks and their troops' living accommodation, warehouses, ammunition stores, defence guns, tanks radio headquarters, transport and other targets had come under the hammer of destruction. Further, more than a few Germans had been taken prisoner, and there was a grim satisfaction among the weary Commandos at the obvious disbelief showing in their expressions. It was the disbelief of men who, for the first time since their awesome Panzer divisions rolled unchecked into Poland, had experienced an upset of their sense of German invincibility.

The British withdrawal was carried out speedily and efficiently, the Navy as unflappable as ever in its supportive role. The RAF, true to its spirit of bravado, had given invaluable help, although it had lost Hampdens. It was the death of the crews, however, that mattered more than the machines.

Major Lucas, having discovered from a sick bay orderly that Tim had suffered nothing worse than a fractured collarbone, was nevertheless having to cope with the painful knowledge that half of his detachment were casualties, including four dead.

Hitler was put into one of his rages by the success of the British assault on the fortified port of Vaargo. It convinced him Churchill was planning a wholesale invasion of Norway. He issued new directives concerning the defence of that country. The directive compelled the German Navy to move part of its fleet indefinitely to Norwegian coastal waters, and forced his Army to detach thousands of men from the divisions serving in occupied France. It meant, eventually, that nearly four hundred thousand German troops were to spend tied-up years in Norway waiting for an invasion that existed only in Hitler's fevered imagination.

It gave Churchill reason to smile and to strengthen his belief in the worth of the Commandos as a force capable of demoralizing the enemy.

He had needed a lift, for Crete had gone and another British force had had to be evacuated.

'I'm damned sorry,' said Boots. 'Not for him, for Matt.'

'Not much of a wedding present, I agree,' said Mr Chapman.

'I'll get him to phone you as soon as he comes in,' said Boots.

'Thank you, Mr Adams,' said Mr Chapman. 'It's a hard knock for Matthew, put out of business by an arsonist, but he's no weakling, and I'm sure he won't ask for a postponement of the wedding. My wife and I, and my daughter and son-in-law, will see you then. We look forward to meeting all of you.'

'It'll be our pleasure,' said Boots.

'Thank you.' Mr Chapman rang off, and Boots returned to the kitchen, where he acquainted Polly and his mother with the reason for Mr Chapman's call.

'Lord,' breathed Chinese Lady, 'it's left Matthew with nothing to call his own. I don't know what he and Rosie can do now.'

'Get married,' said Boots, 'and fight the consequences together.'

'I'm devastated for Matt,' said Polly, 'and so will Rosie be. I only hope the garage was fully insured. But would it cover arson?'

'If it was comprehensive enough,' said Boots.

They talked while waiting for Rosie and Matt to return. It was noon before they appeared, when Boots in sober vein put

344

them in the unhappy picture.

'Oh, no,' breathed Rosie, stricken.

Matt, jaw tight, said, 'Not the best morning of my life.'

'Your father would like you to ring him,' said Boots.

'Thanks, I'll do that now,' said Matt, and went to make the call.

'It's very troubling,' sighed Chinese Lady, thinking Rosie's future looked bleak. 'It's not what ought to have happened to a nice man like him.'

'It's filthy,' said Rosie, 'but he'll come out fighting, Nana.'

'Rosie old thing,' said Polly, 'I'll bet my best shirt on that.'

'There's got to be an answer,' mused Boots.

When Matt returned he said his father had confirmed everything, including the fact that the police were sure an arsonist was responsible.

'Not good, blow my socks off if it is,' he said, 'and do I get the impression you're all in mourning for me?'

'We've all got long faces?' said Polly. 'Well, frankly, the death of your garage should be mourned.'

'We're all very sorry,' said Chinese Lady.

'I'm sorrier for my mechanics, Ben and Josh, than for myself,' said Matt. 'The old codgers are out of work until I can rebuild.'

345

'I'm sick,' said Rosie, 'I like those old codgers.'

'Matt, what insurance did you have?' asked Boots.

'Pretty fair do's,' said Matt. 'It'll take care of rebuilding costs and also pay sixty-five per cent of my mechanics' wages for a year or until the place is operating again inside a year. I'm a fanatic about adequate insurance.'

'How will you go about getting the garage rebuilt?' asked Polly.

'Fair old question, that,' said Matt. 'My chief problem is labour and materials. I'm not sure the rebuilding of a garage would count as urgent or even necessary, unless I could twist someone's arm.'

'Is Sammy into black market operations?' asked Polly.

'If he is,' said Chinese Lady, 'I'll have something to say to him.'

'Any port in a storm, Nana,' said Rosie, 'and I don't mind turning a blind eye in a good cause. Would your rebuilding be a good cause, Matt?'

'Only if the repair of tractors and farm machinery counted for something,' said Matt. 'If not, I'll offer my qualifications to an aircraft or tank-building factory.'

Rosie made a face. She thought Matt had much more to offer his war-torn country than factory work. His education, his talents and his natural intelligence fitted him for something far better, as long as it wasn't behind a desk.

'Something's got to be done,' said Chinese Lady, and looked at Boots who, in a crisis, was always the one the family turned to.

'I've a phone call to make,' said Boots.

'Daddy, are you ticking?' asked Rosie hopefully.

'Dashed if he isn't,' said Polly, 'I can hear his little wheels turning.'

'What did I say? Only that I needed to make a phone call,' said Boots.

'What about?' asked Polly.

'Army business,' said Boots.

'I still think I can hear a tick-tock,' said Polly.

'Polly old love,' said Boots, 'would you help Matt to a Scotch?'

'Love to,' said Polly. Boots smiled and disappeared into the study. 'Fancy a Scotch, Matthew?' smiled Polly.

'Lead me to it,' said Matt.

'This way,' said Polly, and led him to the drinks cabinet in the dining-room.

'Oh, Rosie, a letter came for you by the midday post,' said Chinese Lady. 'It's there, on the mantelpiece. I think I'd best start getting some lunch.'

Rosie took the letter up to her room. She felt she needed to re-orientate herself. She read the letter with her mind mostly on

Matt's problem, but the contents jerked at her consciousness and began to stun her. At the end she sat heavily down and read the letter again. It was from Arnold, Musgrove and Stanley, solicitors of High Street, Godalming, Surrey.

Dear Lieutenant Adams,

It is with sincere and profound regret that we have to convey to you the sad news that your father, Colonel Sir Charles Armitage, fell in action at Tobruk while leading a counter-attack against units of the German Army. For your consolation, we trust, his gallantry was recorded at length in despatches, and there will be a posthumous citation and medal for his outstanding bravery.

We have to inform you that his house and estate will pass to his brother, Bernard Armitage. As you know, Sir Charles's wife died some months ago, and as you also know, you are his sole issue. Out of his personal fortune, he has bequeathed you the sum of Twenty-Five Thousand Pounds, and if you will be so kind as to get in touch with the undersigned and subsequently present yourself at these offices with proof of your identity, we shall be pleased to make the arrangements that will result in crediting you with said amount in due course.

We wish to amplify our regrets at the tragic loss of your courageous father and to send you our deepest sympathy.

The letter was signed by Arnold Harvey, senior partner, the solicitor consulted by Charles Armitage after he had discovered the existence of Rosie, his child by a woman of shallow emotions and vain ambitions.

'Oh, my God,' breathed Rosie, shocked by the death of her natural father and incredulous at the amount he had left her. Had he cared for her as much as that? For all that she had kept in touch and established a quite affectionate relationship with him, she did not deserve a gift of this kind. It would make her a rich woman. It would make her and Matthew rich. Matthew knew everything about her natural father, he knew everything about her. She had told him everything.

Sadness touched her. She had never denied the obvious, that her natural father had been a distinguished and extremely likeable man. Simply, however, he had never meant as much to her as her adoptive father, whom she had adored as a girl and still loved deeply. But it really was sad, her natural father killed in action. Why had he left her so much when she had given him so little?

She came to at the sound of Polly calling her from down below. She had never worried about money, or about having more than others. Twenty-five thousand pounds was almost an embarrassment. But not if she considered how it would help Matthew after the loss of his garage and the work he liked so much. He enjoyed taking engines to pieces and fixing them up as good as new. Without stopping for further thought, she gave in to an unusual impulse. She rushed out to the landing and called.

'Polly?'

'Come on down, old thing, lunch sandwiches are on the table,' said Polly.

'Will you ask Matthew to come up here first, Polly? I need to talk to him. Then we'll come down together.'

After a few seconds, Polly said, 'The gent in question is on his way, ducky.'

Matt, arriving on the landing, said, 'Rosie?'

'Come in here,' said Rosie, and took him into her bright and attractive bedroom.

'Don't tempt me,' he said.

'No, I'm going to tell you something,' said Rosie, unusually flushed. 'Matthew darling, you'll never believe – oh, the tragic news before the incredible.' She told him of the death of her natural father at Tobruk and then of his bequest to her. 'I'm terribly sad about his death,' she said, 'and stunned at what he left me, but it's a silver lining, isn't it? Matthew, we're rich. You need have no more worries about the garage.'

She pushed the letter into his hand, and he

glanced at it.

'I can see you're rich yourself, Rosie,' he said.

'Matt, we both are. Even if it's terribly sad that it's come about through the death of Sir Charles, it's a wonderful wedding present for the two of us, isn't it?'

'Rosie, it's yours,' said Matt.

'Ours as soon as we're married,' said Rosie.

'No, Rosie,' said Matt, 'it was left to you, to make you independent–'

'Independent?' said Rosie. 'That isn't what marriage is about, me independent of you, or you independent of me. Marriage is about togetherness and being dependent on each other for all kinds of things, love, companionship, friendship, help and comfort.'

'I mean I think your natural father wanted to make sure you were financially independent for the rest of your life,' said Matt.

'My God, you're being stuffy at a time like this?' said Rosie.

'I don't think so,' said Matt.

'Well, I do,' said Rosie. 'You're being stuffy and old hat, and letting silly pride ruin your commonsense.'

'I hope you don't mean that.'

'I do mean it,' said Rosie, temper rising. 'I never say anything I don't mean.'

'Well, damn my boots if you can't see the embarrassment of a man who's suddenly found himself with nothing and just as suddenly's given the news that the woman he's going to marry is an heiress,' said Matt.

'I wouldn't take that attitude myself if the situation were reversed,' said Rosie. 'If someone left you a large amount of money, I'd be happy for you and happy for both of us.'

'As it stands, it's not the same,' said Matt.

'I don't see why not,' said Rosie angrily. 'It solves problems for us, doesn't it?'

'It doesn't solve the problem I've got,' said Matt, 'the problem of suitable work, work that ought to be a contribution to the war effort. Rosie, you don't honestly think I like the idea of being supported by my wife, do you?'

'I honestly think it bloody-minded of you to put it like that,' said Rosie, disgusted that he had made her lose her temper. 'Be stuffy, then, be old-fashioned and proud and Victorian, and I hope your cottage roof falls on your head and knocks some sense into you. Goodbye.'

'Goodbye? Where are you going, then?' asked Matt.

'To lose myself in the garden for the time it takes you to pack and leave,' breathed Rosie. 'I know what marriage means to me, it means what it has meant to Boots, to Uncle Sammy and Aunt Susie and – oh, to all of them. To you it only means being independent of each other, and it'll never work, not for me.' She rushed again, down the stairs, out of the house and round the side of it into the back garden.

'Blow my head off,' said Matt, 'that was Rosie, that whirlwind? Hares and hounds, I need another Scotch.'

Down he went. He bumped into Boots, who was just coming from the study. He spoke to him, but not about another Scotch.

In the garden, Rosie trembled with anger, disappointment and the humiliating knowledge that she had lost her temper for the first time in her life.

'Rosie?'

She turned. Boots was there, noting her expression and the glitter in her blue eyes.

'I warn you I'm not at my best,' she said.

'Let me say I'm sorry about the death of your father–'

'You're my father!' Rosie shot the words at him.

'About Sir Charles, then,' said Boots gently. 'Matthew showed me the letter. I understand there's been an argument.'

'Yes, during which I found out he puts a greater value on stupid pride than he does on me,' said Rosie. 'I'm sick. I'm sick because he made me lose my temper. Have you ever known me do that, lose my temper and shout at someone?'

'Did you shout at Matthew?' asked Boots.

353

'Yes, when I said goodbye.'

'Was this a good time to speak to him, poppet? To offer him all you had so soon after he'd been reduced to having nothing?'

'If you're going to be wise at my expense,' said Rosie, 'I'll hate it. I'd have expected faithful support from you of all people.'

'Rosie, you have my faithful support and always will,' said Boots. 'Is a suggestion that you were hasty a disloyal arrow?'

'Make allowances, please,' said Rosie, 'I'm still in a temper.'

'When you said goodbye to Matthew—'

'When I shouted goodbye?' said Rosie.

'Was that to tell him the wedding's off?' asked Boots.

'Yes,' said Rosie through clenched teeth.

'I can't believe you'd make that kind of mistake,' said Boots.

'The mistake isn't mine,' said Rosie. 'I intend, by the way, to tell the solicitors to give that money to a home for fallen women.'

'Rosie, Rosie,' said Boots, and laughed. Rosie stiffened.

'You think the situation is funny?' she said.

'Not to fallen women, I suppose,' said Boots, 'but your temper is, Rosie love. It's not you, poppet, and it won't last. By the way, I have to talk to Matthew. Will you come with me?'

'No,' said Rosie, 'I'll be busy shredding my wedding gown.'

354

'If you see that as the act of a woman scorned,' said Boots, 'you're even more in love than I thought.'

'Would I shred my wedding gown if I were?' said Rosie.

'Yes, you'd do exactly that in these circumstances,' said Boots.

Polly came out.

'Rosie old sport, Matthew's trying to work out what hit him,' she said.

'Lover's quarrel,' said Boots.

'Yes, I know,' said Polly. 'Rosie, you dear thing, what's your next move?'

'Something to do with mangling her wedding gown,' said Boots.

'I'll scream if you make one more joke,' said Rosie.

'Oh, dear,' said Polly. 'Well, never mind, buck up, old thing, storm in a teacup and all that. Boots is going to talk to Matthew about a career in the Army.'

'What?' said Rosie.

Boots did some explaining.

Chapter Twenty-Two

Chinese Lady, getting very touchy about the fact that the lunchtime sandwiches hadn't yet tempted anyone to the table, was talking to Matthew in the hall without getting any sense from him about who was where and what was going on. Matthew wasn't prepared at this stage to let this redoubtable old lady know that he and Rosie had had a serious disagreement.

'Is something else worrying you besides your garage?' asked Chinese Lady kindly.

'Something else?' said Matt.

'Where's Rosie?'

'Here she is,' said Matt, as Boots, Polly and Rosie, in from the garden, came into the hall via the kitchen.

Chinese Lady, turning, said, 'Could somebody tell me what's going on?'

'I need to talk to Matthew,' said Boots.

'Hello again, Matthew,' said Polly. Matthew responded, then said hello to Rosie.

'Hello,' said Rosie coolly, 'are you the plumber?' And she went through to the parlour.

'What did Rosie say that for?' asked Chinese Lady.

356

'Oh, she likes plumbers,' said Polly. 'None of us can do without them.'

'Matthew's not a plumber,' said Chinese Lady. 'I think something's going on that I won't like.'

'Oh, it's all right, Maisie, let's leave it to Boots,' said Polly sweetly. She found it extraordinary to be so fascinated with the ups and downs of the Adams family. Even more extraordinary was the stimulation she derived from now being one of them, having happily exchanged her upper class environment for that of these gregarious suburbanites, who had no hang-ups about their cockney antecedents. The fact was, of course, she had always felt she and Boots were made for each other, that somehow Emily's place in his life had been an act of usurpation. 'Join us in the parlour, do.'

Chinese Lady followed her into the parlour, and Boots took Matthew into the study, where he immediately opened the dialogue.

'Sorry about your disagreement with Rosie, Matt.'

'Well, I had to let you know,' said Matt. 'Damned if I thought my argument would upset Rosie as much as it did.'

'Well, old chap,' said Boots, 'I think you can sort it out on a give-and-take basis. It's the only thing that consistently works, give and take.'

'In this case, Rosie gives and I take?' said Matt wryly.

'In this case, if I were you, I'd start with a friendly chat,' said Boots, 'but not until I've discussed something with you.'

'Well, I hope I can give you my attention,' said Matt. 'At the moment, I'm at sixes and sevens. It's a fair old swine, I tell you.'

'You love Rosie, don't you?' said Boots.

'More than I can put into words,' said Matt.

'Do try a friendly chat,' said Boots. 'Now, you're a holder of the I.Mech.E. certificate, aren't you?'

'Right,' said Matt.

Boots said that made him a top man in his field, an expert, and now that REME was being set up from the old RAOC, they could do with any number of such engineers. Matt pointed out he was an expert with a lame leg. No problem, said Boots. There will be, said Matt, when it comes to trying to get an Army boot on. Boots laughed.

'Still no problem, not in today's Army,' he said. 'We've got men who could alter a boot to fit an elephant.'

'Are you saying that a company of Royal Electrical and Mechanical Engineers would accept me?' asked Matt.

'They wouldn't look hard for an excuse to turn you down,' said Boots, 'and as a member of the Institute of Mechanical

Engineers you'd go in as a staff-sergeant at least, and possibly as a lieutenant.'

'Blow my damned head off, are you serious?' asked Matt. 'I was turned down by all the Services at the beginning of the war.'

'The beginning of the war in the eyes of most oldtime recruiting officers was only a resumption of the Great War,' said Boots, 'a war for footsloggers marching to their trenches. But this war is being fought mechanically, with wheels, tracks and engines. Wheels and engines are your forte, Matt, and even if you could get your garage rebuilt overnight, you'd still have more to offer by way of the REME than repairing farm machinery. Does the prospect of serving with a REME unit appeal to you?'

'Damn right it does,' said Matt, 'but this leg of mine is still going to raise some questions, isn't it?'

'The REME personnel have a maintenance role, not a footslogging one,' said Boots. 'You might be called on to fire a rifle in an emergency. You could manage that, obviously. Can you run?'

'Pretty well and after a fashion,' said Matt.

'The BEF ran after a fashion last year,' said Boots, 'all the way to Dunkirk, cripples, wounded and ablebodied. That was a case of he who fights and runs away lives to fight another day. Matt, the Army can use you. I could contact Colonel Fullerton, CO of

33rd REME at Bovington, about arranging an interview for you. I've already sounded him out, on the phone a little while ago.' He smiled. 'Bovington, as you know, is in Dorset.'

'Have you discussed this with Rosie?' asked Matt.

'I told her and Polly that I intended to have this talk with you,' said Boots, 'but it's your entitlement to consult with Rosie about it. I've a feeling she won't argue, providing you let her know she's – um–' Boots smiled again. 'Um, the light of your life. I think women like a turn of phrase of that kind, even intellectual women like Rosie and Polly. Right, then, if you can get the emotional sixes and sevens sorted out, and if you're willing to be interviewed at Bovington, I'll start the ball rolling.'

'This to me is on a par with meeting a Martian,' said Matt, 'but I'd be Dorset's prime idiot if I ducked out, damn me I would. I just hope the ball won't come to a stop against my gammy leg.'

'Irrelevant,' said Boots.

'My leg?' smiled Matt, liking Rosie's easy-mannered adoptive father. He was coming to a full understanding of why she was so attached to him. 'This old limb?'

'Fetch up, old man,' said Boots, 'it's your expertise the Army needs, and it's Army expertise that will fit you with a left boot inside twenty-four hours. In any case, if you've lived with your leg for years, the Army will live with it for the duration.'

'Fix up the interview, Major Adams,' said Matt.

'There's one more thing I'd like to mention,' said Boots. 'About Rosie's inheritance.'

'Go ahead,' said Matt.

Somehow, Rosie had lost the company of Polly and Chinese Lady. Somehow, she had arrived at the stage of being alone in the parlour when Matt entered. He closed the door. Rosie, reading a woman's magazine, looked up from an armchair.

'Rosie–'

'The plumber again, I see,' said Rosie.

'Shall we talk?' asked Matt.

'About plumbing?' said Rosie.

'About why you're giving me a fair old headache,' said Matt.

'Take an aspirin,' said Rosie, and hid her face behind the magazine.

'I'd like to make a suggestion,' said Matt. 'Don't give your inheritance to a dog's home–'

'A home for fallen women,' said Rosie, 'and someone's been talking to you.'

'Your father, Major Adams,' said Matt. 'He informed me your Uncle Sammy means to form a property company, to buy up

361

bombed sites in shopping centres and develop them after the war. Why not invest the money with him? You've told me yourself that he's one of the sharpest businessmen this side of London. Your father seems to think the postwar return on your investment would be pretty good.'

'Do you have a personal interest in my inheritance?' asked Rosie.

'I can't say I don't,' said Matt. 'It could add up to us being able to buy a beautiful house in Wimborne Minster after the war.'

'Us?' said Rosie, eyeing him from under frowning lashes. 'I think you'd better speak in a way I can clearly understand, Mr Chapman.'

'Clearly understand, right,' said Matt, and chose to take off cockney vernacular to an exaggerated extent. 'Well, yer know, Rosie, it ain't just the dibs, bless yer, it's yer blue mince pies, yer warm bosom, yer fair looks and yer first-class tent pegs, which I ain't seen the like of since me old man took me to a circus and showed me what a fair young piece of female sculpture ridin' an elephant looked like in spangles and fancy tights. Lord love yer, Rosie, me eyeballs near fell out. Might I be so bold as to ask if you've ever worn spangles and fancy tights, and if you've got a photograph of same?'

Rosie came out of her unreceptive state and shrieked with laughter.

'You clown, you can't do cockney,' she said.

'No good?' said Matt. 'Well, I'll 'ave one more go and inform yer with genuine sincerity that you're the light of me gorblimey life, and I'll put me 'ead in me own gas oven if yer don't marry me.'

Rosie, laughing, jumped to her feet.

'Oh, mister,' she said, 'would yer give us a kiss and would yer cuddle me warm bosom that was mentioned in yer first speech, would yer do that, mister?'

'Strike a light, not 'alf I won't,' said Matt.

He went into action.

'Crikey, me respectability,' said Rosie a minute later. 'You ain't decent, Matt Chapman, specially when we ain't 'ardly married yet.'

'Ruddy blimey, ain't we?' said Matt.

Rosie's laugh was of pure delight.

'Love you, you stinker,' she said.

'Bless yer,' said Matt, 'so can I forget me old gas oven?'

'Yes, if you'll cuddle me warm bosom some more,' said Rosie.

All was forgiven in the exhilaration of playing cockney lovers.

Matt said he understood she knew about the possibility of her father getting him a REME interview. Rosie said to tell her everything Boots had discussed with him, so Matt recounted the conversation, and Rosie listened and made little intercessions. She said oh, yes, what a splendid idea. She said my word, yes, REME would want his expertise. She said if Boots was sure they'd take him, then she was sure too. She also said he must never make her lose her temper again, never.

'Ah, well,' said Matt, 'men be all of a cussed kind, and women be all of a sweet kind, but when storms blow strong, the way a wench goes on, weren't never what men had in mind.'

'Women are gracious,' said Rosie. 'Well, I am.'

'Sweet devil more like,' said Matt.

'Look who's talking,' said Rosie.

'Did I do something?' asked Matt.

'Only nearly everything,' said Rosie, 'and in my grandma's parlour and all.'

'Well, blow my hat off,' said Matt, 'and us not hardly married yet.'

Bobby and Helene were talking to Lizzy over a pot of tea. Lizzy was nothing if not a replica of her mother in her belief that any time was a pot-of-tea-time, and Helene was now used to English tea and its refreshing element. Lizzy thought not for the first time how fit and healthy these two young people looked. She also thought how they never stopped engaging in their own kind of cross-talk, with Helene insisting Bobby was still a crazy man.

When Bobby went up to his room to change into casual wear, Lizzy put a question to Helene.

'You're so funny together, you two,' she said, 'what d'you think of each other?'

'We think wonderful things of each other,' said Helene.

'D'you mind me asking if you're in love?'

'But of course, Mrs Somers, very much,' said Helene.

'And?' said Lizzy.

'And we are very happy together,' said Helene, strictly forbidden to mention the real purpose of their comradeship.

Well, that's nice, thought Lizzy, but there's no mention of marriage.

'Do you and Bobby have any plans?' she asked.

'Yes, many,' said Helene. She smiled. 'Also, my parents like your crazy son very much. I write to my aunt in Switzerland sometimes, hoping she will let them know how I am.'

'You must miss them,' said Lizzy.

'Ah, *c'est la guerre*,' said Helene.

'Oh, I know what that means,' said Lizzy. 'It's the war.'

'Yes, the war is responsible for much unhappiness,' said Helene. 'But it's good we have Commandos like Bobby's cousin Tim.'

'Good?' said Lizzy.

'Of course,' said Helene, 'they are going to fight the Nazis where they can find them. They found some this morning, the radio said so. The Nazis refused to come here after our brave Air Force gave the *Luftwaffe* a bloody good hiding–'

'Pardon?' said Lizzy.

'Yes, I like that kind of English, *madame* – Mrs Somers. Bobby has let me know when it's right to use it, and don't you think it sounds right to say what Hitler is, a bleedin' Hun? I think so too. Wait, I was saying that the Nazis refused to come here after our Air Force shot the buggers out of the sky, so we must go to them and–'

'Helene, no!' cried Lizzy.

'Excuse me?' said Helene.

'You mustn't use words like that,' said Lizzy.

'What words?' asked Helene.

'I'll speak to Bobby,' said Lizzy.

'Oh, bloody good,' said Helene, 'he's often in need of being spoken to.'

Boots and Polly were in the garden, and Rosie joined them there.

'Well, ducky,' said Polly to Rosie, 'did you hit Matthew over the head with something heavy?'

'No, he knocked me out with a piece of cockney wordage,' said Rosie, and did her best to quote it in similar style. Polly

366

gurgled. Boots laughed. 'He slew me with mimicry,' said Rosie, who'd left out the bit about her warm bosom. Well, some things were still sacred.

'A Dorset man mimicking cockney must be a gift to the ear on a wet afternoon,' said Polly.

'Any afternoon, I'd say,' said Boots.

'You're bloomin' right, guv,' said Rosie.

'I'm screaming,' said Polly, 'and we can take it, can we, Rosie old sport, that the wedding's on?'

'Did you have a mistaken idea that it was off?' asked Rosie.

'Well, darling, I'm not perfect, you know,' said Polly, 'I do draw mistaken inferences sometimes.'

'It was just a slight hiccup,' said Rosie. Boots lightly squeezed her arm. 'I'm all right now, bless you both. Listen, do you think Tim was on the Commando raid?'

'Bound to have been if his group was part of the force,' said Boots.

'He'll be in touch,' said Polly.

The garden looked green and colourful as Matt came out. No-one was in uniform, and the war seemed far away. Chinese Lady broke that illusion when she too came out a few minutes later.

'There you all are,' she said. 'Perhaps someone could look at that old wireless. It's been talkin' now about our soldiers being in

367

that place in the Bible, Damascus. I don't know what they want to be there for, especially as they don't seem to have enough soldiers fightin' the Germans in Egypt. I just know that that blessed wireless is goin' to give me a nervous breakdown in the end. It's never been a blind bit of use. You'd better have a look at it, Boots, or it'll spoil Rosie's wedding day.'

'No, nothing will spoil that, Maisie,' said Polly.

'Well, I hope that what was going on isn't going on any more,' said Chinese Lady firmly.

'Nana,' said Rosie, 'your only oldest son has made up for the loss of the garage by arranging an Army interview for Matthew.'

'Yes, I know he's done that,' said Chinese Lady, 'but I don't know if that was what everything was about.'

'There was something else,' said Boots. 'Rosie will show you a letter.'

After reading it, Chinese Lady looked ready to faint.

'Oh, my goodness,' she breathed, 'where's somewhere I can sit down?'

Boots assisted her to a garden seat. She fanned herself with her apron and faintly expressed a wish not to pass on until the wedding was over. Boots said he was sure recovery was already on its way, that Polly was fetching her a glass of port. Chinese

Lady said she didn't know if she'd have the strength to drink it.

'Well, here it is, Nana,' said Rosie.

'Yes, here we are, Maisie, this'll buck you up,' said Polly, and handed her the glass.

'Oh, Lord Above,' sighed Chinese Lady, but took it and sipped at it. 'Our Rosie, all that money, would you believe, I don't know I'll ever be the same again. And that poor man, Rosie's natural dad, dying in the desert like that. I only met him once myself, but I can't say he wasn't a gentleman.' The new crisis was already over, Chinese Lady was drinking port and talking her head off, even if she did sound a bit breathless. 'I never heard of so much money in all my life, but what a nice time to know about it, directly after Mr Chapman's garage being burned down. But I'm sure he'll get to be a providing husband, and that will mean you'll both be very comfortably off, Rosie, which I'm sure we're all pleased about. I'll be very pleased myself to tell your Aunt Victoria about it.'

And so on.

The battery wireless set, placed on a bench outdoors, was repeating the news stories of the afternoon, the leading story still featuring the Commando raid on Norway.

'It really is one in the eye for Hitler and his gang,' said Clara.

'That's the third time you've said that,' said Felicity. She'd had a bad night, one of those nights when her sightlessness induced recurrent nightmares that woke her again and again. But she'd made a gradual recovery from depression during the day, and felt elated by the news. She was sure the Troon Commandos had been part of the assault force, and that Tim would have excelled himself. She was certain she knew now why his last letter had ended so abruptly. 'What I'm waiting for is news of Tim.'

'Would they mention individual soldiers?' asked Clara.

'They could mention Tim,' said Felicity, her dark glasses a permanency, for she guessed her eyes were scarred. 'Tim's a tiger.'

'What kind of a tiger?' asked Clara.

'That information is private,' said Felicity. 'Curse it, I've just realized that if he's with the group I shan't get a letter from him for days. God, what a lousy war. I'll get a headache in a minute.'

'When I really think about the war, I don't feel all that happy myself,' said Clara.

'Find one of the doctors, one with an overdose of hormones, and drag him into the bushes as soon as you're off duty,' said Felicity. 'That'll cheer you up, and I don't suppose he'll complain. Believe me, if Tim

370

were here, we'd drag each other.'

'It's not allowed, naughty romps in the bushes,' said Clara.

'Well, hard luck for both of us,' said Felicity. The battery wireless set droned on in the sunshine. 'Switch it off, or find some music.'

Clara used the knob and found music.

'How's that, Felicity?' she said.

'Bloody awful,' said Felicity. 'Look here, Florence Nightingale, when's tea coming out?'

'I'll go and arrange for ours to be brought now.'

'Good show,' said Felicity, 'but I don't want any of that stale cake. Find me a strawberry jam tart like my mother used to make.'

'Will a currant bun do?'

'One of those without currants?' said Felicity.

'It's the war,' said the nurse.

'As if I didn't know,' said Felicity.

She thought about the raid on Norway, and about Tim, a young man of whipcord whose training as a lethal soldier hadn't given a cynical edge to his lovely sense of humour or soured his good nature. She asked herself, not for the first time, if she could really do the selfish thing and marry him.

Yes, I could, he's the best there is, and I

need him. I'll fight all the weaknesses of the blind to make myself a useful wife, not a useless burden. I've already promised myself I would, and I will.

When the tea tray arrived, she said, 'I'll pour.'

'I'm not going to discourage you,' said Clara, 'but I don't want you to end up with hot tea in your lap.'

'I'll pour,' said Felicity, 'you can point me.' That accomplished, she said, 'Listen, Tim's attending his sister's wedding on the fifth of July. He may visit me again. If he does, arrange the use of a private room for us. With a bed.'

'A bed?'

'Yes, thinking about it,' said Felicity, 'I don't fancy bushes.'

Clara laughed.

'Our expert will begin teaching you Braille on Monday,' she said.

'I'll be thrilled, won't I?' said Felicity.

'I hope so,' said Clara, 'then when Tim does visit you'll be able to read him a bed-time story in the private room.'

'That's it, let's have hysterics,' said Felicity, and brought her teacup accurately to her lips.

'Bobby, have you been teaching Helene to use swear words?' asked Lizzy when Ned was home. 'Have you?'

'Perish the thought,' said Bobby, enjoying an evening beer with his dad while waiting for Helene to come down from her room.

'Well, she's using swear words,' said Lizzy, 'but I don't think she realizes it.'

'Oh, those kind of words are flying about all over our unit,' said Bobby, 'and Helene catches hold of them.'

'She told me you were teachin' her,' said Lizzy.

'I probably explained one or two,' said Bobby.

'And did you explain ladies don't use them?' said Lizzy.

'Not many ladies left in this country since the bombing started,' said Bobby. 'They're all using French.'

'French?' said Lizzy.

'Yes, you know, Mum,' said Bobby. '"Hope Goering falls out of bed and breaks his bleedin' fat back, and excuse my French."'

'Is that supposed to be funny?' said Lizzy. 'Well, it's not, and what're you grinning about, Ned Somers?'

'French,' said Ned.

'My mother's right,' said Lizzy, 'it's not just Boots that's a comedian, the war's turned everyone in the fam'ly into a music hall comic. Well, I don't want to have to listen to too many Max Millers, and I won't have you encouraging Helene to use bad language, Bobby, specially as she doesn't realize she's doing it.'

'Right you are, Mum, I'll do what I can,' said Bobby.

Helene came down then.

'Hello, *Madame* Somers. Good evening, *M'sieur* Somers. I am looking nice, don't you think?'

She was. Lizzy had bought new clothes for her from one of Sammy's shops when she arrived with Bobby from France. At this moment she was wearing a tangerine dress that enhanced her brunette colouring. The hem flirted around her knees, her stockinged legs looked long and sleek, and the bodice of the dress had its own appeal.

'Oh, very nice, Helene,' said Lizzy.

'My compliments,' smiled Ned.

'Thank you,' said Helene. 'And what do you say. Bobby?'

'Gorblimey dazzling,' said Bobby, 'if you'll excuse my French.'

Lizzy gave him the kind of look she had inherited from Chinese Lady.

The night was quiet. That is, the skies over the South of England were again undisturbed. Tommy, Sammy, Ned and old Uncle Tom, all ARP wardens, were allowed another peaceful sleep. In Kennington, Jemima and Job Hardy slept in anticipation of enjoying Rosie's wedding, Jemima

374

delighted at being invited. Not far away, neighbours of theirs, Mr and Mrs Skinner, were tucked up, although Mr Skinner had a black eye for opening his Friday wage packet again.

The ships bringing home the weary Commandos and their wounded were steaming for Portsmouth.

On their border with Soviet Russia, Hitler's armies were poised for their attack. British Intelligence and Churchill had up-to-date information on it, but Stalin was still refusing to accept the warnings being delivered to Molotov, his Foreign Minister. He preferred to believe Hitler would honour the non-aggression pact that obtained between Nazi Germany and the Soviet Union. Churchill found it hard to credit a belief in Hitler's honour.

Chapter Twenty-Three

Saturday, 21 June.

The ships bringing the Commandos home were in the English Channel. Tim was nursing his injured shoulder but looking forward to ten days leave in common with all the returning men. Major Lucas was turning over in his mind methods of attack that might reduce casualties. Now and again images of Subaltern Eloise Adams intervened. Sometimes the images contained an extrovert element, a picture of that infuriating young lady over his knees.

In Troon, Eloise woke up and was immediately fretful and on edge. The day ahead offered little in the way of interest to a newly fledged subaltern suffering worries about her half-brother and frightful frustrations about his detachment commander. She had been given charge of six ATS personnel in admin ops, and they were all boring girls. At least, she thought so. That was probably because Boots's French daughter only came to life in the company of men. Admiring men. However, she was the first to whom ops messages were passed for scrutiny, and she realized there were bound to be certain signals today concerning the movement home of the Commando task force. That bucked her up a little.

At home, there was an early morning telegram for Bobby. Briefly, it informed him his leave was up on the 25th, when he was to be back by noon. He knew that meant Helene as well. He also knew they might miss Rosie's wedding.

With Helene, he took a Green Line bus out to Tatsfield in Surrey, and there they walked the lanes of the friendly countryside. The sky was full of running white clouds, the bright, breezy day inviting to walkers, ramblers, hikers and other lovers of the open air in a land whose towns and cities bore the hideous marks of a rampaging enemy. Bobby let his thoughts linger on the years gone by, the years when young people felt they would live a lifetime of peace because their fathers had fought the war that was to end all wars.

'Talk to me,' said Helene, whose own thoughts had been reaching out to her parents in occupied France.

'Lovely day,' said Bobby.

'That's talking to me?' said Helene.

'Serious stuff, then,' said Bobby, and they talked about what they had been trained for, work with French Resistance cells. They speculated on what Major Buckmaster had in mind for them to begin with, and where in France they would land up. If in Northern France, said Helene, there might be a chance to get in touch with her parents. Not if it would put them at risk, said Bobby, and reminded her that part of her parents' farmland and the farmhouse itself had been commandeered for the use of a German anti-aircraft battery headquarters.

'Yes, and what I would like to know is how my parents are being treated by the Nazi Boches,' said Helene. 'Ah, perhaps we may be fortunate enough to receive orders to blow the battery up. It's what our Free French soldiers would do.'

'Following which, we could expect your parents to be arrested,' said Bobby. 'We've had those kind of consequences drummed into us during our training. Himmler's hounds make arrests out of spite if there's no evidence. You know that, Fifi.'

'You don't have to call me Fifi now,' said Helene. 'Speaking of parents, your mother expects you to marry me, do you know that?'

'She expects right,' said Bobby. 'I am going to marry you, so stop talking about Free French soldiers.'

'That is a lie, I never talk about them in the way you mean,' said Helene. 'I speak only of the brave men and women who have managed to get to England to serve General de Gaulle, who is magnificent.'

'Always looks like a gloomy lamppost to me,' said Bobby.

'Ah, you are jealous of my admiration for him,' said Helene.

'The first time I'm jealous of a gloomy lamppost who needs lighting up, you can carry me off to a home for imbeciles,' said Bobby.

'But you are ready now for such a home,' said Helene. 'You have been a crazy imbecile all the time I've known you.'

'How would you like this particular specimen to chuck you into a load of hay and jump on you?' said Bobby.

'What a joke,' said Helene, her long legs carrying her easily along beside him. 'I'm as strong as you are.'

'You're not supposed to be,' said Bobby, 'you're supposed to be a nice feminine female like my Aunt Vi, with a fondness for knitting and needlework.'

Helene laughed. No-one quite knew how happy she was when she had Bobby to herself.

'That is what you think,' she said.

'Well, whatever muscles you've got—'

'Oh, you pig, I don't have muscles like a man, I've told you so.'

'Well, whatever, I cherish you, my French lovely,' said Bobby.

They stopped and turned to each other.

Helene's dress rippled in the breeze, and her eyes looked over-bright.

'Bobby?'

'Well?' said Bobby.

'I love you, *cheri*, always. It will be always for both of us when we're married, yes?'

'It's always for always in my family,' said Bobby, 'but I'm set on us winning this war first.'

A kiss was in the making, but its development was checked by the approach of a boy riding a bike. As he cycled by, he laughed and shouted.

'Join the Army and see Russia! Hitler's been and done it on old Joe Stalin, he's invaded!'

On the lad went, bouncing on his bike in his youthful exultation.

'Bobby, can that be true?' breathed Helene.

'Let's find a pub,' said Bobby, 'they'll know.'

It was true. At four in the morning, and without any declaration of war, Hitler's massive armies had crossed the border on a huge front from the Baltic to the Black Sea, and the unprepared Soviet forces were being overwhelmed.

Churchill, delighted that in the fight against Nazi Germany the Soviet Union was now an ally, albeit willy-nilly, nevertheless prayed soberly for what was vitally necessary, that at some stage the Russians would hold the formidable Panzer divisions. Stalin, in shock, had actually taken to his bed. He was suffering mental paralysis at Hitler's perfidy.

'I don't want to keep on about it, but I just don't know what that wireless is getting up to,' said Chinese Lady, sharing the astounding news with Boots, Polly, Rosie, Matthew and Mr Finch. 'Listen to it, all about Hitler again. It'll turn into that madman himself one day and I'll have him in my kitchen, shouting speeches at me.'

'It's about the Russians as well as Hitler, Maisie,' said Mr Finch.

'And if he does materialize, call Boots,' said Polly. 'He'll pickle him in sharp vinegar.' The long news broadcast finished. 'Did I really hear all that? Did I? Saints alive, an invasion of Russia? I'm dizzy, Edwin old scout.'

'I'm thankful,' said Mr Finch. 'Hitler will lose the war now. Eh, Boots?'

'We'll still have to win it,' said Boots.

'We've more of a fair old chance now,' said Matt.

'Well, I think a fair old chance counts as a lovely wedding present,' said Rosie.

All she wanted now was news of Tim.

At this moment, the Commandos were disembarking at Portsmouth, where ambulances awaited the wounded.

Emma, just in from her Saturday morning's work, was upstairs in her room. Ned wasn't home yet, and Bobby and Helene were out for the day. So it was Lizzy who answered the ringing phone.

Thirty seconds later, she was calling.

'Emma! Emma! Phone!'

'Who is it?' called Emma.

'Jonathan, love. Jonathan.'

Emma let go a little yell of excitement and came running down the stairs. Lizzy, smiling, gave her the phone and tactfully retreated to the kitchen. Emma drew a breath, then spoke.

'Jonathan?'

Her loving country chap came through clear and vibrant.

'Be that my little woman as ever was?'

'Jonathan!' Emma shrieked his name.

'Hello, fox got you by the tail, Emma?'

'Don't make me go potty,' gasped Emma, 'tell me where you are.'

'In bed,' said Jonathan.

'What? What did you say?'

'In bed, in the military wing of the Mitcham General Hospital,' said Jonathan.

'Mitcham? Mitcham?' Emma couldn't believe her ears. 'That's only about ten miles away. What's happened to you? Jonathan, what's happened?'

'Smashed kneecap,' said Jonathan. 'About ten days ago. Downright hurtful, I can tell you. Got medicated and looked at in the British Military Hospital in Cairo, then airlifted home with some other surgical cases for some kind doctor here to fit me a tin kneecap in place of the one that's no good to anybody now. They're doing it on Monday. Got a lovely nurse here. She managed to get the ward phone to my bedside. "Here it be, my wounded hero," she said. After the op, I'll end up a mite stiff-legged, but I think the rest of me will still go up and down the stairs without falling about.'

Stiff-legged? Emma wondered why fate laid such malicious hands on the family. Uncle Boots blinded in the last war, Tim's young lady blinded in this one, my dad fitted with a tin leg after a battle in 1916, and now my Jonathan being fitted with a tin kneecap. Except that wasn't nearly as bad as a lost limb or blindness. Or was Jonathan being too cheerful by half?

'Jonathan?'

'Hope you're still there, Emma. I'm still here.'

'You're not fibbing, it is just your knee?'

'Just that, Emma. A low-down piece of metal did it when Rommel's gunners were shelling our battery. Lucky for me it weren't high up or they'd be fitting me with a tin head.'

383

'Well, I wouldn't like that,' said Emma. 'Jonathan, you really will be able to get about and do other things, won't you?'

'Well, there's a funny old coincidence, Emma, you talking about other things and me thinking of them,' said Jonathan.

'What other things? Oh, you cheeky devil, and over the phone too, with everyone in the ward listening, I suppose.'

'Just four of us, Emma,' said Jonathan. 'The other three have had surgery, but not come to yet.'

'Oh, give them my best wishes,' said Emma from cloud nine. 'Jonathan, can I come and see you tomorrow?'

'Be a treat, that would,' said Jonathan, 'and make me remember our wedding nuptials. Wear something that'll hit me in the eye. Say your honeymoon nightie. I've got happy memories of that.'

'Oh, stop making me feel sexy,' whispered Emma.

'Pardon?' said Jonathan. 'Could you speak up, Emma?'

'No, I couldn't,' said Emma, 'Mum'll hear.'

'What did you say, then?'

'That I wish I was there, in bed with you,' said Emma in an even lower whisper.

'Blessed if I can hear a word you're saying,' said Jonathan.

'Never mind, darling,' said Emma, 'I'll say

384

it all to you tomorrow as long as no-one's listening. Jonathan, was it awful fighting the Germans in the desert?'

'We don't need to talk about that,' said Jonathan.

'Well, will your tin kneecap mean you'll have to leave the Army?'

'I wouldn't want that, Emma, not while we're still fighting this old war, and I've been promised a posting to a training regiment as a sergeant-instructor teaching gunnery, which means the science of artillery.'

'Where, Jonathan, do you know where?'

'A camp down along Zummerzet way.'

'Oh, would I be able to come and live near you, please?'

'You don't have to ask please, Emma, you being my young missus and a rare tidy treat of a girl. I'll find a Zummerzet farmer with room to billet you, and maybe with a wife who needs someone to look after her chickens, which'll put you into a reserved occupation. Would that suit you, Emma, something like that?'

'Jonathan, arranging something like that would be loving of you,' said Emma.

'Well, down in Zummerzet, Emma, I reckon we could go in for a fair bit of loving on my off-duty days, and I'll see my tin knee doesn't get in the way.'

'Jonathan, is it hurting now?' asked Emma.

385

'I've had injections that have knocked it unconscious, but I tell you, Emma, it aren't been a pretty sight. More like a boiled suet pudding the size of a football. Emma, would you be a lovely girl and let my parents know I'm here?'

'Jonathan darling, I'll go and see your mother this afternoon, promise.'

'Well, I'll thank you for doing that,' said Jonathan. 'Your family, Emma, how's your family?'

'Oh, Bobby and Helene have been here on leave, but they're going back on Tuesday. Uncle Boots, Aunt Polly and Rosie are all home on short leave before Rosie's wedding in two weeks, and we've all met her fiancé, Matthew Chapman, a lovely man. And we're waiting to hear from Tim. We think he was on the latest Commando raid.'

'Now wasn't that a fine fighting strike, Emma? Regular knockout blow for old Jerry.'

'But a lot of casualties, according to the news,' said Emma. 'Jonathan, I'll be with you tomorrow, Sunday afternoon. I'm dying to see you. Do you want anything, anything I can bring with me?'

'You bring yourself, Emma, and I won't want anything else,' said Jonathan. 'You're my angel.'

'Your angel wants you,' whispered Emma.

'I don't think I caught that,' said Jonathan.

'Tell you tomorrow,' said Emma.

''Bye, Emma.'

''Bye, Jonathan.'

'Call for you, ma'am,' said the ATS girl on the Troon switchboard.

'What?' said Eloise. 'Oh, yes, all right, I'll take it.' A click. 'Hello?'

'Subaltern Adams, Major Lucas here. I'm—'

'Major Lucas, it's you?' said Eloise, and the boredom of Troon when it was empty of so many of the rough, tough, fighting men of 4 Commando, receded for the moment. 'It's you?'

'Sorry if that upsets you,' said Major Lucas. 'I'm in—'

'No, no, I didn't say it upsets me.'

'Well, if you'll allow me to proceed,' said Major Lucas, 'I'm in Portsmouth and I thought you might like to know that your brother's a casualty—'

'Oh, no!'

'It isn't serious, just a fractured collarbone. He'll spend a couple of rest days in the military hospital here, then go on leave. That's all.'

'What do you mean, that's all?' asked Eloise.

'I mean I've let you know about your brother. There's no more. I imagine the radio has filled you in with all the details of

387

the raid including heavy casualties.'

'But are they heavy among 4 Commando?' asked Eloise.

'Heavy enough. I'll leave you to inform your family about your brother, if you want to. How are you yourself, Subaltern Adams?'

'Unhappy about our casualties, but relieved about Tim,' said Eloise.

'I share your feelings,' said Major Lucas. 'I'll be back in Troon in a day or so before I go on leave myself. Goodbye, Subaltern Adams.'

'Major Lucas—'

But he'd hung up, the beast.

Oh, wait till I see you, just wait, she thought.

It was mid-afternoon when Rosie answered the ringing phone.

'Hello?'

'Rosie? This is Eloise.'

'Hello, sister dear,' said Rosie, 'how are you?'

'Oh, happy to tell you Tim's back from the raid,' said Eloise, 'and that he'll be coming home on leave in a few days.'

'Lovely,' said Rosie. 'I worried a little in case he was one of the casualties.'

'Well, he does have a fractured collar-bone,' said Eloise. 'Major Lucas phoned from Portsmouth to tell me. Tim is spending two rest days in the military hospital there, then he'll be sent on leave.'

'We'll all be thankful it's no more than a fractured collarbone,' said Rosie. 'How kind of Major Lucas to let you know.'

'Kind?' said Eloise.

'Yes, wasn't it?' said Rosie.

'Yes. Yes, of course,' said Eloise, and realized then that she hadn't thanked him for making the call. Oh, bother. 'He was upset about the number of men we lost.'

'I think certain kinds of officers feel personally responsible at losing men,' said Rosie. 'But even our wireless set, which Grandma thinks is all doom and gloom, sounded pleased about the success of the raid.'

'How can a wireless set, a radio, have its own feelings?' asked Eloise.

'Ask Grandma,' said Rosie. 'Eloise, are you getting weekend leave for my wedding?'

'Oh, yes, that's all arranged,' said Eloise.

'Lovely,' said Rosie. 'Bless you, sister dear.'

Chapter Twenty-Four

'Emma?' said Jemima Hardy as she opened her front door and found her cherished daughter-in-law on the step. 'Well, this be an unexpected pleasure, seeing you.' Emma often visited, but nearly always by arrangement. 'Come in, do, my dear.'

'Hello, Mum,' said Emma, and bestowed an ecstatic kiss on her mother-in-law's cheek before going into the parlour with her. 'You'll never believe.'

'Won't I?' smiled Jemima, more than happy with Jonathan's young wife. Emma, nearly nineteen, had inherited her mother's brunette looks, her dad's ability to meet life's buffets with composure, and the Adams' sense of humour. The combination had made her the most engaging girl Jemima knew. 'You're going to tell me the war be over now that that old devil Hitler's tangled himself up in Russia?'

'The rotten warmonger hasn't tangled himself up yet, Mum,' said Emma, 'he's walking over the Russians. No, it's nothing like that, it's about Jonathan. Mum, he's home.'

'Home?' said Jemima. 'Emma, he don't be here.'

'I mean he's back in England, in a hospital in Mitcham,' said Emma, and began to explain quite happily why Jonathan had been hospitalized, and why an operation was necessary without, however, suggesting the damaged knee was actually a thing of joy. But it did mean, she said, that when he was up and about he was going to stay on home service, that the Army was going to–

'Bless us, Emma, not so quick,' said Jemima, 'I be holding my breath at listening to you. Tell me all of it in the kitchen while I put the kettle on. I don't mind too much about Jonathan's knee, considering what this war's doing to other people, but I be very wishful to hear everything, starting from the beginning again.'

'Oh, I'm so excited, Mum, so happy,' said Emma. 'Oh, allowing that I'm sorry about his knee.'

She and Jonathan's comely mother became very happy together in the kitchen over a pot of tea, Emma taking her time to give details and recount some parts of her phone conversation with Jonathan. Each agreed with the other, that a tin kneecap was nothing to seriously worry about when one thought of terrible deaths, terrible wounds and injuries, and what had happened to Tim's young lady and Emma's Aunt Emily.

'We're blessed, Emma.'

'Oh, I do hope Jonathan can get me billeted on a farm close to his training camp,' said Emma. 'Down in Zummerzet, he kept saying, and I bet he'll have both of us talking Zummerzet fashion in a month or so.'

'Jonathan's been a joker all his life,' said Jemima, 'but we've never minded. Well, my husband Job can be that way day in, day out, and when I were young he might have made me blush if I hadn't liked laughing more than any blushing. He'll be downright pleasured Jonathan's home, and won't worry about his knee.' Jemima eyed Emma with a little smile. 'That Jonathan, do he make you blush at times, love?'

'Well, he would, believe me he would,' said Emma, 'only I'm like you.'

'Like me?' said Jemima.

'Yes, I like laughing a lot more than blushing,' said Emma.

Over Saturday high tea, Sammy said, 'For the first time in my life I don't know where I am, and I'm not even sure who I am.'

'Oh, dear, I am sorry,' said Susie. 'But cheer up, you're Mr Sammy Adams, and you're at home. I'm your wife and my name's Susie, and this little girl is your younger daughter, Paula. Paula, say hello to Daddy, to let him know he's at home.'

'Hello, Daddy, you're here at home,' said Paula.

'Well, I'm glad about that, Plum Pudding the Second,' said Sammy, 'it's consoling information. But I tell you, Susie, since Rosie phoned this afternoon to let us know about the garage being burned down and what she's been left in Armitage's will, and what she'd like to do with it, my mind's been taking tram rides to places I've never heard of.'

'I expect the whole family's a bit dizzy, love,' said Susie. 'Who wouldn't be, with that kind of good news coming so soon after the bad news?'

'I wouldn't call the fire bad news,' said Sammy. 'Well, a run-down garage is a convenient write-off if you can collect profitably from the insurance. Rosie was more concerned about her natural dad's death, and sounded more upset about that than glad about the money.'

'Did that surprise you?' asked Susie.

'Not really,' said Sammy, 'Rosie's got deep feelings about people. But I ask you, Susie, yes, and you, little Plum Pudding, twenty-five thousand genuine smackers, probably all lying secure in a highly reputable armour-plated bank just waiting to be picked up by Rosie, and then handed to me for investment at my discretion. As you know, I've touched elbows with a bit of oof in my time–'

'A fair amount, Sammy,' said Susie.

'But twenty-five thousand smackers all at once and at the same time in the near future,' said Sammy. 'No wonder I don't know if I'm coming or going.'

'You're sitting down, Daddy, and eating sausages and fried potatoes,' said Paula.

'Sausages and what?' said Sammy. 'I thought it was faggots and pease pudding. Just shows you. Susie, that twenty-five thousand quid plus some capital from Adams Enterprises is going to make Adams Properties Ltd the owners of streets, stores and postwar building sites of happy potential. Susie, what's in these bangers?'

'Your guess is as good as mine, Sammy.'

'Did the butcher say what he put in them?'

'No, he only said he made them with his eyes shut.'

'It's criminal, what the war's done to honest sausages,' said Sammy. 'Still, san fairy, Joe Stalin's going to have to take some of the weight off Winnie Churchill's shoulders, and I'm going to see that Rosie's investment pays her a packet in a few years. I'll get to profitable work as soon as I've recovered from feeling I've got no legs.'

'Oh, you're off the tram now, are you, Sammy?' said Susie.

'What tram?' asked Sammy. 'Listen, I think I've got a hot flush. Can anybody help?'

'Isn't Daddy funny, Mummy?' said Paula.

Susie smiled.

'We'll buy him a funny hat for his birthday, darling, then he'll look the part.'

Paula giggled. Sammy winked.

'Are you sure Tim hasn't been on the phone?' asked Felicity just prior to retiring.

'I swear it,' said Clara. 'What help d'you want tonight?'

'None.'

'Shall I fold your clothes for you?'

'No, I'll do it, even if I muck it up. Listen, you were on duty from breakfast until six. Now you're back. You'll wear yourself out.'

'I'm only here to wish you good night and see you into bed.'

'Where's the night duty staff, then?'

'They're around.'

'I thought Tim might have phoned. The Commandos must be back by now.'

'He'll be in touch, I'm sure,' said Clara.

'If I'm in a foul temper tomorrow, turn a blind eye, Clara.'

'A blind eye, yes, very droll, Felicity.'

German bombers arrived that night. Hitler, in his fury over the Norwegian raid, had spared a few minutes from directing his invasion of Russia to order, through Goering, a heavyweight attack on London. Not long after the warning sirens had sounded, bombs were dropping in the central district of the capital.

Ned, Tommy and Sammy were all standing by, ready to be called out on ARP duty. Chinese Lady, Mr Finch, Polly, Boots, Rosie and Matthew crowded into the garden shelter of the house on Red Post Hill. Mr Finch had fixed up an electric light in the shelter to avoid claustrophobic darkness. By eleven o'clock, when it was obvious the bombers were concentrating on inner London, Boots, Polly, Rosie and Matthew came out of the shelter, much against the advice of Chinese Lady, and stood in the garden to watch the night sky. It was a star-studded indigo blue, and although the drone of bombers was constant, there were no flashes to indicate anti-aircraft guns were in action.

Polly commented on it.

'Does that mean we're offering no defence?' asked Matt.

'It's more likely to mean RAF night fighters are up there,' said Boots.

'What results have they been getting?' asked Matt.

'Fair to middling, I believe,' said Boots.

'Fair to middling, do we call that good?' asked Rosie.

'Let's say promising,' said Boots.

They fell silent, watching the sky and listening to the disturbing drone of Dorniers and Heinkels. Above the heart of London, the night sky was flushed. Incendiaries, raining down, were creating infernos. Rosie thought how impotent they were. They could give no help at all to the people suffering the bombs and incendiaries.

'It's another revenge raid, isn't it?' she said quietly.

'I feel horribly mesmerized,' said Polly.

'Damn all, listen to them,' said Matt. The drone of the bombers was constant, the sky alive with noisy vibrations.

'Are we silly to be standing here?' asked Rosie.

'Safe, I think,' said Boots, 'it's the City and Central London they're smashing again.'

'The people there are living with hell and the devil again,' said Polly.

A warm arm slid around her waist and Boots murmured, 'Are you all right, Polly?'

She knew he was thinking of the child.

'I'm fine, dear old thing,' she whispered, 'and so is Jack or Jill.'

Chinese Lady and Mr Finch looked up when the four returned to the shelter.

'You've been outside too long,' said Chinese Lady accusingly.

'Taking a look at what the ARP wardens, the police and special constables are up against during every raid,' said Boots.

'Well, you're not special constables,' said Chinese Lady, 'and I don't know what you were up to, Rosie, when your wedding's not far off. And I must say you shouldn't have been out there, Polly.'

'A breath of fresh air,' said Polly.

'An acceptable reason,' smiled Mr Finch.

'It's mesmerizing, looking and listening,' said Rosie.

'Horribly,' said Polly.

'You're all very unresponsible,' said Chinese Lady.

'Who'd like some Navy coffee?' asked Boots. 'I've brought a couple of flasks out.'

'What's Navy coffee?' asked Chinese Lady.

'Coffee with a dash of rum,' said Boots.

'I've got the rum,' said Matt.

'Clever old scout,' said Polly.

'Well, perhaps I'll have a small cup,' said Chinese Lady.

'I'll have a full cup,' said Mr Finch.

'We need something to help us pray,' said Rosie, feeling intensely for Londoners.

They all sat drinking coffee with rum and listening to the muffled sounds of the bombers. Boots thought not only of suffering Londoners, but of suffering Russians pulverized by the fire of German armour and German planes.

Although the Denmark Hill area escaped that night, Walworth and Kennington were hit. Two adjoining terraced houses in Kennington were down, one of which was rented by Arthur and Gladys Skinner. Mrs

Skinner was bitter about it.

'Now don't you fret, Gladys me old Dutch,' said Mr Skinner, 'we'll soon get another place, and I'll do overtime at the fact'ry to 'elp set you up with new furniture and new clobber. Might even be able to buy you a fox fur, eh?'

'That's if you don't spend yer overtime on beer,' said Mrs Skinner.

'Cross me 'eart,' said Mr Skinner. 'Let's count our blessings, eh? That old shelter saved you and me. What's the house matter as long as we still got each other?'

'Well, that's uplifting, Arthur Skinner, I didn't know you still 'ad it in you to say anything like that. But where we goin' to put up till we find another place?'

Jemima solved that question. She offered them rooms in her house, with a gas ring for cooking: Job had said he'd be obliged if she didn't invite them down to meals too often, as Mrs Skinner fair made his ears ache with her carry-ons. Jemima promised she wouldn't, just supper. Job said he'd fashion himself some ear plugs.

Jemima's gesture and the resilience of the Skinners were typical of the ways of people in all bombed towns and cities. The persistent German night raids could have brought the worst out of His Majesty's suffering subjects.

Instead, it brought out the best.

From the beginning, Goering's bombers had failed to induce a mood of surrender in the insular Britons of that stubborn, irritating and frustrating island nation in the North Sea.

Mid-morning, Boots and Polly began their journey back to the headquarters of Sir Henry's new corps. Not long after, Matthew and Rosie began their own return journey, Matthew with his burned-out garage not as much on his mind as his forthcoming REME interview. He could do little about his destroyed garage except conduct negotiations with his insurance company. Everything of real importance to his need to stand on his own feet now rested on a chance to join the Army.

'I know what you're thinking about,' said Rosie after a while.

'Tell me,' said Matt.

'The REME,' said Rosie.

'That and you, Rosie,' said Matt, 'and it's raised an interesting question in my mind.'

'Oh, I regard interesting questions as very interesting,' said Rosie. 'What's yours?'

'Well, your father said if accepted I'd go in as a sergeant or lieutenant. If a sergeant, isn't it a fact that regulations wouldn't allow you, as an ATS officer, to marry me? Am I right?'

'I don't call that an interesting question, I

call it an awkward one,' said Rosie, as they passed through West Norwood.

'One can't fight some regulations.' said Matt.

'Some regulations need a poke in the eye,' said Rosie.

'I've a suggestion,' said Matt. 'If I'm accepted and given the rank of sergeant, I'll ask for time to settle certain matters relating to the garage and its customers, marry you while I'm still a civilian and take up my Army career a week or so later. Will that be a way of poking one particular regulation in the eye?'

'My answer to that,' said Rosie, 'is to tell you how glad I am you're not just a pretty face.'

Polly, talking to Boots, said, 'We had quite a momentous leave, old scout, but I think I like going back to our cottage.'

'It's not actually ours,' said Boots.

'It's ours while we're living there, old love,' said Polly, 'and I'll always have tender memories of it. It'll always be the place where we spent the first year of our married life.'

'Your sentimental side is a surprise to me,' said Boots.

'Don't be rotten,' said Polly, 'everyone should have some sentiment, otherwise memories are only factual entries in a notebook. And you're sentimental, I know you are. Aren't you?'

'Well, let's say I'll cherish our time in the cottage,' said Boots, 'and even have happy memories of your morning sickness.'

'Do me a favour, sweetie,' said Polly, 'don't make memory notes of my morning sickness.'

'Like all husbands, I'm only an observer of my wife for a certain nine months,' said Boots, 'but that doesn't prevent me saying I'll treasure the memory of every part of the process.'

'Bless the man,' murmured Polly, 'he's my friend for life.'

Emma enjoyed an hour with Jonathan in the hospital at Mitcham, an hour that was a reunion of eyes and tongues, although it wasn't possible for them to engage in quite the kind of lovers' dialogue Emma had had in mind. Well, the other three patients were fully conscious, and two of them had visitors, and everything everyone said travelled to the ears of all. However, it was enough – almost – to see each other again. Jonathan's bed blanket looked tented, due to a cradle placed over his injured knee, but he himself looked so brown and healthy that towards the end of her visit Emma scribbled a question in pencil on a blank page of her diary. She tore the page out and gave it to him. He read it.

'When will I be able to come to bed with you?'

He borrowed her pencil to scribble a reply.

'I'm having my op at ten tomorrow morning, Monday. Try to sneak in just after lights out on Tuesday.'

Emma read it and wrote more words.

'What a lovely thought, but don't let this *billet-doux* lie about for everyone to see. Eat it. Love and kisses, Emma.'

'I'll have it with my supper,' said Jonathan. 'What's the latest on the Russian front?'

'Awful for the Russians,' said Emma.

The Russians were shattered and running.

And Stalin was still bedridden.

The orderly arrived at a brisk trot.

'Phone call for Lieutenant Jessop from a Lieutenant Adams,' he said to Clara. 'Matron says OK.'

'It's Tim,' said Clara.

'Not before time,' said Felicity, irritable, and Clara took her into the hospital and to the extension. 'Hello?' said Felicity.

'Hello yourself,' said Tim, his fractured collarbone held in place by a figure of eight dressing, 'how's life today?'

'Bloody,' said Felicity.

'Good, glad to hear you so cheerful,' said Tim.

'Where've you been?' asked Felicity.

'Oh, up and away,' said Tim.

'I thought so,' said Felicity. 'How was it?'

'Bloody,' said Tim.

'But you're all right?'

'Yes, one of the lucky ones. But we lost Sergeant Watts among others.'

'Oh, God,' said Felicity, 'old hardboiled Watts?'

'I'll miss him,' said Tim.

'Tim, come and see me. Will you?'

'Wednesday?' said Tim.

'Where are you now?'

'Portsmouth. I'll be home Tuesday on ten days leave.'

'Wednesday, then,' said Felicity.

'And Sunday?' said Tim.

'Will you do that, Tim, will you visit me on Sunday as well?'

'Love to,' said Tim. 'Put a Sunday frock on.'

'I do have a dress here with a button-up front.'

'Don't put that on,' said Tim.

'Why not?' asked Felicity. 'You'll lose all the buttons,' said Tim, and he liked what came next. Felicity was out of her irritable mood. She was laughing.

Chapter Twenty-Five

Monday, 23 June.

Rachel put her head into Sammy's office at nine o'clock.

'Good morning, Mr Adams.'

'Ah, yes,' said Sammy, looking up from his desk. 'Come in, Mrs Goodman.' Rachel entered. Sammy came to his feet and shook hands with her, noting that her silver-grey business suit of jacket and skirt was highly appropriate. 'Good morning, and welcome.'

'Thank you, Mr Adams,' said Rachel, 'which office shall I use?'

'Boots's old abode,' said Sammy.

'My life,' murmured Rachel, 'I'm to have the office of Mr Adams senior?'

'The elder, I grant you,' said Sammy, 'but would you kindly note, Mrs Goodman, there's only one senior in Adams Enterprises, which is yours truly?'

'Very good, Mr Adams,' said Rachel. 'I did look in on that office and saw a mountain of paperwork in a tray.'

'All yours,' said Sammy. 'I'll come and join you in ten minutes, and go through everything with you.'

'Thank you, Mr Adams,' said Rachel.

'Don't mention it, Mrs Goodman,' said Sammy. 'I am confident our relationship as employer and assistant will be a happy one.'

'And profitable?' said Rachel.

'That, Mrs Goodman, is a sentiment close to me heart,' said Sammy. 'Sometime this week I'll take you to the fact'ry at Belsize Park, let you see how Tommy's running things there, and how we make sure I always know what he's up to, and he always knows I'm right behind him.'

'Mr Adams,' said Rachel, 'haven't you ever thought of housing the factory and the head office in one building?'

'I appreciate that suggestion,' said Sammy, 'but Gertie and the girls wouldn't work this side of the river, and if I moved myself and staff to the north side, my revered Ma would carry on alarming, unless I could rent Buckingham Palace. She'd accept that.'

'Will you make an offer, Mr Adams?' asked Rachel tongue in cheek.

'Only if I get invited to tea,' said Sammy. 'Well, that's all for the moment, Rachel. That is, Mrs Goodman.'

'Very good, Mr Adams,' said Rachel, and they looked at each other. Sammy winked. Rachel smiled. 'You'll have no regrets, Sammy, at bringing me on the staff.'

'Don't I know it?' said Sammy

Tuesday.

By four in the afternoon, Bobby and Helene had finished a long interview with Major Buckmaster. They were now in possession of all the minute details concerning their new identities, and heading for a resort on the Kent coast, to take up residence in a house run by a landlady who would see to their wants but ask no questions. During their time as boarders, they were to digest and absorb every single detail relating to their new identities on the understanding that when Major Buckmaster summoned them for their next interview, they would be what they were required to be.

Major Lucas arrived back in Troon at five in the afternoon. He went straight to his billet, was welcomed by his landlady, Mrs McGowan, drank a double whisky, took a hot bath, drank another double, then tumbled into his bed and fell instantly asleep. He dreamt of German fire-power, huge grey shadows and falling men, all of whom were German, which made the dream a welcome hallucination. He smiled in his sleep. Then a woman got in the way, and everything fell apart. It had to be her, of course, and it was. He growled in his sleep.

Wednesday.

In Troon, Eloise knew that Major Lucas was back, and that along with other detachment commanders he would join a day-long discussion on the results of the raid, the contribution made by 4 Commando and ways and means of reducing casualties in future raids.

Eloise waited, her nerves on edge.

Tim, on leave at home, went to Farnham to see Felicity. On arrival at the convalescent hospital, Clara came to meet him.

'Hello,' he said.

'What's happened to you?' asked Clara. His left arm was in a sling.

'Fractured collarbone,' said Tim. 'A Norwegian frost-proof brick collided with my shoulder. I'm tied up in a figure eight.'

'Oh, that's not so bad when it could have been your head.'

'Ta very much,' said Tim. 'How's Felicity?'

'Come with me,' said Clara, and took him out to the grounds at the rear of the building. She faced him. 'Felicity's crying.'

'Is that bad?' asked Tim.

'I don't know if she wept any tears between the time the bomb struck and the day she arrived here,' said Clara, 'but I do know that no-one has seen her cry here. And no, it's not bad. She's due for tears, and she needs to give in to them. It's

408

therapeutic. She's been worried about you. She doesn't want to lose you, and I do hope you realize that. You're her lifeline. Her worry made her irritable. She knew you were coming today, and suddenly there she was, crying. She's in my room now, letting herself go. Give her half an hour.'

'She can have all the time she wants,' said Tim, and thought. 'It really is good for her, having a howl?'

'Yes, any therapist would tell you so,' said Clara.

'Well, I don't think I'd be much good as a help to a crying woman, especially Felicity,' said Tim.

'No, but the help you're going to give her is what's most important to her,' said Clara. 'I'll go and see her in a few minutes, then let you know when you can see her yourself. Fair?'

'Fair,' said Tim.

It was twenty minutes before Clara took him to her room in the nurses' quarters adjacent to the hospital. She opened the door and put her head in.

'Your bloke's here, Felicity,' she said.

'All in one piece?' said Felicity.

'All shipshape,' said Clara.

'Chuck him in,' said Felicity.

'In you go, Tim,' said Clara, giving him a smile, and she closed the door as he entered.

409

Felicity was on her feet. Wearing a honey-coloured dress with buttons all the way down the front, her head was turned, her dark glasses off, her sightless eyes directed at the door. Her face was quite clear of any lamentations, and her hair shone from a vigorous brushing. She showed the hint of a smile. What a warrior, thought Tim.

'Hello, Puss,' he said.

'Hello, Tiger,' said Felicity.

'You're looking first-class,' said Tim, 'but I thought I told you not to wear that dress on Sundays.'

'It's Wednesday,' said Felicity.

'Is it?' said Tim, slipping his arm out of the sling. 'That's all right, then.'

'You mean Wednesday's all right for you to undo the buttons?' said Felicity.

'Here? I shouldn't think so,' said Tim, taking his time to sum up exactly how she was feeling.

'Clara let me know we wouldn't be interrupted,' said Felicity, and made a face. 'Look, I've had a bloody good howl.'

'Ruddy rotten, Puss, but it doesn't show,' said Tim, and took her hand, pressing it. 'You were due for letting go.'

'Clara helped me repair the damage,' said Felicity. She was looking straight at him, as if she could see. She couldn't see a thing, of course, not one damn thing, but she could hear Tim and she thought she could even

410

pick up the warm smell of his vigorous body. 'You'll have to help me later on, every time I feel sorry for myself.'

'As much as I can, I'm not going to let you feel sorry for yourself,' said Tim.

'So what do we do now?' asked Felicity.

'This is your nurse's room,' said Tim.

'Clara's, yes,' said Felicity. 'What's it like?'

'Tidy,' said Tim. 'There's a bed.'

'Clara's,' said Felicity. 'What's it like?'

'Tidy,' said Tim.

'Are you going to lead me to it?' asked Felicity.

'I don't think we should use someone else's bed,' said Tim.

'Clara wouldn't mind,' said Felicity.

Tim felt she didn't mean that seriously. She'd had a good cry, probably because extreme depression had reared its dismal head, and now she thought, perhaps, that making love would convince him – or herself – that her sightlessness didn't matter. It didn't matter to him, and it didn't diminish his feelings for her.

'I think you'd mind if you were Clara,' he said.

'But we don't have to wait until the wedding day, do we?' said Felicity.

She was braving it out, thought Tim. She probably didn't feel in the least like making love.

'What's really on your mind, Puss?'

'What kind of a wife are you actually getting, Tim?'

'I'm getting you, Felicity, and you're my kind. You always have been. What d'you say to going for a walk? Round and round the grounds? It's a lovely day.'

'Lovely for some,' said Felicity.

'And for you and me,' said Tim.

She smiled then.

'Let's do that, let's go for a walk,' she said.

'Rattling good idea, chum,' said Tim, speaking her language.

With his guidance, she emerged a few minutes later into the sunshine of the extensive grounds, and they began the kind of saunter that was easiest for her. Tim noted the continued improvement she showed in her walk. He noted too how other inmates watched her with interest, and he sensed sympathy and admiration.

'Tell me about the raid,' she said.

'There was some heavy stuff flying about from both sides,' he said. He thought of the smoke bomb that had hit a landing craft and incinerated a number of Commandos. 'And some bloody awful casualties. But we mopped up the opposition eventually, and left the place in ruins. By the way, friends and relatives have been asking what we'd like for wedding presents, so I thought we'd have a chat about what we fancy.'

'I fancy you,' said Felicity.

'Oh, I come with the ring,' said Tim.

'Your father and stepmother have already given us a personal wedding present,' said Felicity, 'a book of funny bedtime stories.' Boots had bought and posted a book of anecdotal stories by Stephen Leacock, the Canadian humorist of international fame. 'You can read it to me before you jump in with me.'

'Wouldn't a book of sexy stories be better?' asked Tim.

'Sexy stories don't make you laugh, they make you wonder what the authors get up to on Saturday nights,' said Felicity. 'Peeping Tom larks, I suppose.'

'On a ladder,' said Tim.

Felicity laughed.

'Kiss,' she said.

'Here?' said Tim.

'Who's looking, then?'

'Everyone.'

'Do you mind?'

'Not if you don't.'

'Kiss, then.'

They stopped and kissed. An inmate whistled.

'How was that?' asked Tim.

'Healing,' said Felicity.

'Fancy another?' said Tim.

'Six more at least,' said Felicity.

'Let's put ourselves out of sight,' said Tim, 'or we'll get talked about.'

A chorus of whistles accompanied their disappearance.

'Now how'd you feel?' asked Tim, after he'd delivered several of the best.

'Saucy,' said Felicity, and they both laughed.

They strolled and sauntered, Felicity's arm wrapped around Tim's, he making sure it was his right arm. They forgot about wedding presents, which weren't important to them at this stage, and they concentrated on the pleasure of simply being together. Clara had tea brought out to them after a while, but it was Felicity who took up the teapot. Clara gave Tim a look that plainly warned him to make sure her patient didn't scald herself. Tim nodded, and Clara left them to themselves.

'Can you manage, Puss?' asked Tim.

'Say when,' said Felicity. She put a hand around a cup, and having established where it was in relation to the pot, she poured.

'When,' said Tim, and she repeated the process with the other cup. 'Take a bow,' he said.

'No spillage?' she said.

'None,' said Tim, who had his sling in his pocket. His fractured collarbone was knitting nicely. 'You'll be hanging out the washing next.'

'I'll get there little by little,' she said.

'Well, wherever, we'll get there together.'

'I'm counting on that,' said Felicity, which was a way of telling him not to go in for winning medals. 'Thanks for coming, Tim, I feel alive again.'

'In that case,' said Tim, 'after we've had this tea and cake, we'll get that book of funny stories and I'll read you one.'

'It's for bedtime,' said Felicity.

'Well, I suppose we can manage without a bed,' said Tim. 'How'd you feel about that?'

'Saucy,' said Felicity, and once more brought a teacup accurately to her lips.

In Dorset, the staff of a brigade of armoured regiments had taken over the mansion near Bere Regis. In charge of the ATS personnel was Major Clarice Robbins, a handsome woman of thirty-three. Horsey, breezy and valiant, one of her first duties was to interview Lieutenant Rosie Adams, who had been awaiting the arrival of her new unit.

'Pleased to have you, Lieutenant. In from the beginning, I see. Good, I like that. Need officers with experience, y'know. Had a bellyful of gels still wet behind the ears. Haven't got the foggiest notion of what the war's all about, some of 'em. What's your notion, Lieutenant?'

'Hit the enemy harder than he's hitting us, ma'am,' said Rosie, correctly summing up her new chief.

'That's the stuff,' said Major Robbins.

'Chop the buggers up. I see, according to your file, that you're a Somerville gel.'

'Quite true, ma'am.'

'Splendid. I've heard damn fine things about Somerville gels working for Intelligence, except I came across a couple who were hollow-chested. Don't like that in a woman.'

'It's addiction to study, ma'am,' said Rosie, keeping her face straight.

'Bent over books day and night, I suppose,' said Major Robbins. 'Not good for any woman's chest, and gives 'em round shoulders as well. Now, I also see you're going to be married. Who's the lucky feller?'

'Mr Matthew Chapman of Bere Regis,' said Rosie.

'Mister? Not an Army chap?'

'Not yet, ma'am.'

'Not waiting to be conscripted, is he?'

'No, ma'am,' said Rosie. 'He's been indispensable to the local farmers up to now, but today he has an interview with Colonel Fullerton of Bovington for direct entry into REME.'

'Good man,' said Major Robbins. 'Have to say, though, I'm not keen on any of my officers marrying. Plays the very devil with routine, y'know, and can muck up the whole works. Got my own wedding day out of the way in the early Thirties. Knew that bugger Hitler was going to land us in the hot soup

416

sooner or later. Had my offspring in quick time, Augusta and Horatio, and handed 'em over to our Punjabi ayah. Hope you won't muck up the works, Lieutenant. By the way, can you drill a squad of gels?'

'Yes, ma'am,' said Rosie. 'Usually in company with an ATS drill sergeant.'

'Good man. You and Sergeant Morris give our lot what for tomorrow. They've all got knock-knees, left feet and sloppy postures. Get 'em to straighten their backs and stick their chests out. Tell 'em to be proud of their bosoms. Glad to see you've got a straight back and a good posture yourself. D'you know what this bumph is on my desk?'

'Yes, ma'am,' said Rosie, 'a detailed inventory of all furniture and effects belonging to the War Department, and distinct from everything belonging to the owners of this mansion. There's a separate inventory for that, of which the owners have a copy.'

'Lot of bosh with a war on,' said Major Robbins. 'I make it a rule to keep my distance from bosh and bumph.' She dumped the sheets of paper in the waste basket. 'Did you see me do that, Lieutenant?'

'No, ma'am,' said Rosie.

'That's the stuff,' said Major Robbins. 'Well, a pleasure to have had this chat with you.'

'Thank you, ma'am,' said Rosie. Hiding a smile, she saluted and left.

She wondered how Matthew was getting on at Bovington.

Matthew, his garage no more than a forlorn heap of ashes and collapsed, fire-scorched girders, his hopes resting on entry into the Army, was standing up well to his interview with Colonel George Fullerton, RAOC. The Colonel, a thickset man with bristly, irongrey hair, was a regular of many years service, but a mechanical engineer first and foremost. It hadn't taken him long to do a severe kind of probing job on this Dorset fellow, and to be convinced he knew what he was talking about.

'But you're a stranger to tank engines,' he said.

'I'm no stranger to internal combustion, the basis of any fuel-driven engine,' said Matt.

'I can't argue with that,' said Colonel Fullerton, who had agreed to interview the man himself as a favour to Major Robert Adams, whom he'd originally met in Belgium before the Germans launched their massive invasion of the Low Countries. 'All the same,' he said.

'Yes, it comes down to that in the end,' said Matt. 'Tank or plane or truck or tractor engine, just a difference in size, horsepower and construction, but all the same basically as far as servicing goes. A simple question of noting the differences.'

'Up to a point,' said the Colonel, and looked again at the letter he'd had from Boots. It asked for Mr Matthew Chapman to be given serious consideration as a favour to the writer, and as agreed over the phone. Boots had left nothing to chance. 'Well, I'll be frank, Mr Chapman, I can't say we couldn't do without you, but I can say we'd like to have you. Major Adams mentioned your ankle, but you're no cripple, are you?'

'I don't even think about it,' said Matt. 'It happens to be there, but it's no problem.'

'I've known one-armed and one-eyed officers who've managed well enough in the right kind of unit,' said Colonel Fullerton. 'I see from your personal details that you matriculated from Dorchester Grammar School with honours. What made you elect for a trade and not a profession?'

'Family business of two thriving garages,' said Matt, 'and my father's wish for me to take one over eventually. Well, I enjoyed tinkering and learning from the time I was twelve.'

'Natural bent, I daresay,' said the Colonel, 'and no finicky distaste for getting your hands dirty. Too many young men turn their noses up at any mention of engineering, but I'm damned if I've ever wanted to work in a bank. You're never much more than a clerk. It's going to be a technological post-war world because of what the war is demanding of technology. The latest developments are awesome.'

'I've heard rumours of a jet engine, Colonel,' said Matt, 'and that it's hush-hush.'

'It is,' said Colonel Fullerton, 'but only in respect of how far we've got with it, since we know the Germans are working on it too. It'll be in aircraft before very long, and make propeller-driven planes look like carthorses. Look here, I'd like you to spend a day in our main workshops. Can you get here again on Friday, say by o-nine-hundred?'

'Easily enough, sir,' said Matt.

'Fine,' said Colonel Fullerton briskly. 'That'll do for now, then. Thanks for coming, Mr Chapman.'

'Thanks for a very fair interview,' said Matt.

Colonel Fullerton, smiling, said, 'But I put you through it for the first ten minutes, did I?'

'There aren't any bruises,' said Matt.

The Colonel liked that. He liked the man himself, a typical product of a grammar school. Pleasant manner and acceptably self-assured, without any public school cockiness. But he had the look of a farmer more than that of a garage proprietor. Well, Friday would tell, when he was confronted with a tank engine in need of some real servicing expertise.

Chapter Twenty-Six

At a little after six, Major Lucas's landlady, Mrs McGowan, knocked on his door. He was in his shirt sleeves, packing his valise. He was due to go on leave tomorrow.

'There's a caller, y'ken,' said Mrs McGowan.

'Who?'

'Good evening, Major Lucas.' Eloise materialized. She was smartly turned out and looking her best. Her make-up was light, as per regulations, but subtly complementary.

'To what do I owe the pleasure?' asked Major Lucas.

'Official business, sir,' said Eloise.

'Official?' said Major Lucas.

'Yes, sir.'

'I've had official business up to my eyebrows all day,' said Major Lucas, 'but very well, come in.'

'Thank you.' Eloise entered and Mrs McGowan took herself off. Eloise closed the door. She was tense, Major Lucas curious. 'How did the inquest on the raid go, sir?'

'Inquest is right,' said Major Lucas soberly.

'It concerned our dead in the main and what can be done to avoid heavy casualties in the future. Not much, apparently, unless we can catch the Hun in bed. Now state your official business, Subaltern Adams.'

'I have to state, sir, it's official just between you and me,' said Eloise, who looked cool but wasn't.

'It's an official complaint directed at me, is it?'

'Major Lucas,' said Eloise, 'it concerns an unfinished conversation between you and me.'

'What the devil are you on about?' asked Major Lucas.

'Major Lucas, last time we were together you seized me in your arms, made my skirt slide up–'

'I did what?'

'Made me show my legs and kissed me several times on my lips,' said Eloise.

'Was that the occasion when you were yelling at me, you baggage?'

'I won't be called a baggage,' said Eloise heatedly.

'Then don't be so confoundingly pro-voking,' said Major Lucas.

'I want to know why you kissed me on my lips if you think so badly of me,' said Eloise, pent-up.

'I kissed you to shut you up and because I always want to, damn it,' said Major Lucas.

'Ah, always?' said Eloise, pouncing on his admission. 'Always?'

'Yes, damn it, even if you are too full of your own importance.'

'Well, I am important to myself, and won't be treated as if I'm a nobody,' said Eloise. 'Major Lucas, I must ask you, if you always want to kiss me, does that mean you love me?'

'Yes, God help me,' he said.

Eloise took a deep breath.

'Then why don't you ask me to marry you?' she said.

'What?'

Eloise took another deep breath.

'That is what an officer and gentleman should do before kissing me like that,' she said. 'If you wish me to marry you, well, although you don't always act like a gentleman, you're a splendid officer and a very distinguished soldier, and I should be happy to be your wife. I'm sure you'll be the one to hang Hitler and be knighted for it. That would make me Lady Lucas, which I should like very much.'

Major Lucas looked as if Martians had arrived and taken hold of his ears. Certainly, for the first time as an adult, he was lost for words. His tongue struggled.

'What did you say?' he asked eventually.

'Major Lucas, I'm sure you heard me,' said Eloise.

'Then you're the most confusing and pre-posterous young woman I'm ever likely to meet,' he said.

'Preposterous? Preposterous?'

'God knows if I'll ever make head or tail of you.'

'But if you love me–'

'That's my weakness.'

'No, no, how can it be a weakness?' protested Eloise.

'Well, I will ask you to marry me, so help me,' said Major Lucas, 'although I know that if it comes about it'll mean you'll rattle my ears for the rest of my life, and that'll be a result of my weakness.'

'Oh, how can you say such a thing?' Eloise was flushed with indignation. 'Do you want me to say no to your proposal?'

'I want you to be my wife with a promise that you won't set about me more than once a week,' said Major Lucas.

'Set about you? Am I a boxer? Major Lucas, do you like upsetting me?'

'Why do you want me to propose to you, apart from thinking you might become Lady Lucas?'

'Why? Why? Because I want to be your wife. Haven't I told you so?'

'I thought you once said–'

'What does it matter what I once said? Yesterday is not the same as today.'

'I simply want to know if you care for

me,' he said.

'Do you think I would marry a man I didn't care for?' demanded Eloise.

'In that case, Subaltern Adams, will you marry me?'

'Ah, you are officially asking me?' said Eloise.

'I am,' said Major Lucas.

'Heavens, I can't believe it,' breathed Eloise.

'You can't what?'

'I mean, this is so sudden,' said Eloise.

'God Almighty,' said Major Lucas, and gave her a helpless look. Eloise smiled. 'Come here, you witch,' he said, and Eloise placed herself in his arms. She was not only over the recent shock of discovering why she had suffered a storm of jealousy, she was remarkably happy with the outcome and what was going on now. She was close to his warm, firm body and he was kissing her. Happily, she closed her eyes.

Opening them, she said, 'Your name is William.' Then, mischievously, 'Am I to call you Willy?'

'Only at your peril,' he said. He was Bill or Luke to his friends, having been called Luke at school. 'The first time you address me as Willy, you'll get your bottom smacked.'

'Heavens, you wouldn't do such a thing, would you?' said Eloise, amazed at how delighted she was with everything.

'God knows how you've escaped it so far, and bear in mind I'm no gentleman,' said Major Lucas.

'Of course you are,' said Eloise. 'Shall I call you William?'

'Definitely not. Try Luke.'

'Oh, I like that,' said Eloise, 'and I would rather be kissed than anything else.'

'I'll settle for that,' he said, and suited his action to his words.

Eloise closed her eyes again and dreamed blissfully.

Imagine it.

Lady Lucas.

Boots answered the cottage phone at nine that evening. Eloise was calling him.

'Papa, you will never believe.'

'I'll never believe what, my French chicken?'

'I'm going to be married.'

'Which I'm not to believe?'

'Yes, of course you are, darling Papa, I am saying so.'

'I'm delighted, then,' said Boots. 'Who's the lucky man?'

'Major Lucas.'

'The bear who growls?'

'How can you say that? Major Lucas is a gentleman and a very distinguished soldier.'

'From where, I wonder, did I pick up my mistaken impression?'

'Oh, we all make some mistakes, Papa, but never mind, I'm very happy and want you to know how glad I am that you found me and brought me to England, which I love. Oh, I love Scotland too. It's very beautiful up here, did you know?'

'Yes, I know, Eloise. A land of shining lochs, a thousand quiet places, a fair number of bagpipes, and a fine people who built our Empire with us.'

'You are fine too, Papa, and very much a gentleman. That's why Rosie and I are out of the ordinary, yes, and Tim too. Are you happy that all of us are going to marry this year?'

'I'll be happy if I can get my breath back,' said Boots.

'Ah, you are amazed?'

'Open-mouthed,' said Boots, 'but not unhappy.'

'Major Lucas wishes us to marry in October, two months after Tim's wedding. Do you approve?'

'You have my best wishes, Eloise,' said Boots, 'but if much more of this goes on, your grandmother will take to her bed.'

'Oh, I know you, Papa, you will have your little joke,' said Eloise. 'Grandmama will be happy, I'm sure, and I'm writing a very nice letter to her. Papa, Major Lucas is here with me and wishes to speak to you.'

'Put him on,' said Boots.

Eloise's distinguished gentleman came through.

'Major Adams? Major Lucas here, Bill Lucas.'

'My compliments, Major,' said Boots.

'I thought I'd better introduce myself and let you know I'd like to meet you and your family sometime,' said Major Lucas.

'If you can get to my home with Eloise the weekend of fifth of July for my other daughter Rosie's marriage, we'll all be delighted to meet you,' said Boots.

'I appreciate that,' said Major Lucas, 'and if circumstances allow, I'll be there.'

'Fine,' said Boots.

Eloise came back on the line, and she and Boots had another little chat before saying goodbye to each other. Boots then spoke to Polly. They were enjoying the quietest of evenings, Polly a pleasant surprise in that she never demanded to be entertained either at home or in the officers' mess. At this moment she was curled up on the old-fashioned sofa, a book in her hand. When told that Eloise was following Rosie and Tim into wedlock, she nearly dropped the book.

'Ye gods,' she said, 'is it the excitement of being attached to a Commando unit or is it love? Or not wanting to be left behind by Rosie and Tim?'

'I've an idea she's actually in love,' said Boots.

'I thought she didn't consider Major Lucas her kind of gentleman,' said Polly.

'Changed her mind, apparently,' said Boots. 'She's a female.'

'Watch what you're saying, old pieface,' said Polly. 'I'm lost for words myself. All I can see in front of me is wedding confetti. I think I need an aspirin.'

'Will a gin and tonic do?' asked Boots.

'In my condition?' said Polly.

'I like it,' said Boots.

'Gin and tonic or my condition?' said Polly.

'Your condition,' said Boots, and leaned over her to apply a fond caress.

'Those,' said Polly, 'are now to be treated with respect, old lad.'

'Miracle woman, I'm devoted to them,' said Boots.

'Love them, do you?'

'I'm their closest admirer,' said Boots.

'Love me too, do you?'

'Hand on my heart,' said Boots.

She smiled, but what she really wanted was to be told he loved her more than he had ever loved Emily.

As at the brigade headquarters where Rosie was working, a new ATS admin contingent was installed at Sir Henry's headquarters. The switchboard girl rang Boots late Friday afternoon.

430

'Hello?' he said.

'Colonel Fullerton of Bovington on the line, sir.'

'Put him through,' said Boots.

'Hello? Major Adams?'

'Don't fall about,' said Boots, 'I've just been gazetted as a colonel.'

'Welcome to our high-falutin' ranks, old man,' said Colonel Fullerton. 'Look, about Chapman.'

'What about him?' asked Boots.

'First-class. On my instructions, Number One workshop chucked a decrepit tank engine at him this morning. He embraced it, asked for the manual, was told we'd try to find one, and then set about the lump of old iron from scratch. Without any kind of help, in fact. By the time I gave instructions for the manual to be produced, it was superfluous to his requirements. Not long after he had that engine running. He's a natural for REME when it's set up. We'll have him. I'll arrange his medical. He'll probably be classed Grade C because of his ankle. That'll disqualify him for combat duties, but not for maintenance and as an instructor. Staff-Sergeant rank, I thought, except I've an idea you had something on your mind when you recommended him. If so, spit it out, old man.'

'He's marrying my daughter, Lieutenant Rosie Adams, next week,' said Boots.

'So that's your game.' Colonel Fullerton let go a bark, the equivalent of a laugh in his case.

'I merely mention it,' said Boots.

'One pip, then? Second Lieutenant?'

'If he's worth it,' said Boots.

'I could beat about the bush, but I won't,' said Colonel Fullerton. 'Yes, he's worth it.'

'Good of you, but don't think I'm twisting your arm,' said Boots.

'Not much as your daughter's father, but you're welcome,' said Colonel Fullerton. 'What's your view on the situation in Russia?'

'Unprintable,' said Boots. Hitler's hordes had overrun the Ukraine, and Stalin's armies were still falling back.

'Is there no stopping those Panzer divisions?'

'That's a question Churchill must be asking,' said Boots.

'I'll have to hang up now,' said Colonel Fullerton. 'Be my guest next time you visit Bovington.'

'Pleasure,' said Boots, and returned to a list of units that were to form another of Sir Henry's new divisions. He was making a study of what they were equipped with in the way of small arms and heavy weaponry. Totally inadequate, and he would have to submit details of extra requirements to Sir Henry, and Sir Henry would have to fight to get them. Boots pushed the list aside after a few minutes, remembering he wanted to phone Rosie. Switchboard made the call for him.

Rosie, contacted, came through. Boots enjoyed the pleasure of letting her know Matthew was to receive direct entry into the REME as a subaltern following a few necessary preliminaries. Rosie, delighted, expressed a belief that her adoptive father was a gift to civilization. Boots suggested she was guilty of a slight exaggeration. Rosie said a slight exaggeration didn't make any real difference. She also said she had contacted the solicitors about her natural father's bequest and was going to present herself in person to them as soon as she could arrange it. Then she asked Boots if he'd recovered yet from the news of Eloise's engagement to a distinguished officer and gentleman. Boots said he was keeping a sense of proportion, that while the event had made the family fall about, the rest of the country was still on its feet. Rosie laughed.

'Eloise has always wanted to marry a distinguished gentleman,' she said, 'but does this one realize he's marrying into a family of cockneys?'

'That's a point,' said Boots. Chinese Lady, Tommy, Sammy, Vi, and old Aunt Victoria and Uncle Tom were unmistakable cockneys. He himself had been a cockney kid until his five years at a grammar school improved his speech and made other kids call him Lord Muck. 'Well, you've never been a cockney, Rosie.'

'Course I 'ave, guv,' said Rosie, 'ain't I?'

'You can take off Harry Champion himself, but you're not a cockney,' said Boots. 'I'm a born one.'

'Some hopes,' said Rosie, 'you talk more proper than the Archbishop of Canterbury. Well, let's see what happens to Major Lucas's face when he's listening to Uncle Tommy and Uncle Sammy.' She laughed again. 'I know there's a war on, Daddy old love, but there's still a little fun lurking around some corners, isn't there?'

'Enough to give the country some cheerful moments,' said Boots, 'and as for your interview with the solicitors, good luck, poppet.'

'I'm still sad about Sir Charles,' said Rosie.

'Yes, that's in your nature,' said Boots. ''Bye, Rosie.'

''Bye, Daddy old sport,' said Rosie, 'and thanks again for being a great help to Matthew. Love you for it.'

Boots put the phone down and spent a few moments reflecting on family marriages and the state of the war. The Germans under Hitler were proving as irresistible as the French under Napoleon. They were in occupation of most of West and Central Europe, of Albania, Greece, Crete and the Channel Islands. They were still advancing in Egypt, and in their latest offensive they were rolling back the Russians.

God alone knew how they could be beaten.

It wasn't the brightest time for any marriage. It was a year of exhaustive effort, with the country badly wounded, yet Rosie, Emma, Tim, Eloise and he himself had all chosen to embrace wedlock.

Boots let a little sigh escape, then returned to his work.

'Good night, Mr Adams, I've enjoyed my first week here,' said Rachel.

'Mutual,' said Sammy, 'and glad to inform you you've proved highly valid to operations.'

'Valuable?' said Rachel.

'That as well,' said Sammy.

'Good night, then.'

'Same to you, Mrs Goodman,' said Sammy.

On arrival home at her Brixton house, Rachel noted a car parked outside. As she reached the steps, a man emerged from the car, a chubby well-dressed man. Rachel recognized him as Solomon Morrish, a family friend and a business colleague of her husband Benjamin.

'Solly?' she said, smiling. 'To what do I owe the pleasure of seeing you on this peaceful evening?'

Solly took his hat off and regarded her soberly.

'Might I talk to you inside, Rachel my dear?' he asked.

'Of course,' said Rachel.

In her handsome parlour, Solly said, 'I don't like this, bringing news not so good, Rachel.'

'The club's gone broke?' said Rachel.

'I should worry about that?' said Solly. 'It's a terrible war, Rachel, full of sadness, and even more now. Rachel, I have to tell you that at a meeting at the club–' He checked, looked down at his hat and sighed.

'Solly?' Rachel's heart missed a beat. 'It's Benjamin?'

'Yes, that's the news, Rachel, and God knows don't I hate bringing it to you? Benjy was himself, so it seemed, and stood up to make a point. Then he fell. He folded, my dear, and fell. Before my eyes he went, without a sound except a little sigh, a little painful sigh. We did what we could while someone fetched a doctor, but he'd gone.'

'Oh, my God,' said Rachel, white.

'That air raid, Rachel, and what it did to him, put him under a collapsed house and broke his legs,' said Solly. 'It damaged him more than we thought, it affected his heart,

436

and his heart gave up just a little while ago. Rachel my dear, did any of us know? No, none of us. When he returned to business, he was the same as always, or so it seemed, didn't it?'

Rachel's knees gave way and she groped for a chair. Solly lent her his arm and she sat down.

'No, none of us knew,' she whispered, 'and nor did any of the hospital doctors speak to me about a damaged heart. He's gone, Solly?'

'He's gone, Rachel, but no suffering, none. All in a split second, believe me.'

Rachel, grieving for a man who had been a good husband, could only thank God that she had never been less than a faithful and loyal wife, that there was nothing for which she would have needed Benjamin to forgive her.

Solly gently insisted on seeing to the arrangements for tomorrow's funeral.

'Susie?'

'Rachel?' said Susie. It was just after seven, and she and Sammy had been listening to the news when the phone rang.

'Susie,' said Rachel, 'I have to ask you to tell Sammy I shan't be in the office tomorrow morning, Saturday, nor for a few days next week.'

'Rachel, what's happened?' asked Susie,

and in a very strained voice Rachel told her of Benjamin's sudden death from heart failure. 'Oh, dear God, how terrible,' said Susie. 'Rachel, are you alone?'

'Mr Morrish has just gone.'

'Rachel, you mustn't be alone, not tonight, or tomorrow night,' said Susie. 'You must come here, especially if there's a raid. I'll talk to Sammy, and he'll come and fetch you.'

'Susie, I can go to stay with Mr Morrish and his wife,' said Rachel.

'Are you going to?'

'I haven't been able to think very well, Susie, and couldn't make up my mind.'

'Rachel, pack some things,' said Susie. 'Sammy will be round in his car in ten minutes or so, I know he will. And I know he'll agree with me that you mustn't be alone. Spend the weekend with us, and we'll give you all the help we can.'

'Thank you, Susie,' said Rachel, 'I would like to come, I would like to talk to you and Sammy, about Benjy and about how I am to tell my daughters, as I must.'

'I'm going to let Sammy know now,' said Susie, 'and you can expect him in a little while. Rachel, I'm so very sorry.'

Sammy moved fast. He fetched Rachel in quick time, talked to her, and himself telephoned the school at which her

438

daughters were boarding. Once through to the headmistress, he handed the phone to Rachel. Rachel spoke to the headmistress, and then to her daughters, Rebecca and Leah. The girls wept, but begged to be allowed home for their father's funeral. Sammy and Susie had helped Rachel make a decision about that, to say yes to what she knew her daughters would want, to bring them home for a week and to risk any air raids.

Accordingly, Sammy left his house at six the following morning to drive Rachel to the West Country to pick up Rebecca and Leah. We can't ask them to put themselves on a train, he had said, and that had turned Rachel's eyes misty. In the boarding school close to a Wiltshire village, she conducted a quiet and gentle meeting in private with her daughters, who had packed in readiness for the drive home.

Sammy made the journey through green countryside bursting with summer life. Against such a canvas, war and death seemed to have no place in the scheme of things. But Sammy drove with sustained control and care, to ensure that fate's ugliest hand did not strike twice at the same family. He greatly valued Rachel as a long-standing, warm-hearted friend, and had an avuncular affection for her daughters.

Rachel wondered, amid her grief, if there

were any people who meant more to her than the men and women of the Adams family.

The journey was completed just after midday, when Rachel and her daughters immediately went out to buy mourning clothes. Sammy drove them to the shop.

Benjamin's funeral took place at four that afternoon, Rachel and her daughters in deep black. Sammy and Susie attended.

There was no raid that night.

Chapter Twenty-Seven

Saturday, 5 July.

There was a light drizzle falling in Camberwell just before dawn, but by seven-thirty the sun was out and about.

'Rosie?'

Rosie awoke. Polly in a negligée was beside her bed, smiling down at her.

'Polly?'

'Good morning, ducky, the sun's arrived and here's a cup of tea for you.' Polly placed it on the bedside table. Rosie sat up.

'Well, isn't that nice of you?' she said.

'Yes,' smiled Polly, 'ask yourself what's happening to me. Old slippers, old dressing-gown, curlers in my hair, fag hanging from my lip and smoke in my eyes.'

'That's not an old dressing-gown, there are no curlers in your hair, and I haven't seen a fag in your mouth for months,' said Rosie.

'In addition to all that, I've made a pot of tea for everyone,' said Polly. 'I'm a domesticated old biddy.'

'You don't look it,' said Rosie, sipping her tea, 'but what made you play the domestic?'

'I thought as this is your big day, I'd do the honours,' said Polly. 'Have a lovely wedding, sweetie, and never forget how much you mean to me. If Boots loves you, so do I. Must dash now to carry tea to the others. Toodle-oo.'

From then on the house hummed with activity.

At twelve-fifteen, Boots called up to Rosie.

'Transport's at the door, poppet.'

'Coming,' sang Rosie, and down she came in her white silk, her skirt floating, her veil up, her blue eyes as clear as a Pacific sky, Lilian watching her from the landing. Boots, in uniform, was touched to the quick by her loveliness. She had been born of a mother who had deserted her and a man who had not known of her existence until a few years ago. Boots had a moment of deep sympathy for Charles Armitage, killed in the defence of Tobruk and robbed of any chance of seeing Rosie in the enchantment of her bridal raiment. Not only should the man be remembered for his battle honours, but for fathering a girl never less than endearing. Within the next hour she would belong to Matthew. Boots was not going to complain. He had had the extreme privilege of knowing her and all her ways for over twenty years as daughter, friend, companion and jewel.

'Poppet, you look superb,' he said.

'Thank you, Daddy old love,' she said, a

442

little catch in her voice. She knew there were going to be times when she would miss him. She walked to the open front door with him, where she was greeted by Mr Eli Greenberg. Dressed in top-hat and tails, a remarkable sight as ever was to behold, he swept the hat off and bowed.

'Might I have the honour and pleasure, Miss Rosie Adams?' he asked. His little green cart and pony stood on the drive.

'Dear Mr Greenberg, you know how disappointed I'd have been if you hadn't arrived,' smiled Rosie.

'Ah, well, it's an old family custom, ain't it, Rosie?' said Mr Greenberg. The custom had begun in 1916 with the wedding of Lizzy and Ned, and if pony had succeeded pony, the cart was the original. 'Requested by Boots and your own self for today, and didn't I do it for Miss Emma only a while ago? Vould I exclude you of all my young lady friends? Never. A picture out of heaven, ain't she, Boots?'

'Granted, Eli,' smiled Boots, and he and Rosie mounted the cart to which colourful bunting had been attached.

Mr Greenberg drove them to the church on Denmark Hill, with Lilian catching them up and passing them in a taxi. Rosie had her veil down, a circlet of silk orange blossom crowning her. People stopped, turned, stared and smiled.

Rachel was talking to her daughters. The girls were over the worst of their lamentations, and were due to return to their West Country boarding school on Monday.

'Mama, weren't you going to the wedding of Uncle Sammy's niece Rosie today?' asked Leah, fifteen and very much like her mother in her looks.

'Yes, you were,' said Rebecca, seventeen and studious. 'Isn't Rosie a favourite of yours?'

'Uncle Sammy's my favourite,' said Leah. She and Rebecca had long adopted Sammy as an uncle.

'I was going to the wedding and reception, yes,' said Rachel, 'but I can't, not now.' She and the girls were still in mourning black.

'No, I suppose not,' said Rebecca.

'It's a shame,' said Leah, 'but Mama simply couldn't attend a celebration yet.'

'Darlings,' said Rachel, 'I've a wedding gift for the happy couple. Would one of you like to take it to the house sometime this afternoon?'

'Of course, Mama,' said Rebecca, 'Leah would love to, wouldn't you, Leah?'

'Rebecca's getting–' Leah checked. She'd been going to say her sister was getting into a bossy habit of ordering her about, but one couldn't make quarrelsome remarks while they were still in deep mourning for their father. 'I'll take it, Mama,' she said, and then thought a bus ride might bring a little relief from sadness. And she might see Uncle Sammy, whom she adored. As her mother's more outgoing daughter, she had no hang-ups about owning affection for a Gentile like Uncle Sammy. 'Yes, I'll go, Mama, I'll take the present.'

'Thank you, darling,' said Rachel, 'I'll wrap it up in a while.'

Because other young female cousins were living as evacuees in the West Country, Rosie had only one bridesmaid. Little Paula. She was waiting in company with Emma and Annabelle, maids of honour. Annabelle, Rosie's most faithful friend ever since they were little girls, had left her children in the care of friendly neighbours in Wiltshire, for she and Nick simply had to be at the wedding. Paula was in Cambridge blue, Emma and Annabelle in primrose, the vicar waiting with them. A posy was clutched in Paula's hand. She gave a little yelp of delight at the arrival of the bride in a polished green cart.

'Oh, crumbs, look at that, Mister Vicar.'

'Charming,' smiled the vicar.

Preceded by the priest, Rosie advanced into the church with Boots, her hand tucked inside his elbow. Paula, accompanied by Emma and Annabelle, trod in awe behind the bride. Every head turned. Lilian, who had found a place in this Christian church, allowed herself a pat on the back for what the wedding gown did for Rosie.

Lovely, thought Lizzy, simply lovely.

Just like I looked for Jonathan, thought Emma. Well, I hope I did. Oh, I wish you were here, Jonathan, and not in hospital with your operation wrapped up in bandages. Never mind, I'm coming to see you tomorrow.

My, thought Vi, our Rosie, she's a picture.

A Gainsborough, thought Ned.

A corker, thought Tommy.

Lord Above, thought Chinese Lady, is this really our Rosie?

Good on you, Rosie, thought Tim.

Bless us, thought Jemima Hardy, Jonathan's mother, these Adams brides be something special. Husband Job thought, here's a reason why this old country still be worth fighting for.

Holy Joe, thought Sammy, that's an Adams princess. We're royalty. Well, good as.

How beautiful, thought Lady Simms.

As for Matthew, he thought he was dreaming when the vision that was Rosie arrived beside him.

Boots relinquished her.

Ye gods, thought Polly, she's exquisite, and that darling man of mine is letting go of her at last, with a smile.

'Hello, my lovely,' whispered Matt.

'Hello, darling,' whispered Rosie, then turned and handed her bouquet to Emma who, because of Paula's enraptured look, passed it to her. Paula clasped the bouquet and her posy to her awestruck self. Mr Greenberg slipped into the back pew next to Lilian.

The vicar began the service, which was graced with the presence of Sir Henry and Lady Simms.

Chinese Lady took hold of a hand that touched hers. Mr Finch glanced at her. Her expression contained a note of lament, and he knew she saw the marriage as one that would take Rosie away from the family. She liked everyone to be within easy reach, and to her even places like Clapham and Norbury didn't fit. Well, from the Denmark Hill area, a body couldn't pop in on someone in Clapham or Norbury while out shopping.

A little sigh escaped her. Mr Finch gently pressed her hand.

The service proceeded, and Lizzy dabbed her eyes as it reached the moment when Boots gave away his adopted daughter to her Dorset man. Ned looked as if nostalgia was overtaking him. Polly looked touched. Sammy cleared his throat. Tommy swallowed. Tim, always so close to Rosie in affection and spirit, felt a little wrench. Bobby seemed serious, Helene seemed absorbed, and Vi was misty-eyed. Eloise thought how fine Matthew looked. Susie experienced a little heartache. Rosie belonged to the family in her own special way, as she had shown when she chose not to live with her natural father.

'I now pronounce you man and wife,' said the mellow-voiced vicar. 'Matthew, you may kiss your bride.'

Everyone who could be at the church had been there, and were now at the house for the reception, including several whom Susie had marked only as possibles, such as Cassie and Freddy Brown, Emma's sister Annabelle and her husband Nick, and two of Rosie's old Somerville friends.

Bobby and Helene had come from somewhere on the Kent coast. On Monday they were to present themselves to Major Buckmaster again, when they would be obliged to convince him they could stand up to any questions concerning their new identities. For now they were intent on enjoying the reception.

Also present was Bobby's brother Edward, who had arrived home yesterday evening with Annabelle and Nick. Edward, seventeen, tended to be lean, like his dad, and undemanding, like his Uncle Boots. He was in his last term at his Wiltshire school.

Eloise was suffering disappointment

because Major Lucas, who had hoped to be there, had gone to London with other senior officers for a Commando conference immediately after his return from leave.

The guests spread themselves around the house and garden, participating in greetings, animated talk and welcome refreshments. Rosie and Matt were circulating. Cassie and Freddy were enjoying a rapturous reunion with Annabelle and Nick. Sammy was having what he considered shouldn't be allowed on such a happy occasion, a verbal ding-dong with one of Rosie's old Somerville friends, Miss Evelyn Harris. What was upsetting him was the one-sidedness of the ding-dong.

Miss Harris, who liked his electric blue eyes but considered he didn't know as much about Nazi ideology as he ought to, had been filling his ears with information he hadn't asked for and didn't really need. As far as Sammy was concerned, Nazism was a wholesale curse, full stop.

'Take the Nazi attitude to women, for instance,' said the earnest Miss Harris. 'It's regarded, Mr Adams, as an affront to every facet of civilization. It looks at women only as breeders. It amounts, basically, to ideological cultivation of the womb.'

Sammy was sure he could do without that piece of news. Womb was a kind of delicate and private word that had never been mentioned to him by Susie in all the time he'd known her as girl, wife and mother. And Chinese Lady would consider the world was collapsing if it was ever mentioned in her presence.

'Well,' he said, 'I–'

'Everyone should be made fully aware of the lowly state of women in Nazi Germany,' said Miss Harris, 'and particularly they should be aware of the fact that what value German women have to the State is primarily governed by their fertility.'

'Well,' said Sammy, who was also not on speaking terms with female fertility, 'I–'

'In short,' said Miss Harris (which made Sammy hope she was running out of breath), 'the perfect Aryan woman in the eyes of the Nazis is one who has the right antecedents and can and will produce children to order, within or outside of marriage, and if outside, then irrespective of whether this involves one father or several, providing every father is a certified true-blooded Aryan himself, which ideology represents State-inspired degradation of women, as I'm sure you'll agree.'

'To be frank,' said Sammy, 'I haven't–'

'You haven't given the subject any thought, is that what you mean?' said Miss Harris. 'Would you like me to send you a pamphlet?'

'I'd like you to excuse me,' said Sammy,

'someone's dropped a cigarette and my trousers are on fire.' He vanished.

'What a funny man,' said Miss Harris, 'I didn't see any smoke or smell any burning.' She made tracks for handsome Tommy Adams, whose respect for the privacy of wombs and female fertility was on a par with Sammy's.

The caterers were dispensing a variety of liquid refreshments, and the wedding breakfast, laid out on tables on the garden patio, was being consumed on a help-yourself basis. The chatter was a buzz of active tongues. Boots and Polly attached themselves dutifully to Matthew's parents, sister and brother-in-law.

Tim, his fractured collarbone well on the mend, thought about Felicity.

Felicity at this moment was talking to Clara.

'Listen, Florence Nightingale, how do you rate me now?'

'High,' said Clara.

'Drunk, you mean?' said Felicity.

'Great,' said Clara.

'Do I have a good chance, then?' asked Felicity.

'Of what?' said Clara.

'Of being a useful wife, of course,' said Felicity.

'Tim doesn't think about you like that,' said Clara.

'Perhaps not, but I have to. Wait a moment, have you been talking to him behind my back, you devious woman?'

'I've talked to him, yes, but not behind your back.'

'What's your verdict?' asked Felicity.

'That you can make him a very happy man,' said Clara.

'How can I do that in my condition?'

'Just by going through with the marriage,' said Clara.

'Oh, jolly good,' said Felicity.

'What does that mean?' asked Clara.

'That you've just made me a very happy woman,' said Felicity.

Edward was talking to Bobby in the hall when the doorbell rang. He answered it. A very pretty girl with gorgeous brown eyes stood on the doorstep. She was holding a nicely wrapped parcel.

'Hello,' he said.

'Oh, hello,' said Leah, wearing a filmy black scarf over her hair and black stockings on her legs. But a light spring coat covered her black dress. She simply hadn't wanted to arrive in full mourning. 'Is this where the wedding reception is?'

'Yes, this is where,' said Edward. 'Have you come to join in?'

'Oh, no, I'm afraid not,' said Leah.

'Well, you're welcome to now you're

452

here,' said Edward.

'That's very kind of you,' said Leah, 'but I can't. I've come just to deliver a wedding present from my mother, Mrs Rachel Goodman, who's a friend of the family.'

'Mrs Rachel Goodman?' Edward felt a sympathetic pang. 'I'm so sorry. We've all heard about your dad. Rotten bad luck, and I expect you still feel rotten. I can understand wedding parties are out for you, but thanks for bringing the present. Would you like to hand it to the bride, my cousin Rosie, or shall I take it for you?'

'Oh, I think you'd best take it,' said Leah, who felt, naturally enough, that she didn't want to suddenly find herself in the middle of the celebrations, even if she wouldn't have minded a little talk with Uncle Sammy. And even then, if all the family were as kind and sympathetic as this boy, she'd be certain to cry, and that would be embarrassing for everybody. She handed over the parcel. It contained an exquisite flower vase.

'Thanks,' said Edward. 'Let's see, I know your mum has two daughters, but as I've never met either of you, which one are you?'

'I'm Leah.'

'I'm Edward, Edward Somers. Tell you what, while you're here, would you like a glass of lemonade and a piece of wedding cake? You don't have to come in, you can

453

have it out here with me. Would you like that?'

'Oh, I–' Leah was a little flustered, but since she was also touched, she said, 'Oh, yes, thanks, I would.'

'Don't go away, then, stay there,' said Edward, and disappeared. He was back inside a minute, with a glass of lemonade and a plate containing two slices of cake. Beside him was the bride herself.

Leah gazed at Rosie in unaffected admiration. Rosie smiled.

'You're Leah, Mrs Goodman's daughter?'

'Yes.'

'Well, you know, don't you,' said Rosie gently, 'how sorry we all are about your father. Thank you so much for taking the trouble to bring the wedding gift. Tell your mother I'll be writing to her. You're sure you won't come in? Edward says you'd rather not.'

'I hope you understand,' said Leah.

'Of course,' said Rosie, 'I'll leave Edward to look after you. Goodbye, Leah. Please thank your mother and tell her we're all thinking of her, won't you?'

'Goodbye,' said Leah, 'and I hope you'll be very happy.'

She found herself lingering. She actually sat down with Edward on the front steps in the bright light of the afternoon, and they shared the cake and also the glass of lemonade. The receding clouds of her grief receded a little more as they talked about their respective schools, which weren't all that far apart, and about their experiences as evacuees.

'You don't mind if I tell you I like you?' said Edward after a while.

'But you hardly know me,' said Leah, slightly pink.

'Well, I know your mum,' said Edward. 'We all do, and we all like her. Now I like you too. Glad to have met you.'

'Oh, it's my pleasure too,' said Leah ingenuously.

Edward asked her if she'd spend her time at home when the school holidays started. Leah knew her mother, having just lost Daddy, would now make absolutely sure that nothing happened to her and her sister Rebecca through air raids, so she said no, she'd remain at the school with Rebecca and lots of other evacuee girls. Edward said he was finishing his own schooling at the end of this term and starting work as an assistant in one of Salisbury's public libraries, that he'd work there until he was eighteen, when he'd volunteer for one of the Services if the war was still on.

'That sounds really interesting, working in a library,' said Leah, thinking what a friendly boy he was and so natural. 'But I'd better go now or Mama will be wondering what's happened to me.' They came to their feet and Edward walked with her over the drive to the open gate. 'Goodbye, Edward, thanks ever so much for being so nice,' she said.

'Goodbye, Leah,' said Edward, and shook her hand in manly fashion. 'I'll write to you sometime when I get back to Wiltshire.'

'Will you really?' asked Leah in a happy way.

'Give you my word,' said Edward. 'Well, I daresay I could come and see you at your school, couldn't I?'

'Oh, my life,' said Leah, who'd never dreamt of having a Gentile boyfriend, 'd'you mean that?'

'Give you my word,' said Edward again. 'Say in a month or so, when perhaps you'll be feeling a bit better about your dad.'

'Well, it's ever so nice of you,' said Leah. 'Oh, I really must go now.'

Off she went, a much happier young lady for the moment. Edward watched her as she walked to the bus stop. Crikey, what a lovely girl.

'Leah?' said Rachel in astonishment.

'Could I have him for a friend, Mama, if he does come to see me?' asked Leah.

'You really want that, lovey?' said Rachel, thinking back over the years to the day when she first met Sammy, a Gentile boy with

456

laughing blue eyes and the friendliest of natures. Nothing could come of their relationship, but how she had wished otherwise.

'Mama, I do like him,' said Leah, 'and I know he doesn't mind about differences.'

'Darling, I'm never going to discourage you in your feelings because of differences,' said Rachel, 'or dictate to you about friendships. If you and Edward want to be friends, I shan't object. I know him, of course, and although I haven't seen him since the war started, I always thought him entirely likeable.'

'Thank you, Mama,' said Leah, 'you're really very nice to your daughters.'

'I simply believe, darling, that our years of being young should be happy and carefree,' said Rachel. 'It's later on that responsibilities arrive and we discover it's necessary to observe certain do's and don'ts.'

'Oh, I'll face up to the do's and don'ts of later on,' said Leah with the blitheness of the young, and Rachel hoped her younger daughter wouldn't find the age of responsibility to her religion as heart-breaking as she had herself.

The time was a little after six. The evening was fine, the skies clear, Hitler's aggressive and dynamic Germans flooding the Ukraine. Rosie and Matthew were ready for

457

departure, everyone calling good luck and goodbye. Rosie was in new turquoise blue, a colour favourite with her, and she was striving to control emotions. She was leaving the home she had known for many years, the home she had shared with the family she loved, to build her own home with Matthew in faraway Dorset. Sammy was still grieving about that, and Chinese Lady still felt she'd have liked Rosie a little closer. However, at least she wasn't going to live in poverty, not now Matthew was going into the Army and Rosie had her inheritance.

Everyone wanted to say a personal goodbye, and amid the crush, Rosie managed to snatch a few moments with each of those dearest to her. Tim, Chinese Lady, Grandpa Finch, Eloise, Sammy, Susie, Lizzy and others. Then Polly, and finally, Boots.

'Oh help,' she said, the catch back in her voice, 'now I don't know if I can stand going.'

'Take the leap, poppet,' said Boots, 'you'll like the landing.'

'I–' Rosie was lost for any other words at this point. All she could do to let him know how much she had always loved him was to hug him. He kissed her. She put herself quickly into the car then, taking her wet eyes out of sight.

'Good luck, Matt,' said Boots, and shook Matthew's hand.

'Damn all if any man could have had more good luck than I've had today,' said Matt. 'Thanks for everything, and thanks especially for Rosie.'

He was away with her a minute later, and the guests swarmed from the drive into the road to watch the going of the newly-weds, good luck charms festooning the back of the car.

'Happy days, happy days!' called young people.

With Polly beside him, Boots was watching in silence, wondering just how many happy days the war would allow Rosie and Matthew. Rosie of all people was deserving of a full quota.

The car travelled on. From out of the open passenger window, a hand in a white glove appeared to wave in a final gesture of goodbye before the vehicle disappeared.

Boots felt a strange sense of loss.

Warm fingers pressed his hand, and a whisper from Polly reached his ears.

'You've still got me, darling, you'll always have me.'

A memory awakened. That was what Emily had said to him many years ago, on a day when he thought he had lost Rosie the child into the care of her grandfather's niece.

'You'll always have me, Boots.'

459

The publishers hope that this book has given you enjoyable reading. Large Print Books are especially designed to be as easy to see and hold as possible. If you wish a complete list of our books please ask at your local library or write directly to:

Magna Large Print Books
Magna House, Long Preston,
Skipton, North Yorkshire.
BD23 4ND

This Large Print Book for the partially sighted, who cannot read normal print, is published under the auspices of

THE ULVERSCROFT FOUNDATION

THE ULVERSCROFT FOUNDATION

... we hope that you have enjoyed this Large Print Book. Please think for a moment about those people who have worse eyesight problems than you ... and are unable to even read or enjoy Large Print, without great difficulty.

You can help them by sending a donation, large or small to:

The Ulverscroft Foundation, 1, The Green, Bradgate Road, Anstey, Leicestershire, LE7 7FU, England.
or request a copy of our brochure for more details.

The Foundation will use all your help to assist those people who are handicapped by various sight problems and need special attention.

Thank you very much for your help.